THE DRAGON AND THE FAERIE

The Vasara Chronicles, Part 1

ROLAND CAPALBO

Dragon Moon Press

Cover Design by Greg Simanson
Edited by Ellen Margulies

This is a work of fiction. Names, characters, places, brands, media, and incidents are either the product of the author's imagination or are used fictitiously. Any resemblance to similarly named places or to persons living or deceased is unintentional.

Print ISBN 978-1-988256-45-0
EPUB ISBN 978-1-988256-46-7
Library of Congress Control Number: 2016905903

To my wonderful family, for their support and inspiration in all I write

And to all who have come along with me on this incredible journey, lifting me up with their kind words and encouragement

Chapter 1

ANDY IDLY WALKED along the path next to the railroad tracks, skipping rocks on the river. He was tall for his sixteen years but not gangly. His body moved with a fluid grace, skimming across the ground like a snake sliding along the sand. The wind coming off the river blew his sandy brown hair in all directions. His hawk-like hazel eyes looked out at the water where bright sunlight reflected off its rippling surface. He tried to imagine those bygone years when tall-mast ships ply the Hudson River on a daily basis, when the land on either shore was inhabited by Indians. That was a time to be alive, he thought, where freedom and adventure were the order of the day. Or so he believed.

Andy lived in a house not far from the river, so making his way down to shore was an easy task. He spent hours walking the trails, hoping to discover something that no one had seen before, like a hidden cove or a game trail where no human had walked. Excitement was his air and adventures, his bread. Some of Andy's escapades could easily have caused his death, but the idea that death was even a possible outcome never entered his mind. As Andy walked farther up the path, the air seemed to compress around him. Something buzzed deep inside his mind, like a thought dancing out of reach. He looked out across the water again and found himself staring at the ruins of Bannerman's Castle. The castle never ceased to fascinate him. He couldn't help but wonder what secrets were hidden inside its walls. The blood in his veins would race in excitement as he pictured himself scrambling along the rocks and rubble.

Andy had collected bits and pieces of the castle's history over the years. In actuality, it was a warehouse built in the style of a Scottish castle to house surplus munitions from the Spanish-American war. A short path up the hill led to a house, erected in the same Scottish style as the castle. Almost forty years ago, a fire had ravaged the island and left the house and castle in ruins, leaving only the walls of brick standing; without its wooden supports, it had started to collapse in places.

"I wonder what really happened there," Andy said aloud to himself for perhaps the thousandth time. No one knew the origins of the fire, which had led to all sorts of speculation. He had heard all the ghost stories that surrounded the place and couldn't help but imagine that some spirit or god of the island would not suffer anyone on its shores.

He remembered a tale his dad had told him of an English war ship that was able to sail beyond the West Point cannons during the Revolutionary War and came to drop anchor near the island. It was dead calm when they put their dories into the water and rowed to the beach on its east side. As soon as their feet touched dry ground, the river became a rolling tempest. The wind rose to gale force and caught the sails, causing the ship to lurch violently and break up on the rocks hidden below the surface. Everyone on the ship perished. Those still on the island jumped into their boats and tried to row for the nearest shore, only to capsize and drown. Andy found it a fascinating tale, but he believed there might have been some duplicity on his father's part, since history did not record such an event.

As Andy stood looking at the castle, his sister seemed to float as she walked up the trail and stood beside him. Emilia was slightly taller and two years older than her brother, and though she had a delicate air about her, she was tough as steel. Her long black hair cascaded down her back, and her dark green eyes reflected the mysteries of a forest pool.

"What are you doing?" she asked her brother.

"Just staring at the castle," Andy replied.

"You always stare at that place whenever we walk here. Why?"

"I don't know," he responded. "I just feel a kind of pull whenever I walk past it. It's like I can hear someone whispering my name. Nuts, I know, but I don't know how else to explain it." Andy was close to his sister, even though she could sometimes be extremely bothersome. He could always share these kinds of thoughts with her, when any other person really would think he was nuts.

"Well, it gives me the creeps," she said. "Let's go."

"Wait! I need to try to get a rock through the entrance arch."

"You always try that, and you can never reach it. I keep telling you, it's too far from shore."

"Yeah, but this time I have the slingshot Dad made for me."

Picking up a good-sized, but not too heavy, stone from the bank, Andy loaded the slingshot and took aim for the stone arch, the entranceway to a brick path that led to the castle and the house. Pulling the rubber band back to his ear, he took a breath and held it, then released the stone, tracing its graceful arc over the river toward its destination.

The sun had just set behind the hills, not yet night but no longer daytime. The dusky light made it seem like the world was in flux and almost anything might happen. That day, something did. The rock fell just short of the arch, but it had enough momentum that it skipped on the ground once and bounced through the opening.

Andy and Emilia stood with open mouths, not because the rock had made it through the arch but because of what happened when it passed beneath the opening. It was as if the rock had passed through a shimmering transparent curtain, igniting colors and sparks, the likes of which neither had ever seen.

"Did you see that?" Andy exclaimed.

"Yes! And now I want to get out of here as quickly as possible."

Andy could tell she was visibly shaken by what she'd seen. It was like something out of an adventure movie, and she wanted no part of it.

"Wait!" he said. "We need to go check it out." He loved a good adventure, and once he had the scent of one, he would not let up until his curiosity was satisfied.

"Are you crazy? First of all, you are not allowed on that island. Second, whatever caused that is likely to be extremely dangerous. And last, you have no way to get out there."

Andy disregarded the first two arguments, because adventurers were not held to such rules; her third point, however, pointed out an obstacle he hadn't considered. The island was not far from shore, and the section of water between the island and the east bank of the river was shallow at low tide—but not shallow enough that you could wade through it. Andy didn't like to swim in the Hudson because of the stories he had heard about the unexpectedly treacherous currents.

The Hudson is what is known as a flooded river. It has an incoming current during high tide from the ocean, as well as its natural north-to-south current. It is sometimes called the river that flows both ways. He had heard of swimmers being sucked under by the current and never resurfacing. This was going to take some thought. He did not own a boat, and he didn't want to ask any of his friends, because that might make their parents suspicious. He didn't want to just float out on a tube, given his fear of the currents. This was maddening. A great escapade lay waiting just across a small strip of water, and he couldn't think of a good way to get out there. *This will take some serious planning,* he thought.

"Okay," he said. "I guess you're right. Let's head back."

"Great. Let's go," she said, relieved.

As they walked away, a pair of golden eyes peered out at them from beneath the arch. The time was fast approaching.

CHAPTER 2

SEVERAL DAYS WENT BY, and Andy had still not come up with a sound way to get to the castle. Day after day, he found himself sitting on a log looking across the water at the object of his frustration. It was as if the castle were daring him to come across and try to discover its secrets.

It had been hot all summer, with no rain to speak of. The weatherman on TV had warned of a severe drought in the area, and the river was running sluggishly, several feet below the usual waterline. Andy stared across the river, absently thinking it was low tide because the rocks were showing. As he watched the current moving north, he suddenly realized it couldn't be low tide. An idea began to form.

"If the water is so low with the tide still coming in, how low will it be when the tide is fully out?" he wondered. "Just maybe it will be low enough that I can wade across." His heart started racing, and he grew more determined than ever, leaping to his feet despite the stifling heat. He had just enough time to prepare before the tide went out again.

* * *

But someone did see him. Two golden eyes stared out through a portal from some other world into this one, exerting all his power to peer beyond the thin veil that separated the two realms. It was he who was causing the water level to be so low near the castle, hoping to lure the boy to cross the space between the two shores. *And now to wait*, he thought.

* * *

Andy came back several hours later to check the water levels. He could see the mud of the river bottom now; the tide was definitely heading out. He wasn't too concerned about sinking into the mud, because there were plenty of good-sized rocks that, with sure feet and carefully planned jumps, would help him to the other side. His heart was pounding now. He knew something wonderful and impossible would happen when he walked through that arch. Taking caution with his footing, he hopped from rock to rock.

He was almost three-quarters of the way across when he heard, "Andy!"

He fell to hands and knees on the rock he was standing on, narrowly avoiding a tumble into the mud. Already amped-up from his river crossing, he nearly jumped out of his skin at the unexpected sound of his name.

He looked back toward shore and saw his sister standing on the bank, hands on hips and fire in her eyes. The hot wind blowing her long black hair gave her the appearance of a storm cloud descending on a warm sunny day.

"You almost made me fall!" he yelled. "What are you doing here?"

Emilia scrambled down the bank and hopped across the rocks to where Andy was crouching. She had a knack for balance and was able to reach him in no time at all.

"Apparently saving you from yourself," she replied when she'd reached him. "Are you crazy? Do you know how much trouble you could be in if someone sees you?"

"Calm down, Em. No one is going to find out. Unless you tell them." Andy flashed his dimpled smile that seemed to disarm most people when he wanted to bring them around to his way of thinking.

"Let's get to the other shore so we're not seen sitting in the middle of the river."

"All right, but that doesn't mean I am in any way supporting whatever crazy scheme you're planning!" She gave him her angry-green-eyes look, which she used to let people know she would not be swayed.

They stepped onto the small beach just in front of the arch and looked around. Kudzu and prickly buckthorn bushes crowded along the water's edge. Andy looked up at the castle walls where the vines climbed like so many fingers looking for a handhold. It struck him with great sadness that the castle was in such a ruinous state. Even though it was essentially just a warehouse, he could envision the great parties held there in its heyday.

"So, why are you here, Andy? If you're thinking of walking through that arch after what we saw the other day, you can just forget it right now."

"Why are you being so bossy?" Andy was clearly agitated. He liked his sister a lot, but not when she got that "I'm older and more responsible" air.

"I'm scared, that's why! And because what happened was not natural. Something is going on here that we don't understand."

"Nothing bad will happen. I'm sure of it. I can't tell you why, but I believe I'm supposed to be here."

"Well, that makes me feel so much better," she said, rolling her eyes. "Thank you."

"If you're going to be that way about it, you can just leave," he shot back.

Andy paused for a moment, considering his sister. When they were younger, they'd shared so many adventures together, and more often than not ended up being grounded by their parents. Not that they weren't good kids, but they'd been known to push their boundaries a little more than they should have. As they grew older, the two-year gap between them seemed to widen somehow. Emilia tended to look at life a little more seriously than she had when she was younger, and she was much more focused on her school work and the promise of adulthood just out of reach. He, on the other hand, was more adventurous than ever.

"I'm sorry," she said finally. "This whole thing just scares me down to my toes. And it scares me that something might happen to you."

"Em, I don't know if I can convince you or not, and I appreciate your concern. I do. But I have to do this. The compulsion to step through that arch is extremely strong now, and I don't think I could turn back even if I wanted to." A power was drawing him, he could feel it.

Andy could see her resolve to thwart his plans starting to waver.

"I can see you're determined in this, so I'm coming with you. If anything, just so you don't kill yourself," she said, smiling.

"Thanks, Em. This means a lot to me. I have to admit I'm just a little bit nervous about going through there."

"Well, if we're going to do it, let's do it before I lose my nerve."

They grabbed each other's hands.

"Ready?" Andy asked.

"Ready."

They took a deep breath, took one step, then another. Just a few more steps and they would be under the arch.

"Last step," Andy said. "You can still turn back if you want."

"No, I'll see it through."

"Right. In we go."

They took the last step in tandem, crossing under the stone archway. They looked around and saw nothing but each other, standing in the setting sun on the other side of the arch.

"What the…?" Andy asked. "I don't get it."

"I don't get it, either," Emilia said, clearly relieved, "but I'm not going to complain about it. We came, we tried, nothing happened. Can we go home now?"

"Wait! Something has to be different. Let me think." He pondered for a moment, looking up into the sky and running his fingers through his hair.

"Look, the sky!"

"What about it?"

"Don't you see? When the rock went through, the sun had just set. What if this thing, whatever it is, only happens at certain times?" Looking toward the west, he could see the last light of the setting sun about to disappear behind the hills. "Come on!" He grabbed Emilia's hand and ran back through the arch.

"Look!" Emilia cried, pointing at the river. The level of the water had risen dramatically. They'd only been on the island for a few minutes, and now it seemed as if the way back were deliberately blocked.

"I guess there's only one way to go now." Taking her hand again, they faced the arch. "Are you ready?"

"I'm about as ready as before," she said, a hint of fear in her voice. "But, ready or not, I believe the decision has been made for us."

"Okay, here we go. See you on the other side, Em."

"I hope so." She squeezed his hand a little.

They stepped through the arch, and this time, they seemed to be passing through some sort of transparent curtain that vibrated and shimmered with a thousand colors. The sensation was strange but by no means painful. Andy's stomach lurched slightly but then righted itself. He looked over at Emilia and saw panic written all over her face. He tried to reassure her but found she couldn't hear him. Andy tried shouting, but still nothing. They seemed to be walking very slowly as they parted the veil. Their hands wrenched apart.

Emilia looked down in horror then looked back at Andy. She seemed to be shouting something, but Andy couldn't hear her. The last Andy saw of his sister was her terror-stricken eyes as she faded into darkness. Andy heard someone screaming her name over and over. He realized the screams were his own.

Something hard smashed into his left shoulder, forcing him to fall face-first onto a hard stone floor. He looked up and found himself in a large room with two wooden doors on opposite sides. The dim light within came from a pair of burning torches set in iron sconces on the walls. He could barely make out a cloaked figure standing over him. The face was in shadow, but two golden points of light stared down at him.

"Hold still, boy," a hollow voice said. "It will soon be over."

His shoulder seemed like it was on fire. The scream that tore from his throat sounded strange to him, almost inhuman. He started thrashing, trying to escape the pain. Suddenly a flash of bright light exploded in the room. He was falling, and just before darkness claimed him, he heard the hollow voice shriek, "Loki, I will kill you for this!"

CHAPTER 3

IT WAS THE SMELL of meat cooking that started to clear the fog in Andy's brain. He did not know how long he had lain there, but he knew he was famished. He remembered, as if in a dream, drifting in and out of consciousness. During those times, he thought he'd seen a man puttering about doing various tasks.

Andy knew he was in a cave. The floor was hard and cool like stone, and even his shallow, nervous breathing echoed in the cavernous space. He could hear water trickling somewhere in the back, yet the cave did not feel damp. Off to one side, a huge fire burned in a stone hearth. A side of beef was cooking there. The smoke rose up, and Andy watched it disappear through a hole in the ceiling that was more than a hundred feet high.

One thing that puzzled him was how clearly he could see the hole that was obviously quite a distance from him. Another was that his head felt like it was stuck on the end of a long pole and was floating back and forth as he looked at things. He also felt extremely heavy. Why he should feel like that, he did not know. He looked back toward the beef, thinking again of how hungry he was.

You may eat, if you like, a voice came from inside his head. And, like it was the most natural thing in the world, Andy responded in kind.

Who are you? Where am I, and how are we talking like this?

"So many questions," the voice chuckled. This time, the voice spoke aloud, and Andy swung his head toward the sound. At the entrance to the cave stood a tall man, his black hair streaked with gray. His dark brown eyes were deep and ageless. He wore a simple brown robe with the hood pushed back. Andy could not guess at his age. He seemed both young and old at the same time. Again, Andy was amazed at how clearly he could see the man, given the distance he was from him.

"I will answer two of your questions," the man replied. "First, as to where you are, you are in my cave. Maybe I should clarify. We are in our cave. In answer to your second question, we can communicate mind-to-mind because of what you are."

Because of what I am? What does that mean?

"Look in that pool over there. But before you do, take a couple of deep breaths and try to stay calm." Andy wished the man hadn't said that, because he was even more apprehensive now than he had been before.

He stretched his neck toward the pool, again having that odd feeling that his head was on the end of a long pole. As he looked down into the water, the image reflected back was both shocking and unbelievable. A triangular reptilian head with horns like spikes shooting out of the back and eyes the color of fire looked back at him. Terror exploded in his brain, causing a great pressure to build up in his head as Andy realized the face he was seeing was now his own. A great roar came from the dragon's throat. A cry of loneliness and separation, a cry of humanity lost embodied in a roar, as the dragon's head perched on that long neck came crashing to the cave floor, and Andy lost consciousness one more time.

* * *

After several hours, he started to stir. The old man came forward and poured some foul-tasting liquid down Andy's long throat. He started to sputter and his head whipped up, lifting the man off the floor before having a chance to let go, causing him to drop from a height.

What is that stuff? his mind spoke angrily.

"Just something to help clear your head," the old man replied, getting to his feet. "Trust me, it will not harm you."

I'm not in a very trusting mood right now, Andy replied wearily. *Who are you?*

"First, eat something. Then I will answer your questions. I took the beef off the fire just before you woke up. Of course, you don't have to eat it cooked, but I do. So let's eat."

Andy watched as the old man got up and walked to a large oak table. In the center was a huge piece of steaming meat. After carving several pieces for himself, he dragged the remaining side of beef over to Andy. "You must eat," he encouraged. "It will help to calm your hunger and give you a clear head for what you must hear. It is always easier to concentrate after the stomach is full. Yes?"

If you say so. Andy tore into the meat, using his foreleg to hold it down while he ripped.

As he ate, Andy took a good look at his surroundings. The floor of the cave was a polished white marble. Several areas had strange circular designs carved on them. The ceiling was even higher than he'd originally estimated, and he noted it was domed. It was indeed a cave built for dragons. *But who built it?* he wondered. Off to the right side of the cave, near the hearth, was a bed, undoubtedly used by the old man. There was also a small desk with several books on it. Next to the hearth was a well-worn wooden chair with goose-down cushions. Judging from the flatness of the cushions, he could tell this chair had seen a lot of use. The sides of the cave were smooth and straight, chiseled from the native stone. The doorway in the front was tall and narrow. Sunlight streamed in and reflected off the floor, washing the cave in light.

An ale barrel stood in the rear of the cave where it was cooler. A rack of hand-crafted smoking pipes stood next to it. The pipes were of various sizes and colors. Also in this area was a small food pantry and shelves of crockery. Pewter tankards were displayed on their own shelf, separate from everything else. Intricate scrollwork and various images were expertly etched into the metal. *The old man must really like his drink,* Andy thought.

He then looked at himself. His scales were black, and his talons were a gold color. He knew his eyes were fire-red from looking into the pool. His leg muscles were thick and rounded. His wings—*My god, I have wings!* he thought—were black as well and spanned about fifty feet. He still could not believe that he was a dragon. "How is this possible?" he asked himself. "Actually, how is going through an arch and coming out in another world possible, for that matter?" Then it all came back to him. *Emilia!* he cried suddenly. *Oh my god!*

"What is it?" the old man asked, concerned. "Who is Emilia?"

My sister! She came through with me, but we were separated. I have to leave! I have to find her! It's my fault. She could be in trouble! Andy started to rise.

"Whoa! Easy lad, slow down. Are you telling me someone else came through with you?"

Yes! That's exactly what I'm saying! I have to go! he replied as he started running for the door, his talons making sparks on the white marble.

"Andros, stop!" The authority carried in that voice brought him up short, and the name seemed to strike a chord in his being. "Listen to me," the old man continued calmly. "You can't just run out of here in your current condition. You need knowledge and training, not to mention the fact that you haven't a clue as to where you are or where she might be. Lower yourself down, and we will talk." Andy turned back and lowered his massive body to the floor.

Very well, he replied grudgingly. *I will listen.*

"Great, glad to hear it. Actually, let's go over by the fire. It's much more comfortable there. I'll just grab some ale and a pipe. Talking is such thirsty work."

Andy got up, walked over to the fire, and found a place to stretch out his bulk. The old man came back carrying a pewter mug full of ale and a long-stemmed pipe the color of obsidian before setting himself in the chair. After lighting the pipe and taking a sip of ale, he began to speak.

"First off, my name is Loki. I am a wizard, one of three in the land of Vasara."

Loki? I heard that name spoken right before I blacked out.

"Yes, my brother wizard Devon was spouting curses at me as I pulled you out of his castle. He was definitely not having a good day." Loki laughed. "A bad day for him is always a good day for me."

That bright light was you?

"Yes, you see, I was waiting for you. In searching the prophecy, I knew the day of your arrival. Fortunately my brother was ignorant of the fact that I would know this, or he would have laid enchantments to thwart me. He never would search the prophecy, believing it to be nothing that could be counted on, except when it suited his purposes."

Prophecies? Enchantments? This is starting to make my head hurt, and it's not at all helpful for finding my sister, Andy complained.

"Let me finish and things will become clearer. It is probably best if I start from the beginning. Afterward, I will answer all of your questions—and I'll have some questions of my own."

I'm listening.

"Excellent. You are already starting to show some promise." Loki paused and puffed on his pipe.

"To begin," he started, "Vasara was created roughly five thousand years ago, give or take a few centuries. The creators number six, five gods and one goddess. The names of the five gods are Aditya, Fallon, Rafael, Trystan, and Cael. We normally just refer to them as the Five. The goddess is called Braylynn, and she never lets you forget that she is the only goddess. Her favorite line is, 'It took five gods to equal one goddess,'" Loki said, smiling.

You have physical contact with your gods?

"Of course, although the Five no longer dwell on Vasara. Braylynn, however, is still here."

What happened to the Five? Andy asked as he readjusted his tail to curl up along the bottom of his claws.

"They left around the second millennium. They felt their task here was done, so they departed. In extreme circumstances, I can contact them, but for the most part, they are gone. It was from them that the wizards received their power. When the Five left, they made sure we would still have an energy source to draw from. I will teach you how to draw from that source." He paused his narrative to drink some ale and puff again on his pipe. "If you would be so kind as to throw a few logs on the fire, lad, I'd appreciate it." Andy stretched his leg toward the woodpile and grabbed several logs with his massive claws then dropped them on the fire, sending up a shower of sparks.

"Thank you, that's much better. Now, after the gods and goddess created our world, they made the various races that populate Vasara. Aditya made the people who inhabit the area known as Fenner. Open grasslands for the most part with few trees and lots of space to run horses. Aditya was always fond of horses, so naturally his people are the finest horsemen in Vasara.

"Fallon, being the god of battle, created a warrior race. They settled the Border Lands to the east. No better swordsmen exist anywhere. They also brew the best ale. This ale is from there," he said, raising his tankard.

"Rafael is the god of healing. His people populate the area near Lake Pleasant and the town of Black River. Pretty obvious what their nature is. They specialize in the study of plants, herbs, and all things to do with healing.

"Trystan is big on study and intellect. His people founded Kensington, where the White Castle is. Here you will find many universities and libraries. The Great Library of Vasara is there. They say at least one copy of every book ever written exists in that library. Most of the original works are there, as well. The people of Kensington felt it their duty to spread learning to all four corners of Vasara. You will find, at a minimum, a library in every major town, each with a Kensington curator overseeing the collection.

"Cael is the creator of all beings nonhuman—gryphons, fauns, satyrs, and the like. The biggest concentration of beasts can be found in the Parma Wilds."

Does that mean he created dragons?

"Yes and no," Loki replied. "All five created dragons for a specific purpose. I'll explain that later. The other nonhuman race that Cael did not create is the faeries. Braylynn created them. It is for them that she stayed behind while her brother gods left. They live south-east of here in Laurel Hollow."

Loki continued to blow smoke rings as he spoke. Although ring is not quite accurate, as some were in the shape of animals. Andy was astounded and a little overwhelmed at all he was hearing. Gods and goddesses, creatures, human and nonhuman—it was all hard for a kid from New York to take in.

Can we stop for a moment? Andy asked. *I would like to stretch my legs and maybe step outside for some fresh air.*

"Very well. I need more ale, anyway."

Andy walked through the doorway. As he did, he saw all kinds of strange symbols and letters carved on the underside of the door that ran from the floor on both sides up to the top of the arch. He was sure it must have some significant meaning. *I'll ask Loki about it later*, he thought.

He stepped outside onto a wide ledge that ran around the circumference of the mountain that the cave was built into; plenty of room for a dragon Andy's size. He walked to the edge, his talons making a clicking sound against the rock. There was a stone wall, chest-high on a man, presumably so no one would fall over the cliff. No human that is, Andy could have easily stepped over it. Looking down, he could see that the cave was near the top of a huge mountain, bigger than any mountain in his world. It seemed to be part of a range of mountains that ran from east to west as far as he could see. Lifting his head, he looked due south and saw what appeared to be a large body of water. It was then that Loki came up from behind to stand at the wall.

"Impressive, isn't it," he said, taking a long drink from his newly-replenished tankard.

What is it called?

"Lake Pleasant." Loki wiped his mouth on his sleeve.

That's a lake? Andy was dumbfounded. *But I can't even see the other side.*

"It's massive. It takes several days to sail from one shore to the other. If you had to ride around it, you would be several weeks on the trail." He puffed his pipe. "On the western shore there is a big shipping town called Black River. The people of Black River have some of the finest sailors and shipbuilders in Vasara."

Andy looked at Loki with profound sadness in his eyes. A huge dragon tear escaped from his eyelid and slid down his scales, making an audible splash as it hit the stone below. *I mean no disrespect, Loki, but these people and places mean nothing to me. I did a stupid thing going through that arch. My mother and father are probably sick with worry, and my sister is somewhere out there, scared and possibly hurt.*

Loki put a sympathetic hand on the dragon's neck.

"Let's go back inside, lad. It is time I told you of the creation of the prophecy and how it works. It is responsible for your being here, and maybe upon hearing what I tell you, it will abate your sorrow somewhat. Come." He turned back toward the cave, tankard in hand, his pipe smoke trailing behind him.

Andy took one last look, sweeping his head from east to west. "I will find you, Em." He sent his thought out. "I swear to God, or in this case the five gods and one goddess—whatever it takes, I'm not leaving here until I do." He then swung his neck around, turned, and walked back into the cave.

CHAPTER 4

ONCE INSIDE, Loki settled back into his chair by the fire. Andy walked over and lowered himself as before, with his tail curled up around his legs.

"I know this is all hard for you to accept Andros…"

Wait a second. Why do you call me Andros? My name is Andrew, or Andy for short.

"In your world, maybe. But here it is Andros, your true name." Loki took a long draw on his pipe. "It was because I knew your true name that I was able to pull you out of Devon's chamber. And Devon must also have known your true name to be able to lure you here. As for how I knew, I searched the prophecy, which only wizards can do."

You mentioned the creation of this prophecy, but where I come from, prophecy is a record of future events. You make it sound like it's almost alive.

"It is," he stated simply. "The Five are responsible for its being. They knew they might not always be around to fix things, so they created the prophecy. Its nature is to provide a way out, should things go wrong, however big or small. It is always striving for balance. It can look ahead in time to a certain event, and then spin out the required people and/or creatures that can do the job. There is a catch, though."

There's always a catch, Andy said cynically. *Sorry, please continue.*

"No need to be sorry." he smiled. "I feel the same way myself. The catch is, even if all the requirements are met, there is no guarantee for success. The prophecy only provides the tools needed to achieve the goal. It is up to those who use the tools to succeed or fail. Should an action fail, the prophecy looks ahead to the next branch and puts in place the participants required for that event."

Branch? Andy asked, puzzled.

"Yes, let me explain. The prophecy is like a never-ending tree with infinite limbs and branches. Say you start on the ground going up the tree. The prophecy can see ahead to where a limb forks. One branch will be followed over the other as the result of some action taken by the participants. The prophecy's job is to make sure the participants exist to take part in that action. How they interact is entirely up to them. If they fail, that fork or possible future falls away and the prophecy looks ahead to the next junction. The time between forks can be years, decades, or even many centuries. So it is possible for evil to hold sway for a long period of time. Understand?"

Not really, Andy replied. Loki let out a sigh. He tapped his pipe thoughtfully against the side of his almost-empty tankard and tried again.

"All right, let's talk about this prophecy, the one that involves you. Devon is a wizard like me, although he's been altered some-what due to certain choices and associations." Loki wore an angry scowl. "I will not go into those now, but he has become an evil being obsessed with power. He will not rest until he rules all worlds that are open to him. He has held Vasara under his oppressive thumb for many centuries now. The day he first turned from servant to master, the prophecy looked forward to the next junction where the two forces of good and evil would come together again in battle. Two possibilities exist—either Devon wins and we have more cen-turies of oppression until the next battle, or you win and an era of peace begins."

Me? Win? Win what?

"The prophecy has chosen you, however long ago, to be the one who confronts Devon and kills him. You will have everything you need in order to win. Whether you succeed or not will rest entirely upon your choices and actions."

But why would the prophecy choose me? I'm not from this world. I don't know anything about this place! I don't want to kill anybody!

The prophecy has the ability to reach across times and worlds to gather what it requires. That your name in the world you came from is a form of your true name is no coincidence. One thing it cannot do, however, is create a thing of this world in a different world."

What do you mean? You don't mean...? Andy's panic was clearly visible in his eyes.

"Yes, Andros, because you are a dragon means you are of this world."

But that's impossible! he exploded, rising and cracking his tail like a whip. *I was born in a hospital in New York, to my mother and father. That's a fact!*

"New York, Old York, your physical birthplace does not matter. Your spirit was created here. You could not be a dragon otherwise."

Andy crashed back to the floor, stunned.

"This is a shock, I know," Loki said kindly. "I have never heard of or seen it happening this way before, but it obviously did. I cannot tell you how it happened. I couldn't even guess. If I knew your parents' history or their parents' history, I might be able to come up with a hypothesis. I am sorry I cannot help you in this regard."

Andy's world had already been turned upside down. Now it seemed to have been flipped inside out, as well. He could process no more. *I need to rest. I can't handle anymore today.*

"Very well, lad," Loki replied sympathetically. And with that, Andy got up and walked over to the far side of the cave and lay down. The last thing he saw before sleep took him was the old man staring intently into the flames of the fire, puffing away on his pipe.

*   *   *

Morning dawned bright and warm, giving promise to a day of new possibilities. Loki was busy in the pantry gathering foodstuffs for breakfast. Andy opened his eyes and breathed in the heavenly scent of coffee. His father was a coffee fanatic; he drank coffee all the time.

And whenever they traveled somewhere, they stopped in at the best coffee shop recommended online in his father's perpetual quest for the perfect cup. The thought of his father brought a smile to Andy's face. True, it was a dragon smile, but it was a smile all the same. He missed his parents, and the smell of something as homey as breakfast made him realize just how much.

He rose up and walked over to where Loki was preparing breakfast. "Good morning!" Loki said cheerfully upon hearing Andy's scales scraping against the floor of the cave.

Is that really coffee I smell? Andy lowered his head to sniff the pot.

"Absolutely. There's a coffee grove just south of Albion that produces the best beans in all of Vasara."

Which god created the coffee growers? he asked jokingly.

"That is the deepest of all mysteries, lad." He gave him a wink. "So, how are you feeling today?"

Better. I think I'm ready to hear more.

"Actually, I've decided today we will rest the mind and work on the body. I want to get you started on some training exercises that you should do every day. We may talk a little, but only if it pertains to the instruction, all right?"

All right.

"Excellent! Now for some breakfast," the old man said, rubbing his hands together gleefully. "Yours is down at the end of the table."

Andy looked and saw a half rack of mutton resting on the far end of the table. His head swooped down and in one bite it was gone.

"By the gods, boy, how about chewing a little and savoring the taste a bit?"

Sorry. I guess I was hungrier than I thought.

"Well, lucky for you dragons only need to eat once a day. By the gods," he repeated, looking at the empty space where the mutton had once been. "Also, you should know this will be the last time I will be feeding you. I cannot store large amounts of meat for you to consume, nor can I be running back and forth to Dragonsgate to get you more. Starting tomorrow, you will hunt for your own food. This will help with your training."

Where is Dragonsgate?

"It is the town just below the Macedon Mountain range. Our cave sits atop the highest mountain in this range. Well, since you've finished breakfast, why don't you go outside and stretch your muscles while I finish mine?"

All right. Andy turned and walked out the door. The sun and warm breeze felt good against his scales. He could hear the cry of hawks far below. *They must have a nest in the cliff face somewhere,* he thought. He figured he might as well try a little jog along the ledge to loosen himself up. He could walk as a dragon without any problem. A run shouldn't be that difficult.

He reared up on his hind legs like a horse and leaped into a trot. He was doing quite well and feeling really proud of himself when all of sudden his legs got twisted, causing him to trip. It was then that he made an amazing discovery. His scales were hard as iron but also smooth like glass, so when his underside hit the flat stone ledge, he took off like a child riding a sled down a huge snowbank.

Whoa! he exclaimed. *This is fantastic! Wow!* Things were going along great until the end of the ledge appeared. Andy's eyes widened in alarm as he tried dragging his talons along the stone to slow his momentum. What eventually stopped him was a natural-rock barricade at the cliff's end. The impact was thunderous, causing several of the rocks to crack. With his head on the ground and his claws in the air, he started to laugh. Looking back the way he'd come, he could see Loki running upside down toward him.

"Well, lad, that's not exactly what I meant by stretching your muscles, but it's a start." He collapsed next to Andy and then burst into laughter himself. "What a sight you are!"

Getting control of themselves, they both stood up. "You actually learned the first things most dragons do—sliding."

It was exhilarating. It felt good to think of something other than his predicament, if only for a moment.

"Now we are going to take that a step further. Your training has officially begun. Turn around and face the way you came. Then lower your neck so I can climb on." Andy did as he was instructed. He could hardly feel Loki's weight. "Now slowly lift your head up, and I will slide into position at the base of your neck. Start running as before, but concentrate on your leg placement to keep from tripping. Once you have a good rolling gait going, I want you to dive and slide. Got it?"

Got it.

"Good. Now go!"

Andy started to run, feeling the rhythm of four clawed feet striking the stones as he went. After gathering enough speed, he dove as if he were sliding into second base. The speed they achieved was tremendous. Andy then saw the other end of the ledge looming before them. But unlike the stone barrier behind, the only thing to stop them was the man-high wall, and Andy, as big and heavy as he was, knew they would smash right through it. He believed it might be a good idea to make Loki aware of this fact.

Loki, ah..., we're going to die!

"Not today, lad!" Loki exclaimed, clearly enjoying the ride. "When I give the word I want you to throw your head and neck straight up then open your wings—but don't flap. Get ready—*now!*"

Andy threw his head toward the sky and extended both wings. The lift on his wings made him airborne but also slowed his momentum considerably. He was able to get his hind legs folded beneath him and lowered his body back to the earth, landing gently.

"Well done, Andros, well done indeed!"

That was fantastic, but why didn't you want me to flap my wings? I could have slowed us more with some backward thrusting.

"I will show you why," Loki answered. "Stand still and open your wings." Andy did. "Now flap."

Andy started both wings flapping and understood Loki's concern at once. Never having had wings before, the movement of his right wing was slightly faster and out of synchronization with his left, causing him to spin.

"Now you see. Had you tried that while we were sliding, we would have spiraled right off the ledge and been dashed on the rocks below. But don't despair—with concentration and practice, you will be flying in no time."

Flying? He looked out over the wall to the peaks far below and felt a little queasy. *How stupid of me not to realize as a dragon I would be expected to fly,* he thought.

"Not afraid of heights, are you?" Loki asked. "I hope not. It would be damned embarrassing having a killer dragon that won't fly."

I'll be okay, Andy promised, swallowing hard.

"That's the spirit! Now, take the rest of the morning and practice moving your wings together. Once you have the rhythm down, we'll attempt to fly." Loki went inside to finish breakfast, leaving Andy to his training.

Andy walked over to the wall and looked down. He spotted the hawks again far below, wings outstretched and circling on the warm air currents. He felt their freedom and total surrender to their element. He would love to be able to do that, to feel that. He made up his mind that he would—he *had* to. If he ever wanted to find his sister again, failure was not an option.

Taking a deep breath, wings outstretched, he began.

CHAPTER 5

SUN PIERCED THROUGH the trees only grudgingly in Laurel Hollow. The green moss by the stream was thick and soft, and the trees were tall with dark red bark. It was sometimes called the Iron Forest, not only because of its color but also because the wood itself was extremely hard to cut.

Leah knelt down on the bank to pluck a white flower floating on the water, and just as she was leaning over, the current took it and pulled it out into the middle of the stream.

"Oh no you don't!" she said, standing quickly, her faerie wings beating so fast they were an iridescent blur. She flew above the water and hovered slightly downstream from the flower, waiting for it to come to her. "Gotcha!"

She flew back to the stream bank and sat cross-legged on the grass, her opalescent lavender wings coming to a stop. Her purple gown, cut just above the knees, was a perfect match for the flower she had just rescued from the water. "I could pin you to my sash," she said softly. "That would look just stunning."

As she sat with her back to the woods, Leah suddenly pushed her blonde hair off her pointed ears and turned her head slightly to the right, listening. Remaining perfectly still, she waited. There it was again: the sound of twigs breaking. She was being stalked, but by what kind of animal she did not know. She smiled to herself.

That was part of the fun, not knowing until the last minute who your adversary was going to be. Whatever was watching her lost its patience and started its charge.

Leah stayed calm and focused. The beast let out a wild cry, and from that cry she knew it was a lynx. She sat perfectly still, and at the last possible instant, she sprang from her sitting position in a flurry of beating wings and launched herself straight up. The lynx came skidding to a halt right before the stream bank and narrowly escaped plunging in. It shook its head from side to side in bewilderment, baffled at where its prey had gone.

After reaching the top of her arc, Leah came rushing back to earth, picking up speed as she went. She reached down along the side of her leg for what appeared to be a small stick. Pressing a hidden clasp, the stick expanded into a six-foot spear sharpened on both ends. She held the spear in both hands and, taking aim, flew straight for the lynx.

The lynx saw her coming and crouched low, waiting to spring once she came into range. Faerie and lynx met in midair, and Leah brought the spear in a swinging arc around her back, expertly slicing the lynx along its jaw. In a spray of blood, the lynx fell back to the ground and sped away. The wound was superficial, and Leah knew it would live. She was not aiming to kill.

"Most invigorating!" she said as she set her feet upon the ground once more. "Damn! I've gotten blood on my sash."

Just then she heard another noise off to her left, in some tall grass. It sounded like a moan, as if someone were in pain. Holding her spear at the ready, she cautiously walked over to the grass and peered in. Lying on the ground was a faerie, not unlike herself in build. Her dress was white with a sash the color of red wine. Her pointed ears were visible through long black hair that surely cascaded down her back, and on her head was a silver circlet. Her wings were dark green shot through with black. Her dress, which would come to the top of her ankles if she stood up, was hiked up on her leg. What drew Leah's attention was the image of a twisting red dragon on her calf muscle.

Leah looked at her intently, trying to figure out where she might be from. She definitely did not come from Cavanah Hall, which is where the queen resided in Laurel Hollow. Leah would have seen her there. She knew most of the faeries in the settlements along the outer edge of Laurel Hollow, too, but she couldn't remember ever seeing this one. Was it possible she'd come from some of the lands up north? Not all faeries lived in Laurel Hollow, and Leah knew some had migrated around Lake Pleasant.

The faerie started stirring. Her eyes opened and then shut again in a grimace of pain.

"Easy, sister," Leah said, slipping an arm around her back to help her sit up. "Can you speak? Do you know what happened to you?"

She opened her eyes and, blinking, looked at Leah. Leah could see her eyes were as green as moss by a forest pool. "My head... hurts."

"You're all right now, you're safe. What is your name?"

The faerie looked at her blankly.

"I, I don't know," she replied. "I don't even know where I am."

"Are you from the north?" Leah prompted. "I don't remember ever seeing you in Laurel Hollow before."

"I don't know. I can't seem to remember." She appeared frightened.

"Don't worry. I'll take you to the queen. She will know what to do. My name is Leah."

"Hello, Leah," she replied with a half-smile. "I wish I could tell you my name, but I just don't seem to remember.

"Do you know how you got that mark?" Leah asked.

"Mark?"

"On your leg." The faerie looked down to where Leah pointed.

"I have no idea. I think I may have always had it, but I am not sure. Things seem so muddled right now." Leah could see she was on the verge of tears.

"It's all right," Leah assured her. "Maybe you just fell and hit your head. A little time and rest will be just the thing to bring those memories back. You'll see."

"I hope you are right."

"Come on." Leah extended her hand to help her up. "Let's walk for a bit."

After retrieving her flower, they walked down a well-worn dirt path that wound through the woods to eventually arrive at Cavanah Hall.

"You are lucky I was here today," Leah said. "There was a lynx about that could have hurt you badly, had it known you were here. I was able to drive it off, though."

"Thank you," she said gratefully.

"Do you know how long you were lying there?"

"I have no idea."

The red trees towered above them. It was a good thirty feet up before any branches appeared. The limbs spread wide, and the leaf cover was dense. There were many different bird songs from the many birds darting in and around the trees. Every so often, the sun would break through a gap in the leaves, anointing the forest floor with its rays.

"What are these trees called?" she asked, watching the birds in their flight.

"They are called talon trees," Leah replied.

Looking at Leah, she asked, "Do you fly?"

Leah was taken aback by the question. "Why, of course I fly. All faeries fly. Don't you?"

"I have no memory of flying. Although I have wings, so I must be able to."

Leah was getting concerned. It seemed she didn't remember being a faerie at all. "The queen will straighten it out," she said aloud.

They walked through a flower-covered arbor and came upon the faerie settlement known as Cavanah Hall. Everywhere the faerie looked, there was activity. Faeries flitting here and there, playing games, chasing one another with wild abandon. There were also men there, dour-looking and carrying weapons, plus some small boys as well. The buildings were arranged in a semicircle around the Hall itself. Most were small dwellings with conical-shaped roofs. The Hall was many-storied, with an east and west wing. It was made entirely out of the talon wood of the forest. Steps led up to two main doors and a porch that wrapped around the building.

"The men are not originally from here, are they?" the faerie asked Leah.

"No, they're not," Leah responded. "How did you know?"

"I don't know. I look at them and see they are displaced, but they are accepted."

"They are from the Border Lands. They are warriors, every one. Laurel Hollow and the Border Lands are the only free places in Vasara." The faerie glanced at Leah, who had fire and pride in her eyes as she said this. "Although I must admit, we are not truly free," Leah continued. "It is true the wizard Devon does not hold sway here. We do not have one of his garrisons or a Baron overseer, mainly because of Braylynn's presence in Laurel Hollow. But he also knows we will not wage war on him. His army is vast, and a third of them are skilled archers. A faerie is formidable fighting on the ground but nearly unstoppable in the air—except when it comes to archers."

"Who are Devon and Braylynn?" she asked.

"Devon is an evil wizard who has ruled Vasara for more than fifteen hundred years. Your memory must truly be gone if you do not remember him," Leah replied as they approached the Hall. "Braylynn is our goddess. I'm sure at some point you will be meeting her."

Just then, something whizzed past their ears, and Leah let out a curse and put a hand to her head.

"Ouch! Tera, you little imp! Will you stop that? I've no time for your games!"

A young faerie was in the middle of a fit of giggling, pointing at Leah. She wore a light pink dress that floated above her knees. Her wings and hair were silver, and her eyes were brown.

"Ha-ha!" Tera laughed. "I got you, but you'll never catch me!" She spun around and flew toward the back of the Hall.

"Will you excuse me for a moment?" Leah said. "I'll be right back." She took off like a shot and circled around the opposite side of the Hall, emerging from the other side with a struggling little faerie clasped under her arm.

"Put me down! No fair! No fair! You saw it, lady! Right? She cheated!" Tera exclaimed as Leah set her down. "You're not allowed to fly that fast around the Hall!"

"And you're not supposed to sneak up behind unsuspecting players and smack them on the head. The game must be agreed to by both participants beforehand. You know that. And had you asked, I would have told you what I said when you first hit me—I've no time for your games!" Leah sounded angry, but it was feigned because Leah was trying to suppress a smile.

"I'm sorry, Leah," Tera said, hanging her head.

"It's all right. This is Tera," Leah said.

"Hi! You're a beautiful faerie. How old are you? What's your name? I don't think I've seen you before. Are you from around here? I've never seen wings that color before. Would you like to race? I'm considered one of the fastest." The boundless energy of this young faerie made them both smile

"Let her be, Tera. She's having trouble remembering. We are going to the queen now to see what may be done."

"Can I come, too? Please? Please! *Please!*"

"Very well, but only because I don't want you sneaking up behind me again," Leah said.

Faeries and men had begun to glance over at Leah and her companion, wondering who she might be. Leah saw their stares and whispered to her, "Don't let it bother you. They just haven't seen a new faerie in the last few hundred years or so."

The dirt path turned to flagstone that ended at the foot of the steps leading to the twin Talon-wood doors that opened onto the Hall. They proceeded down the hallway to the throne room. Benches, chairs, and divans lined the walls for the use of those waiting to see the queen. Today, however, most of the faeries sitting there were spending their time in quiet conversation. They paused as Leah, Tera, and this unknown faerie walked by. Up ahead, at the entrance to the throne room, stood the queen's counselor dressed in a black robe with gold trim on the hem and sleeves. His hair was auburn and his eyes were blue. His facial features seemed both stern and fair, and in his hand was a red wooden staff with strange symbols carved into it. On his hip was a sword in a scabbard. The sword had a serpent hilt.

"Hello, Dain," Leah said.

"Greetings, Leah," the counselor replied. "Greetings, Tera." He looked suspiciously at Tera, not turning his back for fear of some mischief the little faerie might play.

"No tricks today," Tera replied, giggling.

"That is good," Dain replied. "But I still cannot find my good shoes. The walk back from the stream in my bare feet was most unpleasant. It took hours to pull out all the splinters and thorns. Are you sure you saw a beaver run off with them?"

"Oh, absolutely," Tera said, straight-faced.

"*Hmm.* And who is this, Leah?"

"A guest. It is because of her that we wish to see the queen."

"One moment and I will speak to her," he said as he left to inform the queen.

"Did a beaver really take his shoes?" Leah asked with one eyebrow raised.

"No, but he hasn't been looking all over for them, either, because they are under his bed," Tera replied primly.

Leah didn't respond, as she was distracted by the mystery at hand. Something wasn't right. *Who was this faerie? Why could she not remember anything and yet have amazing insight into the things around her?* Leah looked over at the raven-haired faerie who, at that moment, was taking stock of her surroundings. Those green eyes seemed to be able to see more than just the physical world. Perhaps she had a heightened inner sight that allowed her see to the core of a situation. *She is special,* Leah thought. *Hopefully the queen will tell us more.* Just then, Dain reappeared.

"Go in. She will see you now."

"Thank you, Dain," Leah said, giving him a grateful look.

As they walked into the queen's chambers, the first thing they saw was an ornate wooden throne. It was made of the same red talon wood that was prevalent in all aspects of life throughout Laurel

Hollow. Ornate carvings of trees and branches twisted up the legs and arms of the throne. On the floor was a dark blue carpet embroidered with the silver and gold constellations of Vasara's night skies. The obvious thing missing from the throne room was the queen.

"Valencia?" Leah said.

"Over here, Leah," a voice called out from an alcove to the right of the throne. They walked into the small chamber where the queen was standing next to a table, studying a thick stack of documents. She looked up as they entered.

Leah heard the green-eyed faerie gasp. The beauty of the faerie queen was almost beyond description. Her eyes were a stunning hazel-gray. Her hair was red with streaks of gold, giving the impression of liquid flames against her skin. She wore a gown that shimmered with the colors of autumn leaves that left her bare at the shoulders. Her wings, like her hair, were the colors of dancing flames. Encircling the queen's throat was a necklace of gold with a green stone at its center. Her bearing and demeanor were such that they immediately inspired loyalty and trust.

"Welcome, Leah." The queen turned toward the other faerie, embracing her. "You have been too long away from the Hall, sister. I've missed you here."

"You know me, Valencia. I'm not happy unless I have the wind against my wings and the sun on my back. I'm a romantic at heart, although I do love a good hunt."

"Yes, I thought I heard a lynx screaming like a banshee as it sped past the Hall not too long ago. That wouldn't have been your doing, would it?"

"Just keeping in practice, Majesty," she said, smiling.

"Hello, little Tera." The queen greeted her with a smile. "And how many lives have you been making miserable today?"

"All right, I'm getting an unfair reputation here!" Tera responded, stomping her foot and crossing her arms. "The only trick I played today was on Leah." The queen knelt down and gave her a hug. "I apologize, then." Tera collapsed into another fit of giggles.

The queen stood up to look at the unknown faerie.

"And who is this, Leah?" she asked in a tone that was both comforting and disarming, conveying there was nothing to fear.

"She is the reason we have come, Valencia. I found her by the stream near the outer boundaries of Laurel Hollow. She seems to have lost all memory of who and what she is."

"You poor child. Do you have any idea how this happened, dear?"

"I don't," she responded sadly.

"Very well, let's go to my apartments where we can talk of this more comfortably. Dain!" she called.

Dain appeared at the door to the alcove almost instantly. "Yes, Your Majesty?"

"Can you please make sure these maps and documents get back to my library?"

"Of course, Majesty, I will attend to it myself."

"Thank you, Dain. Follow me, ladies."

*   *   *

This was all very confusing to the green-eyed faerie. Passing through a doorway in the rear of the alcove, they took a short walk up the stairs to the queen's apartments.

"Please sit down and I will have refreshments brought in," the queen said.

Leah and the others took chairs next to the fireplace. It was never cold in Laurel Hollow, but the fire gave off a warm glow that lit the entire room, eliminating the need for torches or candles. A small table for placing drinks and food sat between the chairs and the fireplace. On the walls were pictures of faeries who were part of the royal family line. She was looking at these when one portrait to the left of the fireplace caught her attention. That faerie in the picture had chestnut hair and translucent brown wings. Her eyes were large and brown, but she appeared sad, even though the picture showed her smiling. There was something so familiar about her, the faerie thought. The queen returned shortly with a tray that contained four crystal goblets of wine and a plate of pastries and cheeses. After setting the tray down on the small table, there was a knock at the outer door.

"Enter," the queen responded.

Dain poked his head inside. "The documents are safely put away, Your Majesty. Is there anything else you require?"

"Not at present, Dain, just please make sure we are not disturbed."

He nodded in acknowledgement and closed the door. "Please, have some wine." The queen took a goblet for herself and sat in the nearest chair.

Sipping the wine, Leah exclaimed, "This is very good, Valencia. The vineyards must have had a good harvest."

"What do you think, dear?" the queen asked her guest.

"It's fantastic!" the faerie replied, relaxed by a warm glow from her head right down to her toes. She noticed it was very dry but had a hint of spring flowers as it slid down her throat.

"I love these cream-filled things!" Tera said, grabbing up a pastry and ignoring the wine. Everyone couldn't help smiling at her.

"Now, tell me," the queen began, "what is the last thing you remember just before Leah found you?"

"I have been trying to think of that very thing, Your Majesty—," she started to answer.

"Please, you may call me Valencia if you wish. It is true, I rule here, but we are all sisters of the goddess."

"Thank you, Valencia." She relaxed, staring at the wine swirling in her glass. "The very last thing I remember is a feeling of falling."

"There is one thing, Valencia," Leah said, jumping in. "There is a mark on her leg that could mean something."

"May I see this mark?" She pulled up the hem of her dress to reveal the twisting red dragon. The queen's eyes grew wide.

"You're a Summoner!" the queen exclaimed.

"What is a Summoner?" Tera asked.

"It is one with the ability to call dragons," Leah supplied, "although I did not know they were marked so."

"It is a closely-guarded secret," the queen informed them. "The mark is a form of anointing by Braylynn for the faerie chosen as her Dragon Summoner."

"You mean there is only one?" said Tera.

"Yes. There has only ever been one at any given time. Some faeries may share the same kinds of abilities, but the Dragon Summoner is singular in this regard. If you are marked by the goddess, she must know your name," the queen told her.

"Her name is Donella," said a voice from the rear of the room. "My dark-haired one."

They turned as one toward the sound of the voice. All the colors of nature seemed to shoot up from the floor like a cascading fountain, and out of that fountain emerged the divinity of the faerie world. Braylynn was tall, more than six feet. Her hair was a summer gold with streaks of autumn red. A crown of red roses, blue morning glories, yellow daisies, and white carnations encircled her head. Her wings were a deep blue that matched her eyes, and her gown was forest green. Around her neck, she wore a silver chain set with white stones that glowed like the stars on a moonless night. Her body emanated a soft purple aura, like the glow of the sun against the clouds immediately after it has set. To look at her face was to look at love. Tenderness and compassion radiated from her eyes, and her smile was joy itself.

Upon hearing the name Braylynn had called her, Donella felt like she was in a dream as she walked over, tension and fear draining from her tired muscles. The goddess welcomed her, enfolding a weeping Donella within her arms and wings.

CHAPTER 6

AFTER DONELLA'S TEARS subsided, Braylynn took the little face in her hands. "All will be well, daughter. I do not want you to fear. Will you trust me?"

"I will," Donella replied, wiping her eyes.

"Come, let's go join your sisters." Upon reaching the others, Braylynn embraced each in turn. "I am sorry I have been away so long, Valencia," she said. "And I am afraid this visit must be short, as well."

"You are always in our hearts, Braylynn, so you are never truly away," Valencia responded. "I also know I have but to call and you would come without delay."

"You have led my people well, daughter, but your greatest task still lies ahead of you. However, now is not the time to speak of it. Leah, Tera, my blessings on you both."

"It is good to see you again, Braylynn," Leah replied.

"Did you bring me anything?" Tera asked hopefully.

"Actually, I did," the goddess replied. Reaching into the folds of her sleeves, she pulled out a set of pipes. "Pan asked me to give these to you. He knows of your fondness for pipes."

"Oh!" Tera squealed in delight. "Thank you! Thank you! Thank you!" She then proceeded to play a mournful melody.

"Please, Tera, nothing sad today. We should be happy in the meeting of old and new friends."

"All right. I will play it later. Thank Pan next time you see him for me, promise?"

"I promise, little Tera," the goddess smiled. "Please, everyone, sit down. We have much to discuss." Everyone returned to their chairs. Tera gave Braylynn her chair and fetched one for herself from the outer room.

"Now, as I said earlier, this is Donella, and she is my chosen Summoner. But before we go any further," she said, looking hard at Tera, "what we discuss here does not leave this room."

"What?" Tera asked innocently. "I might like to play a good trick now and then, but I know how to keep a secret."

"Very well," the goddess said.

"Since Donella is your Summoner, you must know where she is from," Leah stated.

"I do. I know her entire history."

"You do? Can you please tell me?" Donella pleaded.

"I am sorry, dear, I cannot." Donella's shoulders slumped, and her head went down. She thought this might be the one person who could fill in her missing memories. A hand gently lifted her chin and she lifted her eyes to meet those of the goddess; they were full of pain, sympathy, and also unconditional love.

"I need you to trust me, Donella. As my Summoner, I will be sending you into danger, and a large part of your success will depend on your trust in me. I need you to trust that I will tell you all I can, but some things must remain hidden." The goddess spoke to the quiet places of Donella's heart so she could trust her and would go wherever she was asked to go.

"I will," she replied, "but I have many questions."

"I know, and whatever can be answered will."

"What is it, Braylynn?" Valencia asked with concern in her voice.

"The time has come for the end of Devon's reign. The world groans under the weight of the evil that man has wrought," Braylynn stated. "He is also trying to spread his reach beyond this world into other worlds. Should he accomplish that, we would have no power to stop him in those worlds."

"Who is Devon?" Donella asked. "Leah told me he is an evil wizard, but that is all I know."

"That is probably a good place to start," Braylynn said. "When we created Vasara, my brothers thought it would be a good idea to have stewards to help, nurture, and protect all the various races."

"Brothers?" Donella asked puzzled.

"Brother gods," Leah supplied. "There are five of them."

"And these stewards, or wizards, as we call them, were given powers to fulfill this duty," Valencia added.

"Your sisters speak correctly," Braylynn continued. "There are three wizards. Their names are Devon, Redlin, and Loki. They claim no country as their home but roam freely, helping with their powers wherever they are needed most. Devon and Loki are still in Vasara, but Redlin has vanished. I know that he is not dead, because the wizard count is always three. Should one be killed, his power would go to the next person anointed by my brothers. So far there has been no transfer of power. As to where he is, that is hidden."

"What about Loki?" Donella asked. She reached for her wine and took another sip.

"Since Devon seized power, Loki has secluded himself in the remote north. He will sometimes go about disguised as a vagabond to avoid being captured by Devon. Devon would like nothing better than to imprison Loki and hold him with enchantments, thereby removing any known threat to his power."

"Why not kill him?" Tera asked after taking a bite of another cream-filled pastry. "You've got to try these, Braylynn. They are fabulous."

"I'm sure they are, but as to killing Loki, Devon would not do that except as a last resort. Remember, if a wizard is killed, his power will go to someone else, and Devon would not know who that would be. Better the enemy you know than the one you don't."

"What happened to Devon that made him evil?" Donella asked.

"It might help if I showed you. Stare into the flames of the fire." As they did this, Braylynn touched the necklace at her throat, and it started to glow. A scene began to take shape among the flames:

a man wearing a hooded robe, his face veiled by shadows at first, glanced around furtively, as if he sensed someone was watching him. When he looked behind him, the firelight revealed a thick shock of black hair, a thin beard cut close to his face, and a long, pointed nose.

He seemed to be walking in an arid desert. Upon reaching a spot he deemed appropriate, he dropped down on one knee. Taking a stick from inside his robe, he started drawing strange symbols in the sand. Then, raising his hands in the air, he began to chant. It was not audible to the faeries, but they could see Devon's lips moving, his eyes tightly closed. Soon the symbols on the ground started to glow, emitting a black vapor. Inky tendrils of vapor twisted and turned as they rose into the air, coalescing into an unfamiliar form.

The form was a thing of nightmares. Standing seven feet tall fully erect, the being had three claws on both of its reptilian feet. The tail, body, and snout closely resembled that of a crocodile, although the snout was shorter and this monster could walk on its hind legs. It had double rows of razor-sharp teeth. Devon seemed to be speaking to it. The monster's mouth opened wide as if making a loud roar. Devon spoke some final words and clapped his hands together. The being dissipated back into its black vapor form and floated into Devon's mouth and nostrils. When Devon turned his head again, the faeries could see that his dark eyes had turned a frightening, lurid yellow-gold. Pulling his hood back over his face, he turned and walked back the way he had come.

The scene in the flames changed. This time it showed Devon walking the halls of White Castle. As he turned his golden eyes on all the guards he came across, they became immobile. It was night, and all the royal residents were asleep. With a cat-like stealth, he entered the sleeping chamber of the king and queen. Reaching forth his hand, he drew a sword made of fire out of the air and with it killed the monarchs while they slept.

The scene changed once more. In the castle's Great Hall, a score of richly-attired men were seated around a long table with Devon at the head. He appeared to be speaking. At a nod from him, servants started distributing large canvas bags to each person seated at the table. Upon opening the bags, the men discovered small fortunes in gold coins and glittering jewels. Devon spoke again, and then, as one, the men rose from their seats and bowed. Some sort of deal had been struck. The images faded, and the flames returned to normal. It was some moments before anyone spoke.

"I had no idea that was how he had gotten his other powers," Leah said with a shudder.

"I am not sure I fully understand all that happened," Donella said, clearly shaken by the images she had seen.

"Devon summoned a demon, and then he made a pact to absorb its power. He murdered the king and queen, and since there was no heir, he bought the Council of Baron's fealty, thereby making himself ruler. His powers are great, but he can be beaten." Braylynn looked long at Donella. "You are the one chosen to defeat him."

"Me?" Donella exclaimed. "I know nothing of defeating a wizard!"

"Not yet, but Leah can help you sharpen the faerie skills that are part of your nature. And, as the Dragon Summoner, you can call upon the power of the elements, as well as the aid of dragons."

"I thought all the dragons vanished long ago," Valencia remarked.

"There is one in Vasara again," the goddess said. "He is in Loki's care in the mountains to the north. He is not our concern right now, though." Looking at Donella, she continued. "You bear my mark as my Dragon Summoner, but the powers will not come until you obtain certain talismans and vestments. They are infused with power from me and my brothers, as well as the natural elements. First, you will need to find the dragon crown with a dragon-eye jewel in the center. This allows you to see what the dragons see, as well as communicate with them. Also, if you summon them while wearing this crown, they are compelled to come to you. Next, you must attain the green garment that will prove impervious to many types of assault. Lastly, you will have to acquire the necklace and ring to give you power over the elements. There is one problem, however."

"*Uh-oh*, here it comes," Tera said. "There's always 'one problem.' Can't things ever be easy?"

"Tera, *shhh!*" the queen admonished.

"These items are not in Laurel Hollow. They reside in the manor house of the Baron of Hadley. You will have to go in there and retrieve them."

"How did they wind up there?" Leah asked.

"They were taken off the body of the last Dragon Summoner," Braylynn replied with great sadness.

"Do you mean she was killed?" Tera asked.

"Yes, by a most foul and murderous deed. A Dragon Summoner is extremely hard to kill because of the protection the garment provides. However, there was a person who was close enough to do it, a so-called friend, a faerie who is no longer a daughter of mine. Her name is Zana. She and my Summoner Layla were inseparable growing up, but when Layla was marked as the Dragon Summoner, pride and envy entered Zana's heart. They traveled together and fought many battles, but as soon as Devon seized power, Zana conspired with the Baron of Hadley and lured Layla to his manor as a place of safety while they plotted how to overthrow Devon. But Devon had enthralled Zana with promises of prestige and power in his new order. Devon knew he had to eliminate the Dragon Summoner if he were to maintain control. One night, as Layla slept, Zana crept upon her and slit her throat. The crown, jewels, and dress are there still, in a closet in Zana's chambers at Hadley Manor. They're of no use to Zana, because she is not the Summoner. You, Donella, must go and retrieve them." Braylynn shared a long look with her Summoner. Donella knew her goddess was aware of the pain and confusion she was going through and also of the pain that was bound to come.

Donella stood up and walked over to the only window in the room. It had a wide sill to sit on, and the view overlooked the circular courtyard below, with lush green grass and a bubbling stone fountain in its center. Faeries sat along the fountain's edge, splashing their feet in the water, as the bright sun warmed their faces. Several others were flying up to branches of nearby trees, picking fruit. It seemed hard to believe that, in a place of such peace, murder and darkness hovered just outside its borders. Donella was overwhelmed by all she had heard, and even more so by what she was expected to accomplish. She felt a hand touch her shoulder and, turning, saw compassion in Leah's eyes.

"You don't have to do this alone, sister. We will all help you, for as far as you need to go." Donella looked at each one in turn, and a kinship was awakened in her heart. These faeries shared a bond, and she was a part of that. Donella gave Leah a hug, and with that embrace let her know that her friendship was both welcome and accepted. She then walked over to Braylynn and looked directly into those deep blue eyes.

"You are my goddess," Donella said with resolve. "And I am your Summoner. I will do what you ask of me."

"I know you will," she said with pride. "And as Leah says, you need not go alone. If Leah consents, I will have her accompany you."

"You don't even have to ask. I had already planned on going," Leah said.

"I will not be able to go with you, Donella," the queen said. "But I will send Dain. Aside from being my counselor, he is also my personal protector. He was a high-ranking general with the warriors of the Border Lands when Leah found him bleeding from many wounds and near death. When he was whole again, he told me Braylynn had convinced him to stay. He is one of the finest swordsmen in Vasara and would better serve us if he were with you." The queen looked thoughtful for a moment. "I wonder, Braylynn, could this be why you wanted him to stay so badly?" she asked with a sidelong glance at her goddess.

"I do sometimes have foresight, daughter," the goddess replied slyly. "Before you go to Hadley, you will first need to travel to the Parma Wilds, which is to the west of our lands. There is a hermit who lives there whose special talents may prove useful. His name is Diminitus. Dain will be able to guide you. Once you have retrieved the dress, crown, and jewels return here, and I will instruct you in their use."

"When are we to start?" Tera asked, not leaving any doubt that she was going, also.

"You are most certainly *not* going," the queen told her in no uncertain terms.

"But..." she started.

"No buts, young lady. You are too young for this kind of danger, and that is final."

"I fear the queen is right, Tera," Braylynn explained. "No one doubts your courage, and your time will come soon enough."

Tera ran across the room and flew out the window.

"Oh, dear," the queen said. "I didn't think she would take it that hard."

"Don't worry, Valencia. I will speak with her," Leah said. "She has an adventurous spirit, and it is hard for her to be left out of something like this."

"Thank you, Leah," the queen replied.

"I am afraid I must leave you now," Braylynn said. "Donella, there will be much planning and instruction before you set out. I will leave that in Valencia's and Leah's hands." Turning to the queen, she added, "When you feel they are ready, send them with Dain to find Diminitus."

"Why do they need Diminitus? You never really explained that."

"Oh, just call it another one of those foresight things." She smiled enigmatically. "Farewell, my daughters, and stay safe." Unlike when she arrived, Braylynn faded into a blur of color and disappeared.

"When will she come back?" Donella asked.

"Probably not before you are ready to leave," Valencia replied. "Certainly by the time you get back from Hadley. This has been a busy day and full of revelations. You are probably exhausted, dear. Leah, will you take Donella to the house directly behind the Hall? That house was specifically built for the Dragon Summoner. It is connected to a path that leads to a wide glade where the dragons land. Go and rest, dear. Leah will stay with you until you are comfortable in your new surroundings." With that, she stood up and embraced each of them.

Leah and Donella left the queen's chambers and went back outside. Even though the day's events were swimming around

Donella's head, she had a feeling of peace and of coming home after meeting with Braylynn.

Upon reaching the house of the Dragon Summoner, Leah opened the door and ushered them inside. A great weariness seemed to come over Donella, and instead of looking around her new dwelling, she found a high-backed chair by the fireplace and, folding her wings, collapsed into it. Unable to keep her eyes open any longer, she fell asleep as Leah grabbed a coverlet from the bed and placed it over Donella's sleeping form. She then crept from the room and silently closed the door, standing guard outside lest anyone disturb the house's weary occupant.

Chapter 7

DONELLA WOKE to the morning sunlight streaming in through the window. She must have slept through yesterday's afternoon hours and all through the night without stirring. Her legs were covered with a dark green coverlet that had circular designs in silver thread woven into it. She stood up and stretched, moving her wings in and out while taking in her surroundings. It was a one-room dwelling with stairs leading up to a loft. On the floor was a circular green carpet with a white dragon emblazoned on it. A small table with two chairs sat in one corner. On the table was a bowl of fruit. The house was very clean and tidy. The fireplace mantle held various statues of dragons and faeries. Grabbing a piece of fruit from the bowl and taking a bite, she headed outside.

There was no one around the immediate vicinity, so she walked the dirt path down to the glade. When she got there, the enormity of it struck her. *A host of dragons could fit in this space*, she thought. The talon trees encircled the entire area. The grass was thick like a carpet. Donella's urge to take flight and circle the field was strong. Braylynn was right: her faerie nature was emerging. She moved her wings slowly back and forth, testing the movement in the center of her back. She could feel a certain rhythm as she sped them up. Soon she started to lift off the ground. At first, Donella was startled by this, but the joy and freedom of flight took over, and she started to propel herself higher. She tilted her wings from side to side to get the feel of turning, all at a slow and steady pace. She then climbed higher and allowed herself to glide down.

Now for a little speed, she thought. Staying low to the ground, she started going faster. Right at the midway point of the glade, a flash of blonde and lavender streaked in front of her. She was momentarily startled, and her flight was thrown off course. She looked over and saw Leah flying around the rim at an incredible speed. As she reached the far end, she turned and headed back to where Donella had landed.

"Good morning, Donella! Now, that was fun!" she said, smiling, her face flushed.

"Good morning, Leah. I see Tera is not the only one who likes to pull surprises."

"Well, it is somewhat part of the faerie nature. Tera just takes it to the extreme. Speaking of the faerie nature, I see you have remembered how to fly."

"Yes, although I don't think I could fly as fast as you can," she replied.

"Oh, I bet you could if you were pushed to it. I have something for you." She handed Donella what appeared to be a stick that was about the length of her palm.

"What is it?"

"Hold it up horizontally with the ends not pointing toward your body," Leah instructed. "Now, you see this small indentation along the grain? Push there."

Donella pressed on the wood, and the ends opened and expanded into a six-foot faerie spear.

"This is the faerie weapon of choice. There are others, but most of us have these. There are straps that attach to your arm or leg to hold it while you fly. Want to learn how to use it?"

"Yes, I would," she replied enthusiastically.

Over the next several days, Leah taught Donella how to block and attack using the spear. She also taught her how to spin it in front of herself at such a high rate of speed, it would act like a shield against other spears and arrows. All this was done on the ground, and Donella proved to be an apt pupil. Soon she was ready to try these skills in an aerial fight.

The sun was a few hours before noon in the sky when they met back at the glade.

"Are you ready?" Leah asked.

"I think so."

"These spears have no tips, so we won't accidentally cut each other. Now, try to catch me!" Leah launched herself into the center of the glade and hovered about thirty feet off the ground, waiting for Donella to make her move. And move she did. Donella did not fly right at Leah. Instead, she flew low to the ground, and when she judged she was directly under Leah, she changed her path and flew straight up, holding the spear diagonally across her body and turning like a corkscrew.

This movement took Leah by surprise. Anywhere she tried to strike was met by the rotating spear. She quickly moved to the side and dropped down. As she did this, she stuck her spear into Donella's midsection. The spear slid along Donella's body as it turned and lodged against her spear as it came around. Once Leah felt it lock, she turned her spear and pulled, sending Donella's spear flying.

"Ha! Now what will you do?" Leah laughed triumphantly.

Realizing she was weaponless, Donella arched her back and did a half-loop in hopes of putting some distance between Leah and herself. Righting herself, she streaked to the opposite end of the glade with Leah in hot pursuit. She then flew around the outer edge until her flight brought her full circle, back to where her spear had fallen. Coming in low, she made ready to grab for it. All the while, Leah was swinging her spear inches above her head.

"Got it!" Donella cried as she turned around to meet Leah's attack. The spears made a loud crack as they hit. It then became a match of swing, thrust, and block, neither faerie gaining the advantage as their battle climbed higher.

Leah suddenly broke off and started speeding toward the ground. Donella was not going to let her get away and followed close behind her. Then, with a quickness Donella didn't think possible, Leah stopped in midair and turned, bringing her spear up and pointing directly at Donella's chest. Donella realized her mistake too late and prepared herself for the fatal blow. But at the last instant, Leah dropped her spear and wrapped her arms around Donella as she crashed into her. They spun for a little bit, but Leah was able to slow their speed before they hit the ground. They both landed with a gentle thump. Donella and Leah were both breathing heavily, sweat glistening on their bodies from all their exertions.

"My wings are aching," Donella said when she was able to catch her breath. Both fairies lay on their backs with their wings spread out beneath them.

"Mine as well." She turned to look at Donella and smiled. "That was a great match!" Donella smiled back. "The last maneuver I did was something I couldn't teach you on the ground, but it is the one thing you must always be prepared for. Always assume your enemy will turn suddenly, because if you're not able to check your speed or veer away, you will impale yourself on whatever weapon they are holding."

"I will remember that," Donella replied, turning to look at the clouds floating by. After a few minutes' contemplation, she turned back toward Leah. "There is something I've been meaning to ask you."

"Ask away."

"Who are these warriors from the Border Lands, and why are they here?"

Leah sat up and, gathering her blonde hair behind her pointed ears, tied it into a ponytail with a piece of vine.

"The men and women who live on the Border Lands serve a very specific purpose and have since their creation. From what Braylynn has told me, demons touch every world, even this one. Sometimes they can manifest themselves into such monstrosities, and they will try to invade Vasara. The gate they come through is on the Border Lands. It is the duty of the people living there to fight back the creatures. They have specialized skills in weapons and warfare to meet this demand. Sometimes they get overwhelmed and send for us to help. It is not often, but we always go when asked. That is why there is such a special bond between us, and that is why they are accepted here. Some faeries fall in love with the men and have families with them. This is not really practical. Any female born will be a faerie, but the father and any sons will have normal human lifespans. Since the faerie life is extremely long, it makes for eventual heartbreaks. Some faeries are willing to risk that, though. I am not that strong. I may enter into an occasional relationship, but nothing long-term." Leah looked extremely thoughtful as she said this. Donella wondered if there was someone to whom Leah wouldn't mind being attached. She figured the best course of action for now would be to change the subject.

"I've not seen Tera since that day in the Queen's chambers. I hope she is all right."

"I talked to her the other day. She is still not happy about being left out, but I think she is starting to understand. You will probably see her around in the next day or so," Leah said.

It was actually two days later when Donella saw Tera. Donella was sitting on the fountain wall in the courtyard, peeling an apple with a talon dagger that Del the weapon master had made for her. The talon wood held a fine edge and could slice as well as any steel blade. She looked around at all the activity about her. The faeries were an extremely social group and had befriended her as if she had always been a part of their clan. Though she did not know them all by any means, those she had met treated her like a daughter, a sister, or a friend.

"Good morning, Donella," said a voice from behind her.

"Oh, good morning, Brie," she replied, turning around. Brie was one of the first faeries to introduce herself during her initial days in Laurel Hollow. She liked Brie, who had a sweet, honest face. Her hair was chestnut brown, and her wings were red. Brie also had a special ability. She could talk to birds.

"How is the training coming along?" she asked.

"Very well," Donella replied, "although Leah pushes me to near exhaustion."

"You couldn't ask for a better teacher." Just then, a crow flew down and landed on Brie's shoulder. It put its beak toward her ear and started making piping bird noises. Brie listened intently and made a few bird noises in response.

"What did it say?" she asked.

"She was telling me she thinks your long black hair is beautiful. And she would love nothing better than to feather her nest with it. That is a high compliment among birds."

"Thank her for me. And tell her I think her feathers are beautiful, as well." Brie relayed this to the bird, which puffed out her chest and gave a few flaps of her wings before taking flight.

"She appreciated what you said," Brie told her, smiling. "I bring a message from Leah. She says when you have a moment to come to the queen's library."

"I'll go now. Take care, Brie."

"See you later, Donella."

Donella got up, took a bite of her apple, and started walking toward the Hall. Along the path, she saw the top of a silver-haired head ducking around a corner. There were not too many faeries that Donella knew who had silver hair, so she had a pretty good idea who it was. She walked over and peered around the corner.

"Hello, Tera. I hope you are well. I've missed you." Tera looked up from where she was crouching.

"You did?" she said. "Truly?"

"Of course! You were one of the first faeries I met when I got here. You were with me when I met my goddess and learned my name. That forms a special bond between us."

"I'm sorry I haven't been around. I just couldn't stand the thought of being left behind. Everyone thinks I am too young. Compared to human years, I'm old enough. Just because I haven't lived a thousand years, like some, I'm considered immature."

"I don't think that's it at all, Tera. I believe Valencia and Braylynn feel the danger we may encounter will be beyond what is normal. I would be willing to bet they would be reluctant to even allow someone like Brie to go."

"I guess you're right, but that doesn't make it any easier."

"I know." Donella sat on the grass next to her. "Would you like my apple?"

"Yes! I love apples."

Donella looked at Tera while she took several bites. The young faerie had an infectious smile and a way about her that made Donella want to laugh at the world.

"Listen, I have to go see Leah and the queen. Why don't you come with me?"

"You mean it?"

"Sure. You were here when all this started. I don't see why you can't be there."

"Thank you, Donella," Tera said shyly, picking idly at a blade of grass.

"What for?"

"I know I'm a little flighty, and people don't think I take things seriously, so they in turn don't take me seriously. But you treat and talk to me like an equal, and I appreciate that." They both stood up, and Donella gave Tera a hug.

"You know, we probably have a few minutes if you want to play 'catch me if you can'." And without waiting for a reply, she lightly smacked Tera on the head and flew off.

"Hey! That's not fair." Tera dropped the apple and took off after her.

* * *

Leah and the queen were in the library, studying some maps. The room itself was not very large. Every bit of wall space was packed with books, scrolls, and maps of every kind. In the center of the room was a table with six chairs placed around it. There were also some high-backed chairs in each corner for casual reading. Valencia walked over to a set of shelves with scrolls at the very top. Giving a slight thrust of her wings, she flew up to one scroll with a red ribbon tied on it and pulled it out.

"This is the one we need," she said to Leah as she glided back down. The queen unrolled the scroll on the table. "This one has more detail of the Parma Wilds than the others." There came a knock at the door.

"I'll get it," Leah said. Upon her opening the door, Donella and Tera entered. "Ah, there you are. I was just about to send another messenger."

"Sorry, I was delayed. Tera claimed to be the fastest faerie alive, and I just had to see for myself," Donella said.

"And is she?" the queen asked, smiling.

"If she isn't, she is probably running a close second."

"I know. I have seen her fly in and out of trees like a stormy gust," Leah added. Tera was blushing from all the praise.

"Well, I'm glad you are both here," the queen said. "We were just about to search out the best route to find Diminitus. I am just waiting for Dain."

Donella walked over to the table to view the map. It had been drawn in great detail, with striking colors representing forests, marshes, dells, and hills. The Parma Wilds did have a wild look about it just from the map. Everything seemed to blend into one another: forest into marsh and grassland into jungle and so on. There was no set boundary that told where one part ended and the other began. A purposeful knock sounded at the door.

"That will be Dain," the queen said. "Let him in, Leah." Leah opened the door to allow Dain to enter. After all the greetings were out of the way, Valencia got down to business.

"Her greatest assets when it comes to battles and quests are planning and tactics. She is an excellent fighter, but in laying out a plan, she is without peer," Leah whispered to Donella. "It is also rumored she has a special ability that no one is allowed to know and that can be used in only the most extreme circumstance. As far as anyone knows, she has not had to use it yet."

"Dain, please come over and look at the map," the queen said. Dain walked over to the table where Valencia and Leah had put their heads down to consider the possible routes they would take. As he came near, he stole a glance at Leah. A stray strand of blonde hair had slipped from behind her pointed ear to fall across her pink cheek. His hand unconsciously started to rise, as if to push it back, but then fell down to his side in resignation about something that could not be.

Donella happened to be looking directly at him, and her ability to see to the heart of a situation told her at once how this man regarded Leah. She also knew Leah was totally unaware of Dain's affection for her. Recalling her previous conversation with Leah about her attitude toward long relationships with humans, she held out little hope for this warrior from the Border Lands. Donella looked over at Leah and wondered what her reaction would be if she knew how Dain felt. There definitely was a friendship between them. Leah had saved his life, after all. Looking back at Dain, she could see his days as a military leader had taught him to hide his emotions well, but Donella saw the undercurrent of pain running just below the surface.

"Donella, you should look at this, as well." The queen's words brought her back to their present situation. "You should enter Parma at its northernmost tip," she said, pointing to a section on the map that read Northern Gate. It was not a physical gate but a stream that flowed out of Laurel Hollow and into the Wilds between two hills. "It will increase your total distance, but the stream will take you to the heart of the Wilds with little contact with some of the more dangerous beasts that inhabit that place. Dain, it will be up to you to use your skills and knowledge of Parma to find Diminitus, once you leave the stream." Valencia looked at Leah and Donella. "You two must use your skills in concert with Dain, but follow his lead on the trail. He's the best there is, even if he is only human," she said affectionately.

"Pan lives in those woods," Tera added. "If you happen to see him, you can probably get him to help you."

"Who is Pan?" Donella asked.

"He is king of the fauns," Valencia said. "He sometimes visits Laurel Hollow. Tera is right, though—if you can find Pan, he could probably lead you to Diminitus' house or at least tell you his whereabouts."

"Where do the fauns live in Parma?" Donella asked, looking at the map.

"There are several forest locations in the Wilds where fauns can be found. One of them is just south of where you will leave the stream. Dain should be able to track them. Once you find them, they should be able to contact Pan for you."

"Braylynn has obviously had contact with Pan before," Donella said, remembering the pipes she gave Tera. "Can she not find him for us?"

"I will not be able to do that," Braylynn said from the doorway, causing everyone to jump.

"I know you're a goddess and all, Braylynn," Dain said, "but I wish you wouldn't do that. A man of my temperament and training expects to hear someone sneaking up behind him, no matter how silent they try to be. You gave me such a start, not to mention shaking my faith in my training."

"Forgive me, Dain," Braylynn said. "In my case, though, I don't think you need to question your abilities." She smiled at him and, being as tall as he was, easily put a hand warmly on his shoulder.

"Why can't you contact Pan?" Tera asked.

"Because the quest has begun," Braylynn started to explain. "From this moment on, secrecy will be our greatest ally. I will not go abroad in Vasara, in either body or spirit. I do not want to give Devon any reason to be looking too closely at faeries. Your approach to Hadley Manor will be difficult enough, but it would be near impossible if the enemy knew you were after the vestments of the Dragon Summoner. It would also tip our hand that a Summoner was in the world again, and I would rather he not know that yet. Of course, once you have obtained all the items, he will most certainly hear of it and what it means."

"I still don't understand," Donella said, puzzled. "You're a goddess. You can do anything."

"That's right, I can, but my brothers and I purposely put limits on ourselves."

"Why would you do that?" Leah asked.

"By defining limits, we also limit any other beings with our kind of power. In this case, demons. Also, this is your world. You would not come to value it if you did not share in the struggles to make it a better place."

"I can understand that," Dain remarked, as his face took on a proud aspect. "In the Border Lands, we watch for evil every day. Man, woman, and child, each will do their part. And we do not do it for thanks, which we get precious little of from the rest of Vasara. We do it because we are tied to the land and one another in ways that I am not eloquent enough to explain. Above all, we value our freedom. I do not think we would cherish this if the gods just continually stepped in to solve all our problems."

"Well said, Dain, and if that is not eloquence, I do not know what is. If my brother Fallon were here, I am sure he would be bursting with pride. But now back to the issue of Pan. You will need his help to locate Diminitus, and so," Braylynn said, placing her hands over her ears, "Tera will be going with you."

"*What?*" Tera screamed happily, launching herself from the other side of the table into Braylynn's arms. "Braylynn, are you serious? Do you really mean it?"

"I thought we were in agreement that it would be too dangerous for her," Valencia said.

"I was in agreement, but events are starting to move more rapidly than even I anticipated. They must have Pan's help to find Diminitus, and they don't have a lot of time to achieve this. Tera will be able to find Pan more quickly than any of you."

"How can she do that?" Dain asked, clearly skeptical.

"If I am not mistaken, Tera, Pan taught you a special song on his pipes," Braylynn said, putting Tera back on the floor.

"That's right!" she said, her cheeks flushed with excitement. "The last time he was here, he taught me the song of Calling. If I play it in the Wilds, eventually he will hear it and come to us."

"Why can't Tera just teach us the song?" Leah asked, clearly not liking the idea of exposing Tera to danger.

"Because the song has to be in an exact tone and rhythm, and there are also special notes that only Tera is able to play. Sound and music are Tera's special ability." She looked fondly at the little faerie. "I have heard her mimic the sound of a sparrow so perfectly, I spent quite a while looking for it before I realized it was her. I think she even fooled Brie once, until she realized the sound Tera was making was pure gibberish."

"I can imitate the sounds, but I don't know the words," Tera explained.

"She must go with you, and I have every confidence that you will be able to protect her."

Valencia looked hard at the three of them. "Very well, but you better keep her safe. She is very precious to me. And you, young lady, you do everything the others tell you to do, understand?"

Donella could see Tera was overcome by the queen's sentiments. She knew Tera enough that she would hide her emotions behind her silliness, but not today. Tera walked over and gave the queen a hug. In turn, Valencia bent down and kissed both her cheeks. She looked at her like a mother bird pushing her chick out of the nest, hoping she will be able to fly before she hits the ground.

"I will guard her with my life, Valencia. I promise you, no harm will come to her," Leah said with steel and resolve in her voice.

"I know you will, Leah," the queen responded with a hint of melancholy. Donella assumed Valencia couldn't help feeling responsible for these brave souls in sending them into what could possibly be their deaths. As queen, such decisions were hers to make, and she did not shrink from them, but that didn't mean she had to be happy about it. Still, if any faeries had a chance of making it, it was these three. It also helped knowing Dain would be with them.

"You will need a couple of days to get everything together for your journey," Valencia said. "Dain, I will trust this task to you. When you feel you are ready, set out for the Northern Gate in Parma. There will be a man there to provide you with a boat to go downstream. I will get some money from the royal treasury for the expenses of your journey."

"Very good, Your Majesty. I will start the preparations at once. Farewell, Braylynn. I will see you when we return."

"Goodbye, Dain. My blessings on you. I must take my leave, as well. Keep one another safe. Donella, once you have what you seek, return here as fast as you can."

"I will, Braylynn."

"Goodbye for now, and my blessings on you all." Braylynn slowly faded out of sight like a morning glory closing its petals in on itself after the sun has moved on.

"You all know what you have to do. I believe a lot of your planning will have to be made on the spot, since we don't know exactly what you will encounter. Donella, you and Tera go back to your cottage and make the preparations you deem necessary. You should also visit Dev before you leave. He can probably tell you what weapons will best suit you. But tell him nothing of your mission. We are the only ones who know, and it needs to stay that way until your return."

"I will do as you say, my queen," Donella replied with affection and loyalty. Valencia couldn't help but smile at this green-eyed faerie. In such a short time, she had embraced the inhabitants of Laurel Hollow as her own.

"Come on, Donella, let's go visit Dev first. I think I could use a good dagger. Bye, Valencia, and don't worry. I will take care of them," Tera replied, smiling.

"I'm sure you will, dear. Be careful. Leah, Donella, would you stay back please?" Valencia rolled up the map and flew it back to its spot on the shelf.

"I'll be right behind you, Tera," Donella said.

"What is it, Valencia?" Leah asked when Tera had left.

"When you get to Hadley, there is a good chance that you will run into Zana. What would you do if faced with the prospect of killing another faerie?" Valencia asked.

"In my eyes, she is a traitor and murderer. She is a faerie no more. Hopefully, she will not get in our way, but if she does, I will do what is necessary," Leah said matter of factly.

"You must be careful, Leah. I know Zana, and she is your equal in fighting skill."

"Don't worry, Valencia. I won't underestimate her."

"I don't know if I have the same confidence as Leah," Donella said, "but I will do what must be done."

"That is all I can ask of both of you."

Leah and Donella left the queen alone in her library, looking out the window to the courtyard below, contemplating their chances of success.

CHAPTER 8

THE POUNDING OF HOOVES sounded like thunder as the chestnut mare raced along the half-mile span known as the Palatine Bridge. The bridge crossed the chasm that divided the White Castle and the city of Kensington from the rest of the mainland. Unless one could fly, it was the only way to enter the city. The rider was tall with sandy blond hair and brown eyes. His facial features would be considered handsome by most women, and his skin was tan from the long hours of riding that his occupation demanded.

The rider was whipping his horse into a lather in order to report to Devon on the progress of the search. Upon reaching the other side of the chasm, the guard working the barricade quickly lifted the pole to allow the rider to pass. It was not the speed of the horse nor the determined look in the rider's face that made him move so swiftly, but instead the symbol embossed on the rider's shield. A raven with outstretched wings and claws on a bone-colored background let him know he was part of Lord Devon's special guard. And unless one was getting tired of life, one did not stand in their way.

It was nearly dawn, so there was not much activity on the cobbled streets as he rode past the shops of the market square. Shop owners were lifting up awnings and setting up tables for the morning crowd that would soon descend. The rider flew by the great library, with its silent stone sentinels on the front steps that led up to the main door. The statues were polished black marble, which made them stand out against the building's white facade. One statue depicted a woman wearing a flowing robe with hair cascading down her back. Her arms were open in a gesture of welcome. One hand held an open book representing knowledge; in the other hand was a map of Vasara, representing the idea that knowledge belonged to everyone.

The second statue was a man in full armor, visor raised, a sword firmly grasped in his hands with its blade pointing straight up in front of his face. Inscribed on the blade were the words *Preserve and Protect*. This statue represented the guarding and perpetuation of knowledge for future generations. The rider did not pause to admire these but pressed straight on to the castle gates. The portcullis was down when he reached the guard tower.

"Open the gates!" the rider yelled. A balding silver head appeared from a nearby window.

"State your name and business, sir," the guard shouted down, somewhat annoyed to be made to work this early in the morning.

"For my name, all you need to be concerned with is this," the rider said, showing his shield. "And my business is for Lord Devon's ears alone. Now open this gate, for if I have to do it myself, it will be because you no longer have any arms!"

"Yes, sir! Right away!" the guard replied nervously. The portcullis came up, and the messenger rode through. As he reached the castle steps, he jumped off his horse and gave the reins to a groom standing nearby then strode up the steps at a brisk pace to the great iron doors of the palace. As he pounded on the entry door, set in the middle of the great door, he happened to look up to see a raven circle and then disappear through a window in the high tower. The door was opened by a youthful-looking porter in red robes with yellow trim. He was tall with red hair, and his eyes were quick and alert.

"Greetings, Lieutenant Nyle. Lord Devon has been expecting you," the porter said with a slight sneer.

"Hello, Tolbert. Yes, I know. I saw the raven. And how is your wrist feeling today?" Nyle hated Devon's porter. He was such a sycophant and an informer. He had foolishly challenged Nyle to a duel with foils after Nyle insulted him in front of the Council of Barons. It was quickly over, and Tolbert had received a nice slice on the wrist as he was disarmed.

"Please follow me, Lieutenant," Tolbert said sourly, ignoring Nyle's question. Nyle followed behind, smiling to himself. They walked the long hallway that extended all the way to the throne room, but that was not their destination. Many doors opened up off the hallway, and it was through one of these that they entered. It led to a spiraling staircase. After climbing to the top, Tolbert knocked on the door.

"Enter," a hollow-sounding voice called from inside. Tolbert opened the door. "Come in, Lieutenant Nyle. Leave us, Tolbert."

"As you wish, Lord Devon," Tolbert replied, casting a dark look at Nyle before closing the door.

"Have a seat, Lieutenant." Devon had his back to Nyle as he tended to his ravens. Nyle took a moment to take in his surroundings. Most people were not allowed in Devon's room of ravens. There seemed to be about ten of them perched on what appeared to be a wide ladder with four rungs. The birds were eerily quiet as Devon stroked each one in turn. Except for the birds, the only other things in the room were a desk and two chairs. "How is the search going?" he asked without turning around.

"In Dragonsgate, there has been no sign of him. Before coming here, I rode to Black River and consulted with General Kyle. Several riders had reported in from some of the other garrisons. Nothing so far."

"He may still be in the mountains with Loki," Devon mused. "What have the common soldiers been told?"

"Exactly what you ordered, my Lord. To keep a lookout for anyone acting strangely. And if they see someone, they are to report it to a Raptor."

The Raptors were Devon's elite fighting force. It was actually five units made up of ten men each. Each unit took a designation from one of the five main raptor birds. Nyle's unit was known as the Kestrel. The training to become a Raptor was rugged and ruthless.

Potential candidates were put through rigorous physical and psychological trials. At the end of the training, two candidates engaged in single combat. Only the survivor could become a Raptor. It was a lifelong assignment; the only way out was by death. Nyle had had the misfortune of facing off against a boyhood friend. He had not known whom he was fighting until he'd entered the combat ring. The fact that Nyle was still alive gave testament to the fate of his friend. But it had left a scar on his heart that he knew would never truly heal.

Devon turned around and pinned his golden eyes on Nyle. Nyle did not fear Devon; a man could not be a Raptor if he held fear for anyone. But Devon's eyes, because of their unusual color, pulled any eyes right to them. Even if you looked away for a moment, your eyes inevitably wound up staring back at those two golden orbs, which were so like a cobra's when it hypnotizes its prey just before it strikes. "And what were you told, Lieutenant?" Devon asked with intensity.

"General Kyle had a meeting with the heads of each of the Raptor units and told them to be on the lookout for a boy of about sixteen years of age, tall with brown hair. If we find anyone fitting that description, we are to examine the left shoulder for your mark. Once we have the boy, we are to return immediately to the White Castle."

"Alive, Lieutenant Nyle. He must be alive! You may tell your brother Raptors that the man who kills him or lets him be killed will find his entire unit put into a pit and set on fire!" Nyle shrank inwardly at that thought.

"Who is this boy, my Lord?"

"You do not need to be concerned with that. Just find him."

"It might help if we knew his name, my Lord," Nyle said.

"I know his name, Lieutenant," Devon snapped, "but Loki would not be foolish enough to let him use it in public. Also, I don't want you looking for a name. That is how mistakes and false leads are made. Do I make myself clear, Lieutenant?"

"Yes, sir." Nyle had never seen Devon like this before. Devon was a wizard with enormous power and always in control.

"How are things in the outlands, Lieutenant?" Devon asked calmly. Nyle was surprised by the sudden change of topic.

"Well enough, my Lord, although you might want have a talk with your barons."

"Oh? And why is that?" Devon asked, smiling knowingly.

"They are becoming heavy-handed with some of the punishments they deal out to the peasantry, my Lord."

"Order must be maintained, Nyle. Don't you agree?"

"Absolutely, sir, but your barons take it a little farther than that. One of the farmers in Black River was not able to recover from his failed crop the previous year and so could not pay his taxes. He went to the Baron of Black River to see if something could be worked out, and the Baron chopped off his head right in the town square in front of all his neighbors," Nyle said with disgust.

"You don't seem to like my barons, Lieutenant," Devon said, smiling.

"Sir, it is not my place to like or dislike, but if things go unchecked, you could have a revolt on your hands."

"Your point is well taken. However, do you know one of the reasons why I have been able to maintain power? It is because I've kept the barons and every subsequent generation of barons corrupt. I feed their greed and desires. By having each one believe he holds a special place in my good graces, they will always be pitted against one another. Never would they be able to come together to form a plan to overthrow without someone informing me. If ever I get a baron who is having noble or moral thoughts, that person is removed and replaced with someone of more questionable character. Like Tolbert. Tolbert will make a good baron someday, if one of the current barons should happen to lose his office... prematurely."

Nyle scowled at the mention of the porter's name.

"You don't much care for Tolbert, do you, Nyle?" Devon asked. "You don't need to answer that. It's plain on your face you don't. However, such men are necessary to me, Lieutenant."

"With all due respect, sir, such men can cost you a kingdom. Was there anything else, sir?" Nyle was growing tired and wanted to start his journey back.

"No, that will be all, Lieutenant. Thank you."

* * *

Devon turned his back on Nyle as he left and resumed his contemplation of his ravens. Nyle had a point. He could not allow things to get out of hand. Another reason he had stayed in power so long was by keeping the economic status quo. He was ambitious and craved power but was neither stupid nor insane. He knew of no quicker way to lose power than by making everyone's life miserable. Such conditions fostered heroes and causes. He didn't concern himself too much with the peasantry; in fact, he ignored them altogether. The merchants and nobles, however, were a different matter. He reasoned that, if he kept them in financial security, they would be very reluctant to rock the boat.

Devon turned his attentions back to his ravens. The raven was considered a bird of ill omen. But for Devon, it was only an ill omen for whomever he sent them after. Devon stepped back a couple of paces so he would have all the ravens in his field of vision. He then began the spell that would allow him to hear and see everything the birds witnessed today. These were his true spies. When the spell was complete, every bird was locked onto his golden eyes. Then the images started coming. If something interested him, he would open himself up to hear any potential conversations. Today's images yielded few results.

"Loki must still have him up in that damn cave," he said aloud. "No matter. He will have to come down sometime. In any case, he will have to come to the castle if he wants to get back home. And then my work will be accomplished. Go, my pets, and be my eyes and ears." The ravens took flight out the window, each heading in a different direction. One he held back. "I have a special job for you, my dear. I haven't seen what has been going on around Laurel Hollow for quite some time. Fly down and see what the faeries are up to." He kept his gaze on the bird and fed it images of the area he wanted it to survey. Satisfied that the raven had the location, he released it on its mission.

As Devon headed back toward the door to exit the tower, he doubled over in pain. He put one hand on his desk in an effort to keep himself from falling. His breath came in raking gasps. He quickly recited the chant that kept the beast within him chained. His breathing slowly returned to normal.

That was close, he thought. Usually there were little warning signs that let him know the demon was stirring. If the demon should ever break free, his life would be over. This was another reason to get into that other world. Once that was accomplished, the demon would be sealed within him forever, and nothing would be able to stop him. Not even the Gods. But first, he needed to recapture that boy.

"It won't be long, Andros. I will have you, and we will finish what we started when we were rudely interrupted by my errant brother." He walked out of the tower with a malicious grin on his face, certain of his success.

CHAPTER 9

IT WAS A MOONLESS NIGHT, and the stars shone brightly on the herd of deer foraging in the fields. A large antlered buck walked over to the stream and started to lap up some water. It lifted its head suddenly in alarm and looked around. There was a fluttering sound, like a cape billowing in the wind. It swept its head left and right and saw nothing. Too bad it didn't look up. Never even feeling the impact because it was dead instantaneously, the deer was suddenly gripped firmly in the golden talons of a black dragon.

Sorry about that, big guy. Circle of life and all that, Andy said as his wings beat a steady rhythm back toward the cave. Each day, Andy's hunting and flying skills got better and better. He remembered back several weeks to his first flight. He had been so terrified about jumping off the cliff that Loki had had to use magic to push him off. He looked like a duck, flapping like mad, trying to slow his descent.

"Stop moving your wings and glide!" Loki had yelled down to him. Once he did this, things had improved dramatically. Like huge sails, his wings had caught the warm air currents, giving him the necessary lift to stop falling. Andy had then moved his wings in a single thrust and been amazed at the sudden increase in height and speed. Like rowing a boat, the longer and more powerful the stroke, the farther and faster the boat goes. It was in that first flight that he had experienced the joy and freedom the hawks below the cave knew. It had felt so natural, as if he had been doing it all his life. He only flew at night. Loki had explained that his presence must be kept a secret for as long as possible. Eventually, someone would see him, but the less foreknowledge Devon had the better.

Loki, I'm coming in. I have dinner.

Well done, lad! I'll be right out to give you a hand. Loki had explained many things in those first couple of weeks. For one thing, Loki had told him he could "mind speak" with anyone, but only if he made contact first. He also showed him how he could carry on a conversation with several people and allow everyone to hear everybody else, so all were part of the conversation. Although when they first practiced this, the only other participant had been a frog, which had made it quite difficult to get the hang of it, because the frog had refused to connect at first, not knowing what was going on. But once Andy had connected and the frog lost its fear, both he and Loki could hear the croaks together. "This will come in handy later on. You'll see," Loki said with prophetic wisdom.

Loki had also told him more of his brother wizards, about Devon's pact with a demon and Redlin's disappearance. Loki did not know where Redlin had gone but said the Five had assured him that he was safe and alive.

"I miss Redlin," Loki said with a hint of sadness. "He was a great brother and an even greater friend. Devon was always aloof, but the three of us could work together when the need arose." He looked thoughtful, retracing his path of memories. "I really miss my brothers, both the one who vanished and the one who is lost to me forever." He had not spoken anymore that night. Andy had found him the next morning, still sitting in his chair, smoking his pipe, and staring into the flames.

One thing that came as a shock to him was when Loki told him that his own brothers were safe. His world had started spinning again when he heard that. *Brothers? I have no brothers!* Then he braced himself for another one of Loki's shocking revelations.

"Actually, you have nine brothers," Loki said. "Nine dragon brothers. They vanished shortly after Devon seized power. Don't ask me where they went, because I haven't a clue, and the Five are not talking about it. I guess you could say in this regard we are akin, since we have both lost our brothers." Andy didn't know his brothers, but he knew his sister, and she was out there waiting for him to find her. His sister was in trouble all because of him, making it difficult to focus on anything else.

He brought his mind back to the present. As he neared the cave entrance, he started his hovering maneuver so he could land upright without crushing the deer in his foreclaw. Loki emerged from the cave.

"Now there's a big brute," he said, examining the buck. "Bring him inside, and I'll skin him and cut some steaks for dinner." Loki went back inside as Andy dragged the buck after him.

After dinner was over, Andy felt stuffed. He thought that, being a dragon, he would naturally have a huge stomach that would need constant filling, but Loki was right: one meal a day was all he needed. That deer was so tasty he had made an absolute pig of himself. Andy settled into what had become their nightly routine. He curled up by the fire while Loki sat in his chair with his pipe and ale. Tonight, Loki had selected a dark red pipe with images of faeries carved into it and a tankard to match.

"That was some good meat, lad," Loki said, sighing contentedly. He took a long sip of his ale and puffed leisurely on his pipe. Andy didn't know when it had happened, but somewhere along the way, he had developed a great fondness for this old man. And he trusted him with his life.

What shall we talk about tonight? Andy asked, absentmindedly swishing his tail back and forth.

"Nothing tonight, Andros," he said, looking at him fondly. "Tonight we will just have idle chit-chat and quiet contemplation. I want you totally relaxed tomorrow, because, in the morning your world will change again."

I don't think I can handle any more surprises, Loki.

"You can, lad. You are more than ready. You have done every-thing I have asked without question, which tells me you don't need reasons. And someone who can do a task without needing a reason as to why they are doing it is someone who can handle the unexpected. You're ready, boy, and I am extremely proud of you." Andy felt a lump in his throat hearing praise from this kind old man and for the confidence he had in him. Andy hoped and prayed he would never have the occasion to let him down.

He awoke the next day before the sun came up. This was his favorite part of the morning. Loki was still sleeping. He gave himself a little shove and slid out the doorway as silent as a snake, so as not to disturb him. He liked to come outside and feel the first rays of the sun hitting his horned head as it came over the mountains. It reminded him of the times when his family—his human family—vacationed in Cape Cod. He and his father would get up before everyone else and drive down to the shore to watch the sun come up over the ocean. The thought made him wonder what his mom and dad were doing right now. Probably out looking for him and Emilia. He needed to get this done, find his sister, and get home.

Andros, are you here?

I'm outside, Loki, watching the sun come up.

I'll be right out.

Loki emerged from the cave wearing a dark blue cloak with the hood pulled up over his head. Andy thought he looked like a monk from an ancient monastery.

Cold? Andy asked.

"A little," Loki replied. "At my age, it takes my bones a little longer to warm up." They both stood watching the sun clear the mountains and shine full on the world, its rays warming body and earth.

"Ah, that feels good!" Loki exclaimed. "A positive way to start off the day, and we need a lot of positive energy for what we're about to do."

Andy took a deep dragon breath. *I'm ready when you are. What are we going to do?*

"I am going to teach you to tap into the energy source the Five left for us. Only wizards and dragons can touch it, and once you learn to use it, you will be able to do fantastic things with it, as well as deadly things."

I understand, Andy said.

"Excellent, lad! Now, I am going to walk you through this. I am going to place my hands on your head, and I want you to allow me to enter your mind. You need to turn all your thoughts inward. Do you think you can do that?"

I think so, he replied a little hesitantly.

"You'll do fine. First, it might help if you close your eyes." Andy did this, and then he felt Loki's hands on his forehead. He tried turning his thoughts inward. Slowly, an inner vision was revealed to him. It was a misty place, and Andy saw a figure in the fog coming toward him. The figure then coalesced into the familiar form of Loki.

"What do you think, lad?"

Is it always so misty?

"It is just because this is your first time here. We are spirit walking, and we are in an altogether different place. It will start to become clearer. Follow me." Dragon and wizard proceeded to walk toward a glow just a short distance ahead. Andy noticed the mist was thinning and objects were becoming clearer. They seemed to be walking along a forest path, with trees on either side forming a tunnel of branches high overhead. When they reached the end of the path, Andy looked up. Hovering just above the ground was a glowing orange sphere with five rays radiating out of its center. It reminded him of a bicycle tire with a hub and spokes but no wheel. The air around it was electric. The power emanating from it was both terrifying and awesome. Andy felt sure that if he were to stretch forth his claw, a bolt of lightning would connect the tip of his talon to the source.

Is that it? Andy asked in awe.

"Yes," Loki said reverently. "It contains attributes of all five gods."

What about Braylynn? Is there some of her power in it?

"There was no need, as she is still here. Also, dragons and wizards are a creation of the Five, and it is for us that they left a portion of their power behind." Andy noticed a silhouette standing off to the side. It had the shape and size of a human, much like his own shape and size had been before he became a dragon.

Loki, what is that standing over there? He pointed at the silhouette.

"We will get to that soon. First, I want you to try touching the source. Imagine yourself as an empty glass, and try to fill your glass with energy from the source. Your mind becomes the conduit that the power will flow through into the glass, which in this analogy is your body."

Andy did as Loki instructed, reaching out with his mind as if trying to lay hands on the energy source. He attempted several times, but it was like trying to hold a glass ball covered in oil. Every time he tried to link with it, his mind slid off.

I can't seem to do it, he said, frustrated.

"That's because you are trying to pull the source to you, but it is the other way around. You need to push yourself to the source. Then, once the connection is made, the power will flow through you. Give it a try. It might help if put yourself in a calm state."

Andy tried to relax, and this time, instead of trying to grasp the source, he pushed his thought and being into it. The source, accepting him, released its power back through him. Andy gasped, and his eyes went wide. The feeling of strength and power flowed through him like a fast-moving river rushing through a narrow gorge and then free falling over a mile-high waterfall. He felt like his blood was moving so fast that at any moment his skin was going to set itself on fire. He believed he could do anything; all he had to do was channel the source toward whatever task he wished. He could breathe fire if he desired. *I'm going to try it.* Loki must have sensed his thoughts.

"Andros! Don't do it. I'm standing right in front of you! You'll burn me to a cinder!" Loki yelled. "Listen carefully. Just as you pushed yourself into the source, now you need to pull yourself back out. You are going to feel reluctant to do so, but don't think about it and just do it." Andy did so, and the flow of power stopped like a faucet being turned off. He felt drained.

Sorry, Loki, I just didn't want to let go, Andy replied, a little shaky now that he realized he'd almost turned his friend into a charred stick.

"It's all right, lad. We all do that the first time," he said reassuringly. "Your only mistake was that you went in too fast and put your whole self into the source. You don't have to go slow, but your thought should be controlled and deliberate. Do you know what I mean?"

Yeah, I think I do.

"All right, let's try something." Loki took his hands off Andy's head. Andy opened his eyes and blinked several times to adjust to the bright sun. "Now you know how it works. You don't have to spirit walk there as we just did to utilize the source. We did that so you would know where it was and what it looks like. It helps to be able to visualize it. In the waking world, it will all seem automatic. There are certain circumstances that will require you to turn your thoughts and being inward, as we did, but we will get to that later." Andy looked at Loki a little apprehensively. That was the second time he'd said they would "get to that later." How much more lay ahead?

"Now, since you are having incendiary urges, we will start with that." Looking over the cliff's edge, Loki spotted what he was searching for. "Do you see that dead tree jutting out from the rock face?" Andy looked toward where he was pointing.

Yes, I do, he replied, excitement beginning to build.

"Fly out a short distance then circle back and hit it with fire." Andy leaped into the air and, spreading his wings, dropped and circled away from the cave. Feeling he had gone far enough, he made a wide turn as he sought his target among the rocks. Locking onto the tree, he sent his thought back to the source but in a controlled way, as Loki had cautioned him. The connection was made, and he felt prickly all over from the enhanced sensation of the power flowing through him. He'd never felt more alive. He was coming close to the tree, and when he judged the distance ample, he opened his mouth and allowed the power to pour out in the form of liquid fire. The flames incinerated the tree instantly and blasted away a good portion of the rock face in the process. He veered off and made his ascent back to the cave where a smiling Loki was waiting.

"Well done, lad! Well done!" Loki exclaimed after Andy had landed.

That was awesome!

"You controlled it extremely well. I am very proud of you," he said, smiling.

It's like nothing I have ever felt. I just can't describe it with words.

"I know exactly how you feel, Andros. Now it is time to get to that thing I said we would talk about later." Andy felt as if something ominous were going to happen. "I hope you won't be too mad, but there is a reason I did what I did."

What are you talking about? Andy asked.

"That silhouette you saw at the source," Loki said, pausing. "That was your human form. Dragons are shape-shifters. You have the ability to switch between being human and being a dragon. Both are real, and both are you."

Andy was stunned. All this time he'd been led to believe he was a dragon forever. For a split second, he was very angry at Loki. But then he let peace and calm flow through him. He trusted Loki with his life. He would hear him out.

Why? Andy asked. *Why didn't you tell me when I first came here?*

"Because then your only thought would have been how to change back. You never would have accepted that part of you that is a dragon. You would have come to look at yourself as a human who can transform into a dragon. If anything, it is the other way around. You are a dragon who can transform into a human. But, as I said before, both are equal parts of you, and you need to see it that way and accept yourself as you are, otherwise you will not succeed in anything you do here. So let me ask you, Andros, what are you?"

Andy knew the answer to this question was extremely important to Loki and himself. Nothing short of honesty would do. He thought of what things were like when he'd first come here, of his first steps as a dragon. He thought of his first flight and his first hunt, things that now seemed so natural to him. He thought of touching the source that first time, and in that moment, he felt totally a part of this world. Andy tried to imagine what it would be like if he could no longer be a dragon. The thought made him feel like half his body was cut off. He would not be wholly dragon without his human side, and he would not be wholly human without his dragon side. Loki was right: had he known at the start, all thought of being a dragon would have left him. He looked Loki straight in the eye, and everything clicked into place.

I am a creation of the five gods, and whatever is required of me to restore Vasara back to the free and peaceful world it once was, I will do, he said solemnly.

"Yes!" Loki cried jubilantly. "You are a wonder, my boy!"

Does this mean I've forsaken my mother and father, my sister? he asked, a little downcast.

"Not at all, lad! Nothing has changed in regards to them. Your father is still your father and your mother is still your mother. And you have a sister out there waiting for you to find her." Andy felt better hearing Loki say this, and he was ready to proceed to the next step.

What do we do now?

"Now we go back to where your human form is. You should be able to get back there with no problem. I will meet you there."

Andy turned everything inward and found himself standing at the source. Loki was next to him. As before, he saw the outline of his human self.

"In your day-to-day use of the source, you are connecting with only your mind. To change forms, you have to send in your spirit as well, and make it fit inside the outline that is you. As you do this, your human side will become substantial, while your dragon side will become insubstantial in terms of form only. It might help to think of it as changing clothes. Your spirit is the same no matter what clothes you are in. Can you visualize it? Do you think you can do it?"

As Andy was listening to Loki's description, he had the image of a wax candle melted down and then poured into a mold of a totally different shape. *I can do it,* Andy replied with confidence. He started to make the connection. Once he had it, his spirit flowed through and merged with his human form while at the same time his dragon self faded until it became the outline.

When it was done, Andy pulled himself out of the source and opened his eyes in the physical world. He saw his hands and fingers. He looked down at his feet. He then ran inside to the pool of water to examine his reflection. Staring back up at him were his own familiar hazel eyes and sandy brown hair. He couldn't help rubbing his hands along his face. There was a little fuzz there. He would need to start shaving soon. He was wearing a black shirt with pants to match and a gold band around each cuff. Both shirt and pants had tiny dragon-scale designs on them.

"Where did these clothes come from? My god! That's the first time I've spoken with my mouth since I don't know how long."

"It's not been that long, lad," Loki said, smiling as he walked up to the pool. "The clothes are a gift from the gods, you could say, so you won't transform and suddenly find yourself naked. And it doesn't matter if you take them off. Anytime you switch from dragon to human, you will have these clothes. A word of warning," he added with a serious tone. "When you change forms, make sure no one is around, and if there is, make sure it is someone you trust with your life."

"Why?"

"When you are changing shape, your awareness is turned inward, just like everything else. You cannot see what is going on around you in the moments it takes to change. An enemy could harm you, and you wouldn't know it until it was too late."

"I'll remember that." Andy still couldn't believe he had hands and feet again. But something was different. It took him a moment to realize that he missed being a dragon. He missed soaring in the open sky and the feeling of freedom when he was up there. He reminded himself that his dragon self was still part of him, and he could change back anytime. Something else was different, though. Ever since he'd changed, he'd had a slight burning sensation in his left shoulder. In all the excitement, he had ignored it, but now it was intruding on his awareness. He rubbed the back of his shoulder and felt the skin was raised there. He pulled his shirt down to try to see what it was, but he couldn't get his head around far enough. "Loki, can you tell me what is on my shoulder?"

"A raven brand," Loki replied. "Devon branded you just after you walked through the door in the castle. His plan was to have you go back to the world you came from bearing his mark. That would have provided him the link he needed to pass through the door with the power of demons behind him. Eventually, he would have enslaved your world and set himself up as a supreme ruler." Andy remembered that day—the intense pain in his shoulder as he writhed on the floor. He would now have a raven forever on his back.

"Then I can never go back, can I?"

"Only if you kill him first, lad," Loki replied sympathetically.

Andy knew there was no way around it. The prophecy had brought him there for this purpose. He could choose to either accept it or not. He decided that he would do what was necessary to get himself and his sister back home, and if it freed Vasara in the process, all the better.

"How do I do it, Loki?"

"I don't know, my boy. But the prophecy has either placed the knowledge to accomplish the task in you or it will be revealed in its proper time. If you want my advice on what you should do first, I think you should go out among the people and creatures of Vasara. Get to know them and their stories. You will need to speak to them in any case, if you wish to find your sister." He looked thoughtful for a moment. "You should go down to Dragonsgate and visit the library. Learn some of the history and at the very least obtain a map. The Kensington curator will be able to help you with this."

"Do you think I should leave now?" Andy asked, a little apprehensively.

"Well, you don't have to leave this minute, but you should probably start out in the next day or so. Something tells me that events are starting to move out there."

"All right, I'll get some supplies together, and we'll leave in the morning."

"Just you, Andros. I will not be going with you."

"Why not?" he asked, a little alarmed.

"If Devon sees me, he will know you are close by. I will be out there but disguised and traveling alone. I will contact you from time to time," Loki assured him. "I have a lot of confidence in you. However, you don't have to be totally alone. When you get to Dragonsgate, go to the Red Bull Inn. Ask the man at the bar if he has seen Bart the Archer. Tell him that I sent you and that you need his help. Then the two of you should travel to the Border Lands. Ask for Lyson. He's the best tracker on the Border. He is also very good with a sword and could teach you a lot. Show him this," he said, handing Andy a gold coin stamped with the image of a lion pawing the air.

"Lyson's father gave me that. Lyson will recognize it and offer you aid. Between the three of you, you should be able to locate your sister and, of course, somewhere along the way, figure out how to get rid of Devon. Also, don't go using your real name except with people you trust. Devon knows your name, and he will have people on the lookout for anyone speaking it. Do you have any other names?"

"My middle name is Edward," Andy replied.

"Splendid. That will do just fine. Now, let's get your things together. I'll grab myself a pipe and ale, and we'll sit by the fire while I tell you some of the old stories." He smiled, and, for the first time since arriving in Vasara, Andy sat down.

CHAPTER 10

IT WAS EVENING the following day before Andy left the cave. Instead of walking the path down the mountainside, he waited for darkness and then changed back into a dragon and glided down to the road that led to Dragonsgate. It was somewhat of a relief to him that he could still be a dragon. It was so much a part of him now that he didn't know how he could have been so unaware of this part of his nature.

After he landed, he got out of sight as quickly as possible. Loki had warned him that Devon's troops would most likely be watching the roads for any sign of him. Andy went under the cover of the woods and walked parallel to the road. Whenever he heard a horse or voices, he melted farther into the forest to avoid detection. Loki had also warned Andy about Devon's Raptors, an elite fighting force that was highly skilled in tracking down and assassinating enemies of the realm.

"If they are in uniform, you will know them by the raven insignia on their weapons or clothes," Loki had told him.

Andy walked in the woods for several hours before seeing the torches on either side of the bridge that led into Dragonsgate. He could see a sentry on duty watching for anyone trying to enter the town at night. He would wait until morning. He was very good at living off the land, having camped in the mountains near his home many times. He picked out a spot farther away from the bridge that was screened by huge boulders. He unrolled his blanket and was soon dead to the world.

The morning dawned sunny and warm. Andy packed his things and started back toward the bridge. He and Loki had come up with a story, in case he was approached by anyone wondering about his business in Dragonsgate. He was to tell them he was a craftsman from Albion trying to find work. As Andy (now *Edward*, he reminded himself) neared the bridge, the sentry was nowhere in sight.

Walking as naturally as he could, he crossed the bridge without incident and entered the town of Dragonsgate. There was a lot of activity for the early morning. The open-air market reminded him of the weekend farmer's market back home. He proceeded down the main street of town but stayed close to the buildings, hoping not to attract too much attention. He figured, if he had to, he could quickly duck into a nearby store or shop to avoid notice.

As he watched the people walking up and down the street, something struck him as odd. He couldn't exactly pinpoint what it was, and then it hit him. There was not much conversation going on. Everyone was going about their tasks, not paying much attention to one another. One would at least expect a greeting from a shop owner to a potential customer, but none of that was evident. Andy didn't wonder too much on it, though, but instead kept an eye out for the Red Bull Inn. Loki said he couldn't miss it. "Just look for a statue of a red bull out front," he'd explained.

Andy reached the center of town. To his right and across the street was the library. He knew this because the word *Library* was chiseled into the marble above the doorway. What first drew his attention to the building was not the white marble of the structure, but a young girl about his own age who was sitting on the steps, singing and playing what looked like an oddly shaped guitar. Her voice was crystal clear, hovering somewhere between soprano and alto. One of Andy's favorite classes in school was music. His teachers always told him he had a great ear for tone and pitch, and the sound coming from this girl's throat was achingly beautiful. She had shoulder-length brown hair and wore a loose, long-sleeved white shirt with a dark burgundy vest. Her pants were the same color as her vest, and she wore leather boots that came up to the top of her calves. To Andy, she looked like what he imagined to be a female pirate. He was so taken by her that he was not looking where he was going and walked right into the rump of a chestnut mare. The horse shied away as Andy made contact, causing her rider to let out a string of curses.

"What's the matter with you, boy?"

Andy looked up into the stern visage of a garrison soldier. For a moment, his eyes opened wide, and he froze. He was not a Raptor, though, Andy quickly noted, figuring he would probably be all right as long as he didn't look too flustered.

"I'm sorry, sir," he replied, quickly thinking up a lie. "I tripped on a rock and was trying to brace myself so I wouldn't fall."

"Well, watch where you're going, fool! I ought to take you in for questioning," the imposing soldier said. Andy momentarily panicked but quickly lowered his eyes in an act of subservience. This seemed to appease the soldier, who didn't give him a second look as he wheeled his horse around and rode down the street. Andy cast his eyes over to the object of his distraction and saw her holding her sides and laughing. Embarrassed, he was a little put out by her amusement at his expense. He needed to visit the library anyway, so he crossed the street to where the girl was sitting.

"I don't see what's so funny," he stated in a firm voice that said he would not tolerate being laughed at. This made the girl laugh all the harder.

"Sorry, boy. That was just one of the funniest things I've seen in a while," the girl said, wiping tears of laughter from her eyes. Her speaking voice was just as lovely as her singing voice, Andy thought.

"And no need to call me 'boy,' either. I'm at least as old as you are," he said a little snippily.

"Whoa, take it easy. I meant no offense. My name is Abby."

"My name is And— Edward," he replied, cursing himself for almost forgetting his alias, and softened his tone. He was in a strange land alone and could use a friend.

"Nice to meet you, Edward," Abby said, smiling. "You're not from around here, are you?"

"Is it that obvious?" He smiled back. He wasn't the type of guy to be awestruck just by a pretty face, but this girl was infectious. "I'm actually from Albion. I've come north looking for work."

"Albion, you say?" she asked a little skeptically. She looked him up and down as if she were trying to find some flaw. "Have you lived there all your life?"

"Yes, of course," he replied nervously, wondering if he had given himself away.

"Have you ever had the opportunity to meet Baron Ogden?"

Andy figured that he had better answer questions in as neutral a manner as possible.

"No, I've never had the chance to meet him, as our paths seldom cross."

"Well I should hope not, since he is the Baron of Hadley, not Albion," she said with a satisfied smile. Andy's face went pale for a moment.

"What game are you playing at?" he asked angrily.

"No game, Edward, if that is your name. I'm just showing you what a terrible liar you are."

Andy was furious at himself for being tricked so easily. He was not going to last, at this rate. He needed to speak to her privately and see if he could trust her. "Can we go somewhere and talk?"

"Sure. Come into the library," she said, rising and walking up the stairs.

"Isn't the curator in there?"

"Not yet, but once I step inside, she will be."

"You're the curator?"

"Surprised? You were probably expecting an old man with a gray beard and scholarly-looking robes."

"Actually, yes."

"Well, if you had been here about a year ago, that is who would have greeted you," she said somberly.

"What happened?" he asked, noting the tone in her voice.

She stopped in front of the library doors and looked him full in the face. "He was killed," she replied fiercely, "because he wouldn't force his daughter into marriage with a man she didn't choose or love." Andy was somewhat taken aback by her manner.

"Let me guess," he said. "You are the daughter." Abby lowered her eyes for a moment. "I'm sorry. It's really none of my business."

"No, that's all right. I'm the one who brought it up."

Andy was finding it hard to breathe with her being so close to him. *What's the matter with me?* he thought. *I can't be getting involved with someone from this world.* He shook his head, as if that would shake the feeling.

"Something wrong?"

"No, I just got a chill, that's all," he replied.

Abby opened the doors, and they both stepped inside and walked down a short hallway, where they came to a room that opened up onto a small but ornate rotunda. The top of the dome was made of colored glass. To Andy, it looked kind of like the stained glass windows he had seen in a church. The images on the glass represented all the major races of Vasara. One in particular caught his eye. It was a dragon flying with a faerie astride its back.

Off the rotunda were several corridors each marked by a plaque over its entryway. On one was written *Philosophy* and on another, *History.* A third had the words *Natural Science* and another *Literature,* and so on. Abutting the wall on the far side of the rotunda was a lone desk with a quill pen and parchment on it.

"So, what did you want to talk about, Edward?" Abby asked.

"I was wondering what you were planning to do." A lot could depend on her answer. If she said she would turn him in, he wasn't sure what he would do about that. He couldn't kill her; he wasn't even sure he could kill Devon. He didn't want to kill anyone, but it seemed that that decision had been taken out of his hands long ago. In any case, he wasn't going to think about that any more than he had to. Meanwhile, however, he couldn't just let Abby turn him over to the Raptors, either. He wondered if the source could help him somehow. Loki had told him that what a person could do with the source depended a lot on their personality and creativity. Perhaps he could use the source to restrain her, at least temporarily, while he made good his escape. He hoped it wouldn't come to that; he desperately wanted to trust her, to trust someone.

"Do? I am not planning to do anything. What you do is your own business. I will tell you this, though. You look and act like someone trying very hard not to be noticed. If that soldier had been more alert, he would have arrested you on the spot. If you are in some kind of trouble, you should do whatever you need to do here and leave as quickly as possible, because, unless you are a better actor than I have seen so far, it won't be long before someone in authority takes you in for questioning at the very least."

"They would really do that here? What about people's rights and all that?"

"What do you mean 'here'? Where are you from, the moon? You're not making any sense," she said incredulously. "The Baron and the soldiers can arrest anyone they want for whatever reason they want." Suddenly wary, Abby eyed Andy closely. "Listen, maybe you'd better leave. I can see trouble is following you, and I don't want any part of it."

Andy was very disappointed. He had hoped he'd found someone he could confide in, but she was obviously spooked. "You're right, my problems are my problems. I will leave. I was coming to the library to see about getting a map of Vasara. There are several places I need to go, and I don't want to get lost."

"Such a request is usually made a week in advance, to allow time to make a copy. All materials remain in the library. However, since you are obviously in a hurry, there is one I can let you have. It's very general, but it should do. Wait here and I'll go get it." She left to walk down the corridor marked *General Information*. It wasn't long before she came back with a scroll tied with a leather band.

"Look, you seem like a nice guy, but I have my own worries," she said, handing him the scroll.

"I understand. Do you mind if I ask you a couple of questions before I go?"

"Sure," she said kindly. "Information is free here."

"Thanks. First, did you happen to see a girl, around eighteen years old, long dark hair and green eyes? She would seem lost."

"No, I'm sorry I haven't. Is she a friend of yours?"

"She's my sister." He'd known it wouldn't be that easy, but he had to start somewhere.

"Oh, I am sorry. I will watch for her," she said sympathetically. "What was your other question?"

"I need to find the Red Bull Inn."

"That one I can answer. When you leave the library, go left and walk past two side streets and go down the third. You will see a statue of a red bull. You can't miss it."

"Thanks," Andy said as he made to leave.

"Good luck, Edward. I hope you find your sister," she said warmly. Andy found it hard to turn away as he stared into Abby's eyes, but he managed it and was soon out the doors of the library.

What is the matter with me? he thought.

*   *   *

Abby stood looking at the space the boy had occupied long after the door had shut behind him. She felt some kind of connection with him. She thought maybe it was because they had both lost someone about whom they cared very deeply. Abby had been alone since her father died and hadn't had the companionship of someone her own age in quite a while. Edward seemed kind and decent, and for some reason she wanted to muss up his hair. She smiled at the thought.

*   *   *

Outside, Andy walked down the third street as Abby had instructed and saw the statue of the bull. It was definitely red and made of wood. The horns were pointing down as if in a charge, ready to lift its head at any moment to impale its intended victim. In the alley next to the inn, Andy saw a pair of legs sticking out from the shadows and heard the sound of loud snoring.

Probably one of the inn's late-night patrons, he thought as he stepped inside. Except for a couple of candles burning on the bar, the only light was from a fireplace and the sunlight streaming in through an east-facing window. This gave the effect of shadows in the corners of the inn's main room. Someone could be concealed in those shadows. He would have to watch his step and not give himself away.

There were several tables spread out across the oak floor. Chairs were in a semicircle around the fireplace. Off to the right of the bar was a staircase that led up to what Andy assumed were the many sleeping rooms of the inn. The common room was not empty. Aside from a bartender and barmaid, there were three others seated about enjoying their breakfast. One man was by the fireplace, stirring up the embers and trying to get a better burn going. Andy walked over to the bar.

"Excuse me, sir," he said, getting the bartender's attention.

"What'll you have, young man?" the bartender asked. He was a short, stocky man wearing a stained white apron over his clothes. His demeanor was friendly but business-like.

"Just some information."

"Sure thing, son, as soon as you tell me what you'll have."

"I'll take a coffee." He put one of the coins Loki had given him on the bar. The bartender took it and gave him three different coins in return, but Andy returned one of them to help put the bartender in a generous mood for information. Andy didn't know all the currencies in Vasara, so he trusted the bartender had given him the correct change. The man turned toward a wood-burning stove and grabbed what looked like a coffee pot then poured Andy a mug of coffee and set it on the bar next to him. Steam was still rising from the top when Andy took a sip. "Very good," he said, and he actually meant it. He was expecting something strong and burnt-tasting.

"Thank you, kind sir," the bartender said, smiling. "Now, what question do you have for me?"

"I was wondering if you might know where I can find Bart the Archer," Andy said.

"Why, you're in luck, lad. That's him sitting over by the fire." Andy turned around and looked at the man stirring the embers. He was tall and thin with long but powerful-looking limbs. Andy had shot a bow several times in his life and could imagine the amount of force this man's draw would generate. His red hair was secured in a ponytail, and he was dressed in buckskin. A huge knife was strapped to his hip. Andy picked up his mug and walked over to the fire.

"May I sit here?" he asked.

"Sit where you like, boy. I don't own this inn," Bart replied without looking up. Andy sat down in the chair next to him.

"A mutual friend told me to seek you out."

"Is that a fact. And just who might you be?"

"My name is Edward. My friend said you would be able to help me get to the Border Lands."

"And just who is this friend who is so free to offer up my services?" Bart looked over at Andy, squinting with one eye as if he were aiming at a target.

"I'd rather not say his name in here." Andy looked around the room to see if anyone was watching them.

"Let me get this straight. You want me to pack up and head off with you to the Border Lands, but you won't tell me who sent you, and yet you claim that he is a friend of mine. I'll tell you, I can't think of one of my friends who would ask such a thing of me without discussing it with me first," Bart said skeptically.

"There is a reason I can't say his name, but he gave me something to show you." Andy reached into his pack and pulled out a small, metal arrow painted red with yellow fletching. Bart took the arrow and looked it over.

"Nice craftsmanship, but if this is supposed to tell me something, I don't know what it would be." Andy didn't understand. Loki had said he would know the arrow and its significance.

"This means nothing to you?" he asked, confused.

"Sorry, I think you better find someone else to help you." Bart handed him the arrow and returned to his contemplation of the embers.

Andy didn't know what to do. This day was just going from bad to worse. *What should I do now?* he wondered. He couldn't tell him Loki had sent him; Loki had warned him against using his name in places where Devon's soldiers held authority. Then he thought of something.

"Could I hire you?" Andy asked.

"Do you have money?"

"A little, but I could get you more when we reach the Border Lands."

Bart shook his head in the negative. "Only a fool makes that kind of arrangement, lad. Besides, something tells me that taking up with you would not be the healthiest thing to do. Troubles are following you, and I don't think any money you offered would convince me to go along," he said, adding finality to the conversation.

Andy put the arrow back in his pack and left the inn. Once outside, he walked back onto the main street. The only thing he could think to do now was to get out of town and wait for nightfall. Then he would change and fly back up to the cave and talk to Loki. He hadn't walked more than five steps when he heard a shout from behind.

"You, boy! Halt!"

Andy turned around and saw a garrison soldier with a spear in his hand walking toward him. He didn't dare move.

"What's your name, boy, and what's your business here?" the soldier asked sternly.

"Well, I...," Andy started to reply.

"Edward!" Andy turned and looked back down the street and saw Abby running toward him. "Edward, I'm glad I saw you when I did. I've been waiting at the bridge all morning," she said, catching her breath.

"You know this boy?" the soldier asked.

"Why, of course. He's my cousin Edward from Albion. He came up to help me with the yearly inventory at the library," Abby lied smoothly. Andy knew to keep his mouth shut. One misstep could ruin them both.

The soldier looked back and forth between them. Finally, he made up his mind. "Very well. You may go." Andy slowly let out the breath he was holding.

"Come along, cousin. We have to hurry." Abby took Andy's hand and started to walk briskly back to the library.

"Thank you," Andy whispered as they hurried along.

"Not yet. Wait until we are inside."

"Stop!" Andy and Abby whipped their heads around, and Andy's heart sank. Coming from the direction of the inn was a man who was unequivocally a Raptor. There was no mistaking the raven symbol on his shirtsleeve.

"Run!" Abby said. Andy didn't hesitate. He leaped ahead like a deer being chased by a wolf. He was worried he might outdistance Abby, but she flew past him like a streaking comet. "Follow me!" They ran down the street and up the library steps. Once inside, they slammed the doors shut, and Abby grabbed a stout board that was used to brace the doors and placed it in the holders just in time. The Raptor slammed into the door, but the brace held.

"What now?" Andy said.

"This way." They ran through the rotunda and into the corridor marked *Philosophy*. The end of the corridor opened up into another circular room with several tables and chairs. Every bit of wall space was taken up with bookshelves from floor to ceiling. Abby walked over to a section of books on the left, running her fingers along the spines of the books, perspiration glistening on her forehead. She knew there wasn't much time. Already she could hear them pounding and hacking away at the front doors.

"*Ah*, got it!" Andy read the title on the thick volume Abby had her hand on: *Escapism: A Self-Help Guide to Reaching the Heavens* by Redlin. Abby pulled the book part of the way out, and Andy heard a click. The bookshelf opened to reveal a passageway beyond. "Quickly. Inside!" she hissed at him. They both squeezed in, and Abby deftly pulled the bookshelf shut, plunging them into total darkness. They were just in time. The doors splintered and gave way as several Raptors rushed in.

"Search everywhere!" one of them said.

"We will have to feel our way through the dark," Abby whispered with a slight tremble in her voice. When the bookshelf shut, she had immediately sought Andy's hand and held it.

"Hold on a second. I'm going to try something," Andy said. There was no fear in his voice. He liked exploring dark places and finding out their secrets. He reached into the source and, when he connected, held his free hand palm-up then channeled the energy to form a glowing ball. The ball appeared above his upraised palm and began to float, giving off a luminous glow that lit the tunnel.

Abby was astounded. "How did you do that?" Even though the tunnel was now well lit, she still held his hand.

"I'll explain later. Pretty soon they'll start tearing down book-shelves, trying to figure out where we went."

"They won't be able to do that. The wizard Redlin laid down enchantments to prevent that very thing. It was he who created the tunnels long ago. But we can talk more about that later. Let's go." Hand in hand, they proceeded down the tunnel, following the ball of light. The corridor was wide enough that they could walk side by side. The entire tunnel was made of stone, and the floor was level and even. They walked for about twenty minutes before coming to a stone door.

"Do you know where this comes out?" Andy asked.

"I believe it comes out in the woods somewhere west of Dragonsgate," she replied. Andy did not see any handle on this side of the door, so he tried pushing. The door opened effortlessly, and once they were outside, it closed by itself. The door on this side was made to look exactly like the rock it came out of, masking the fact that there was a tunnel behind it.

They walked farther west together, keeping their eyes and ears open for any pursuit. It was hard to move with any stealth, because the forest floor was littered with twigs and dead leaves, but they managed as best they could. Andy had many questions to ask Abby, but he knew now was not the time. He looked over at her. Even with her face flushed and her brown hair plastered to the side of her head with sweat, she was still strikingly beautiful. He was debating whether or not to tell her this as they rounded a boulder and a spear suddenly appeared inches from Abby's throat.

"Don't move," the Raptor hissed, "or she's dead."

They froze, wide-eyed and not daring to move a muscle.

"That was a neat trick you pulled. The others wanted to give up, but I knew, if you weren't in the library, you had to have escaped through a secret passage." The man had scars on both his cheeks, and his head was completely bald. He also smelled like he hadn't bathed in weeks, reminding Andy of the pig stalls he use to clean out when working on a farm during summer breaks from school. "Now, boy, suppose you be real cooperative like and show me your left shoulder, and maybe the little lady gets to live." Andy didn't know what to do. Any wrong move would end Abby's life instantly. Just then, something like a bee buzzing went flying by his ear. He looked back at the Raptor, who now had an arrow extending out of the front and back of his neck and a surprised look on his face. Eyes wide open, the Raptor toppled to the ground. The sight made Andy's stomach lurch. He looked behind him to see where the arrow had come from. Up on a rock stood the tall, gangly form of Bart the Archer. He pulled another arrow from his quiver and loaded his bow. *Is he going to shoot me now?* Andy thought. Bart's aim was not at Andy but up in the trees. He let fly his arrow, but it missed its intended target.

"Damn!" Bart said as the raven left its perch and started winging toward the White Castle. Andy turned back toward Abby, concern written all over his face.

"Are you all right?" he asked.

"Yes, I'm fine. A little shaken but all right." She brushed the hair away from her eyes.

"Ho, Edward! Just in time, I see," Bart said, jumping down and walking over, grinning broadly.

"I thought you didn't want to get involved in my troubles?" Andy said, one eyebrow raised. "Actually, both of you said you didn't want to be involved."

"How about we save explanations for later. Right now, we need to put as much distance between us and this place as quickly as possible. That raven I missed will no doubt reveal our position to Devon before several hours have passed."

Andy looked up in the direction the raven had flown. He felt sure he could change into his dragon shape and catch the raven and kill it, but he would risk having people see him. He didn't know how Abby and Bart would react to such a change without any foreknowledge. He felt the prudent thing to do was to let the events play out and see where they took him.

"All right, let's go," Andy said. The three of them ran at a brisk jog deeper into the woods, heading west. Andy hoped and prayed he wasn't making a mistake.

CHAPTER 11

THEY CAME TO A CLEARING where the woods were dense and tight around them as they made camp for the night. Bart made a fire and dug the pit a little deeper to help hide the flames, though the chances of anyone seeing it were extremely remote. Abby sat on a log, looking at her two traveling companions and wondering why she had let herself get involved in Edward's troubles. She couldn't pinpoint the exact reason, but she somehow felt that helping him was the right thing to do. He obviously needed her, although he did display some unusual powers. She had seen Bart in Dragonsgate before and knew of his reputation as an archer. Why he'd thrown his hat in with them was a mystery to her, as well.

She looked up at the stars. They seemed unusually bright tonight. Since her father's death, the stars had been her only constant companions. They were always patient and would listen for hours on end to anything she had to say. She imagined her father had become one of them, and she would direct much of her conversation toward him. Abby's mother had died in childbirth, so she had no memory of her. Her father used to tell her stories long into the night, and, being a curator at the library, he'd had a lot of material to draw from. The stories had filled her with thoughts of adventure, and since she was little, she had longed to be a part of some great quest. Maybe that was partly why she had thrown in her lot with Edward. She knew she didn't want to play out her life as a library curator.

* * *

"Abby?" Andy said.

"*Hmm?*"

"It looked like you were somewhere else just now."

"I guess in a sense I was. Sorry."

"No need to be sorry, young lady," Bart said. "What a dreary place the world would be if we couldn't be alone with our thoughts once in a while. Why, some of my best conversations are with myself." He smiled.

"I think now would be a good time to discuss the questions each of us must have," Andy said, throwing another log onto the fire.

"Quite right, lad. Quite right," Bart responded. Andy had the feeling that Bart was the sort of man who liked to hear himself talk. But, all in all, Andy liked him. He was not a talker himself, and Bart seemed to be good at filling the awkward pauses.

"One thing I would like to know, Bart, is why you're helping us. I thought you wanted no part of this."

"It was all a ruse at the inn. I knew Loki's arrow the moment I saw it—I gave it to him, after all—but I couldn't let anyone there make an association between you and me. My plan was to wait until you were gone about ten minutes and then follow you and tell you everything. One thing I hadn't counted on was a Raptor hiding in the shadows of the inn. I saw him leave shortly after you. When I heard the commotion, I went outside to see if I could help. Three Raptors had rushed the library door and were trying to break it in. When they came out without you, I knew you must have escaped. Then one of the Raptors jumped on his horse and rode across the bridge heading west. I followed him on foot. His trail was easy to follow. He must have heard you walking, because he was already ahead of you, waiting, when I came upon him. I untied his horse, led it a short distance away, and then spooked it so he could not escape. And the rest you know."

"What does the red arrow mean?" Andy asked.

"Very simply, I'm to give whatever aid is necessary to the bearer of the arrow," Bart replied.

"Have you known Loki long?" Abby asked, jumping into the conversation.

"It feels like all my life. He came to me when I was sixteen. I was already a better marksman than most men twice my age." He said this not as a boast but merely a statement of fact. "Loki told me he was putting an army together to go up against Devon someday, and he wanted to know if I would be part of it. I told him I would, but I had serious doubts he could raise enough men to go against Devon. He told me his plan was to recruit leaders, and the leaders would in turn start the fire that would ignite the spirit of freedom in the hearts of all the inhabitants of Vasara. The only thing we lack is a supreme leader, but Loki said the time would be approaching when that leader would reveal himself." Andy wondered uneasily if Loki hadn't already nominated him for the job.

"Well, that explains your interest in this, Bart, but what about you, Abby?" Andy turned his hazel eyes on her.

"Truth is," Abby started, "I can't really lay it on any one thing. I was outside when that soldier approached you, and I knew you weren't going to be convincing, so I thought I would provide a way out. Don't ask me why. It was almost like a compulsion. In any case, I'm not sorry I'm here. There's nothing left for me back in Dragonsgate, no family or anything, and I'm sure someone would have soon figured out you had visited me and taken me in for questioning." She picked up a stick and started drawing idly in the dirt. The night sounds seemed extremely loud in the sudden silence.

"Let me ask you something, Edward. Who are you, and what are these mysteries that seem to surround you? And what is on your shoulder that a Raptor was so intent on seeing?" Abby asked.

Andy sat silent, staring into the fire. He didn't know where to begin or what to reveal. Loki had said he would eventually have to trust someone. On the whole, they seemed honest and trustworthy, but what if it were all an act? He thought hard on it. In the end, he came to the only conclusion he wanted to come to. Instinct told him he could trust them, and whenever he was in doubt, he could always rely on his gut. Instead of answering Abby's last question, he stood up and removed his shirt and then turned around so they could see the mark.

"Wow!" Bart exclaimed. "That's Devon's mark. How is it that you are branded with the raven?"

Andy was about to answer, but then he looked over at Abby. It was hard to read what she thought. She stared for what seemed like an eternity at the mark on his shoulder. Then she got up and walked over to where he stood. She placed a hand on his raised skin, slowly tracing the outline of the raven. Her touch was electric. Andy looked at her eyes and saw tears standing there. She then took off her vest and pulled the shirt down on her shoulder. There, on that lovely white skin, was a branded dragon. She pulled her shirt up and put her vest back on, tears streaming down her face, and then turned back to face them.

"Abby, who did this to you?" Andy asked in disbelief.

She lowered her head and sat back down. Staring into the flames, she answered, "The person who killed my father is the Baron of Dragonsgate. It was his son Tolbert whom I would not marry. Tolbert left to become Devon's porter, but before he departed, he came to the library and marked me with the branding iron of Dragonsgate. He told me that since I wouldn't consent to be his wife, any man I marry after would forever see his mark on me."

Andy was enraged that someone would do this to Abby. Without even thinking about it, he plunged himself into the source. With a feral look, he created a whip of fire and lashed out at a nearby tree. The tree was sliced neatly near the base, popping and cracking loudly as it fell into the forest.

"By the gods!" Bart said, startled. "Well, I guess, if you chop it up some more, we'll have our firewood for the rest of the trip." He chuckled, easing the tension in the air around the camp. Andy stopped channeling, and the whip disappeared.

"I'm sorry. Sometimes my emotions get the better of me." Looking at Abby, he said, "If I ever run across this Tolbert, he will pay for what he did."

"Thank you, Edward," she said, wiping her eyes, "but Tolbert is not worth it."

Andy made up his mind. He would tell them everything. They'd already proven themselves trustworthy and loyal. He came and sat down on the log next to Abby. Her closeness brought him a sense of peace. She seemed to relax, as well, and so he began. He told them where he came from and how he'd ended up here. He told them of his sister and his search for her. He told them of the prophecy and everything Loki had explained to him. He told them that here his name was Andros, but back home his friends called him Andy. He said they could keep calling him Edward, if they wanted, since that was one of his names. They both decided they would call him Andros; it seemed to fit. Finally, he told them he was a dragon. This they found hard to believe.

"Are you serious?" Bart asked skeptically. "You mean you're not human?"

"It's complicated," Andy replied. "I guess you could say I'm both. This is all new to me, as well, so I don't fully understand it."

"But the dragons disappeared fifteen hundred years ago," Bart explained. "I'm sorry, Andros, I don't want to doubt you, but it's just hard to believe."

"And you, Abby, what do you believe?"

"Like Bart, it is hard to imagine you as a dragon. But I've seen you have powers, so I guess anything is possible."

Andy thought it might come down to this. He scanned the area where they were camped. He would fit if he kept his wings in close. He walked over and stood midway between the fire and the forest's edge. Closing his eyes, he turned himself inward, focusing all his thought and being into his dragon self. When he opened his eyes, he could see Bart and Abby no longer had any doubts. They both were staring wide-eyed and slack-jawed at the enormous black dragon that suddenly filled their camp. Moving his neck, he brought his face close to Abby's. She fell off the log and started to back up as the horned reptilian head came nearer.

Do not be afraid, Abby, Andy spoke to her with his mind.

"Andros, is that you?" she said aloud. This whole thing was very unsettling for her.

Yes. Speak with your mind.

All right, can you hear my thoughts? Abby asked, not sure if she was doing it right.

I can hear you. Bart, can you sense my thought?

Yes, I can. Well, if this isn't extremely convenient.

Now, I am going to try to make it so we can all hear together. The only other time I did this was with a frog, so hopefully we won't have any problems. Then, just as Andy was the conduit for the power of the source, he became the conduit for Abby and Bart.

Say something, Abby, Andy said.

I think you're a handsome dragon, she said with a smile on her face. She was definitely warming up to him.

Slightly embarrassed, Andy asked Bart if he'd heard Abby's thought.

"Oh, I did, lad, but I'm not sure if I was supposed to."

Ok, I'm changing back now, Andy relayed, gently disconnecting them from the source and turning inward once again to complete his transformation back into his human form. For some reason, his face felt very hot. "Any more doubts?"

"Oh no, Andros, I think we are both thoroughly convinced. Does that mind speech work when you are human?" Bart wondered.

What do you think? Andy sent without moving his mouth.

"Like I said, lad, very convenient." Bart slapped him on the back. "What are you wearing?"

Andy looked down at the now familiar black shirt and pants. He had forgotten about that. Any clothes he had been wearing were ripped apart when he changed into a dragon. He only had one change of clothes left. He would have to be careful or buy more clothes, as he explained to Bart and Abby.

"If you run out, I have a hooded cloak you can borrow," Bart said. "So what's our next move?"

"We need to get to the Border Lands and find someone named Lyson. Loki said he could help us."

"Well, we're going the wrong way for that, but, actually, it might work out. We need horses, and the Fenner plains are not far away. They have the finest horses around."

"Sounds good to me," Andy replied.

"Great. We'll set out when the sun is up. We should get some rest," Bart said

Abby started to stretch out on the bare earth next to the fire. "Abby, take my bed roll," Andy said.

"Andros, I couldn't. What would you sleep in?"

"I'm going to change. As a dragon, I will stand watch to keep wild animals away, along with any unwanted guests." He paused for a moment. "Abby, I'm sorry I got you involved in this."

"*Shhh.*" She gently placed her fingers over his lips. "It was my choice to make, and I am not sorry I made it. Don't think you dragged me into anything or that you're responsible for my life." She looked deep into his eyes. "Goodnight, Andros." She touched his cheek before turning and walking back to the fire.

Andy stood there a moment. He could still feel the softness of her hand. He'd never felt this way about someone before. He was not a believer in love at first sight, but he certainly had a strong connection to Abby. He took these thoughts with him as he walked to the edge of the wood. Making the change, the dragon lowered his body to the earth and kept a silent vigil as the stars made their march across the heavens.

* * *

The raven spiraled around the great tower, finally coming to perch on the window's ledge. Devon looked up from what he was writing when he heard the raven's caw.

"Hello, my pet. And what have you found for me?" He cast the spell and the images came flooding in. A smile creased his face. "So, Andros, you have come down from your mountain top. And you have some new friends." He took note of whom these new friends were, and an idea began to take shape in his mind. "If I can't catch him, perhaps I can lure him here." Devon went to the door and told the guard standing by to fetch Tolbert. After he arrived, Devon explained the raven's vision.

"I want you to take five men. That should be adequate. They are near Dragonsgate for now, but I doubt they will be for long. I want you to capture the girl and bring her here. Oh, and you might be interested to know this girl is familiar to you." Devon whispered into Tolbert's ear. His eyes lit up and his face took on an evil leer. "Your goal is the girl, nothing else. She will be our bait, should the Raptors fail to get the boy. Kill anyone else with them, but I want the girl alive. Once I am finished with her, she's yours to do with as you please."

"I will not fail you, Lord," Tolbert replied, relishing the thought of gaining what had once been denied him. He left quickly to form his squad of men.

Devon turned his attention back to his raven. "You have done well, my dear," he said as he gave the bird some scraps of meat. What had started out as a disaster was slowly coming back around to his favor.

* * *

The trio rose early and made the trek to the forest's edge, walking for three days. Arriving at nightfall, they made camp and, upon rising, got their first good look at the grass ocean of the Fenner plains.

"Whoa!" Andy exclaimed. "There's nothing but grass. We can't cross that without being seen."

"We don't need to cross," Bart explained. "And it is not as endless as it looks. Once you're five miles inside the border, you will start to see the edge of a wood on the horizon. This is Fenner's biggest defense—no enemy can approach without being watched by the plainsmen who inhabit this land." He gave two short whistles, and up from the tall grass twenty yards away sprang a man. His hair was the color of wheat, and his clothes were much like Bart's, made of buckskin. He wore a cloak that matched the color of the grass, which is why they had not seen him. "His name is Maccus. I've met with him before many times. Ho, Maccus!" Bart called in greeting. Maccus raised his hand and waved as he started to walk toward them. "Maccus is one of those leaders I told you about that Loki recruited," he explained to Abby and Andy.

"Hello, Bart!" Maccus grinned at him, shaking his hand and pulling him into a big bear hug. "It's been a long time since I saw you last. How are you?"

"I'm well, Maccus. I would like you to meet some friends of mine. This is Abby."

"Hello, Abby. It is a pleasure to meet you," Maccus said, bowing deeply and kissing her hand. The plainsmen of Fenner are romantics who hold women in high regard. They often wrote poetry and sang as they herded their horses from range to range.

"Well, it is very nice to meet you, Maccus," she said, enjoying the attention. Andy felt a stab of jealousy. Where he came from, he would call this man a player.

"And this is Edward." Andy had instructed that they use this name while traveling.

"A pleasure, Edward." Maccus gave him a firm handshake.

"Hi," Andy said in a neutral tone. He saw Bart's eyebrow raise in his reaction to Maccus. He wondered if Bart could tell what he was feeling.

"How are Lily and the boys?" Bart asked with a slight smile at Andy.

"Very well," Maccus replied, oblivious to Andy's stiff greeting. "We are expecting our third child any day now. In fact, if you had come in another week, you would not have found me here. It is getting close to her time, and I'll be staying close to home soon." Andy felt like an idiot for assuming the worst of a man he'd just met. "But I am sure this is not a social call."

"It's not," Bart replied seriously. "We need four horses as quickly as possible. It has to do with the struggle we all share."

"No problem." Maccus put two fingers in his mouth and blew a string of whistles. Farther out in the grass, almost indistinguishable, another man popped up and repeated the call, and so it went from man to man until the call reached its destination. "It will probably be a couple of hours before the horses get here. Let's go sit by the edge of the wood and talk a bit.

"What is happening in Fenner these days?" Bart asked as he sat down, laying his bow and quiver on the ground but within easy reach.

"The people are ready. They want to go back to the way it was with their ancestors, when the tribal chiefs each had a say in the governing of Fenner and when a king and queen sat in the White Castle. We're tired of sending our best foals yearly to Devon. We could expel the soldiers in the garrison if we chose to, but then we would have to face the totality of Devon's army, not to mention his magic." Maccus wiped his brow and cast his eyes across the grass. "We are ready to be free. We just need someone to counter Devon's magic, and we need to join forces with more of the provinces who wish to be free, as well. Something tells me that time is close at hand." He looked long at Andy.

"What makes you say that?" Abby inquired.

"The soldiers have been stopping and questioning every new person coming into Fenner," Maccus began. "There are also several units of Raptors in Fenner, as well, and any males under the age of twenty that the garrison soldiers stop are taken in for further questioning by the Raptor generals, which makes me wonder about young Edward here. I've traveled to just about every corner of Vasara, and I can usually place a person as to their country of origin, but him I cannot." Andy started to become nervous at this point. Would anyone else be able to recognize that he was not from this world?

As if sensing his thoughts, Maccus said, "Don't worry, though. Not too many people have this ability. The difference is very slight, and it would take an expert to see it." He looked at Bart with hope in his eyes. "Is he the one?"

Bart looked over at Andy, weighing his words. "I believe he is."

"Bart!" Andy exclaimed.

"Now keep your hair on, lad. Maccus here is not going to betray us, and he has already guessed it, anyway."

"Don't be mad at Bart, Edward. I'm sure Loki would've come and told me eventually. Your secret is safe with me."

"Do you know of the prophecy?" Andy asked.

"I know some of it, but the part I remember most is that Loki said someone was coming to be the counter to Devon's magic. He didn't say who or how." Andy decided it was probably best if he didn't know the how just yet.

"Can I ask you something, Maccus?"

"Sure, Edward, what is it?"

"Since you can place a person's origin, have you seen another like me? A girl with long dark hair and green eyes?" he asked hopefully. "She's my sister."

"No, I haven't." Maccus could see the disappointment in Andy's eyes. "But it's been six months since I've traveled out of Fenner, with Lily expecting. She could be in one of the other provinces. I'm sorry."

"It's all right. I just have to keep looking."

They sat for a while and talked of idle things. Bart and Maccus did most of the talking. Andy first felt the faint thumping on the ground before he heard it, the sound gradually growing louder. He looked out across the grass and saw several riders galloping with four horses trailing behind. One of the horses had saddlebags on it. As the riders reached them, one dismounted and walked up to Maccus.

"The horses and supplies you ordered, Chief," the rider said.

"Thanks, Red," Maccus replied.

"Everyone, this is Red, one of my clansmen and my best friend growing up. You can probably guess why we call him Red." Instead of the wheat-colored hair predominant among the Fenner, Red's hair was indeed red. Introductions were made all around.

"Did anyone see you bringing the horses, Red?" Bart asked.

"No one, and even if they did, they would have assumed we were moving them to a different range."

"Were you able to get all the supplies?" Maccus queried.

"Everything you asked for, Chief. Food, small tools, clothing—although we had to guess at sizes, since we couldn't actually measure them, especially the girl."

"You said all that in those whistles?" Andy asked, astounded.

"We've been communicating that way since our forefathers first came to these plains," Maccus said offhandedly. "You should all probably get mounted. Do you know how to ride, Edward?"

"I have ridden some, although I'm no expert." Andy started to mount one of the horses, but as he got nearer, the horse reared and whinnied in fright.

"Whoa, big fellow. Easy now." Red spoke soothingly to the animal as he narrowed his eyes at Andy. "There is something about you he doesn't like. Hold your hand out and approach slowly." Andy did this. The horse skittered backward a couple of times, but he eventually calmed down and allowed Andy to put his hand on his nose. He then stroked it and whispered softly to it.

"Man, that horse acted like you were about to eat him," Maccus said. Andy could guess why the horse thought that, but then, just as he had done with the frog, he sent images to the horse's mind, images of rolling fields and peaceful streams. The horse's ears picked up, and then he started to lick and nibble Andy's palm.

"Well, that is the strangest thing that I ever did see," Red said, scratching his head.

"You should leave now and make good use of the daylight," Maccus said. As they all mounted, Maccus walked over to Andy's horse and placed a hand on its neck. Looking up at Andy, he said, "The gods go with you, Edward, and may Aditya protect you as you ride. There is a power about you, and I do believe the time for freedom's fight will be soon. When you are ready, I have six hundred horsemen ready to move. Get word to me, and we will come to wherever you are. Even if my wife is about to give birth, I will come. She has told me before that, if ever a chance came to help our children live free, I was to take it. Of course, if you could manage to wait several weeks before you start, I would appreciate it." He shared a wink.

Andy's heart was in his throat at the devotion and dedication this man had to ensure his family and people became free. It reminded him of his own mother and father. They would sacrifice everything, if it would ensure a better life for their kids. Andy reached down and shook Maccus's hand. "When the time comes, I will let you know. I promise."

"Take care, Maccus," Bart said. "I'll get word to you when I can of what's happening."

"Thank you, Bart. You take care of yourself and try not to get killed. Goodbye, Abby. It was a pleasure," Maccus said, kissing her hand once more.

"Thank you for all your help," she replied, "and for the change of clothes. We left Dragonsgate with nothing but what we were wearing."

The three riders turned their horses toward the woods. Andy took one last look back and could see Red and his riders heading for the horizon. Of Maccus, there was no sign. Andy assumed he had melted back into the grass to take up his vigil once more.

They'd been on the trail half the day from Fenner's border when they saw a bent figure on the road ahead. They approached cautiously. Bart scanned the surrounding area for any sign of an ambush. Seeing none, he moved his horse toward what turned out to be a blind beggar man. He wore a simple brown monk's robe and carried an oak staff.

"Good day to you, sir," Bart addressed him. "What brings you so far out in the countryside?"

"Just trying to earn my way, kind master," he replied in a gravelly voice. "I accept charity or do any odd job." Bart fished out a coin from his coat pocket and gave it to the man. "Oh, bless you, sir. Bless you." They started to ride, and as Andy passed the beggar, he heard in his mind, *Just because a man may seem harmless, Andros, doesn't mean he is.*

Andy stopped. "Loki, is that you?" The man stood up straight and tall, the filmy blindness gone from his eyes.

"Well, I'll be," Bart said, turning around. "You fooled me, old friend. And that takes some doing. I can usually see through your disguises."

Loki chuckled. "I was surprised when you gave me that coin and started to ride off."

"Speaking of which, I'll take my money back, if you please." Loki flipped him the coin.

"And who is this, Andros?" Loki asked.

"This is Abby. She is, or rather was, the library curator of Dragonsgate. She risked her life to help me escape from the Raptors," he said with affection.

"It's great to meet you, Abby."

"I've heard a lot about you, Wizard Loki. Mostly, stories handed down from curator to curator as told by the wizard Redlin."

"Ah yes, that would make sense," Loki said. "The god Trystan and Redlin spent a great deal of time together, getting the libraries and universities going. They were both bookworms." He smiled.

"Does this mean you're going to be traveling with us?" Andy asked hopefully.

"No, lad. I'm sorry. I just came to tell you that you're about to be surrounded, if you keep going this way."

Andy looked around quickly.

"What do you mean?" Bart asked.

"Raptors are moving out and heading west from Dragonsgate. Also, a small detachment left Kensington several days ago, headed for this spot. Whom they are I do not know, but I do know the only avenue open to you is southeast, toward Lake Pleasant. I assume you are heading for the Border Lands. That is your only route now."

Bart thought for a moment. "There is a trail to get there that is not well known. It's a little rough, but I believe the horses can make it."

"Excellent! And while you are heading that way, I will arrange a few diversions to keep your pursuers off your back for a little while," Loki said with a wicked grin.

"What are you planning, old man?" Andy asked.

"Just a little fun, lad. That's all. Off you go. I will try to get word to you when I can."

* * *

Loki watched the three of them ride out of sight. He waited under a tree for thirty minutes. "That should be a good enough head start," he said to himself. He reached into the source and, once he had the images in his head, released them into the woods, two heading toward Dragonsgate and two in the direction of Kensington. Anyone who saw them and heard them roar would not fail to recognize them for what they seemed to be—bears. However, if they tried to stab them, the illusion would be broken. The purpose was to frighten the horses, and should that fail, he had a couple of other nasty little surprises in mind.

CHAPTER 12

THE BOAT GLIDED along on the stream. Pulled by a steady current, there was little need for the oars. The Parma Wilds was teeming with plant life on both banks. There were spots where the trees on either side arched out over the water and the branches merged, growing into one another and forming a bridge for the tree-climbing animals above and a tunnel to those on the water below. The faeries and Dain had been several days in the boat. The faeries had folded their wings in and wore hooded cloaks to disguise their features. Dain sat in the stern, manning the tiller, while Leah stood in the bow, watching for any sign of trouble. Donella was on the port side, leaning over to watch the fish following the boat. The stream was crystal-clear and deep. Some of the fish were as long as the boat and rainbow in color. Tera sat on the starboard side, watching the sky. The first day out, she'd spotted a gryphon. Its lion's body and eagle head had looked majestic against the backdrop of the blue sky. She'd also wanted to see if she could spot its nest, because it was rumored gryphons hoard gold.

"I think it's time to send out the call again, Tera," Dain said. Every hour or so, Tera played the song Pan had taught her, just in case Pan was close enough to hear it.

"Will do." Tera then began to play a complex melody for about three minutes.

"How much farther are we going to take the water route?" Donella asked.

"We should reach the center of Parma soon. If it starts getting close to sunset, we will find a place to beach the boat and camp inland," Dain said.

"Why do you suppose we need Diminitus?" Tera asked Leah when she finished her song.

"I have no idea, but if I know Braylynn, we probably won't find out until the last possible moment."

Just then, there was a buzzing sound and a plop, as something hit the water on the right side of the boat.

"What was that?" Leah said, looking around and trying to identify the source of the sound. There was another buzzing followed by a splash on the left side of the boat.

"Everyone down!" Dain ordered "Those were Alfar arrows. They're on both sides of the stream."

"What is an Alfar?" Donella asked from her place in the bottom of the boat.

"Wild wood elves," Leah replied. "They are very territorial, and their arrows are usually dipped in poison."

Soon there was the sound of multiple hits on the sides of the boat and in the water.

"Dain, we're not going to last like this," Leah said.

"My thought exactly." Dain peered over the top of the gunwale, but he could not see the Alfar. He assumed they were just close enough to the bank for their arrows to be in range but far enough away to hide their exact position. Looking downstream, he came up with a plan. "There are two hills on either side that come right up against the water about a hundred yards down. I'm guessing that is the edge of their territory. If we make it past that, we will be safe. Leah, can you make us a shield?"

"Excellent idea!" She smiled at him. "Donella, I'm going to need your help."

"No problem. I see what you have in mind." Both faeries removed their cloaks and extended their spears.

"We are going to need to balance on the edge of the boat to give the bottom of our spears enough clearance from the water. Lock your knees and, whatever you do, don't let your spear hit the water, else you're liable to take an arrow in the chest. Are you ready?" Leah asked.

"Ready," Donella replied with determination.

"Let's go!" They both jumped up, spears spinning, and alighted on the gunwale. Using their wings to maintain their balance, they were effective in protecting the boat from both sides. Arrows would ricochet as they came in contact with the rotating spears. Dain felt the boat wasn't moving fast enough for Leah and Donella to maintain the shields until they cleared the space between the hills. Then he had an idea.

"Tera, are you really the fastest faerie alive?"

"You better believe it, Dain!" Tera replied with excitement. "What have you got in mind?"

"Take off your cloak and grab the seat by the tiller with both hands and hold on tight. Then I want you to beat your wings as fast as they will go."

"You got it, General. I aim to please," she replied with a salute. Dain rolled his eyes toward the heavens.

"Leah, Donella, get ready. We're about to have a burst of speed. Now, Tera!"

Tera held fast to the boat, her wings beating so rapidly, they appeared to form a solid arc. The boat shot forward, and Donella almost lost her balance. The arrows were coming furiously now, the Alfar wanting to leave no question as to whose land this was. Once they were beyond the hills, the rain of arrows stopped. Leah and Donella sank down into their seats, breathing heavily.

"That was hard work," Donella said. "I wouldn't want to have to do that too many times." The boat drifted into a wide-open bay of calm water. Dain happened to see blood on the boat seat and followed it to Leah's leg.

"Leah! You've been hit," he said.

"Yes, I know. One of the arrows got through and grazed me."
She must have noticed the worry in Dain's eyes. "It's all right, Dain.
Those arrows weren't poisoned."

"Thank the gods," he said, relieved. He reached into the pack and
took out a cloth, which he handed to Leah.

"Thanks," she said, applying pressure to stop the bleeding.

"Do you think this is the center of Parma?" Tera asked.

"I believe it is," Dain replied. The bay was a perfect circle with an
outlet on the far southern side.

"I see a beach," Donella said, pointing. Dain moved the tiller and
headed for it while Tera provided some thrust in the calm waters.
They beached the boat and started to scout the surrounding area.
The faeries figured the time for stealth had passed, so they left their
cloaks in the boat. It was getting too hot to wear them, anyway. Dain
was on the ground, examining the tracks of who had come and gone
to the water.

"What do you see?" Leah asked, squatting down next to him.

Dain found her closeness distracting. "There were some wild
boar here early this morning. And over here are some leopard prints
at least two days old. Fauns were here, as well. Tera, give one more
call on your pipes, and then we'll call it a day." She played her song
one more time. "Let's go inland and try to find some shelter."

"Aye, aye, Captain!" Tera replied. Dain groaned. This was going
to be a long trip.

Dain took out his sword, and the faeries used their daggers to
beat back the brush and vines blocking the trail. They had gone
no more than an hour into the woods when they came upon some
stone ruins. They climbed the steps leading up to a flat expanse
and walked through what was left of a tunneled archway. Looking
around, they could see ancient debris sticking up among the grass
and bushes everywhere. The structure looked like it had been part
of a larger keep. Off in the distance, they could see stone walls still
standing, though mostly covered with moss and lichen.

"What was this place?" Donella asked. "Who could have lived here?"

"On the Border, there is a legend that, not long after Vasara came into being, Parma had a functioning government, with all the creatures having a voice," Dain explained. "This was probably the central location of the government buildings. The capital, I believe. They say, at one time, commerce thrived here. Parma culture and arts were felt beyond its borders. But then something happened. Whether it was a natural catastrophe, war, betrayal or something else, no one knows. Whatever it was crushed the government, and it never rose again. It became the Parma Wilds we know today. No inhabitant here will speak of it. I asked Braylynn about it one time, and she got very sad, would not say a word about it. Old-timers have told me that Braylynn's brother god Cael had his heart broken that day, as he was the one who created the creatures of Parma."

"That's so sad," Tera said. "Did Parma once have a king?"

"If it did, I never heard of whom or what he was."

"Parma is shrouded in mystery," Leah said, looking around at the ruins. "I've crossed the border from time to time to see if I could discover some of her secrets. I never have. Even when you talk to Pan, there is very little discussion about the land itself."

Dain saw that Donella seemed to be concentrating on something. "What is it, Donella?"

"There was a great wound here," she said. "And it is still as fresh as the day it happened. But I can see that, one day, in the not too distant future, that wound is going to be healed."

Dain wasn't sure what to make of that observation. He sometimes felt Donella walked in a world apart from their own.

"Let's make camp over by that wall with the overhang," he said, taking the pack off his back. Once the camp was set up and night had fallen, Dain got a small fire going, and they ate a light meal. When dinner was over, he built up the fire.

"Aren't you worried about alerting others to our location?" Tera asked.

"No, I think we're all right. I haven't seen so much as a squirrel within the confines of these ruins since we got here. Something tells me nothing comes in here. Still, we should be on our guard. I will take the first watch."

The faeries found places on the ground next to the fire to sleep. Dain walked over to the edge of the ruins and sat with his back against the stone and his sword resting on his knees.

A couple of hours into the night, Dain heard footsteps coming up behind him. He turned and looked back, sword hand on the hilt until the moonlight illuminated Leah's familiar features. The full moon shone down on her head, giving off a silver glow that surrounded her body. She came over and sat down beside him. They were quiet for some time, just staring out into the woods. Finally, she broke the silence.

"Donella spoke to me the other day," she began.

"Oh? What about?"

"She said you have feelings for me."

"I didn't tell her that," he said, not looking at her.

"I know. She said as much. But she has a gift of being able to read people. Apparently a lot better than I can."

Dain did not have it in him to lie. He either said exactly what he felt or kept it to himself. He could not say a falsehood just to make someone feel comfortable. He did toy with the idea of just denying it and hoping things would stay the same between them, but he had too much respect for Leah to do that, even if the truth strained their friendship.

"You don't have to worry. I won't pursue it," he said in resignation. He continued to stare straight ahead, his face looking as if chiseled from granite.

"And why not? Am I not worth it?" she asked with a light tone in her voice.

"What are you saying?" he asked, turning his head to face her. "Don't toy with my feelings, Leah."

"Oh Dain, you big oaf." Leah smacked him on the shoulder. "I've always had feelings for you. Ever since I found you near death on the border. But then you became Valencia's counselor and protector, and I figured you would be forever bound to Laurel Hollow, and I wouldn't be able to stand that. I need to be able to roam at will. I'm afraid I discounted you because of that. I'm sorry." She paused for a moment and looked up at the moon and stars before continuing. "And on another level, I was afraid of falling in love with you and then having to watch you grow old and die."

He placed his palm on her cheek and gently turned her head to face him. "Couldn't we take it moment by moment and deal with the years as they come?"

"But what about you, Dain? Wouldn't you rather one of your own kind, a woman who will age as you age? Someone who will sit at home while you read her stories and sing sad songs?" she asked, looking deep into his eyes.

"Leah, I'm a simple soldier. I'm not a romantic. I can't sing or write poetry. I will be a soldier until the day I die. I had never planned to marry. But when I saw you and got to know you, all of those plans went out the window. And it is not because you saved my life. It's because you are beautiful and intelligent. You are a warrior, like me. And like you, I cannot stay in one place for very long. It was only by divine intervention that I stayed in Laurel Hollow. You should probably know I spoke to Braylynn. I won't be coming back when this is over. Does that not address one of your concerns?"

"It does, but what do I do when you die and it breaks my heart?"

"Leah, people of my race could be together for a month, a year, or a lifetime. One or the other might die at any time for any number of reasons. But they take that chance, if only for that brief moment of happiness."

Leah smiled. "For someone who doesn't know poetry, you speak very eloquently." She contemplated the ground at her feet. "There is merit in what you say, Dain, and if there is anyone I would take such a risk with, it's you." Dain was a quiet and reserved man, not one to shout his undying love to the heavens. Instead, he pushed back that lock of golden hair that always seemed to slip off her pointed ear, and, with his hand combing through her hair, he leaned in and kissed her. Leah returned his kiss, all her reservations melting away like a candle thrown into a blazing forge.

They stood watch together through the night, saying little but enjoying the closeness of each other as Dain enfolded her in his arms.

* * *

As the sun rose, Donella and Tera awoke to a whistling Leah as she whittled away at a piece of wood by the morning fire.

Tera had not slept at all well. It had felt like a root was digging into her back. "Leah, do you have to be so damn cheerful? You're giving me a headache." Donella had a knowing smile on her face.

Dain walked in from scouting the area. "I think we should head south. The faun prints I saw yesterday lead off in that direction." After they packed everything up and put out their fire, Tera played her Song of Calling as they set out.

Half a day's walk from the ruins, they found the trail encircling the base of a small grassy hill. All of a sudden, the thunder of many hooves surrounded them, coming up the other side of the hill as well as in the front and back of the trail they were on. Dain pulled out his sword, and the faeries extended their spears. Cresting the hill was a white centaur.

"My god!" Donella exclaimed. She had never seen a centaur and was taken aback by this half-human half-horse creature. The one who she assumed was the leader had a white coat and white skin, with hair as black as midnight streaming down his back like a mane.

"Don't move!" he yelled with a deep booming voice. Centaurs streamed over the hilltop and from the left and right, encircling the travelers. There were about twenty in all, mostly males but a few females, as well. They had swords and bows at the ready. "Stay on the ground, faeries, or by Cael we will shoot you out of the air. Now, suppose you tell us why you are walking in our range. Are you spies?"

"We are just travelers," Dain replied, never taking his eyes off the leader. "We are no threat to you."

"And yet you seem very well armed for travelers. I would be willing to bet you have had military training, human. Stop the lies, and tell me what you are doing here," he said with a snarl.

"All right, listen, horse face. What we do is our business, so why don't you leave us alone!" Tera said, hands on hips clutching a talon dagger. Dain gave her a withering look. The white stallion pointed at Tera.

"Kill that one," he said dispassionately. One of the bowmen drew back and let his arrow fly. Donella already had her spear spinning and jumped in front of Tera, deflecting the arrow just in time.

"Well, that was a neat little trick."

"We have plenty more where that came from, if you want to try us," Leah said, spinning her spear in intricate patterns around her body.

Suddenly, the sounds of more hooves closed in. The white centaur smiled to himself. "Now let's see how you do against forty of us." Dain and the faeries looked up, but cresting the hill were not centaurs but fauns. One leapt from the top of the hill to land dead center in the circle next to Tera. He was huge, standing more than seven feet tall. He had the hind quarters and horns of a goat. His skin was bronze and smooth, and his eyes were as black as forest pools. His fur was as black as his eyes, and his horns were dark red.

"Pan!" Tera yelled. "What have you got to say now, horse face?" Then she stuck out her tongue at him.

"This is not your quarrel, Pan."

"Oh, but it is, Silas," Pan responded, smiling and pawing at the ground with his hooves. "This faerie is under my protection, as are her friends."

The centaur seemed uncertain. "You're still outnumbered," Silas said.

Donella looked from one to the other to see who would make the first move. She tried to determine where the most vulnerable spot was, should it come down to a fight. But it never happened.

"I think you better count again, Silas," Pan said looking up the hill.

The centaur followed his gaze. Arrayed on the hilltop and down its slopes were at least fifty fauns with drawn bows. Silas knew he was beaten. He cast murderous eyes at the group, gave a yell, and galloped back down the trail with his followers close behind. Pan watched them go and didn't order the bows lowered until he was sure they were all gone. He turned around and suddenly found himself entangled in the hugs and kisses of Tera.

"Oh, Pan, I knew you would come. But what happened? Haven't you heard my calls? Were you delayed? Captured? In a fight somewhere? What's been going on? Thanks for the pipes, by the way."

"Slow down, Tera," Pan said, laughing. "And how about I ask the questions, since you are in my country? But first, let us do our customary greetings. Hello, Dain. You're looking well." Pan shook his hand.

"Hello, Pan. It has been a long time. I hope all has been well in Parma."

"It has," he replied. "And dear Leah, it is especially nice to see you again," he said, giving her a hug.

"And you, Pan. Thank you for your help with those brutes."

"My pleasure, my dear. And who is this?" He looked long at Donella, his black eyes probing, as if to pierce some possible disguise.

"This is Donella. She is helping us in our quest," Leah told him.

"A pleasure, Donella," Pan said with a slight bow of his head, as if paying homage to royalty.

"I'm glad to meet you, Forest Lord," Donella replied with a head bow of her own. "I've heard a lot about you."

"I've not borne that title in quite some time. I'm surprised you know of it."

"I didn't. Your entire manner and bearing tells me you could be nothing else," she said.

"Ah, you see things others cannot. You know, Donella, whenever I see individuals from outside of Parma, I see their animal aura as well—the animal inside, so to speak. With Tera, I see birds. Leah, the wildcat. Dain, the clever fox. You want to know what I see when I look at you?"

"Yes, I would," she said a little apprehensively.

"Dragons. There are only a few whom I have seen with that aura over the centuries." He turned to Leah. "A quest, you say? I'll bet she is central to it all."

"We need your help, Pan, but what we are doing is best known to few," Leah said.

"I understand." Pan gave a signal, and the remaining fauns disappeared back over the hill. "Come, there is a place a short distance down the trail. We can sit and eat while we talk."

He led them down a worn, hard-packed dirt path through a white birch forest, his hooves making a *clip-clop* sound as they went along. After about ten minutes, the forest opened up into a grass clearing. He led them off to one side that had a few boulders with seats chiseled into them.

"Please sit," Pan instructed. "We use this field sometimes for our festivals." He went over to a nearby tree and rubbed his horns until they were bright and glossy. "Ah, much better." Then, reaching up, he picked several fruits from the tree's branches that were blue on the outside, but their insides were white and juicy, like a pear. He handed them out. "Now, tell me why you are here. It must be something very urgent for you to have brought Tera into the heart of Parma."

"We had no choice in the matter," Dain replied, sheathing his sword. "Braylynn said we needed your help, and having Tera call on her pipes was the quickest way to find you." The object of their discussion was currently flying in and out of the boughs of the trees.

"How may I help you?" Pan asked, removing some twigs from his fur.

"We need to find Diminitus," Donella replied. "He is to accompany us on our journey."

"Ha!" Pan laughed. "Good luck with that."

"What makes you say that?" Leah asked.

"Because he's a cranky old man who will only do something for others if there is a benefit in it for him."

"I was wondering why does he live in Parma?" Donella asked. "He's human, isn't he?"

"He is," Pan replied, "and he has lived here since the beginning. How that is possible given the short life spans humans usually have is unknown to me. Perhaps the gods wanted to have at least one human always here to irritate the rest of us. No offense, Dain."

"None taken, but we need to try to convince him to come with us." The sound of pipes came floating down from the treetops. Tera had perched on a high limb and was playing a cheerful melody. Pan looked up and smiled.

"Well, I guess you can try," he said skeptically. "Braylynn was right, though. You do need me to find him. He is in my secret grotto. You could have been here years and still not have found him without me to guide you."

"Why is he in your grotto?" Leah asked.

"There are certain plants and herbs that grow in and around my grotto that he wanted to cultivate. He can be annoying at times, but he is an expert on plants. Is this perhaps why you need him?"

"We have no idea," Leah replied. "He just needs to come."

"I will take you to him. Now, what are you allowed to tell me about this quest?"

"Would you mind if we wait until we are in your grotto?" Dain asked. "We would be away from prying eyes, and we can also tell you and Diminitus at the same time."

"Sound reasoning, Dain," Pan said with approval. "If you are ready, we can go."

"Excellent," Dain replied. "Tera!"

"Present, Lieutenant!" Tera shouted in true military fashion.

"Gods give me patience," Dain pleaded. "Come on, we're leaving." Tera jumped off the limb and glided down to alight on Pan's shoulders.

"Do you mind if I ride on your shoulders?" Tera asked sweetly.

"Normally, I would impale anyone who made such a request. But you are always the exception, dear Tera. Easy on the horns, though." Donella smiled. Tera's charm had that effect on everyone.

Pan led them south for what seemed like hours. Several times, it felt like they were walking in circles. Donella was further confused when they wound up back at the clearing where they had started.

"How come we are back here?" Donella asked, thoroughly perplexed.

"We aren't," Pan replied with a mischievous grin. "It is part of the illusion that hides my grotto. Someone setting out to find it will feel as if they've covered the same ground several times. Eventually, they will think they have come back to where they started and give up. Follow me."

They walked through the imaginary clearing where they had eaten fruit earlier. Even the tree with the blue-colored pears was there. But as they reached the other side, the landscape changed suddenly and dramatically, as if they had parted a curtain with the clearing painted on it and stepped into a totally different place. They were standing on the bank of a wide, fast-moving river. It was several hundred yards across, and on the opposite shore, they could see the dark mouth of a cave. This part of the river was shallow. Rocks protruded from the water, spaced roughly six feet apart, all the way across to the other side.

"The faeries can fly across, but you might have some problems, Dain, trying to jump from rock to rock."

"Don't worry, Pan. I can fly him across," Leah replied. "It will be low, but I know I can keep him out of the water."

"Very well, let's go." Pan started to jump from rock to rock with such speed and agility, it looked like he was running on dry ground. Donella and Tera followed.

"Are you sure about this, Leah?" Dain asked anxiously.

"Don't worry. I'm not going to let you fall." She put her arms under his and encircled his chest. She stood for a moment and rested her head on his back, enjoying his warmth.

"Whoa! This is a new experience," Dain said nervously as the water flew by dangerously close to his feet. Once on the other side, Leah set him gently down on the bank next to the others.

"What took you so long?" Pan asked. "Had to work up the nerve, Dain?"

"Something like that," Dain replied.

As they walked up to the cave entrance, they heard a voice bellowing from inside.

"Pan, is that you? Where the hell have you been? I'm starving! What kind of host are you?"

"That's your man," Pan said sympathetically. They walked into the cave entrance, which was actually a tunnel hewn out of the solid rock. As they emerged from the tunnel, what they had mistaken for a cave actually opened up into a wide airy space with beautiful gardens laid out in a circular pattern. The actual grotto was on the far side. In the center of the garden was a man with gray hair sticking up in all directions. He was wearing no shirt. He was thin, but his skin was not sagging. Instead, it was tight and muscular. His pants were brown and loose fitting. Diminitus had shears in his hands as he carefully cut some leaves off a plant with bright orange flowers.

"Dim, you have some friends here to see you," Pan said.

"That's impossible. I don't have any friends. Tell them to go away!"

"See what I mean?" he told the others.

"It's all right. Braylynn gave me something to show him that would guarantee his cooperation," Donella said with confidence.

"Let's go into the grotto where it is cooler," Pan suggested. They walked the garden paths into the grotto. Donella was awestruck by the natural beauty of it. The rock was a white limestone. The roof of the grotto had several holes in it to allow sunlight to stream through. Decorative columns lined both sides of the walls and the back. The size of the space was immense. There were several reflecting pools with green plant life on tiered rocks throughout. Two small waterfalls on either side spilled out of the rock and into a trough that ran through the grotto, irrigating the gardens beyond before disappearing into a subterranean stream that eventually emptied into the river. One particular pool caught Donella's eye, and she walked over to it. It was rectangular, and a stream of water came out of the rock to empty into a statue of a dragon's head. The mouth was open in a silent roar as the water spilled into a stone bowl below until the basin filled and water overflowed its sides. In the middle of the bowl, a white flower floated in stark contrast to the dark water. Donella found it curious that the flower stayed directly in the center of the bowl, neither moving from rim to rim nor spilling over the edges. She thought of asking Pan about this but decided against it. She found its mystery very appealing and didn't want to spoil it.

"Wow! This place is amazing, Pan!" Tera exclaimed.

"Thank you, Tera. I like it," Pan said with pride.

"Pan! I got the leaves I wanted," Diminitus yelled as he walked into the grotto. "Now, how about something to eat?"

"You know there is always a bowl of fruits and nuts over by the waterfall. Help yourself. And you don't need to shout. I'm not deaf."

Diminitus walked over to retrieve the bowl and came back to where everyone was standing, munching an apple as he walked. "So, what is it you people want with me?" he asked grumpily.

"Braylynn sent us here to seek you out and have you accompany us on a quest," Leah replied.

"Look, I haven't crossed these borders in hundreds of years, and I really don't see why I should now, just because Braylynn wants me to." He grabbed another piece of fruit from the bowl. "So, unless you come up with a better reason, I'm staying put," he said with a mouthful.

"Come on, let's go. We don't need this," Dain said, clearly not liking Diminitus's attitude.

"No, wait," Donella said, looking at Diminitus. "Braylynn impressed upon me to make sure you came, and to that end, she told me to give you this." Donella handed him a gold medallion. Etched on the front was a talon tree, and on the back was a faerie in flight. Diminitus took it, frowning.

"That sneaky little deity," Diminitus exclaimed.

"Do you know what this is?" Donella asked.

"I should. I made it over a thousand years ago," he replied. "It was during one of my sappy periods when Braylynn just happened to save my life. In gratitude, I made her this and told her if there were anything I could do for her to just name it. I'm beginning to suspect now that she probably saved my life so she could black-mail me later." Diminitus absently studied the medallion. "Well, I've been accused of many things, but going back on my word is not one of them. Today's your lucky day, little lady. It looks like I will be coming with you. Now, suppose you tell me what it is we are doing."

Donella, with the assistance of Leah, Dain, and Tera, filled both of them in on what had transpired, from Donella's arrival in Laurel Hollow to their arrival at the grotto. Both Pan and Diminitus were surprised when she told them she was the Dragon Summoner, and even more so when she told them there was a dragon in Vasara again.

"I used to know the dragons," Pan told them. "There were nine of them. They were nice enough, but they disappeared when Devon came to power."

"A lot of things changed when Devon came to power," Diminitus said. "I'm still unclear on what help I am going to be in retrieving your garment from the Baron's house in Hadley."

"I don't know, either, but perhaps we will find out when we get there," Donella replied.

"Speaking of which, we should probably get going," Dain said. "Something tells me we need to make haste.

"Will you be coming with us, Pan?" Tera asked.

"No, I will stay here, but before you go, I have something for you." He walked over to a column that had a stone peg near the top. On the peg was a necklace with a stone the color of obsidian. He took the necklace down and put it around Donella's neck. "This stone has some of Cael's spirit in it. While you wear it, no one in Parma will do you harm nor those who travel with you. However, it may not go beyond the boundary of the Wilds. When you reach that point, take the necklace off and fly it up to the highest branch nearby. I'll retrieve it from there."

"Thank you, Pan. You have been a big help to us." Donella gave him a kiss on both cheeks.

"My turn!" Tera said before covering him in kisses.

"Take good care of her," Pan said of Tera. "She's the delight of my eyes, and I would be extremely wroth with anyone who would try to harm her." He then made his farewells and saw everyone across the river. He explained the enchantment would not affect them while they were going out then waved goodbye until the forest took them from his sight.

He threw a quick prayer to Cael to watch over them then turned and headed back to his grotto. Before entering the tunnel, he turned once more, feeling watchful eyes upon him. Seeing nothing, he went in. Had he lingered a moment longer, he might have spied the raven lifting off from a dead stump and winging its way north to its master.

CHAPTER 13

DEVON WENT STORMING down the halls of the White Castle. He had just finished witnessing what his raven had seen in the Parma Wilds.

Why would three faeries and a Border Lands officer be visiting with Pan?

The raven had not been able to enter Pan's grotto to hear what was said there, because the magic that surrounded it was too powerful, but he'd seen them come out, and this time Diminitus was with them.

What possible reason could that crazy old hermit have for taking up with that bunch?

He went down several levels, exited the castle, and entered the training ring. The ring was forty feet in diameter made of bare earth and enclosed by a six-foot wall. Above the wall were tiered seats for people to sit and watch the contests. Devon took a seat midway up. Not too many people had come to watch that day.

He looked down in the ring at the two combatants. One was from the elite Raptor fighting unit. He was shirtless and wore brown leather trousers. In his hands was a staff, which he was using to block the well-aimed thrusts of his opponent's staff. His adversary was a woman, a faerie to be exact. Her shorts were also made of leather. Her midriff was bare, and a leather halter covered her chest. Her wings were as black as a moonless night and she had hair to match. Her eyes slanted at the edges, giving her a feline look.

She clearly was on the attack, forcing the Raptor to fight for all he was worth. It was a foregone conclusion, how it would end, but Devon was a little surprised at how quickly the end came. The Raptor, after a series of counter thrusts, took a swing at her feet to take out her legs. But the faerie had been expecting it and leapt above the staff. Using her wings to give her some altitude, she somersaulted over his head and hit a perfect strike at his throat on her way up, crushing his windpipe. The Raptor went down, fighting for breath. The faerie left him there as she walked toward the exit, wiping the sweat from her forehead, while the surgeons rushed into the ring to help the struggling soldier.

As she exited the ring, Devon called out to her from behind.

"Well done, Zana," Devon said with pride, as if Zana were his personal creation.

"Thank you, Lord," Zana replied, breathing heavily.

"Although I would appreciate it if you would limit your contests to the garrison soldiers. It takes a long time to replace and train a Raptor."

"If they get beaten so soundly, Lord, they don't deserve to be Raptors," she said fiercely.

"Point well taken, my dear. How are things in Hadley Manor?"

"I am growing weary of Hadley, Lord. Ogden is a spineless pig of a baron," she said in disgust. "I'm tired of being referred to as the Mistress of Hadley. Especially by humans, who barely make an impact on the world and then they are dead. I've lost count of how many barons there have been. Lord, you promised me power, and yet you have not taught me any of your magic."

Devon's golden eyes narrowed to slits as he burned holes in her mind. Then every muscle in her body cramped, causing her excruciating pain. Zana went down to her knees. "Please, Lord!" she hissed through clenched teeth.

"Are you making demands of me, Zana?" he asked, his deadly voice booming through the vaults of her mind. "Is this the magic you wish to learn? Perhaps I should give you to Braylynn. I'm sure they would love to have the only faerie in the history of the race who killed another faerie. You owe me your life, Zana. You can't go back to Laurel Hollow, and you only live outside of it at my pleasure." He released her. Her breath came in raking gasps, and tears streamed down her face. Once her breathing returned to normal, she slowly stood up. Her face was an unreadable mask.

"Did I make a mistake trusting you, Zana?"

"No, Lord."

"I'm very glad to hear that. I wouldn't want to be disappointed a second time. I have a task for you. And if you do it well, you may move into the castle, and we'll begin your training as my apprentice in the demon arts."

"Truly, Lord?" she asked with a glimmer of hope in her eyes.

"Yes, I think it's time. But first, I need you to travel south. Outside Parma, three faeries are traveling with two humans, and they are heading north. I want you to watch them and find out what they are doing. Take no action unless your life or mine is in imminent danger."

"Why not kill them and be done with it?"

"I don't want to give Braylynn any reason to take action. While I doubt she would risk upsetting the balance of magic, I can't be too certain what she might do where her faeries are concerned."

"I will find out what they are up to, Lord. I won't fail you," she said with zeal.

He looked deep into her eyes and held her, like a cobra hypnotizing its prey just before it strikes. "See that you don't, or you will not get a chance to fail me again.

* * *

It had been eight days since they'd left behind the borders of Parma.

"How is she doing?" Leah asked, concern written all over her face.

"She still has a fever, and her body is alternating between chills and sweats," Diminitus said.

Donella lay on a litter made of branches with a blanket stretched across it. Another blanket was pulled up to her chin. Her teeth were chattering, and her skin was pale and sweaty. She had taken sick two days out of Parma. As they were walking through tall grass, Donella had given out a strangled cry and collapsed. Diminitus had been beside himself, trying to figure out what was wrong with her. He'd tried several different herbs in various combinations but to no avail.

"We need to get to Black River and find a healer."

"I thought you were an expert on plants and herbs!" Leah said accusingly.

"Now look here, missy! I don't like to see anyone in this state any more than you do. But just because I am an expert in plants does not make me an expert in diagnosing illnesses."

"I'm sorry," Leah replied. "I just hate to see her in pain."

"Best thing to do right now is to wait for Tera and Dain." Tera and Dain had gone ahead to the nearby farms to see if they could purchase a horse to pull the litter. Leah and Diminitus took Donella off the road, away from prying eyes. "Has she said anything?"

"Every now and then she'll mention a river and a castle, but I can't make any sense out of it," Leah said.

"She's probably hallucinating. I'll give her something that will make her sleep without dreams. I'm afraid that is the best I can do," he said sadly. Leah had revised her opinion of Diminitus since traveling with him. He sometimes talked like an old crab, but he had a great regard for life and great contempt for those who threw it away needlessly.

After Diminitus gave Donella his concoction, Leah went back toward the road to keep watch. Twenty minutes later, she heard the sparrow's morning song in the late afternoon.

She is good, Leah thought, giving three quick whistles in answer. Dain appeared around the bend, leading a huge, heavy, black draft horse with Tera on its back, the kind of horse whose primary function was to pull heavy loads. The horse was currently pulling a light wagon.

"Wow! He's enormous!" Leah exclaimed when she reached them. "Everyone will note his passing as we go along."

"It can't be helped," Dain explained. "The farm we got him from was the first we had seen in miles, and since time is of the essence, we felt we didn't have a whole lot of choices. Also, Tera was absolutely taken with him," he said, smiling.

"Leah, isn't he just precious?" Tera squealed with delight. "When this business is all done, I'm taking him back to Laurel Hollow. I named him Demon Chaser, but I'm going to call him Chaser for short."

"Why Demon Chaser?" Leah asked.

"Well, I always thought of Devon as a demon, and this fierce guy is going to chase him down and stomp on him. He'll be the hero of Vasara," she said confidently. Chaser, at that moment, had a mouthful of grass and, with his tail swishing back and forth happily, looked anything but fierce. He also was a gelding. The main purpose for gelding a horse was to make them gentle. Leah didn't see any need to spoil the image for Tera, however, and besides, Devon had a way of making people or animals want to stomp on him, whether they were gentle in nature or not.

"Any change?" Dain asked.

"No. Diminitus gave her something to help her sleep. He says we need to get to Black River soon."

"Well, Chaser here should help speed things up. Two can sit up on the driver's seat, and the rest ride in the wagon."

"How much longer do you think it will take?"

"Using the horse and wagon, about two days," Dain replied.

"Hopefully she doesn't get worse in that time," Leah said, downcast.

Dain put a hand on her shoulder. "Don't worry, we're going to make it."

"You better believe it," Tera said cheerfully. "And then we'll ride to Kensington and stomp on Devon."

True to his word, they reached Black River on the evening of the second day. Black River was a port city on Lake Pleasant. There were small villages all along the lake, but everything funneled through Black River, it being the business center for the region. The lake provided the biggest fishing industry in Vasara. It was also home to most of its healers, although some traveled to other cities and towns, offering their services. Dain went into the city first to secure lodgings. He found an inn that had a rear entrance to the rooms upstairs. He returned for Diminitus and the faeries, and they moved

Donella into the room as quickly as possible, while Diminitus took Chaser and the wagon to the stables.

"Easy does it," Dain said as they lifted Donella off the litter and into the bed. She gave a moan as they set her down. The room was actually quite spacious. Dain explained he had gotten the biggest room at the inn so they could all stay together. It cost more, but he didn't want them splitting up. A short while later, there was a knock at the door. It was Diminitus.

"Something's been going on here," he said when he came through the door.

"Why do you say that?" Leah asked, going to the window and checking on the activity below.

"There are two Raptor units in the city. I heard a couple of farm-hands in the stable say they were looking for someone."

"Us?" Tera asked worriedly.

"I don't know," Diminitus replied.

"Everyone stay here," Dain said. "I'm going down to the common room and see what I can learn."

"Do you want me to come with you?" Leah asked.

"Better not. You would have to wear your cloak to hide your features and would certainly be noticed and remembered for keeping a hooded cloak on indoors." He took his sword off and handed it to her.

"Be careful," she told him. "I don't want to have to come down and rescue you again." He gave her a wink and slid out the door.

Tera, Leah, and Diminitus kept silent vigil while they waited for Dain's return. Tera had wetted a cloth in the room's water basin and gently dabbed Donella's fevered skin. Dain returned a few hours later.

"Been having a drink or two I see," Leah said reproachfully as he staggered a little through the door.

"Sorry, love, but these people don't open up unless you have a drink with them."

"I don't care about that," Leah said. "The least you could've done was bring me a pint."

"Forgive me. I wasn't thinking. You actually could've come down with me. There was another patron wearing a hooded cloak sitting at a corner table, and no one was paying that much attention to him."

"How do you know it was a him?" Leah asked.

"Never mind that," Diminitus said, losing some of his patience. "What did you find out?"

"Well, it's not us," he began. "The Raptors were looking for a party of three, two men and a woman, who passed through about two weeks ago. They think they may have taken a boat onto the lake. In any case, we're clear. Tomorrow, Leah and I will go to the Temple of Healers."

"Where is that?" Tera asked.

"On the north end of the city," Dain replied.

Leah walked over to Donella's bedside. Her breathing was shallow, and her dark hair was plastered to her damp brow. "Don't worry, sister, we'll find a cure for this. I promise," she said, gently stroking her hair.

The next day, Leah and Dain walked north along the shoreline until they came to a wrought iron gate. Inside, a stone path led up to a pristine white building with many columns. It resembled a university more than a temple. There was a bell pull by the gate, and Dain gave it a few tugs. It wasn't too long before a woman in a blue dress with a belt of white flowers came walking down the path. Her hair was brown and cut short.

"Good morning. My name is Ala. How may I help you?" she said once she reached the gate. She smiled and had that kind of face that always seemed to be happy about everything she saw.

"Good morning," Dain said. "We are in need of a healer. Our friend is very sick. We left her back at the Shipyard Inn. Would you be able to come there?"

"Is she human or a faerie, like your other friend here?" Ala asked. Leah was astonished. She was wearing her cloak with the hood up. She pushed the hood back, revealing her pointed ears and showing the healer she had guessed correctly.

"How did you know?" Leah asked.

"The healers of this temple are well versed in the anatomy of all the races of Vasara. Even seeing you covered, I know the features that give your cloak its current shape. If you are trying to keep your identity a secret, you may rest assured the common folk of Black River will not guess you are a faerie. Although why you would want to conceal your race is a mystery. Faeries are not uncommon here. In fact, you draw more attention to yourself this way."

"It was necessary," Dain explained, scanning the surrounding area as if searching for someone unseen.

"Your business is your own, and I will not pry. Why don't you come into the courtyard and tell me your friend's symptoms." Ala opened the gate and allowed them to enter. They walked up to the temple and passed through a breezeway that opened into an inner courtyard. The stone path meandered through a small garden that had benches on grass patches and babbling little streams running throughout. It was the perfect place to sit and meditate, which several of the garden's current occupants were doing. They found an empty bench, and Leah and Ala sat down. Dain remained standing.

"Now I said before," Ala began, "that I don't want to pry into your business, but if I am to help your friend, I need as much information as you can give me. What was she doing before she took sick? What area of Vasara was she in? Things like that."

Leah felt she could trust this woman. Without alluding to where they were headed, she told Ala of their journey from the Parma Wilds to Black River. Then, with Dain's help, she described all of Donella's visible symptoms.

"*Hmm*, there are a variety of things it could be, so I won't really know until I see her. It bothers me that the plants and herbs your friend tried had no effect. There are a couple he didn't try which I will bring with me. Please wait here while I get my kit." Ala walked over to one of the doors off the garden and disappeared.

"Do you think she can do anything?" Leah asked with a worried frown.

"She has to," Dain replied, clasping her hand. "I don't know where else to turn otherwise."

Ala returned and together they walked back to the inn. Once inside the room, Ala wrinkled her nose. "The death smell is in here," she said. "I fear I may be too late." Diminitus and Tera were beside themselves.

"She gave out a loud cry," Tera said sobbing. "Then her body started jerking around like she had no control over it."

"Once that was over," Diminitus said taking up the narrative, "she went dead still, as you see her now. Her scream was so loud, the owner of the inn came running up to see if everything was all right. I nearly jumped out of my skin when I heard it."

"I am Ala the healer, and you must be Diminitus. Do you have any theories at all as to what caused her illness?"

"At first, I had lots of theories, but I've watched them all get shot down as each remedy I tried failed," he said sadly.

Ala walked over to Donella's side. Placing a hand on her forehead, she leaned down and rested her head on her chest. After a minute or so, she lifted her head. "Her heart is slowing down, and her fever is still rising. You are Tera?"

"Yes, I am," Tera answered, biting her lower lip. "Can you help her? She's my good friend, my sister."

"I'm going to do everything I can. I need you to take this bucket and fill it with water from the lake. The lake water is very cold. Leah, I need you to stay here and help me undress her. Dain and Diminitus, I need you to leave."

"We understand, Ala. Come on, Dim. I'll buy you a drink, and I'll bring one back for you, Leah," he amended quickly after catching her raised eyebrow.

After Dain and Diminitus left, the women took Donella's clothes off. They adjusted her body so her wings were open and flat beneath her back. Tera returned with the bucket of water. Ala put her finger in to check the temperature.

"Excellent. It's nice and cold." She went to her kit and took out a cloth, which she handed to Tera. "I want you to dampen the cloth and start wiping down her entire body, and don't stop unless I tell you. Keep the cloth damp and cold. This will start to bring down her body temperature. While you are doing that, I will try to figure out the cause."

Ala went to her kit and took out several leaves. They were teardrop in shape and of different colors. She placed one on the base of Donella's throat, another on her abdomen, and one on each leg. She paused as she studied the dragon mark on her leg.

"What are the leaves for?" Leah asked, puzzled.

"The leaves react to the illness when put in contact with the body," Ala explained. "Each leaf is different, but whichever one turns black will help us to understand how the sickness entered her body. For example, if the red leaf on her throat turns black, then some food or drink is responsible." They both watched and waited. Tera kept rubbing the cloth on Donella's skin, trying not to disturb the leaves. After several minutes, the green leaf on her leg turned black.

"What does that one mean," Leah asked.

"It means she was bitten by something, probably venomous. Now I need to look for any possible bite marks. Stop for a moment, Tera." Ala searched her body from head to toe, finding nothing. She let out a sigh of frustration. "Tell me again where you were walking right before she took sick."

"We were walking through tall grass just north of Parma," Leah explained.

"I'll check the legs more thoroughly." She began a closer examination. "*Ah!* I got it. It was near this red dragon mark. That is why I couldn't see it at first, because it blends."

"Can you tell what kind of bite it is?" Leah asked anxiously.

"Of course, but that only deepens the mystery. She was bitten by a skull spider. This spider's bite is small and shaped like a skull."

"But that doesn't make any sense," Leah said. "All faeries have been bitten by skull spiders one time or another, due to the fact that we live in woods and wander fields."

"My point exactly. Faeries usually get their first bite at a young age, when the immune system is strongest. You may have a slight fever for a day, but that's about it. The venom then mixes with the blood, and you are immune forever. This faerie has never been bitten, and her body is trying to burn the venom out, but it is burning her along with it."

Leah was very puzzled. *How could a faerie go through life on Vasara without ever coming in contact with a skull spider?* she wondered. Mysteries seemed to abound where Donella was concerned.

"Is there anything that can be done?" Tera asked, continuing her rubdown.

"There is, but I need to hurry and talk to Diminitus. Time is of the essence. I'll explain when I get back." The two faeries stood staring at a closed door as footsteps descended the stairs.

"I'm worried, Leah. I feel like something bad is going to happen," Tera said.

"Don't worry, Tera. I have to trust that Braylynn would not send her Summoner out only to die by a spider bite. What was that?" Leah got up and ran to the window. She looked down to the street below but she didn't see anything. A couple of the rooms had balconies; one was right next to their window, but no one was there. She looked around one more time before pulling her head back into the room and closing the window.

"What is it?" Tera asked, frightened.

"I thought I heard a fluttering and some steps by the window, but I couldn't find anyone. We will have to be more cautious."

* * *

What Leah had heard was the fluttering of black wings and the running of feet as Zana launched herself up and onto the roof of the inn. When she gauged enough time had gone by, she flew toward the nearest woods.

"Now I have you!" she crowed, congratulating herself. She had been following them for days, which had been made all the easier when the green-winged faerie fell sick.

Zana had been in the common room when Dain came downstairs. After he went back up to their room, she had marked it in hopes of listening in on their conversations. She had heard Ala talk of the dragon mark, and her suspicion had been confirmed when Leah mentioned the Summoner. Zana knew from Layla that only the Dragon Summoner bore the dragon mark on her leg.

"Braylynn's so-called anointing," she spat out with venom. She now knew where they were going. They would need the garment and jewels of the Summoner. They would need entrance into Hadley Manor. She smiled an evil smile. "Perhaps I can help them with that." She decided not to tell Devon. She would set a trap that would net all the traitors, thereby assuring her position as Devon's apprentice. She flew off to the west to put her plan in motion.

*   *   *

Back at the inn, Leah heard the approach of footsteps on the stairs. The door opened, and Ala stepped inside.

"I've sent Dain and Diminitus south to fetch some dragon root for me," she said in answer to their questioning looks.

"What's dragon root?" Tera asked.

"Well, it's not technically a root, more like a stem. There is only one place in all Vasara where they grow. About two hours ride south of here, next to the shores of the lake, is a grove of black trees that we call dragon trees. Everything on the tree is black. Even the leaves are a shiny black. The roots extending above the ground closely resemble dragon's talons. Growing among the roots is a stalk with a fire-colored flower on top. Dain and Diminitus will pick these and bring them back."

"How will this help?" Leah asked.

"We are going to give her body something more deadly to fight."

"You're going to what?" Leah thought maybe she'd heard wrong.

"She's going to poison Donella!" Tera said in horror.

"In a manner of speaking, yes," Ala replied, matter-of-factly. "Listen, her fever is burning out of control. If we don't stop it, she will die. We also have to give the skull spider venom time to mix with her blood, so she will have that immunity. The body's natural response to dragon root is to lower its core temperature. This will offset the fever. Don't worry, it will not be a lethal dose, and I will mix it with other herbs to help dilute it. The important thing is to get her body temperature going in the other direction."

Leah thought that through. "It does kind of make sense. How many times have you done this?"

"None," Ala replied.

"None?" Leah said incredulously.

"Don't worry, the theory is sound. Besides, this is the only thing that I believe will save her life." Ala put a consoling hand on Leah's shoulder. "I promise you, I will use all my talents and gifts as a healer to see her get well. Now help me fetch some more water. We need to keep rubbing her down until the men get back."

"All right." Leah put her trust in Ala as she went out back for water.

It was late afternoon by the time the men returned. They handed Ala the dragon root and went back downstairs to wait. The plant was exactly as she'd described. She cut a small piece off the end, and the juice inside was blood-red in color. Ala squeezed a couple of drops into a small bowl into which she had placed additional herbs. After adding some water, she stirred until the contents were well mixed. Leah tilted Donella's head back until her mouth opened. Ala then poured a very small amount onto her tongue.

"We should see a change almost immediately," she explained. True to her word, Donella's skin started taking on its natural color. The tightness around her eyes relaxed and her breathing became strong and steady. She looked to be in a peaceful sleep, but she did not open her eyes.

"We need to watch her to make sure her body doesn't go in the other direction. The fever and the dragon root seem to be in balance."

Tera breathed a sigh of relief. "When will she wake up?"

"I don't know," Ala replied. "We just have to wait."

They got her dressed, and Ala went down and informed the men the worst was over then left to go back to the temple. She left instructions to watch her through the night and, if anything changed, to come and get her. They were short-handed at the temple that night and needed her to get back. She said she would return in the morning.

* * *

The next day, Ala walked to the Shipyard Inn. As she climbed the stairs in the back, she could hear voices and laughter coming from the room above, which was always a good sign to a healer. She lightly knocked on the door and announced herself. The door opened, and Tera flew into her arms.

"Ala! She's awake and talking. Come in, come in. See for yourself," Tera exclaimed. Ala couldn't help smiling as she walked into the room. Donella was sitting up. She looked relaxed and alert. As she turned her head toward the door, Ala was amazed at how green her eyes were. She was wearing a silver circlet on her head that made her look like a faerie princess.

"You must be Ala," Donella said smiling. "I understand I have you to thank for saving my life."

"It was a group effort. I'm just glad we were in time. How are you feeling now?" Ala asked, walking over to the bed to get a better look at her patient.

"I'm tired and hungry, but otherwise I feel much better."

"I've asked them to bring some food up. It should be here shortly," Dain informed her.

"Excellent," Ala replied. "Tomorrow you should be able to get out of bed and move around."

"When can she leave?" Leah asked.

"If you mean this room, tomorrow is fine. If you mean Black River, probably not for a month," Ala replied.

"A month!" Diminitus exclaimed. "Is she that frail that she can't travel?"

"I didn't say that," Ala explained. "She would have strength enough to travel in two or three days. The reason she needs to stay at least a month is because I don't know how long it will take for the spider venom to work through her system. I will need to continue to periodically give her doses of the dragon root until it does. Otherwise, the fever will come right back. I am sorry," she said, looking at Donella.

"It is not your fault," Donella said. "But I have to leave by the week's end."

"Says who?" Leah asked.

"Braylynn," she replied.

"What...?" Leah began.

"Wait, Leah," Dain said, as though sensing something else might be going on here. "Can you explain to us how this is possible?"

"In my sickness, I had some dreams and visions. Some were not very pleasant, and I will not speak of them. In one, Braylynn came to me. She told me not to be afraid. She said that the priestess of her brother would cure me. She also said the priestess would travel with me to Hadley Manor."

"No priestess cured you!" Diminitus said, slipping into his cranky voice. "Ala here did, and very ably I might add, so your vision must have been a false one."

Everyone looked over at Ala, who was strangely silent. "Well, Ala, did a priestess cure her?" Dain asked.

It took a moment for Ala to find her voice. "She did," Ala said quietly. "And the fact that your goddess told you this tells me she has been in communication with her brother Rafael, because only he knows the identity of his priestess. Each of the Five has a single priest or priestess who is given the power to communicate with the god's spirit directly and beseech their aid in extreme circumstances. As a general rule, no one knows who they are. I don't even know who the priests of the other gods are, nor do they know me. And now that all of you know this, I trust you will keep it to yourselves." It was just by coincidence that she happened to be looking at Tera.

"Why does everyone always look at me?" Tera asked with a pained expression. Everyone in the room burst out laughing.

"Well, I guess I'm going to Hadley," Ala said, resigning herself to her fate. "But not before the week is out," she said sternly to Donella.

"Not until the week is out," Donella agreed, smiling.

"Well, Dain, I guess we better get some provisions together," Diminitus said. "I for one am going to the armory to get a sword. Did I ever tell you that, at one time in my life, I was a very good swordsman?"

"When was that?" Leah asked.

"I can't remember, but I know I've done it," he said.

"Well, hopefully techniques haven't changed too much since the thousands of years ago when you learned them," Dain said with a perfectly straight face.

"I don't have to take this abuse," Diminitus said, stomping off and acting highly offended.

"You seem to have struck a nerve there," Ala said.

"Oh, I don't think so," Dain said. "Most of his gruffness is for show. He's probably down at the bar right now, waiting to buy us a drink."

"Since we aren't being stealthy anymore, I believe I will go down and take him up on that," Leah said, moving toward the door. "Coming Dain?"

"I'm in," Tera said, running out the door.

"I was thinking perhaps one of us should stay with Donella," Dain suggested.

"Go ahead, Dain. I'll be all right."

"I'll stay with her," Ala said. "You all should go and get something to eat and drink. Besides, it will give me uninterrupted time to get to know Donella."

"Very well, I'll have something brought up for you," he said as he closed the door behind him.

Ala went and got a stool and brought it over to sit by Donella's bedside. After some cursory checks of her body, she looked again into those green eyes. "Now, I want you to tell me all about yourself, and why you and your party are here. Something tells me that if I am going to be traveling with you, I better know what to expect. For one thing, why are we going to Hadley Manor?"

Ala watched as Donella returned her stare, looking as if trying to decide how much she should tell her. As Donella shared her true identity, something stirred in her breast and awakened in her spirit. The edges of the faerie's green eyes took on a fiery aspect. Her dark hair glowed with traces of silver, the color of moonbeams.

"I am the Dragon Summoner," she said.

There was a crash as Ala's stool tipped over and put her on the floor, from where she looked up in disbelief.

Chapter 14

CHASER MARKED A SLOW and steady pace three days out of Black River. The main highway was well-worn, giving the occupants in the wagon a smooth ride. Tera played a soothing forest melody on her pipes as they rode along. Leah had flown ahead to scout the area.

Ala looked at the individuals whom fate had thrown her in with. Dain was clearly the leader of the group. The tall, handsome Border Lands general was the epitome of military efficiency. Diminitus reminded her of a crazy uncle she had. He was highly intelligent but could explode in anger in an instant and then calm down just as quickly. Tera was a delight. Ala thought that if she ever had a daughter, she would want her to have Tera's love and joy of life. Leah, though not there at the moment, was a warrior through and through, yet around Dain her rough exterior relaxed and took on a softer aspect.

Donella was an enigma to her. The dark-haired faerie had stunned her with the news that she was the Dragon Summoner. She had heard the tales, passed down over the centuries, of the faerie who commanded dragons. The stories were so clouded in legend, however, that one did not know where fact ended and myth began. And no human currently alive had ever seen a dragon, except maybe Diminitus. But, according to Donella, a dragon was in the world again.

There were other things that puzzled her from a healer's standpoint. Donella's memory loss, for one; another was the fact that she was not immune to skull-spider venom. Ala had given her a dose of Dragonroot that morning, when her temperature had increased slightly. From the time of the first dose to now was eight days. Ala hoped the next span would be longer. She figured, at most, Donella would need two more doses and then her body should be able to manage on its own. She glanced over at Donella, who happened to be looking up at the trees and the birds roosting there. She felt Donella was just about the kindest person she had ever met.

The cart went around a bend. It was then that Leah glided in and landed on the road in front of them.

"Whoa, Chaser," Leah said as the horse's nose came in contact with her palm.

"Anything?" Dain asked from the driver's seat.

"No, it's strangely quiet for the next five miles."

"I don't like this," Diminitus said irritably. "Black River and Hadley are two major commerce cities, and yet we hardly see anyone on the road."

"Whatever the reason, we don't have a choice. We must keep going," Dain explained. "We'll keep a close watch."

"May I make a suggestion?" Ala said.

"Suggest away," Dain said.

"Not too much farther up the road, there is a narrow trail that goes through the woods. I believe the wagon can pass over it. It leads to a small village, about two days drive. I get called there from time to time. It is nestled in a valley with a ring of hills around it. There is also a trail that leads out of the village and comes near the south woods of the Hadley Manor house."

"Ala, that's perfect!" Dain exclaimed. "It gets us off the road and brings us right where we want to be without having to go through the city of Hadley." There was another reason she had suggested this route, but she thought it better to discuss that once they were off the main road.

"I'll fly up ahead and scout out a place to camp," Leah stated.

"Mind if I come with you?" Donella asked. "I really need to stretch my wings."

"Me, too?" Tera asked hopefully.

"Sure, let's go." The three faeries took off down the road and started flying up the trail Ala had mentioned.

"I guess us non-flying creatures will just have to plod along," Diminitus said grumpily.

They caught up with the faeries just before sundown. Leah showed them a clearing in the woods, back away from the trail. They moved the wagon into the trees as best they could and removed Chaser's harness. All of them pitched in to collect firewood, and it wasn't long before they had a fire blazing. They ate a hearty meal, and when it was done, everyone settled in to get comfortable. Then Tera provided Ala the opening to tell what she knew of the village and its citizens.

"This is quite a distance from Black River, Ala. How do you know when people are sick out here?" Tera asked.

"I don't. The visits are scheduled, because of who lives there."

"And who lives there?" Diminitus asked, taking a sip of wine from the wineskin.

"The king and queen," Ala replied simply. Diminitus started to sputter and choke.

"The king and queen of what?" Dain asked already guessing the answer.

"Vasara, the high king and queen," Ala replied.

"Has anyone informed Devon?" Diminitus asked sarcastically.

"Dim, please," Dain said. "Perhaps you better tell us the whole story, Ala."

"Certainly. I would have told you earlier, but I wanted to get as far off the road as possible, and, given what Donella has told me of your quest, I felt you should know." She gathered her thoughts as the fire crackled and a few cinders fell outside the stone fire ring. The crickets were unusually loud as she began.

"When Devon killed King Baldric and Queen Galatea, he assumed there would be no one to lead a rebellion, since they had no children and Baldric had no brothers or sisters. But one thing most everyone forgot was that Baldric's father had a brother, Calan, who in turn had fathered a son, named Taiyo. Calan had died in a duel shortly after Taiyo was born, and the boy and his mother moved back to her native home in Black River. They lived in that remote village we are heading for, and Vasara forgot them." She paused in her narrative to take a sip of her herbal tea.

"Taiyo was the adventurous type," she continued. "When he became a man, he traveled the breadth of Vasara, seeing what he could discover."

"I remember him," Diminitus put in. "He came down to Parma once and pestered me for a week to show him some secret caves and groves and other such nonsense. I told him to get lost. I was extremely cranky that year."

"Is there ever a year when you're not cranky?" Leah said smiling.

"Now see here missy!"

"Please continue, Ala," Dain said heading off the impending argument.

"Taiyo traveled to Fenner, where he met the woman who would be his wife. Once they were married, they traveled back to his village home and raised their children. It was not long after that that the wizard Redlin came looking for a specific healer in Black River. Redlin was the master of history, so he knew Taiyo's lineage. And he knew, if the royal family was to ascend the throne once more, the line had to be protected until Devon was overthrown. So he petitioned Rafael to reveal the identity of his priest. After telling him the circumstances and his plan, Rafael agreed and sent him to find Kendra, his priestess at the time. Redlin charged her with the knowledge of Taiyo's line and asked that she check on them periodically, staying aware of their health and numbers. He told her this knowledge had to be passed on to each priest or priestess of Rafael, which is why I know the story. The current heirs to the throne of Vasara are Paolo and Acacia."

"Do they know?" Donella asked.

"Yes, but only whoever is in direct line is ever told. There is no need for anyone else to know. And the heirs always seem to come back and settle in that village. They may travel from time to time, but it seems, when children are born, they come back here to raise them."

"That is most uncanny," Diminitus said. "Why have they never pressed their claim?"

"There was no way they could match Devon's power. And the heirs figured, if they are meant to have the throne, the inhabitants of Vasara would put them there."

"Well, let us hope we succeed in our quest so they get that chance," Dain said. "We should get some sleep. I want to leave just before the sun rises, so we can reach the village by late afternoon. I'll take the first watch." Everyone went to find his or her sleeping places. At some point during the night, Leah got up and walked over to where Dain was keeping watch.

Ala awoke around midnight and saw the general and the faerie keeping a silent vigil together while a pale moon rose over the tree tops. She smiled to see two people finding happiness in each other then turned toward the fire and went back to sleep.

The ride was uneventful as they crested the rise and came upon the tiny village. Everyone, except Ala, of course, was amazed at what they saw. The homes, about fifteen in all, formed a perfect circle. In the center was a statue that, from this distance, appeared to be a rearing horse. Radiating out from the center of the village were five narrow, white, crushed-stone streets. Small trees and flowers lined the sides of all the streets; stone benches showed up every thirty yards or so, giving everything a park-like quality. It was a tribute to beauty and symmetry. If someone were expecting to find a dirty backwoods village with villagers to match, they would've been sorely disappointed.

There were people about, some leisurely walking the streets, others sitting on the benches, talking or reading. Children ran and played games. There was a spirit of happiness and contentment here.

Dain gave Chaser a gentle slap of the reins, and they descended on the town. The villagers who were outside saw them come down and ran over to greet them. Living in such isolation, many others would have been fearful or suspicious of strangers. These people, however, were outgoing and friendly. They recognized Ala right off and made their hellos. Ala, in turn, introduced everyone. She then asked where she could find Paolo. They told her he was with Acacia in the fields. Ala bade them goodbye and proceeded to the north end of the village, where the fields were located. When they reached the village center, Dain stopped the wagon by the statue.

"Wow!" Tera exclaimed. "It's a unicorn!" The statue was white marble with a polished sheen. The detail on it was amazing; from the horn to the tail, every facet of the animal had been captured.

"That is a beautiful work of art," Leah said in awe. The unicorn stood on its hind legs with its forelegs pawing the air as if in battle with unseen demons.

"It is the symbol of Taiyo's house," Ala explained. "Taiyo was an artisan, and it was he who chiseled this piece."

"Well I'll be," Diminitus said, clearly not believing what he saw.

"What is it, Dim?" Dain asked.

"Remember I was telling you Taiyo came pestering me to help him find some secret groves. One of them was the grove of the unicorns. It is surrounded by enchantments and is never in the same place twice in a row. It moves. I found it once totally by accident. I have never seen it since. It appears Taiyo has seen it, too. This statue is too detailed for him not to have seen a unicorn."

"There is something else. Redlin told Kendra a prophecy," Ala said, "that when the unicorn stands on the western hill, Devon's end is near and Taiyo's house can go home." She pointed toward the western hill. "That is the trail that leaves this village and comes out behind Hadley Manor. It eventually leads to the White Castle."

"Let's go and meet Their Majesties," Dain said. "I, for one, want to get a good look at the future king and queen of Vasara."

They rode the wagon to the edge of the village, left it there, and walked a dirt path beyond the houses to the fields where all the food was grown. On the way to the fields, they saw a man and woman walking toward them, each with a bushel full of vegetables. They were talking animatedly with each other and did not see Ala and the others until they were almost on top of them.

"Oh! Hello, Ala." The man was surprised to suddenly look up and see a group of people in front of him. "I'm sorry, I didn't see you there. It's Acacia's fault. She had me distracted," he said smiling.

"Paolo, stop that," Acacia said, putting her bushel down and embracing Ala. "It is good to see you, Ala. It has been too long." She was a petite woman standing a little over five feet tall. She had long dark brown hair down to the small of her back, currently done up in a braid. It was long enough that, if she wanted to, she could whip Paolo with it.

Paolo was over six feet tall and very muscular. His tanned face and sandy blond hair gave testament to the fact that he spent a lot of time walking and working in the sun.

"Hello, Acacia," Ala said. "Paolo, good to see you. I'm sorry if we startled you."

"Not at all, dear. Who have you brought with you?" Paolo asked, looking toward the others.

Before Ala could begin the introductions, Dain came forward, pulling his sword from its sheath. Paolo seemed taken aback by this action, and Ala was unsure what Dain intended. Dain sank to one knee and placed the sword at Paolo's feet in a sign of fealty. "Your Majesty, my life is yours to command," he stated.

Ala knew the blood of kings ran in Paolo's veins, and he would in no way belittle or make light of this man's action.

"Please rise, good sir," Paolo said in all seriousness, placing a hand on Dain's shoulder. He looked at the sword and then at Dain. "If I were to guess, I would say you are a soldier of some rank from the Border Lands."

"General Dain at your service, sire," Dain said getting to his feet.

"I see Ala has told you our secret," Paolo said, giving a questioning look to Ala. "In any case, General, I do not occupy the White Throne, so I am unable to accept your fealty. If one day that should change, I or my heirs will accept it gladly and with honor."

"I understand, Your Majesty," Dain said. "I am amazed, though, that you knew me for what I am, being as isolated as you are."

"Please, for now call me Paolo. As to your identity, I traveled all throughout Vasara in my youth. It is a requirement we make of all possible heirs, so they know the people and the world they live in. My eldest son is out there now, doing this very thing. I spent time in the Border Lands and got to know the people there. Your bearing gives away your military training, and the golden serpent wrapped around your sword's hilt told me you are an officer."

"I'm most impressed, Your Maj— Paolo," Dain said.

"Come, let's go to our house, for, if I am not mistaken, some major event is happening here that is probably best not spoken about in public. We can make further introductions once we are inside."

Paolo led the way to a two-story cottage with dark green shingles. Once inside, Ala introduced everyone. She told Paolo and Acacia everything she knew about the quest, even Donella's identity. They listened without interruption. When Ala finished, Acacia went over to the fireplace, took the teapot off the fire, and poured cups for those who wanted some. Paolo sat in quiet contemplation then turned toward Donella.

"You really are the Dragon Summoner?" Paolo asked.

"Yes," Donella replied simply.

"Then perhaps it is not by chance that you are here."

"What do you mean?" Leah asked.

"As I said earlier, I traveled a lot in my youth. One of the places I visited was Hadley Manor. I had met Baron Ogden and told him I was a Black River nobleman, which technically is the truth. It was there that I met Acacia. She was completing her five-year fostering at Hadley Manor. If anyone knows the layout of that place, it's her," Paolo said, nodding toward his wife. Everyone turned to where Acacia was busy tending the fire.

"Have you seen the Summoner's dress, the dragon crown?" Dain asked eagerly. "Do you know where it is located?"

"Yes, I do," Acacia said with a shudder, remembering her time there. "And getting it out of Zana's apartments will not be easy."

"Did you know Zana?" Tera asked.

"I knew her, but we were not friends," she said with some heat. "On my very first day there, I accidentally walked into her room. She had the dress on display in the middle of the floor, like it was some kind of trophy. She walked in as I was staring at it. She threatened my life, saying, if I didn't want to suffer the same fate as the previous owner of that dress, I had better stay away. I never spoke a single word to her afterward."

"Can you tell us how to find her rooms?" Donella asked.

"If you are thinking of scaling the walls or storming the front gates, forget it. It is too heavily guarded."

"We need to find some way in," Dain argued. "We can't turn back now."

"There is another way," Acacia stated. "There was one other time I was in Zana's room. She had been away at the White Castle for weeks. I was bored and needed a diversion. I went into her apartments again to seek out the dress." She looked down a little guiltily. "I was very young then. I had been there only a few minutes when, out in the hall, I could hear the servants scurrying and saying Zana had returned. I quickly ran to her innermost sitting room near the south wall and hid behind a tapestry. But instead of a stone wall, my back came in contact with a wooden door. I didn't waste any time wondering why it was there. I opened it and descended a narrow wooden staircase that brought me to a tunnel opening. I followed it to the end. It came out at the mill, just below the manor."

"Can you tell us how to find the tunnel?" Dain asked.

Acacia thought for a moment. "I don't think I could adequately describe it to you. The mill has many levels, and it is easy to get confused. Also, I was only in there once, so I doubt I would remember all the twists and turns." Dain's face fell a fraction on hearing this. "Unless," Acacia said continuing, "I was to come with you. If I were there, I'm sure I could find it."

"I couldn't ask you to put yourself in that kind of danger," Dain said, shocked.

"You didn't ask," Acacia said, smiling. "I just volunteered."

"Paolo, sire, you cannot permit this. It is too dangerous!"

"General, my wife goes where she pleases, and even if we sat on the throne as king and queen, I would not stifle such a spirit." He smiled at her. "She's small, but she is more than able to take care of herself. And don't let her talk you into a duel so she can demonstrate her skills. She has no reach, but she is quick and agile as a cat. I have several scars from her rapier that I got during our courting years to prove it."

"My husband is too kind," she said, beaming at him. "Now, down to business. You will all sleep here tonight, and in the morning, we will take your horse and my own to carry supplies and head for Hadley."

"I thought you were the leader of this little band," Diminitus whispered to Dain.

"I think I've just been outranked," Dain replied.

* * *

After making their goodbyes, the travelers set off for Hadley Manor. A better day could not have been asked for. The trail was narrow, so bringing the cart was out of the question. Acacia rode her white mare, Starling, with Ala, while Dain and Diminitus rode double on Chaser. The faeries took turns scouting the trail ahead. On the evening of the second day, they reached the edge of the wood that bordered the south wall of Hadley Manor. They left the horses tethered back among the trees. The manor loomed dark against the night sky. Some of the first-floor windows and many of the upper floors had candles burning. People could be seen moving in and out of rooms.

"Do you see the window on the extreme lower right, the one with a single candle? That is Zana's room," Acacia explained. All the other windows around it were dark, and no movement could be observed in Zana's window.

"Where is the mill?" Dain whispered.

"We must follow the edge of the wood until it comes to the stream and then follow the water up to the mill."

"Right. Let's go," Dain said. "Tera, you stay in the middle. Leah, bring up the rear." Everyone did as instructed as Acacia led the way. Donella was in the back of the line, near Leah.

"I'm worried, Leah," she said as they walked along. "We are about to enter the lion's den. What if something should go wrong?"

"I wouldn't let your mind worry on it. Besides, Zana might not even be around. It will all work out. You'll see." Donella couldn't tell if Leah was trying to reassure her or herself.

The mill was huge. The stream that ran by it powered several water wheels, supplying energy to various woodcutting machines and a massive, stone grinding wheel. It was clear now why Acacia felt she had to come with them. It took about fifteen minutes and countless doubling backs before she found the door in a false floor of the mill. The mill was empty; everyone had gone home for the day, but they maintained as much stealth as possible as Dain slowly opened the trap door.

"Does the tunnel run straight?" he asked.

"Yes," Acacia replied. "I ran straight through without a turn."

"Good. We will not use the torches, then. Everyone follow me."

The tunnel was straight as an arrow. Acacia told them she assumed Zana had had it built ages ago, in case she needed a quick getaway. Dain came to the end and felt the door that led to Zana's room. Turning the latch and opening the door as quietly as he could, he stepped through. He moved the tapestry slightly and peered into the sitting room Acacia had fled from many years ago. There was a thin, green, oval carpet on the floor with a small, round table and two chairs. A divan sat near the window that looked out onto the south lawn.

Dain did not see or hear anyone about, so he whispered for everyone to come in. Acacia led the way to the room that held the dress. Dain looked in and saw it was empty. With sword drawn, he motioned everyone to follow.

The dress was there, just as Acacia had described, hung on a faceless statue and displayed as a trophy. Donella walked toward it, hand outstretched, as if she reaching for her birthright. It was the most beautiful thing she'd ever seen. She knew each thread and weave had a purpose, since it had been spun by the goddess and gods. It was a rich green color with intricate designs in the hem and on the shoulder. The necklace was an emerald color chain of three strands with green stones hanging from them. On the hand of the statue was a ruby colored ring, and on the head was the dragon crown. Two dragon heads came up on the sides to meet at the centerpiece of the crown, which was the green dragon eye.

"Wow! That's so striking, I'm afraid to touch it," Tera exclaimed.

"It is best that you don't," said a voice from the doorway.

Everyone whipped around, weapons drawn.

"Zana!" Acacia said, rapier at the ready.

Zana stood with four grim-looking soldiers armed with swords. "I never thought to see your face again, Acacia. Are you still living with that Black River peasant?" Acacia did not respond to the insult. "Aren't you at least going to introduce me to your friends?" she said with a sneer. "No? Well, it doesn't matter. I know who they are. I've followed them since they left the Parma Wilds. Especially you, Donella. And if I understand correctly, you are here to steal my property. Stealing is very unbecoming to a faerie, my dear sister."

"I am no sister of yours," Donella said with calm and confidence. She found that she was not afraid. "These are mine by the right of Braylynn, and I will claim them." At the name of the goddess, Zana took one of the knives out of her belt and flung it straight at Donella's forehead. Donella did not even move, but Leah was there to deflect the knife with her spear.

"And you are the mighty Leah," Zana said with a laugh. "I have known of your reputation in battle for quite some time. I had hoped we would meet one day in the ring at the White Castle, but I guess now that will never happen."

"Enough!" Dain said with a snap like a whip in his voice. "What are your intentions here, Zana?"

"My intentions, dear general, are to hand you all over to Devon on the crime of treason. If you all come along peacefully, you will live. If not, you will die. Simple as that."

Donella knew how this was going to go. Zana's soldiers were slowly moving into position, forming a ring. Zana herself was making ready to spring. Before she was able to do that, Leah lunged, bringing her spear whistling over her head and coming down toward Zana's shoulder. Zana's skills, however, were highly developed. She was caught off guard only for an instant and was able to bring her own spear up to meet Leah's, deflecting the strike and suffering only a smart rap on her knuckles. Zana let out a curse and started to engage Leah.

"You will die this day," Zana said through clenched teeth.

The room turned into a battlefield. Dain and Diminitus each took a soldier. Diminitus, true to his word about his swordsmanship, had his adversary backpedaling to the far wall with a series of fast overhead strikes. It was all the man could do to hold his sword up and defend against the blows raining down upon him.

Dain's opponent was much more experienced and obviously the captain of this small detachment. They circled each other in the space available, parrying thrust after thrust, trying to find a weakness. But Dain had fought demons, and once he settled into his rhythm, the man never had a chance. Dain's arm became a blur of movement. At one point, it looked as if he were standing still, staring dead ahead while his sword moved about his body. The soldier never saw the stroke that severed his head, and with cool dispatch, Dain went looking for another target.

Ala, Acacia, and Tera were having some difficulty with the two soldiers who had them cornered and were giving them little room to maneuver. Acacia, with her rapier, was able to inflict some minor cuts on her attackers. Ala, not having any experience with a sword, merely held it in front of her. Tera, when the opportunity presented itself, darted in and stabbed with her dagger, but this had little effect, since the soldiers were wearing chain mail.

Leah and Donella were circling Zana, trying different combinations of attacks. Zana, however, had fought several opponents at once before and was holding her own as Leah swung at her head while Donella attacked her legs. At one point, Zana was able to knock Donella's spear away and, with amazing quickness, wedge her own spear between Donella's legs then twist, causing her to sprawl on the floor. Leah tried to follow up while Zana's spear was entangled in Donella's legs, but Zana was ever-resourceful. Reaching down to her left leg, she retrieved another spear, extended it, and brought it around to meet Leah's blow. Donella rolled, keeping her legs wrapped around Zana's other spear, causing Zana to lose control of it. Donella came up and started an attack on Zana's blind side, but Zana was fast and able to block her blow and still come back and defend against Leah's attack. Now it was Zana's turn to go on the offensive. With agility and speed, she forced Donella back against the wall and landed several shots across her knees, causing her to drop to the floor, crying out in pain. Leah, seeing Zana turn, leapt into the air and swung with all her might at Zana's unprotected head. But once again, Zana's speed proved too quick for her.

Damn! Leah thought. *How can I get in there?*

* * *

Zana gave Leah an evil smile, seeing the frustration in her eyes. Now it was time to finish it. Before she did that, though, she looked around. Diminitus had just run through the soldier he was fighting, and Dain, who had gone over to help the other women, had killed one soldier while Acacia dispatched the last. She was alone now, as they all turned as one and started to advance on her. Hope fled as she realized she would not be able to defeat so many at once.

Zana's greatest asset was her ability to think and act quickly. She was not one for last stands; she was a survivor. Sizing up the situation and realizing she was beaten, she thought of a way that would give her the greatest chance at escape. She needed to give them a reason to be delayed there while she fled. Looking around, she found her target. Knocking Leah's spear wide, she somersaulted backwards, pulling out her talon dagger midair and coming to land directly behind Tera. Grabbing her silver hair, there was a sickening crunch as Zana plunged the dagger into Tera's back, and the bloody point emerged from her chest. She pulled the blade out and let Tera slump to the floor. Tera never cried out. Then, turning, with a single leap she flew out of the open window, heading west. For a moment, everything seemed frozen.

* * *

"No!" Leah's scream tore through the halls of the manor as she witnessed the brutal murder of her friend. Running to Tera, Leah's knees hit the floor as she rolled Tera up onto her lap. The others formed a circle around her, stunned that their friend had fallen. Even Diminitus had tears streaming down his face as he saw the gash over that lovely heart.

"Tera, can you hear me?" Leah was crying hysterically. Tera's eyes opened. They were filmy and unfocused, and blood was seeping into the corners. Her breathing was labored.

"Leah... I'm..." Tera could not get out anymore as her eyes rolled into the back of her head.

"No! Tera, no!"

Valencia's charge came back to Donella. *You better keep her safe.* She had failed. Guilt and grief flooded her soul. Leah's mind snapped. She needed to kill someone, and that person had fled. Gently laying Tera down and smoothing her hair around her ashen face, Leah stood up. Her face like stone, she flew out the window Zana had escaped through.

"Leah, *wait!*" Dain yelled, looking back and forth between the window and Tera.

Donella could see his indecision on whether to chase after Leah or remain with them.

"Go after her, Dain," Donella said sympathetically. "We'll manage here. Leah's going to need you." Dain, his expression grim, made no reply. He turned and ran out the nearest door. The gods help any soldier foolish enough to get in his path. Donella felt spent. They had achieved their goal, but it had come at an extremely high price. Dawn would be breaking, and soon Hadley's inhabitants would be rising to go about their daily labors. She knew they must leave soon.

Ala was on her knees by Tera, feeling for a pulse and listening for a breath. After a few moments of searching, she found it: a faint flutter of a beat.

"She is still alive, barely," Ala announced.

"Is there anything that you can do?" Donella asked hopefully.

"No," she said sadly. "She is beyond any healer's skill." Ala took only a second to reach her next decision. "But she may not be beyond a god's." She pulled out a medallion on a chain around her neck. On it was stamped the image of the Dragon Tree. She held it in her hands and closed her eyes. After a few moments, the air in the room took on a sweet fragrance, and a red glowing nimbus appeared before them. The shape was like a man, but the features were indistinct. Then they heard the voice. It was rich and vibrant, and each one felt happy just to hear it.

"Why have you called, my daughter?"

"Lord Rafael, we need your help," Ala began. "A daughter of your sister is mortally wounded and beyond my skill to heal. She has sacrificed much in the furtherance of the aims of the prophecy you and your brothers put in place upon leaving Vasara. I would ask that you restore her to us," she pleaded.

"Ala, what you ask is not as simple as you may think." Rafael's voice echoed as if from a great distance. "I can sense her spirit is about to leave her body and begin the final journey," he said with great sympathy.

"Please, Lord," Donella said, throwing in her plea as well. "As Ala has said, she has sacrificed much for her goddess and for you and your brothers. Surely it is not a hateful thing to restore her to those who love her." Tears were running openly down Donella's face as she laid out her case to the healing god. She felt a touch on her mind.

"Ah, you are Braylynn's Summoner." He paused for a moment. "There may be a way. You must get her to Laurel Hollow. She is Braylynn's daughter, and only there, in the center of my sister's power, can her spirit be called back and her body restored."

"But they will never make it, Rafael," Diminitus put in. He had known Rafael when the gods walked in Vasara. They would spend months on end talking about plants and herbs. "It is hundreds of miles, and she will be dead before the sun is fully up."

"Have faith, Diminitus. The Dragon Summoner has the power to get her there in time." The god's radiance became an even brighter red. A nimbus then settled over Tera's body. After a few moments, it disappeared. "I have done all I can. I slowed her heart even more, and the blood will only flow at a trickle's pace. You have three days to reach Laurel Hollow. Otherwise, not even Braylynn can bring her back. You can do it, Summoner, and Diminitus must help you." Rafael once again addressed his priestess. "I must go now, Ala. Know that I am well pleased with you, my daughter. Call me whenever you have need. Farewell." The red light faded until it was a single line that shrank in on itself and disappeared.

"Why me?" Diminitus said incredulously. "You gods and goddess appoint me to these tasks, but you never tell me what it is I'm supposed to do!" he shouted at the ceiling.

Donella looked down at Tera. She did not see any noticeable change. "How can I get her to Laurel Hollow in three days?" she asked no one in particular. "Even if I were not encumbered with another, I could not fly there in three days."

"If I heard the god correctly," Acacia began, "he said the Dragon Summoner could do it." She looked over at the clothes of the Dragon Summoner, which remarkably had not been knocked over during the fight. Everyone else followed her gaze. "I have a feeling a dragon could cover the distance in three days."

"That's got to be it!" Ala exclaimed.

Donella's eyes were downcast. "I can't do it," she replied.

"What? Why not? You're the Dragon Summoner," Diminitus said in disbelief.

"Yes, but I do not know how to use these tools that are part of being the Summoner," she said, referring to the dress, crown, and jewels. "The plan was to bring these back to Braylynn, who would instruct me in their use."

Ala put a comforting hand on her shoulder. "You have to try."

"Is there no one else who could help you with this?" Acacia asked.

"The only other faerie I know who would have the knowledge died in this very manor fifteen-hundred years ago. The Dragon Summoner before me. And unless we can bring her back from the dead, we have little hope." Suddenly, Diminitus started to laugh.

"Diminitus, this is no time for laughing!" Ala said, becoming cross.

"Forgive me," he said, getting a hold of himself, "but that divine little fox knew all along, or at least she suspected something like this might happen."

"What are you talking about, man?" Acacia said, starting to lose her patience. "You're not making any sense."

"Let me explain. Braylynn told Donella she would need me on this trip, though we never knew why. Rafael said the Dragon Summoner could get Tera to Laurel Hollow, but she would need my help. Donella just said the only other one who could help her died in this very house. You're an educated woman, Ala. What would you say Donella needs right now?" He couldn't help smiling to himself.

"A necromancer?" she said, the light suddenly dawning on her.

"A Necromancer," he affirmed. "Of which I am one."

"What exactly is a necromancer?" Donella asked.

"Someone who can raise spirits," Acacia answered, "though I must confess, I did not think such people existed."

"As far as I know, I am the only one," Diminitus said. "Now, we have no time to lose. What was your predecessor's name?"

"Layla," Donella responded.

Diminitus lifted and moved part of the area rug to reveal the stone floor underneath. Then, wiping his index finger along a cut he'd received in the fight, he drew a small circle, about one foot in diameter, with his own blood. Once that was complete, he wiped up some more blood and started drawing strange-looking symbols inside the circle.

"What exactly are you doing?" Acacia asked.

"I am calling on the elemental powers of Vasara to compel Layla's spirit to come to us."

"If you are the only necromancer, how did you learn to do this?" Ala asked.

"I was bored one year, so I pestered the god Trystan to teach me something no one else knew, and this was it," he said, continuing to draw. Once satisfied he had all the proper symbols, Diminitus began moving his hand over them and, under his breath, began the incantation that would summon Layla's spirit. After several minutes, there was a shimmering in the air just above the circle of blood. It coalesced into the form of a faerie with auburn hair and yellow wings. She wore a white robe with a black sash that had white stars on it.

"Who are you, and why do you do this?" Layla asked, looking down at Diminitus.

"Please, Layla, he does this out of my need," Donella replied. Layla looked over at Donella.

"Speak, sister. I will hear you out."

"Thank you," Donella began. "I, like you, am Braylynn's Dragon Summoner. We are here in Hadley Manor to retrieve the clothing items Zana stole when she killed you." Layla's face took on a hard set at the mention of Zana's name. "Zana has tried to take another faerie life in order to escape us, and even now, our friend's life ebbs away unless we can get her to Laurel Hollow in three days' time. We believe a dragon can accomplish this. The only problem is I don't know how to summon him."

"I understand your need, sister, and I will help you," Layla replied. "What Zana did to me was vile and evil, and she must not be allowed to succeed again. Listen carefully, because my time here is extremely limited. Go and put on the dress and necklace. You, sir, avert your eyes." This she addressed to Diminitus. Donella took off her clothes and put on the dress. "Don't worry about size. Everything will adjust to fit you." Donella then undid the clasp and removed the necklace, putting it around her neck.

"Now, this is all about connections. The dress and necklace represent the earth and life and your connection to it. You need to reach out to the life force of all living things. The powers of the dress and necklace will help you do that. Try it now."

Donella looked at her friends. She started to see an aura of energy surrounding them. She could feel its power. She closed her eyes and allowed her mind to roam to the grass and woods outside. She could feel their life force, as well. She also knew she could tap that power, if she had to.

"Excellent!" Layla said. "I can see you have achieved this. Now, put on the ruby ring." Donella did this. "This ring has to do with the connection of fire and blood. Try to really feel the blood flowing through your body. Feel the heat it generates." Donella turned her sight inward. Her blood sounded loud in her mind, as she envisioned it traveling through her veins and into her heart then out again. The heat of the friction of the blood against her veins seemed so intense that she wondered why she didn't burn to a cinder.

"Now for the dragon crown," Layla said.

Donella removed her own silver circlet and placed it gently on Tera's head. She kissed her forehead then rose and was about to put the crown on her own head.

"Wait!" Layla exclaimed. "This is the hardest part. This will allow you to connect with dragons, but first you must see that dragon that is in you. That base aggression, those dark places you are afraid to go, that elemental raw power. Everything must be brought to the surface. You must have the courage to accept this as a part of yourself. You needn't be ashamed or loathe yourself afterwards." She looked hard at Donella. "Are you ready?"

Donella was shaking a little, but she was resolved. "I am," she replied.

"Put the crown on," Layla instructed.

Donella was not prepared for the sensation she got when she placed the crown on her head. She sank to her knees as if a great force was pushing her into oblivion. She screamed and fought to stay in the light.

"Do not fight it," she heard Layla say in the shadows of her mind. "Your darkness is a part of you. Flow with it, but know that you control it."

Donella stopped struggling; she rode the darkness as she would a horse. In her spirit, she saw that she was riding something. It was dark and had wings. Then it started to glow. It took on the form of the red dragon that was marked on her leg. The head turned around and looked directly into Donella's green eyes. There was malevolence there, as if this creature wanted to hurt something or someone, to inflict pain. Realization then came to her. This red dragon was an extension of herself. It was her own desire to cause pain, specifically to Zana and then to Devon. She loathed herself. This was not her. She thought on it for a moment and then accepted the truth of the matter. It was her. She *did* want to inflict pain on Zana, a lot of pain.

Donella brought herself under control and bent her thought on the red dragon to take her back to the light. When she opened her eyes, her friends were staring at her openmouthed. Like before, when she had told Ala she was the Dragon Summoner, the edges of her green eyes took on a fiery aspect and her dark hair glowed with traces of silver the color of moon beams.

Layla spoke one last time. "You are ready, sister. Bend your thought as you did with the dragon inside you, and the dragons of Vasara must come to you. Focus your inner sight through the eye in the crown, and you will see what the dragon sees. There is still much for you to learn, but this will help you get our sister to Laurel Hollow. One more thing. Zana has a weakness. She cannot handle a direct overhead assault well. Hopefully, this will prove useful for you. Good luck and farewell."

Layla's spirit faded away, but before she was fully gone, Donella exclaimed, "Farewell, sister. I promise I will avenge you." Layla raised a hand in acknowledgement and then faded out of sight. For some reason, Donella felt it important to say that. As a Dragon Summoner, she shared a common bond with Layla, one that no other faerie alive could share.

"Now what?" Ala asked.

"I will attempt to call the dragon. I don't know what will happen, so be prepared for anything." Donella focused her thought through the dragon crown and the eye. Her mind was searching, calling out

She felt an impression coming from the east, toward the Border Lands. An impression of dragon thought. She reached out farther, and the feeling became stronger, and just like a key fitting a lock, it clicked. She had his location.

She sent out her summons, and, as with the red dragon, she compelled her will upon him. This dragon was black, and she could feel great puzzlement along the link. A name came floating back to her. She used it to compel him harder.

"Andros, I have need of you," she sent. Now she could feel great reluctance. "Andros, you will come to me." He was in the air now, winging his way toward Hadley Manor. She could feel a new emotion coming through the link. Unbridled rage.

CHAPTER 15

THE AIR WAS COOL coming off the lake as the boat sailed on toward the eastern shore. Andy stood at the rail, the wind blowing his hair in all directions. Their flight from Black River was just in time; Raptors had been closing in and were only two days behind when they boarded the ship.

The ship's name was Grey Morning. Not a very pleasant sounding name, Andy thought, but as long as it got them to where they needed to be, he didn't care what they called it. Bart had told him it was larger than most ships on the lake, but she had two extra-large sails that gave her greater speed. She also had seven guns on the port and starboard sides. The guns were mainly for when Grey Morning took the Tear River outlet from Lake Pleasant and headed to the open sea, where piracy was not uncommon. Loki had given Andy enough money to be able to buy passage for the three of them and their horses.

The ship had a crew of about fifty men and a very able-bodied captain named Captain Bowen. He was tall with a closely cropped beard and black, curly hair. He was currently working as helmsman at the ship's wheel. Bowen was not afraid to work side by side with his sailors, which made him well-liked and respected. He had started his career as a cabin boy and worked his way through every sailing job there was. Through some very lucrative business decisions, he was able to buy his own ship at the age of thirty-six, making him the youngest captain on Lake Pleasant.

Andy had told him the Raptors were after them just before they boarded but not why. He figured he could not expose the ship and its crew to that kind of danger without fair warning. The captain merely spat on the ground and said, "That's for the Raptors. You're welcome aboard my ship."

Andy heard some footsteps behind him. He knew who it was without having to turn around.

You know it's me, don't you? Abby communicated just before she reached him.

I do, Andy replied, smiling, as he continued gazing over the water. He liked it when they spoke mind to mind. He felt so much closer to her.

"Do you know how much longer?" she asked aloud, slipping her arm through his on the rail.

"The captain told me probably around noon tomorrow." He looked over at her and brushed the hair out of her face, only to have the wind blow it right back. She was wearing a long-sleeved white shirt with black trousers; a rapier that Bowen had given her was strapped to her hip. *Now she really looks like a pirate,* he thought.

They talked a great deal on the ride from Fenner to Black River. There were so many odds against them having any kind of relationship, but events kept sweeping them along together. He knew it was foolish to form any kind of attachments here, but the thought of going on without Abby seemed to take the breath from his body. He tried not to think about his having to return to his own world; instead, he focused on being in the moment and taking whatever happiness they could. Perhaps it wasn't his smartest choice, but when it comes to affairs of the heart, who makes smart decisions?

"Do you think that we'll find your sister at the Border Lands?"

"I hope so, or at least word of her. I asked Captain Bowen, but he hasn't seen her or heard anything connected to her. I keep thinking she's out there, alone and friendless." He turned sad eyes toward Abby. "At least I had Loki to help me get adjusted to Vasara.

I'm worried she has no one." He looked back toward the horizon. "Lately I've been praying to the Five to watch over and protect her. I figured it couldn't hurt," he said, shrugging his shoulders.

"She'll be all right, Andros. As Wizard Redlin once wrote, 'The gods and goddesses tend to reward those in their service.' And if your being here to set Vasara to rights is not 'in their service,' then I don't know what is."

"I hope you're right, Abby," he said, looking into her soft brown eyes. He leaned in and gave her a light kiss on the lips.

"Ho, Edward! Abby!" Captain Bowen yelled from the wheel. "Come on up. I want to show you something." Abby and Andy left their place at the rail and walked up to the quarter deck.

"Good morning, Captain," Andy greeted him. "How will the weather be today?"

"Should be good sailing for the rest of the day," he said, smiling. "I want you to see something. Look over on the port side and see what's running parallel to us." Andy and Abby looked over the left side of the boat and saw four powerful wakes keeping pace with them.

"What is that, Captain?" Andy asked.

"Give it a minute. You'll see."

They watched a little longer when, suddenly, four creatures leapt out of the water simultaneously, flipped twice, and then dove back beneath the waves. Members of the crew who had been working on deck saw the creatures as well and stood with open mouths.

"Unbelievable!" Andy exclaimed. The creatures resembled sea horses in his own world but on a much larger scale. They were pony-sized, their dragon-like heads studded with long, flexible spikes that cascaded down their muscular backs like a horse's mane. Their undersides were scaly and yellow, while their backsides were silver with a red stripe down the center. Their intelligent eyes were red and yellow, like the sky just before sunset.

"What are they called?" Andy asked.

"Don't know their proper names, but we call them sea dragons."

"They are called tagen," Abby said, astounded at what she had seen. "I've read about them, but most of what I read was from books written more than a thousand years before Devon seized power. I figured they must be a myth."

"Oh, they're real all right, but sightings are very rare. That is only the second time I have ever seen them. The unusual wakes alerted me," Bowen explained.

"Thank you so much for showing us, Captain. That is a sight I would not have wanted to miss," Abby said.

"Not at all, Abby. Take it as partial payment for the singing you have been doing for the crew. I believe you've stolen all their hearts. They think of you now as a little sister."

Abby had been singing for the crew each night on deck after their daily labors were done. She didn't mind; she loved to sing. She'd had them eating out of the palm of her hand the very first night. She sang about sweethearts and home, something dear to every seaman. There wasn't a dry eye on the ship, including Bart's, who had never heard Abby sing.

"Since this is your last night, the crew was hoping you would sing one more time," the Captain said.

"It would be my pleasure, Captain."

All of a sudden, they heard thumping against the side of the ship.

"What the...?" Bowen started.

Oh no, Andy thought to himself. When Bowen had mentioned that the creatures were called sea dragons, his mind instantly tried to reach out to them. He had made contact, and now the tagen were coming to say hello.

Everyone ran to the side of the ship and looked down. Four tagen were bumping their heads against the ship's planking. When they looked up and saw Andy, they went wild, racing around in circles at incredible speeds. Their high-pitched chattering sounded like dolphins, Andy thought.

He tried to get them to leave. *Shoo! Shoo! Go away.* They did a couple more summersaults before disappearing back into the deep.

"Well, that was the most amazing thing I ever saw!" Bowen exclaimed. "I wonder what made them act that way." Abby cast a sidelong glance at Andy. He tried his best not to look guilty. After the tagen show was over, everyone went back to their duties. The captain unhooked the rope that kept the ship's wheel from spinning freely and manned the helm once more.

"Have you seen Bart?" Andy asked.

"I believe he is still in his bunk. He stayed up late last night, drinking and gambling with some of the crew," Bowen replied, smiling.

"I think we better go check on him," Andy said.

"Once you get him out of his hammock and sobered up, come join me in my cabin for some food and refreshment. There are some things I need to tell you about."

"Certainly, Captain. We'll be there."

They proceeded down the stairs to the lower deck, where the sleeping quarters were. Andy had to duck his head most of the way because of the low-hanging beams. They reached the crew's quarters, where hammocks were lined up in rows of ten. Only one was occupied. Andy walked over to where Bart was sleeping.

"Rise and shine, Bart. It's a beautiful day outside," he said a little louder than he needed to.

"Ouch! Don't speak so loud, lad," Bart said through squinted eyes as he gripped his head tenderly. "Don't ever let me drink with those people again. That grog is nasty stuff, although you don't realize it until the next day. Was someone hammering outside earlier?" He sat up and proceeded to rub his temple.

"You could say that. When you pull yourself together, the captain wants us to join him for lunch," Abby said.

"Please, Abby, don't mention lunch to me right now," he said, rubbing his stomach. "Give me an hour and I'll be ready."

Andy and Abby left Bart and went topside. It was more like two hours before Bart appeared on deck, his eyes blinded by the bright sun.

"Any better?" Andy asked, trying to suppress a smile.

"Some. I think I'm able to see the captain at any rate."

Bart walked around on deck for a few minutes, breathing in the fresh air, then the three of them proceeded to Bowen's cabin and knocked on the door.

"Come in," Bowen called. The captain's cabin was in the stern. Windows looked out on the ship's wake. There was a bed anchored to the floor against the port wall and a table with four chairs in the center of the room. On the starboard wall were a desk and a bookshelf laden with books strapped down to prevent them from falling during rough weather. Scattered about the room were various nautical devices. Four candle lanterns swung from the beams as the ship rolled with the swells. There was meat, bread, and cheese on the table along with four silver goblets filled with wine. "Please, sit down."

"If you don't mind, Captain, I'll just have some water," Bart replied.

The captain served the others himself. Andy couldn't help but admire this man. He didn't think any task was beneath his position as captain. He took great pleasure in playing host to his guests, which contrasted with what Andy had heard about him from some of the crew members who had seen Bowen in battle. They said a battle aura came over him and he became like a shadow, unable to be touched and able to disappear at will. Andy was sure the description had grown in the telling over the years, but he had no doubt it was founded in some truth.

"This wine is very good, Captain!" Abby exclaimed, her cheeks starting to take on a rosy color after a few sips.

"Be careful," Bowen cautioned. "It can go to your head very quickly. It comes from the Mistral Islands, just off the Kensington coast in the Scio Ocean. We travel there three times a year by way of the Tear River. There is a wine merchant there who always gives me several cases free because I transport his goods to the mainland."

"Captain, what is it you wanted to tell us?" Andy asked, curious.

After swirling his wine around in his goblet, Bowen took a sip before answering Andy's question.

"Loki came to see me several weeks back," he replied.

Andy carefully kept his face blank. He figured his best course of action would be to keep silent and hear what the captain had to say before speaking.

Bowen continued, "He told me to be on the lookout for a young man who might be seeking passage to the Border Lands. He asked me to give whatever aid I could. So when Bart came looking for a ship to carry three passengers and horses, I had a feeling you were the ones Loki spoke about. When you told me your name was Edward, that confirmed it, for Loki said you would be traveling under that name."

Andy got up and walked over to the window. The lake had calmed, and the water made a gentle lapping sound as it brushed against the ship. Seagulls were darting in and out of view, hoping to catch scraps from the sailors on deck. Andy was puzzled that Loki would confide so much in Bowen. He had a thought.

Bart, is Bowen like Maccus? Andy sent.

I don't know, lad. I'm sure there are a lot of people Loki has in his service that we know nothing about. The fact that Loki told him to look out for us tells me he can be trusted, he replied.

Andy decided to trust his gut and not dance around what Bowen might or might not know.

"Did Loki say anything else?" Andy asked.

Bowen smiled. "I see you've decided to trust me. And it is well you should, because it may be that we can be a benefit to you."

"We?" Abby said, wondering who else might be involved in this.

"The other merchant captains," Bowen replied. "We are kind of a professional band of brothers, watching out for each other's interests. Loki wanted me to tell you about us. We are tired of the taxes and tariffs we pay to the barons every time we come into port," he said, scowling. "And the boarding and inspections done by Devon's soldiers—they seize whatever they desire by declaring it contraband, and then they turn around and sell it. Some captains have tried to argue the tariffs and boardings, only to be questioned by the Raptors and then thrown in prison. Don't get me wrong, I don't mind paying my share, as long as every other merchant vessel does the same."

"You mean not all do?" Bart asked.

"No, some are in the employ of the government. They pay little taxes and no tariffs, which enables them to undercut our prices. We also suspect some of them engage in piracy in order to eliminate competition."

"What exactly are you saying, Captain?" Andy asked.

"That the lake and sea captains are ready for change, and we are willing to fight for it. Vasara should be a free and open land where every person has a fair shot at making a prosperous living for him or herself. Loki told me that time may be fast approaching and that you were the key to it. He didn't go into detail, but am I to assume that there may be a change in management at the White Castle?" he asked with a raised eyebrow.

"That is our hope," Andy said.

"Then, when you are ready, there will be a navy with ships of all sizes waiting for you. We can easily lay off the coast of the castle and hit it with a barrage of cannon fire the likes of which Devon has never seen," he said fiercely.

An idea was beginning to form in Andy's mind. Loki had said that a plan to defeat Devon would reveal itself to him. With Maccus, he had a cavalry; in Bowen, he had a navy; and next he was heading to a place that had an army of swordsmen. It seemed no one province wanted to stand up to Devon alone, but if they all banded together, they might somehow be able to manage Devon's army. That just left him to handle Devon. How he was going to manage that, he did not know. He extended his hand to Bowen.

"I accept your help, Captain. I don't know when or where this will begin, but I will get word to you somehow."

"Excellent, Edward!" Bowen said, pounding his fist on the table. "I will get word to the other captains to be ready to move when the time comes."

"Captain, please don't take your enthusiasm out on that poor table," Bart said, wincing. Everyone burst out laughing, causing Bart to hold his head even harder.

Around noon the following day, just as the captain had predicted, they reached the eastern shore of Lake Pleasant. It was a small port town that only seemed to exist as a transfer station for goods. The captain made his farewells on the wharf while his crew cheered wildly for Abby from the rail. On their last night aboard ship, she had sung to them of the sea and heroic deeds, filling the sailors' hearts with courage and pride.

"I think you've made a conquest there, Abby," Bart said, smiling while looking up at the crew. "If you snapped your fingers, I believe they would fall in single file and follow you anywhere."

"I think that might be a slight exaggeration, Bart," Abby said.

"Maybe, but not by much," he replied with a wink.

The three travelers gave their horses a light thump in the flanks and headed them toward the east. Three days later, they found themselves at the gates of the Border Lands. Two sentries stood guard outside. They wore chain mail with armor breastplates and swords strapped to their hips, and they each held a spear.

The tallest one with a graying beard stepped forward to challenge them. "State your name and business, otherwise turn yourselves around and head back to where you came from," he said in a tone that was firm and all business.

"My name is Edward," Andy began, "and this is Abby and Bart of Dragonsgate. We are looking for a man by the name of Lyson."

"General Lyson?" the younger one asked. Andy wasn't sure how to respond. Loki had never told him what rank he held, if any. Last time he had played this game had been with Abby, when they first met, and he had lost. Well, he figured he had a fifty-fifty chance.

"Yes, General Lyson." He held his breath.

"He is on patrol. You may however go to the guard station and wait for him there. He should be back before sunset. Just ride straight down this road, and you will see another sentry."

"Thank you," Andy responded.

"May Fallon's peace be with you."

"That wasn't much of a challenge," Abby said when they were out of earshot.

"If your business sounds legitimate," Bart said, "they have no cause to stop you. Besides, no one is going to interfere with the people of the Border Lands and the job they do here, which is in the interest of all Vasara."

"You mean fighting the demons," Andy said.

"Yes," Bart replied. "Not even Devon will interfere with them, because he knows, should they fail to keep the demons in check, the demons would overrun Vasara, and not even he could handle that many at once. He does not even have a garrison here. The people will not allow it. So we don't have to worry about Raptors popping up."

The road was wide as it cut through the woods. When they emerged from under the trees, they did not expect the sight that greeted their eyes. Andy assumed, with a warrior race, the land would be as hard as its people. Instead, what Andy saw was how he'd always imagined paradise. He stopped his horse and just stared for several minutes, not saying a word. Gentle rolling hills with lush green grass seemed to stretch for miles. A stream meandered through the countryside. Trees of all kinds were evident. Some had long, outreaching limbs just right for sitting under on a hot day. Others were small, leafy trees with white blossoms, and more than a few were fruit-bearing trees, as well. A gentle breeze made long grasses dance like waves upon the ocean. A riot of colorful wildflowers grew the banks of the stream. Birds of every color trilled and flitted among the trees and crisscrossed the stream. A sense of peace pervaded this place.

"I can't believe this," Andy said, in awe.

"How can a place such as this exist right up against such evil?" Abby asked in wonderment.

"That evil is probably why it does exist," Bart explained. "To give these people a reason to fight and die for their land."

They rode slowly to the guard station, not wanting to miss any part of the beauty around them. Eventually they came upon a brick house flanked by small towers on either end. To Andy, it looked like a miniature castle. They found the guard on duty and repeated their names and business. The guard in turn told them they could wait for General Lyson. As it turned out, they didn't have long to wait.

One look at Lyson and you could not mistake him for anything but a general. His eyes were blue but with a hard edge to them, as if there was nothing they hadn't seen. He gave several orders when he came in, his voice crisp and firm without being demeaning or being overbearing. He knew his orders would be carried out without question. He wore a chain mail shirt and breastplate. He also had a pair of greaves on his legs. Around his hip was strapped a sword with a serpent on the hilt.

"General, these people are here to see you," the guard said by way of introduction. Lyson turned around and sized up the trio.

"I'm General Lyson. How may I be of service?" he asked.

"General, my name is Edward. These are my companions, Bart and Abby. A mutual friend sent us," Andy said, showing Lyson the coin Loki had given him. "Is there somewhere private we can speak?"

Lyson raised one eyebrow, as though recognizing the coin immediately and knowing what it meant. "Very well, follow me." He led the way to the back of the guard house where some stone steps led to the roof. It gave an even more breathtaking view of the surrounding area.

"This is the most beautiful place I have ever seen," Andy remarked. "The Border Lands are a very nondescript name for a land such as this."

"The name is just a designation for where our country lies. We have our own names for the various places within the Border Lands. For example, our chief city is called Bolivar, which is about twenty miles from where we are now. This guard tower is in Spring Valley."

"That name truly fits this area," Abby commented. "Now I sorely regret not taking the time to study this land and its people more when I was learning my geography."

"Most people really don't want to know too much about the Border Lands because of the horrors we keep at bay," Lyson said sadly. "We do get visitors here, but mostly merchants who buy our weapons to sell in other markets on the other side of Lake Pleasant, and of course the faeries, with whom we have had a long history. But I sense the reason you came here has nothing to do with our land. And the fact that you have a coin of my house suggests you need aid."

"We were told by the wizard Loki to seek you out," Andy said. "He believed you might be able to help us." Andy then went on to explain everything about himself and their situation, about his sister and his real name, and also about using the warriors to go up against Devon.

"That is an amazing tale," Lyson said when Andy had finished. "Don't get me wrong, I don't doubt your word. I just never expected this to happen in my time." He sat on the roof's wall and contemplated all he had heard.

"It's a lot to digest all at once," Bart said. "I know it was for me. But he is a handy guy to have around."

"I'm sure he is, but there is more to it than that, actually," Lyson said seriously. "I think you should come to my home in Bolivar. There is a lot to discuss, which may take a while, and I think it would best serve us all if we did that in the comfort of my home."

They mounted their horses and rode to Bolivar. They were tired and hungry by the time they walked into Lyson's house. It was a large house with many rooms. Lyson explained it had been in his family for many generations. He escorted them into his library, where his house staff brought some food and drinks. A fire was burning in the hearth, and everyone moved their chairs close around it.

Abby got up to look at the books. Having been around books most of her life, she couldn't help but pull one or two down and leaf through them. One book caught her eye; it was titled *Parallel Worlds*, by Redlin. She took it down and thumbed through it.

"Would you mind if I borrowed this one?" she asked, showing it to Lyson.

"Please, accept it as my gift," he replied.

"Thank you."

"Now, what is it you wanted to discuss?" Andy prompted.

"Well…"

Just then, the front door of the house opened and closed with a slam.

"Lyson, where are you?" a woman's voice called from the foyer.

"In the library. My sister Cleo," he told the others.

As she entered the room, Bart's mouth dropped open slightly. She was strikingly beautiful. Her dark hair was pulled back in a braid to the middle of her shoulder blades. Like her brother, her eyes were blue and her skin bronzed from many hours in the sun. Cleo wore leather armor from pauldrons to cuisse. Here leather breastplate was burgundy with small silver steel spikes that ran from her shoulder to sternum. Her armor was light and provided for greater freedom of movement. Strapped to her back were two short swords in silver scabbards. She moved with a fluid grace and an air of self-confidence.

"Oh, I'm sorry. I didn't realize you had guests."

"It's all right, Cleo. This is Andros, Bart the Archer, and Abby of Dragonsgate."

"Please to meet you," Andy and Abby said. Bart, however, got up and took her hand and kissed it.

"Madame, it is my pleasure to meet the most beautiful woman in Bolivar," Bart flirted outrageously. "The sparkle in your eyes puts the sun to shame." He had always considered himself a ladies man, although more often than not he had found himself on the receiving end of a slap to the face.

"My, aren't you the pretty talker," Cleo replied with a hint of steel in her voice. "It is a good thing you are a guest of my brother, otherwise your hand would be on the floor next to your feet right now." Bart's face registered shock, and he quickly dropped her hand and took a few steps back.

"I am sorry," he said hastily. "I meant no offense."

Cleo looked stern, and then she laughed. "I'm just funning with you, archer. You can say pretty words to me anytime, but don't expect me to just melt like butter on a hot rock."

"What is happening on the Plains?" Lyson asked.

Her brother's question brought back the seriousness to her voice.

"Forgive my levity, brother, but I bring sad tidings. Tavon is dead."

Lyson's face visibly paled.

"How?" he asked with downcast eyes.

"He fell, and one of them pounced on him. He died quickly," Cleo answered soberly.

"Please excuse me for a moment," he said to Andy as he got up and left the room.

"Where is he going?" Abby asked Cleo.

"I assume he is going to send a rider to inform his family. They live about three days' ride from here."

"Did they know each other well?" Andy asked.

"They were best friends growing up. They trained together and received their commissions together," Cleo replied.

"He was killed by a demon then?" Bart said.

"Yes."

"What do they look like?" Abby asked.

"Most of the time, they take the form of some hideous monster they dream up, but they can assume any shape, even a human. You can always tell them, though. They have a sulfur smell that gives them away."

Just then, Lyson came walking back into the room. He had regained his composure.

"I'm sorry about your friend," Andy said sympathetically.

"Thank you, Andros," Lyson replied.

"If you wish, we can continue this in the morning," Bart said.

"No, it's all right. Besides, we need to talk tonight. Tomorrow I head back to the Plains."

"I'm going to go and get out of this armor. I will come back and join you in a moment," Cleo said as she left.

Lyson went over to a sideboard to pour some wine. He filled three other glasses for his guests and offered one to each of them. He also took up the plate of meat on skewers and gave these to his guests, as well. They all ate some and then settled down to hear what Lyson had to say.

Taking a sip of his wine, he began. "I don't know how much Loki has told you about us and the demons we fight, so I will give you a brief overview. Demons touch every world and manifest themselves differently in each one. Here, they exist in the Plains of Desolation. At least that is the place where they take physical form. But to enter Vasara, they have to come through the Corridor."

"What is the Corridor?" Abby asked.

"It is a strip of the Plains that is a ten-mile square. On each corner is a pillar with a power stone on top. They are called the Pillars of

Fallon. The ruby-colored stones have a power in them that creates kind of an invisible shield that severely limits the number of demons that can take form and attack. But all four must be in place for it to be effective."

"Let me guess," Bart said, hoping he was wrong. "Devon has stolen one."

"That's correct. When Devon made his pact with the demons, he took one of the stones and still holds it in the White Castle. The result being, many more demons can enter the Corridor."

"Which forces us to patrol deeper into the Plains and attack them before they reach the Corridor," Cleo finished. She came in wearing a long-sleeved white tunic with a blue star design along the neck line. Her hair hung loose, which made her features even more striking. "Brother, could you bring me up to speed on our guests here before you go further?"

"Certainly. We are going to need your input, and it is best if you know in full what we discuss here. If you would?" he asked Andy. Andy repeated everything he had told Lyson. To her credit, Cleo had no trouble accepting the story he told.

"Well, now I can say I've actually met a dragon," she said, smiling. "I'm sorry about your sister. I will keep an eye out for her. But Loki was right about one thing. Lyson is the best tracker in the Border Lands."

"You are just as good as I, sister," Lyson said with pride.

"Do you think you will be able to help us?" Andy asked hopefully.

"That brings us back to Devon's theft of the stone," Lyson said. "By doing this, he nailed our feet to the floor, so to speak. Ever since that day, it has been a constant battle to keep the enemy back. Devon knows we won't leave and allow the demons to overrun our land, which basically takes us out of the picture for any uprisings."

"So, in answer to your question, Andros, there is no possible way we can help you mount an attack against Devon," Cleo said regretfully. "Not that we wouldn't want to."

Andy sat thinking. He knew what the next step would be.

"What if the stone were returned?" Andy couldn't believe he was saying this.

"Andros, no! You can't be thinking of going into Devon's lair. That's exactly what he wants," Abby said with a pained expression.

"Abby, I don't see that I have much choice in the matter. We need the Border Lands warriors if we are to succeed."

"I believe you are right, lad," Bart said in support, "and I will help you, if I can."

"Thank you, Bart. Will you at least be able to come?" he asked Lyson.

"No. I am the Supreme General of the warriors, and with Tavon's death, I will have to see to the reassignment of his men until a replacement is found and trained." He paused for a moment and looked over at his sister. "However, Cleo could go with you."

"*What?*" Cleo shouted.

"Listen to me," Lyson told her. "What they are doing is important, and should they succeed, think of what this will mean for us. I would send another if I thought there were someone better qualified than you, but there isn't. You have the skills that will serve them best. I say this as your general and not just your brother."

"Are you ordering me as the general?" Cleo asked, looking her brother in the eye.

"Do I have to?"

"I think you just did. I'll go prepare, and we will leave in the morning," she said as she turned and left the room without a backward glance.

"It seems she's not too happy about going," Bart said.

"It's not that she doesn't want to go. It's that she doesn't want to leave."

"All right, that went right by me," Bart said, confused.

"Cleo would love nothing better than to see the stolen stone back on the pillar. But she is a captain of an elite force, and she feels personally responsible for the warriors under her command. If one is hurt or killed, she will feel it was because she was not here to lead them." Lyson looked sadly at the empty space his sister had just occupied. He didn't want to order her to do this, but obviously Loki thought it important someone from the Border Lands help this young dragon.

CHAPTER 16

IT WAS A GRAY, overcast morning when they left Lyson's house. Andy had seen Cleo and Lyson talking just before they departed. Cleo seemed to be in better spirits when they rode out, so he assumed some kind of reconciliation must have taken place. Before they left, Lyson had given them some gifts. "To help in your struggle," he'd said. To Bart, he'd given a set of arrows with silver tips. The arrowheads, he'd explained, were forged from godstone, which was mined in the northern Border Lands. He'd given Abby a small dagger also made from godstone. Godstone was much stronger than steel and was the only metal known to pierce the skin of demons. As a rule, only Border Lands' warriors possessed weapons made from godstone.

To Andy, he'd given a talisman. It was a small metal disk about the size of a coin, engraved on one side with a pair of crossed swords and an eye in the middle. "This has been in my family for a very long time, since Fallon walked among us. He gave it to my ancestor just before the Five left. Its power can only be released once and will only last a short time."

"What does it do?" Andy had asked.

"When the need arises, take out the disk and concentrate on it, and it will show you where your enemies are," Lyson had replied.

"Thank you, Lyson. This is a priceless gift."

"Use it well, Andros. Farewell to you all."

As they left the gates of the Border Lands behind, Bart and Cleo rode ahead to be sure the way was clear. Abby and Andy rode silently for a while, the only sound the clip clop of the horses' hooves and the singing of the morning birds.

"Have you thought of how we are going to get into the White Castle?" Abby asked, breaking the silence.

"No. Any ideas?"

"None that I can think of," she replied.

Andy looked over at the beautiful young scholar and wondered if he wasn't making a mistake, taking her into danger like this. *Scholar*, he thought to himself, as an idea began to form in his mind.

"Abby, the tunnel we escaped from in Dragonsgate, you said it was made by Redlin, that he created all the tunnels."

"That's right. Why?"

"Do you know the one that leads into the Kensington library?" Andy asked.

"Yes." Abby nodded, as though seeing where he was going with this. "Just on the edge of the city are the ancient tombs. There is a memorial tomb with Wizard Redlin's name on it. The entrance is through there."

"Now, do you think it is possible that there may be a tunnel from the library to the castle?" Andy asked hopefully.

"Yes, that is very possible, but we would have to search for it. The curator of the Kensington library might know, but I do not know if he is an ally of Devon. We would have to take our chances."

Just then, they could hear the sound of hooves pounding on the trail ahead. Andy assumed it would be Cleo and Bart, but he tapped into the source and stood ready to make a fire sword if the need arose. As it turned out, it was Cleo and Bart. The Border Lands warrior, her braid flying behind her, skidded to a halt in front of Abby and Andy with Bart close behind.

"Did you see anyone?" Andy asked.

"We didn't see a soul," Cleo responded with a worried frown as she looked back down the road. "But we did see some tracks leading into the woods about three miles up. Bart thought he heard twigs breaking farther in the forest."

"We thought it best to come back and make sure everything was all right before we investigated any further," Bart added.

"We haven't seen or heard anything on the road except you two," Andy said. "We'll continue at a slow pace until you have a chance to check it out." Andy tried to sound calm, but in the back of his mind, he couldn't shake the image of Raptors closing in on them.

"Bart and I will explore a couple of miles, and if we haven't spotted or discovered what it is, we'll turn back. I think it is important that we are not separated by too great a distance."

Andy was grateful that Cleo was with them. She had that sound military mind to plan things out as they went along. He would definitely need her help when it came time to assault the castle.

*   *   *

With an evil smile, Tolbert watched from his place of concealment as Bart and Cleo rode away. So far, his plan was going like clockwork. Ever since tracking them to the Border Lands, he had formulated a plan for when they came out. One of his men would provide a false trail for some of them to follow, in an effort to split them up. He assumed Abby would not be in any scouting party, since she was only a library curator. He silently congratulated himself as he saw the desired effect transpire.

Devon had given him some magical items before he left, one of which provided invisibility. It worked best in an area with some cover, as opposed to sitting on the open road. Tolbert and his men were cloaked amongst the trees just a short distance off the road. He shadowed Andy and Abby in the woods until he judged that enough time had passed so Cleo and Bart wouldn't be able to come to their rescue. Spurring their horses onto the road, they quickly encircled Andy and Abby.

*   *   *

Andy heard the horses too late. Before he had a chance to react, they were surrounded. Abby gasped.

"Tolbert!" she cried, shaking. Andy looked at the man who had caused Abby so much pain. In his mind, he flashed on Tolbert's leer and evil smile as he'd pushed the burning brand onto Abby's back. A white-hot fire seared his brain as he plunged himself into the source. He was going to make this man pay.

All of a sudden, his thoughts were scattered.

"What the…?" Andy said in puzzlement. Something was pulling at his inner being. He looked around wildly for the possible cause.

"Andros, what is it?" Abby asked in alarm.

Andy couldn't speak. Something was forcing him to change. He couldn't change here. With the trees in close proximity to the trail, he would smash everyone against the trunks as he expanded into his dragon shape. He tried with all his will to hold himself together.

"Seems like your little friend is having some kind of crisis, Abby," Tolbert said, laughing.

Andy looked around the ring quickly and spotted a hole. With what little concentration he could summon, he sent his need to the mind of his horse. The horse's ears perked up, as if listening. Then, wheeling around, he charged the man in front of the trail. As he got close, Andy's horse reared, and a foreleg struck the man in the face, killing him instantly. He urged his horse onward to give himself room. In his mind, he heard Abby call him.

Andros, what's wrong? Where are you going? Please don't leave me! she cried. Andy felt wretched. He couldn't respond. In the vaults of his mind, he heard another voice, one that was commanding him.

Andros, I have need of you, the voice said. He tried holding back, refusing the call, but when he did, he felt excruciating pain. The voice came again. *Andros, you will come to me.* Whoever it was knew his name.

When he judged enough distance had passed, he got off his horse. He slapped the animal on the rump to make him run. He then took on his dragon form. Trees collapsed as his body grew.

With the change complete, he launched himself into the air, black wings beating out a steady rhythm to give him altitude as he headed west. He looked back and saw Tolbert grabbing Abby by the wrist. He could do nothing. Anger consumed him as he felt himself compelled toward the source of the summons. He vented his anger on several hundred acres of forest, setting them ablaze as he flew by, releasing his dragon roar.

Secrecy is gone now, he thought. Tolbert had seen him fly off, and anyone looking up as he passed would spot him as well.

* * *

Tolbert was shocked that Andros got away so easily, but it didn't matter. Abby was the one he needed.

"Some protector," he sneered. "The coward runs off at the first sign of trouble."

"You're the coward!" Abby snapped back. Her courage was returning, and her blood boiled at the sight of this pompous ass.

Just then, they heard a lot of trees crashing to the ground. Looking up, Tolbert saw a black dragon soaring through the sky. His mouth dropped open at the sight. "This is something Devon will definitely want to know about." He quickly grabbed Abby by the wrist and hauled her onto his saddle. Taking a black orb from his saddlebag, he pressed Abby's hand against it. She took the opportunity to slap his face with her free hand.

"Why, you…!" he said rubbing his jaw. "Punishment is only postponed. Once Devon is done with you, you're mine. Think on that. I know I will," he added with evil relish. Tolbert then took the orb and threw it down the trail, where it burst open, and a gray, vaporous cloud poured forth. It coalesced into an exact duplicate of Abby and Tolbert astride a horse. "Something for your other two friends to follow. We, however, will be heading for the White Castle."

Abby's face fell at the pronouncement, and she prayed to the god Trystan to keep her safe. She looked up at the retreating black dragon as a single tear slid down her face.

* * *

Andy flew on through most of the night. Passing over Lake Pleasant, he saw several ships heading west. He wondered if one of them was

Bowen. Black River was coming up. He came in low and brushed the garrison fort, smashing a wall with his tail as he flew by, spraying rock and mortar on the startled soldiers below. Andy figured, since Devon was going to know he was abroad, he might as well give him something to worry about. He passed a small village nestled in a ring of hills as he started to descend on the manor that was the source of the compulsion. He landed in the field between the mill and the manor.

Come out! he growled. He looked to the back of the mansion as a postern door opened and a dark haired faerie came out carrying a smaller faerie in her arms. She was followed by three others, a man and two women. The two women seemed hesitant at first, but the man strode right up as if he had been consorting with dragons all his life and came to stand next to the dark-haired faerie.

Who are you, and how are you able to do this? Andy spat with venom. He knew he was being irrational, but he didn't appreciate being called like a dog.

"My name is Donella, and I am Braylynn's Dragon Summoner," she said aloud. "My friends cannot hear your thoughts. Can you make it so they will hear our conversation?" Andy did so, connecting each mind to his and Donella's, learning each of their names in the process.

I don't know what a Dragon Summoner is, but, obviously, you have some power over me. He brought his horned head close to her face. *You should know that your summons probably cost my friends their lives, or at the very least imprisonment in Devon's tower.*

"The god Rafael told us you would be the only one able to save the life of our friend," Ala explained.

Andy lowered his head down near Tera's body, examining the gash the knife had made.

I know nothing of healing, Andy said.

"We don't need you to heal," Acacia added. "We need you to fly Donella and Tera to Laurel Hollow. Braylynn is the only one that can heal her now. We spent most of the day waiting for you, so you have just over two days to get her there or she will die."

Andy searched Donella's mind. There was something familiar about her, but whenever he tried to look closely, his thoughts were brushed away, as if a gentle hand were passing in front of his eyes, preventing him from seeing what he wanted to see. His demeanor changed somewhat after seeing Tera. He could understand why Donella had summoned him; she had no way of knowing that her summons had come at the worst possible moment. It didn't make his predicament any easier, but it cooled his anger toward her.

He looked at the windows in the mansion. Startled servants hid behind the curtains, sneaking glances at the huge beast that had landed in their lawn. *What place is this?* Andy asked.

"Hadley," Diminitus answered. "And this is Hadley Manor, although its chief occupant, Baron Ogden, is currently not at home. So the servants say."

"We should leave as soon as possible," Donella said urgently.

I can't take all of you, Andy told them.

"That's all right," Diminitus said. "Ala, Acacia, and I will head back to the village. Besides, I have no desire to go dragon riding."

Very well, but you will have to tell me the way. I've never been to Laurel Hollow.

"I will be able to guide you," Donella said.

"One more thing, Donella," Ala said. "When you get there, Braylynn should be able to keep your body in check as far as the skull spider venom goes. However, if you leave before she has a chance to do that, have Andros fly you back to Acacia's village, and I will give you more Dragonroot there."

Now hold on, Andy said, outraged. *I'm not some ferry service to be transporting passengers all throughout Vasara. Besides, I have friends that need my help.*

"Don't worry, Andros," Donella said sympathetically. "Once Tera is back in Laurel Hollow, I will help you find your friends. I sense your pain and the loss of someone you love. You are helping me in my need, and I will help you in yours."

Andy looked into the green eyes of this faerie. She had power, too. He could feel it. *What are you?* he asked, puzzled.

"As I said before, I am the Dragon Summoner, and if I understand things correctly, you and I are destined to overthrow Devon." She could feel his confusion. "I know you have many questions, but time is pressing. We can talk more once we reach Laurel Hollow."

Very well, Andy relented. *But on the way, if we happen to spy a crazy old wizard named Loki, I think we will pick him up and bring him with us. He has a lot of explaining to do.*

Donella handed Tera to Diminitus while she flew up to sit at the base of the dragon's neck. Diminitus then handed her up to Donella, and she held her tight against her lap.

"Thank you all for your help. I will see you again as soon as possible. Please keep an eye out for Leah and Dain. Let them know where we have gone," Donella said.

"We will," Ala replied.

Andy lifted off and caught a warm-air current to help lift him higher. He circled Hadley once before winging his way southeast. He flew straight through the first day and most of the second before Donella pointed out a huge glade in the middle of a forest.

He started to circle, and, as he got closer, he saw a figure standing on the edge of a path. It was tall and had horns like a goat.

Someone you know? Andy asked.

"Why yes, I believe it's Pan," she said, surprised, the wind blowing her long black hair like a comet tail behind her. Andy flew to the far end of the glade, banked, and came in to land in the middle of the field. Pan trotted over and saw Tera draped over Donella's lap.

"Donella, what happened?" Pan asked in his big, booming voice.

"Tera's been stabbed through the heart by Zana," Donella replied, handing her to him.

"Monstrous!" he shouted. "Poor little Tera." He was near tears. "Is she...?" He wasn't able to finish.

"Not yet. We need to get her to Braylynn as soon as possible."

"I will take her there right now. Please excuse my poor manners, Master Dragon. I will come back and greet you properly after I've seen to my dear friend."

I understand, Andy replied.

Donella flew off Andy's back and alighted on the ground. Andy then turned back to his human shape. This took Donella by surprise.

"My god! You can change shape?" she said, aghast.

"Yes. You mean you didn't know that?"

"No, I didn't. I'm afraid I don't know very much about dragons."

Andy thought this very strange. She knew enough to pull him away from his friends; one would assume she had an intimate knowledge of dragons. Andy started to feel a little faint. Dragons need to eat at least once a day, and he had flown two days straight without eating anything.

"Is there somewhere we can get some food?" he asked.

"Sure, follow me." Andy fell in step behind Donella. Now that he had brought them there safely, all his thoughts turned to Abby. What pain and anguish might she be enduring? He also thought of Cleo and Bart. Had they been captured, as well?

They walked into Donella's cottage. Unfortunately, all she had were fruits and nuts. *This will have to do for now*, he thought. He sat in the chair by the fireplace and turned his thoughts inward to walk the forest path and stand by the source. Andy had found this extremely relaxing, when stress and pressure from the outside started to be a little too much.

He was not at the source long when he sensed a presence. He looked back down the path and saw a tall, beautiful faerie with deep-blue wings and flowers in her hair walking toward him. He knew, without being told, that this was Braylynn, the faerie goddess.

"Hello, Andros," she said by way of greeting.

"Hello, Braylynn," Andy responded, letting her know he had no doubts as to her identity.

"Very astute, my young dragon," she said with a smile.

"Not really. I know the only ones able to come here are me, Loki, and you."

"Well said, lad! Well said," a voice replied.

Andy looked past the faerie goddess down the path to see Loki striding toward them with a huge smile on his face. Andy ran to embrace him. After a quick hug, Andy held him at arm's length and looked him long in the eyes.

"You have some explaining to do, old man," he said.

"I guess I do, but I am not entirely to blame here," Loki said, casting a glance in Braylynn's direction.

"Why didn't you tell me about the Summoner?" Andy said

"Because I didn't think there was one. She hasn't picked one for over fifteen hundred years," Loki said, tilting his head at Braylynn. "So you have to forgive me if it wasn't exactly on my mind at the time."

"Why wasn't it in the prophecy?"

"The prophecy was created by my brothers," Braylynn answered. "Because of that, I am able to work outside of it but always in harmony with it."

"Well, I found out about it at the worst possible moment," Andy said as he turned back to look at the source, melancholy stealing over him as he thought of Abby.

Loki came over and stood next to Andy. "I have a message from Devon."

Andy looked at him in surprise.

"He can contact you?"

"Only if I want to listen. He told me he would return Abby to Dragonsgate alive and unharmed if you just go back to your own world."

"Or else?"

"You don't want to know 'or else'," he said sadly.

"Does he have Bart and Cleo, as well?" Andy asked.

"No, I am actually traveling with them now. We are going by ship to Black River."

"At least they are safe."

Andy looked over at Braylynn. She was the first deity he had ever met. Her eyes stared into his. It was as if she knew every pain he carried and made it her own while, at the same time, bathing him in healing and love. Andy felt like he was wrapped in a warm blanket sitting by the fire at home. He felt safe, and he visibly relaxed.

She touched a hand to his cheek. "Do not fear, my dragon. Though you are the youngest of your brothers, you shall be chief among them. You and your friends have the power to save her.

Whether you succeed or not, I cannot see, but take heart that you are not helpless."

Andy took comfort in her words. Then he remembered why he was in Laurel Hollow. "Oh, forgive me. I forgot to ask. How is the little faerie?"

"You got Tera here just in time, thank you. She has a very resilient spirit. She should be up and around in a day or so. I am forever grateful to you."

"It was definitely a team effort," Andy said. Team effort… An idea was beginning to form in Andy's mind on how to free Abby. "Loki, when you get to Black River, can you wait for us in a village not too far from there? I think I flew over it when Donella summoned me, but I couldn't tell you how to get there on foot. One of Donella's companions, Acacia, lives there. We were supposed to meet her and two others, Ala and Diminitus, should Donella require more Dragonroot."

"Diminitus? What is that old crab doing out and about? He hasn't come out of the Wilds since I can't remember when."

"He was needed to help Donella come into her powers as the Dragon Summoner. They can fill you in on the how and why," Braylynn added. "Also, Andros, you will need to take her back to receive the Dragonroot she requires. I will explain it to her."

"I know the village you're talking about, Andros, and its significance," Loki said.

"Significance?" Andy asked, puzzled.

"I'll explain when I see you."

"How long before you reach Black River?" Andy asked.

"I'll have to ask Bowen, but I wouldn't think more than a day or so."

"You're on Bowen's ship? That's perfect, because I am going to need his help. Can you tell him to gather as many of his captain friends and their ships as he can and head down the Tear River to the ocean? I'll come to him and explain my plan."

"I will tell him," Loki assured him with a smile.

"What are you grinning at?" Andy asked with a raised eyebrow.

"Nothing at all, General. Nothing at all," he said with a straight face.

"That is something else we need to talk about, your promoting me to the head of the free armies of Vasara. So what are our next steps?"

"You will need to give Devon an answer," Loki said.

"How long will he wait for a reply?"

"Probably no more than a couple of days," Loki replied.

Andy thought for a moment. "Very well, wait that long and tell him I will do as he says. He is not going to release Abby in any case, is he?"

"He won't," Braylynn said. "And he will not hesitate to kill her if he thinks that will bring you to him seeking revenge." She put a hand on his shoulder. "May I make a suggestion? I know you are eager to go and free her, but if you stay here for a couple of days, I can give you and Donella some instruction on how to use your powers together. Once Devon has your agreement, he will give you time to reach him."

"All right, we'll do that." Andy turned to Loki. "We will catch up with you in about four days' time."

"I'll be waiting. I'm going back now to relay everything to Cleo, Bart, and Bowen. Take care, Andros, and be careful."

"Just out of curiosity, how did you know I would be here?" Andy asked before he left.

"Braylynn told me," Loki replied, and with that, he went down the path and disappeared from sight.

"Thank you," he said to the goddess.

"I thought you could use a friend about now." She smiled warmly.

"I guess I better head back, as well." He paused before turning to leave. "There is something I would like to ask you, and my gut tells me you can probably answer it."

"Where is your sister?" she said

"Yes."

"I do know where she is, and you needn't worry about her. She is safe," she said assuredly. "I've watched over her since she first came here."

"Can I see her?" Andy asked anxiously. "I've been terribly worried about her."

"I know you have, and you don't need to beat yourself up any longer about bringing her here. Other forces were at work that helped bring that about. As for seeing her, it is better for the safety of you both that you not see her for now. You must trust me in this," she said, eyeing him critically.

Andy looked into her deep blue eyes and knew he couldn't do anything but trust her. "I will," he replied. "I feel much better knowing a goddess is watching over her. I wouldn't want her exposed to any of this danger."

Braylynn said nothing but inclined her head in farewell as she faded from sight. Andy walked back down the path and opened his eyes.

"You were gone for a while there," Donella said when he got up out of the chair.

"Yes, and now I'm starving. I'll be back shortly," he said as he left the cottage to go hunt.

CHAPTER 17

WHEN ANDY RETURNED from hunting, he faced a whirlwind of introductions as the faerie queen gave him a warm welcome in the Hall. Pan was there, as well, but he did not stay long. He was extremely upset that Tera had been nearly killed. He said that he was going to make sure someone paid for that and promptly left. What he planned to do, he did not say. Andy brought everyone up to speed on what had been happening and shared his plan for going up against Devon. Valencia told him that any plan involving faeries would have to include neutralizing the archers. Andy assured her, once they had freed Abby, they would go over everything in detail.

When Andy arrived back at Donella's cottage, they talked long into the night. He found it very easy to talk to her. She told him all about herself, including her memory loss and their travels from the Parma Wilds to Hadley. She told him about Leah and Dain and what had happened when Zana stabbed Tera. Andy then proceeded to tell her everything that had happened to him since entering Vasara. She narrowed her eyes slightly when he told her, in his world, they called him Andy, and she opened her mouth as if to say something, but then the moment passed.

The next morning found them walking to the glade, Andy in his black shirt and pants and Donella in her Dragon Summoner clothes.

When they got there, Braylynn was waiting for them. She had an inexplicable expression of pride on her face.

"Vasara has waited fifteen hundred years for you two and you two specifically," she said. She didn't give them any opportunity to reflect on that pronouncement. "Now, since time is of the essence, we will get right down to it. First, though, I want to say one thing about dragon etiquette." She looked hard at Donella. "What you did when you compelled Andros to come to you was necessary because of the circumstance, but you must never do that again, except in a life-or-death situation. By compelling him, you supplant your will over his. In most cases, you have but to send your need to the dragons and they will come willingly."

Donella looked into Andy's hazel eyes. "I am sorry. I promise I will never do such a thing again."

"It's all right," Andy replied. "I know who and what you are now. And, as Braylynn says, you just have to call, and I will wing my way to wherever you are."

"All right, let's get started," Braylynn said. "The whole purpose for the Summoner and dragon link is battle advantage. Andros, go fly out for ten minutes and return."

"You got it," he replied as he took off running to the middle of the glade. Once there, the black dragon emerged, and he took flight over the treetops, disappearing from sight.

"All right, dear," Braylynn said. "Use the dragon crown and reach out to his mind. See with his eyes."

Donella did this. The green eye on top of the crown started to glow. She kept her own eyes open, but the glade before her faded, and a forest with a river running through it came into view. She could see a goat grazing on a hillside. All of a sudden, the goat started getting closer and closer until it filled her entire vision.

"*Ugh!*" Donella said with revulsion. "He just ate a goat!"

Braylynn smiled. "What is he doing now?"

"The landscape is dropping away. He must be climbing higher. Oh my! He has to be thousands of feet up. Everything is so small, but I can see it with such clarity. I even see our glade and us." Donella watched as the countryside rolled by below her. It was an amazing sensation. She knew what it felt like to fly, of course, and had only just ridden the dragon's back, but faeries could never reach such heights on their own.

Andy then dropped like a stone, and the ground came rushing up. At the last possible moment, he banked and veered away. Donella's stomach gave a lurch as the sight played out before her eyes. Andy did a few more acrobatics before landing in the glade once more. Donella let go of her inner sight, and her vision returned to normal.

"Andros, you might as well stay in your dragon shape," Braylynn said.

Sure thing, he said, giving his tail a whip-like crack on the ground.

"Donella, I want you to get on his back." Donella flew up and sat at the base of his neck. "Now slowly fly around the glade. We will talk mind to mind once you start." Andy lifted off.

Donella, connect with the elemental forces around you, specifically the earth and sky. I want you to think of lightning streaking from the sky to the earth. Once you have that image, command the elements to go where you want them. I will make a target for you.

Braylynn made a hand gesture as if commanding someone to stand up. Out of the earth rose a hideous figure. It looked like an upright lizard that stood more than eight feet tall with clawed hands and feet. Its hide was scaly, and its teeth were razor sharp. It made a chilling scream as it advanced on its muscular legs. In its hands, it carried an iron spear.

My god! Andy exclaimed. *What is that thing?*

"I don't know, but we better do something!"

The creature stalked them around the glade, waiting for the right moment to let loose its spear.

Donella could feel the electric current going from sky to earth. She grabbed it and held her palms open, facing the creature. She then focused it on the monstrosity, and two lightning bolts shot out of her palms, hitting the being square in the chest. It dissolved and sank back into the earth.

"Amazing!" Donella exclaimed.

Nice shot, Andy complimented.

Very good! Braylynn praised them. *Now, let's see how you do against two.*

Again, the lizard creature rose up out of the earth, this time followed by a second. The other monster was identical to the first with one exception: this one had wings.

Uh-oh, I think we better split up, Andy said. *I'll fly around the rim of the glade, and then you jump off. If fly-boy takes off after you, I'll get the one on the ground and vice versa.*

"Got it!" she replied, getting excited. She could see why Leah liked this so much; putting all your skills to the test was exhilarating.

As Donella jumped off and flew in the opposite direction, the flying lizard kept going after Andy. She was tempted to use her spear on the other one, but she was there to hone her skills as the Dragon Summoner. As she got closer, the beast threw its spear straight at her. Donella made a shield of air and pushed it against the oncoming spear. The spear deflected and fell harmless to the ground. In that same spirit, she started creating air currents, whipping them around, making a small and localized tornado that settled on the creature and pulled him skyward. Donella then allowed the tornado to dissipate, causing the creature to crash to the ground and dissolve once more.

Andy was having quite the time with the flying lizard. The much smaller creature was able to maneuver more quickly than Andy could. Andy found his tail extremely useful in this kind of situation. Barbed at the end, it made an effective sword against whatever was behind him. Several times, he was able to knock away the lizard's spear.

It's time to finish him, he thought. Giving himself some quick, powerful thrusts on his wings, he pulled farther ahead of the creature, and then, throwing his hind legs in front of him as if he were sliding into second base feet first, he looked between his legs and, with his head upside down, shot a burst of flame. The lizard flew right into it and disappeared into a vaporous cloud that was blown away on the wind.

Andy and Donella flew over to where Braylynn waited. He switched back to human form.

"That was marvelously done!" Braylynn exclaimed. "You two are really getting the hang of this."

"Yeah, we make a pretty good team," Andy said, smiling. Donella smiled back.

"What you need to learn now is how to combine powers. You two are the first Dragon Summoner and dragon to be able to do this."

"Why is that?" Donella asked. Braylynn seemed not to hear the question, and Donella sensed she shouldn't ask again.

"Andros, you will be channeling my brothers' power into Donella, amplifying her control of the elements. You need to use your imagination to think of ways to augment each other in order to make your powers increase. Do you think you can do that?"

"I'll give it a try," he said.

"Donella, hold Andros's hand," Braylynn explained. "It might help the first time if you are actually touching." Donella did this. "Now create a little wind." Gathering the air around them, Donella started a breeze moving through the forest, gently blowing the leaves. "Now I want you to open yourself to Andros. You will feel his presence. Just let the energy coming from him flow through you." She did this, feeling his awareness. "Now Andros, let the power flow."

Andy reached into the source, filling himself up, and then he released it into Donella. She was not prepared for what happened next.

"My god!" Donella exclaimed when the power was fed into her. She could hardly contain it as she used it to augment her breeze, which suddenly became a gale, knocking down several trees at the forest's edge. When it was spent, she slumped to her knees panting. "I'm sorry," she said between breaths. "I wasn't expecting that."

"No, I'm sorry," Andy said, concerned. "I sent too much. I'll have to work on that."

"Which is precisely why you are here—to practice," Braylynn said. "Now, you don't need to be touching to link. I just wanted to make sure the first time was the easiest. When you are out there flying, you might find it a little more difficult. I'm going to leave you now so you can practice the rest of the day by yourselves." And with that, she started to leave the glade.

"Are we going to be practicing on any more targets?" Andy called after her.

"Oh yes, I almost forgot." Without turning her head, she clapped twice and twenty lizard creatures sprang out of the earth, some with wings and some without.

"Big mouth," Donella said, flying to the other end of the glade. Andy changed and flew in the same direction.

Braylynn smiled to herself as she kept walking. She wondered if she should tell them that the creatures couldn't actually do them any harm. *No*, she thought. *They'll have much more fun this way*, and she kept right on walking.

* * *

It was a tired faerie and dragon who collapsed in Donella's cottage at the end of the day. It took a while, but they had defeated all twenty creatures. In the process, they had learned how to raise shields, attack singly or combined. Now they felt totally drained. The goddess only knew what tomorrow would bring. And she did know.

The next morning, Braylynn was waiting for them in the glade, as she had been the day before. She was dressed in a white robe with a blue sash. Her wings were folded in and covered. In her hand, she held a talon staff with a pearl white sphere mounted on the top. Instead of the usual crown of flowers in her hair, she wore a golden circlet with a small green stone in the center.

"So, how many monsters are we fighting today?" Andy asked.

"None," Braylynn replied.

"Thank goodness," Donella exclaimed with a sigh of relief.

"Just me," Braylynn said with a slight smile. She took off her robe, and underneath, she was dressed for battle. She had on a brown leather vest that left her arms bare, and a soft leather skirt that came to her mid-thigh. She had sandals on her feet with leather straps that crisscrossed up her calf. On her forearms were gold bracers with intricate designs etched into them.

"What the...?" Andy never finished what he was going to say. Braylynn lowered her staff, and a burst of energy shot out from the pearl sphere, hitting Andy square in the chest. The blast propelled him up and backwards twenty yards. Braylynn flew to the middle of the glade and hovered.

"*Why did you do that?*" Donella shouted.

"Because you are going up against Devon and the demon power within him. I will not let you out of this glade until I am sure you are ready. Defend yourself!" Braylynn shot another blast at Donella. Seeing the staff leveled in her direction, she jumped at the last instant, avoiding the strike, then she tried to fly to the safety of the trees, only to meet with an invisible wall. She flew over to where Andy was. "She's blocked us in."

"That hurt! She's not playing around," he exclaimed, getting to his feet.

"It's a test. Until we prove ourselves, she won't let us leave."

Andy didn't like this. He needed to get to Abby before something terrible happened to her.

"I'm going to change. When I do, climb up and hold on!" He transformed into his dragon self. When Donella flew onto his back, he beat his wings for all he was worth in order to get high fast. His plan was to fly above Braylynn's barrier. But when he reached a thousand feet up, he crashed into something solid.

There is a barrier up here, as well, he said incredulously. *She seems determined for us to fight her. So be it.* He went into a steep dive, heading straight for Braylynn. *Can you make us a shield?*

"Yes," Donella replied. She made a barrier not unlike Braylynn's but smaller and focused straight ahead. No sooner had she gotten it up when two lightning bolts slammed into it.

"Now you're thinking!" Braylynn shouted as she started to maneuver out of Andy's path. Andy let loose with a stream of fire, narrowly missing her. He doubted very much he could harm the goddess, but he knew she would want them to hold nothing back in trying to defeat her.

It was attack and counterattack for the longest time, neither one gaining the advantage. Donella sent multiple lightning strikes at Braylynn only to have them deflected by her staff. Andy took several direct hits, and, although his dragon skin seemed to protect him, they still hurt like hell.

Andy made another strafing run at the goddess, but instead of fire this time, he shot ice. It started to coat Braylynn, making her wings very heavy. But then her sphere burned white hot and melted everything around it. He veered away.

As the dragon made his turn, Braylynn sent a sonic blast of air at Donella's shield, knocking her off Andy's back. With the shield gone, she caused a large net to appear and cast it over Andy, making his flight spiral out of control. Andy impacted with the ground, dazed but unhurt. Knowing he only had seconds, he changed back to human and started to run. He created his own shield as Braylynn started to fire energy blasts at him.

Donella, I need you to create a ground fog.

Great idea! She worked quickly and soon had a blanket of fog high and thick filling the glade. Andy changed. With his dragon sight, he could see through any fog. He knew, to end this game, he needed to get Braylynn's staff. All the power she was using seemed to be coming from that. Donella hid in the fog, as well, watching through Andy's eyes.

The goddess was now sending blasts of air at the fog, trying to scatter it. The fog would blow apart for a few seconds but then fill back in. Andy waited, hardly daring to breathe for fear of stirring the fog and giving away his position.

Braylynn flew low, and when she was right above him, he sprang silently, his long neck darting out as he grabbed the staff in his powerful jaws. Once Donella saw he had the staff, she flew from concealment, as well. Andy tossed her the staff. Once she had it, she could feel the energy in the pearl sphere and knew she could direct its power. She leveled it at Braylynn and shot a blast at her chest. Braylynn erected a barrier around herself. She was smiling as Donella continued to pound at her from one side while Andy sent jets of flame from the other side.

I yield, she sent, so both would hear her. Andy and Donella stopped their attack. As they all settled back to the earth, Donella dissipated her fog. Andy turned human once more.

"That was well done," she complimented them. "It wasn't so much the powers you used as the way you thought through your situations. That is what it will take to beat Devon."

"There were a couple of times there when I thought you might accidentally kill us," Andy said, rubbing his shoulder.

"I am sorry to test you so, but you need to know what you are going up against." She looked long at both of them. "I'm very proud of you both. Be careful, and stay safe."

"Here is your staff back," Donella said, holding it out to her.

"It is for you, dear," she replied. "The newest weapon in the Dragon Summoner's arsenal. Just as Andros draws on my brothers' power, the pearl sphere allows you to draw on mine. Hand it to me for a moment." She did this. "Now hold my hand and follow my thought." Donella was amazed as the staff seemed to shrink in on itself and, in the end, transformed into a comb made out of pearl. Braylynn made her turn around, and she put it into her hair.

"For ease when traveling or in combat, when you do not require it," she told her. "Use it well."

She gave them both a hug and bade them farewell, but instead of just disappearing, she leaped into the air and flew over the treetops and out of sight.

Donella took the comb out and turned it back into the staff. She put her hand on the sphere. She remembered what Layla had said, that it was all about connections. She allowed her mind to join with it, become part of it. It was like pure energy filled her entire body. She took her hand off the pearl sphere.

"Whoa! That was amazing," she exclaimed.

"Be careful," Andy said. "If it is anything like the source and you draw too much for too long, you're not going to want to let go."

"I think I understand it now," she said. "Come on, let's go back and make our preparations to leave. Also, I want to see Tera before I go." They left the glade and made their way to the Hall.

* * *

Paolo was tending the flowerbeds near the unicorn statue. He took great pride in his flowers and went to great pains to make sure no weeds tried to choke the life out of them. Suddenly, he felt eyes upon him. He turned his head slowly and looked toward where he thought the feeling was coming from. He stared with an open mouth as he saw, on the western hill, a white unicorn. It was standing tall and straight, looking right back at him. It seemed like they held each other's gaze for an eternity. The unicorn then reared and whinnied and, with a graceful leap, took to the trail that disappeared over the hill and headed toward the White Castle.

Paolo stood watching for several seconds after the unicorn left. Then he was met with another surprise. Shooting over the hill the unicorn had just left and circling the village was a black dragon. Something seemed to detach from it and glided straight for him. The dragon flew back over the hills and disappeared.

As the other figure got closer, he could tell it was a faerie, and, upon closer examination, he saw it was Donella and started waving his hands furiously. She alighted right next to him as she brought her wings to a stop.

"Hello, Paolo," Donella said, giving him a hug.

"Donella!" Paolo replied, holding her at arm's length and taking in her appearance. "You seem very different now. You truly are the Dragon Summoner. Positive proof of that just flew over the hills," he said, tilting his head in a westerly direction. "Acacia told me about Andros. It is quite another matter to see him in the flesh."

"The others are here then?"

"Yes, they are up at the house. Loki the wizard is also here, along with two others I have never met. From what I gather, they were traveling companions of Andros's. Bart the Archer from Dragonsgate and Cleo, a warrior from the Border Lands."

"Andros has told me of them. Come, let's go to your house where I can explain to everyone what has transpired. Has there been any word of Leah and Dain?"

"Acacia told me about that, as well," he replied sympathetically. "There has been no word from them."

* * *

Half the day had passed by the time Andy landed in Paolo's village. He had caught up with Bowen and explained his plan to him. Now it was time to fill in the others. He was staring at a statue of a unicorn when he noticed out of the corner of his eye a figure walking toward him. It was Cleo.

"Cleo!" he shouted as he started to run to her. But something was wrong. Her shoulders were slumped, and her head was down. When he reached her, she took out her swords and laid them at his feet, kneeling with her neck exposed.

"I have failed you, Andros," she said with all the bitterness of the tomb. "Abby has been captured and is suffering torture and possibly even death because of my incompetence."

"Cleo, that's nonsense. Tolbert used magic to deceive you, and had Donella not summoned me, I would have been able to handle things. It is no one's fault."

"I have also failed my brother and my people," she continued as if she hadn't heard him. "My life is yours to take, if you wish it, my Lord Dragon."

"Lord Dragon?"

"Loki has explained to me your role in the coming war. You will be chief leader and as such have charge over my very life."

He could not believe that he had to deal with this. Loki would definitely need a talking to. "Cleo, stand up, and put your swords away. And I am no lord, so please continue calling me Andros." He could see the guilt and self-loathing in Cleo's eyes as she rose. He needed to snap her out of it and show her how much he needed her. Grabbing both her shoulders, he looked straight into her blue eyes.

"Cleo, if you want to look at me as this leader, fine," he began, firmly but kindly. "Then there is a task for which I want only you. But I must know, can I trust you?"

Hope was rekindled in her eyes. "Name it, Andros, and I will do it."

"It is going to be your job to find the ruby stone that goes on the Pillar of Fallon that Devon stole and take it back. It will be you who will free your people so they can fight in the battle that is coming."

Andy was appealing to her sense of loyalty and national pride. He could see it was working, as the fierceness and determination blazed back to life in her eyes.

"It shall be done or I will die trying, and though you don't want to hear it, you are my Lord Dragon." She put her swords back in their sheaths, and they walked to Paolo's house.

The house was crowded with people. The only person Andy had not met before was Paolo. Andy had heard about some of Paolo's lineage from Donella; Loki had filled in the missing gaps. He liked Paolo right from the start. He was a king who would elicit not just loyalty from his people but love, as well. He knew how to talk to people in a way that made them feel like they were a part of the government he would lead and that their opinions mattered. Andy thought about Maccus and how happy he would be that someone like Paolo would soon sit in the White Castle.

"What are the next steps?" Andy asked Loki.

"You must tell Devon when you will surrender yourself to him. On that day, you are to walk alone across Palatine Bridge. He will make sure it is clear of traffic when you cross. If you arrive as a dragon or show signs of changing into one at any time, he will give the signal to kill Abby instantly."

Andy thought for a moment on how to present his plan. "All right, this is what we are going to do," he said. "Tell Devon I will be at the bridge four days from now. Before that time, you all need to find your way into the city." Andy then told them about the tunnel that lead from the tomb of Redlin to the Kensington library. He also told them how Redlin built tunnels in all of the libraries.

"That sneaky devil," Loki exclaimed. "He never told us."

"From what Abby says, only the curators know of them, and they guard that knowledge jealously. She thinks there could be a tunnel from the library to the castle, but the Kensington curator would be the only one who would know of that one."

"If there is one, I will get him to tell us," Loki said with determination.

"What do we do once we are inside?" Paolo said.

"Paolo, what do you mean?" Ala asked. "You're not thinking of going?"

"I've seen the white unicorn, Ala," he said solemnly. "It is time I got into this fight."

"I am coming with you, husband," Acacia said, slipping her arm through his and giving him a look that dared him to say no.

He surprised her when he said, "I wouldn't have it any other way, love. I've sent a messenger to find Brayton."

"Brayton?" Diminitus asked, scratching his wild gray hair.

"He is our eldest son, and should anything happen to me, he will need to be here."

"All right, we need to time this correctly," Andy began. "Four days from now, at noon, Bowen is going to lead a sea assault against the castle. I am going to try to be with Devon before he starts. In either case, once Bowen starts, most of the guards should run to the battlements. That will be when Cleo will retrieve the stone." Andy had already told them about the stone that went on top of the Pillar of Fallon and how Devon had stolen it.

"We are going to have to move fast," Diminitus said. "Any ideas as to where we start looking?"

"There is a treasure room off the royal apartments," Loki said. "It is most likely that Devon put it there."

"Also, keep an eye out for Leah and Dain," Donella said.

"That won't be necessary," a voice said from the doorway. All heads turned toward the sound.

"Leah!" Donella cried as she jumped up from her chair and ran to embrace her faerie sister. Andy watched the exchange closely. Leah looked haggard but whole. Her blonde hair was tangled, and she had several cuts on her arm. Dain was right behind her, looking just as ragged. Donella had told him of how Leah had found her and the bond they shared. "Leah, what happened?"

"I chased Zana. I knew I had to catch her before she reached the Palatine Bridge, or I would be exposed to the archers who guard both ends. I managed to catch up to her. We battled for quite a while. She is extremely skilled. I could never gain the advantage. Then Dain showed up on horseback."

Dain picked up the narrative. "After I left the mansion, I knocked a garrison soldier off his horse and followed after Leah. When I got there, Leah had already taken several wounds. I drew my sword and joined in. I've fought flying demons before, and, using both my horse and sword, we pressed Zana hard."

"Then she saw something that terrified her beyond reason," Leah continued. "A black dragon. We assumed it was the dragon that was with Loki. It was a sight to see. Fear entered Zana's eyes, and she fought with reckless abandon to flee. In the end, she succeeded, and we could no longer follow her."

"I think you should meet the dragon that saved Tera's life," Donella said, looking toward Andy.

Leah followed Donella's gaze, but then her words registered. "Tera is alive!"

"Yes, sister, and there is the dragon that flew us to Laurel Hollow, so Braylynn could heal her. His name is Andros."

Andy sensed a weight had lifted from Leah at the news of Tera. She walked over and greeted him, offering her thanks for saving Tera. Dain did likewise then Donella filled Leah and Dain in on everything that had happened since Tera had been stabbed.

"So you are truly the Dragon Summoner now," Leah said, smiling with admiration.

"Yes, and there is something I want to do. Come, sit." As Leah sat down, Donella held the staff while running her hand over Leah's wounds. The sphere began to glow as she channeled the healing energy of the goddess. Leah's cuts and bruises slowly began to fade away, giving her renewed energy and leaving her feeling as refreshed as a flower after a rainstorm greeting the warm rays of the sun.

"By the goddess," Leah exclaimed, "I've never felt the like."

Donella did the same for Dain, and he looked as if a few years had fallen away.

"All right," Loki said getting down to business. "We need some ideas on how to get into the city."

"I know one," Bart said, jumping in and turning toward Paolo. "Was that a forge I saw on the edge of the village?"

"Yes, it is," Paolo answered. "I work with the iron to make weapons and anything else we need."

"Perfect!" Bart exclaimed. "We can use one of the wagons, load it up with tools, and pose as weapon-makers at the general market."

"Excellent idea, Bart," Loki said. "But I don't think we should all go in together. We can disguise ourselves as various merchants heading for the market and enter the flow of traffic at different points."

"Once in the city, make your way to Redlin's tomb and investigate the tunnel," Andy said. "If there is no tunnel from the library to the castle, you will need to think of a way in before I cross the bridge. Donella must be inside before me. Together we worked out a plan for handling Devon. Of course, that could change once we are in the heat of things. I think some should stay in the market area to create some diversions, should we need them."

"I think Ala and I should do that," Diminitus said. "I don't believe you really need us in the castle, anyway."

"I think I will stay outside, as well," Acacia added. "That tunnel sounds pretty crowded as it is."

Andy looked at each of them in turn. *Would any of them be killed in what he was proposing?* He hadn't asked for this responsibility, but it was his nonetheless. "Let's get some rest. When night falls, I will scout the area to make sure there are no ambushes before you set out." After the meeting broke up, Andy stepped outside to breathe in the fresh air. Loki followed him out.

"Are you all right?" Loki asked, looking on him as a father would a troubled son.

"I am. I'm just trying to take in the immensity of it all. Believe it or not, Loki, my life before this was very simple and uncomplicated."

Loki put an affectionate hand on his shoulder. "Lad, you were made for this task. You needn't worry if you have the skill to do it. All you need to worry about is if you have the will to do it." Andy was grateful that he had Loki there with him, and so he was able to manage a smile. They stood there, watching the sun make its trek across the sky and sink behind the hills. All the while, Andy's thoughts were on Abby.

CHAPTER 18

THE TORCHES CAST an orange glow on the walls where Abby found herself shackled. Her hair was matted and pasted to her face with sweat. The hot, stuffy room was bare and had two oaken doors on opposite sides. Abby felt like she had been there for an eternity. Tolbert would come in now and again to torment her with visions of what he was going to do once Devon was done with her. She felt, no matter which way things went, she was going to die. Hope had left her on that count.

Abby knew that she was bait to bring Andros there. She also knew that he had not abandoned her in the forest, and he would obviously try to rescue her. Then Devon would capture him and kill her regardless. Her thoughts were interrupted by a key rattling in the lock, followed by a click. The door opened, and Devon stepped inside. His golden eyes gleamed down on her coldly.

"Resting comfortably?" he said sarcastically.

"What do you want?" she said, turning away.

"I just wanted to inform you that your lover approaches." She looked at him sharply. "Don't bother to deny it," he sneered. "I know you love him and would probably do anything to warn him. I am here to tell you that, should you speak a single word to him, you shall both die instantly." His voice was deceptively calm. "If everyone does what they are told, no one needs to die."

"Do I have a choice?"

"Actually, no," he whispered, leaning close to her face.

Abby knew the situation was hopeless. Devon would not let her live. She decided to take herself out of the situation. She had given up hope of ever seeing Andros again. Lunging as far as her bonds would allow, she raked her fingernails across Devon's cheek.

"*Aghh*!" Devon shrieked as he pulled her hand away from his bloodied face. His golden eyes burned fiercely. "Die, then, if that is your wish!" He made a swinging motion with his hand and slammed Abby's head against the stone wall. Bright lights exploded behind her eyes, and she felt herself start to lose conciseness. She waited for the fatal blow, but it never came. She started slumping over to the floor but kept her eyes closed. It hurt too much to open them. Then she heard a quiet chuckle.

"Very clever, my dear," Devon said. "You will not die yet. But, because of your foolishness, when it comes time to kill you, I promise it will be slow and long."

The door slammed closed and the key turned, locking her in once more. Despair filled her as she lay crumpled on the floor and darkness engulfed her.

* * *

Andy stood at the entrance of the Palatine Bridge. He hoped the others had found their way in by now. He walked a little way onto the bridge and looked over the low wall into the chasm. Even with his dragon's eyes, it would have been difficult for him to see the bottom. He lifted his head and looked toward the castle as he heard the sound of a horse approaching. The bridge was clear, and the rider rode on unimpeded. He had sandy blond hair and rode a chestnut mare. The symbol on his shield let Andy know that he was a Raptor. The rider stopped a few feet from where Andy stood and dismounted.

"I am Lieutenant Nyle," he said, all business. "I am to escort you to Lord Devon."

His bearing did not seem to indicate that he was a cold-blood-ied killer, which was the image Andy had of the Raptors. The lieutenant's eyes would not look directly at his, as if he were not entirely in agreement with what he was doing.

"I'm ready," Andy replied. He walked next to the lieutenant as they started across the bridge. In the distance, he could see ravens circling. He noted one would fly off toward the castle as another one circled back. Andy looked at Nyle but remained silent. He wanted to see if curiosity might prompt the lieutenant to talk. It worked.

"So, you are a dragon," Nyle said, looking at him with a sidelong glance.

"I am," Andy replied. "But you must have known that."

"Only recently," he replied. "You should know that, if you attempt to change, I am to slay you instantly."

"Don't worry, Lieutenant. I am not going to do anything that would jeopardize my friend's life."

"It might be better if she were dead," Nyle said.

"Why do you say that?" Andy asked, looking at him quickly.

Nyle looked straight ahead as they kept walking. A constant breeze was swirling across the chasm, pushing their hair in all directions.

"After Devon is done with her, he plans to give her to his porter, Tolbert. It was he who captured her."

"I know," Andy said, his blood starting to boil at the thought of that monster with his hands on her. "Why are you telling me this?"

"Because I have no taste for these plots and intrigues. I prefer a good clean battle."

Andy could sense some kind of conflict in the lieutenant's mind. "You deserve a better master, Lieutenant," Andy said.

"Perhaps, but I have a feeling it is too late for that."

"Always keep your options open," Andy said quietly, hoping to create more doubt in his mind.

They did not speak for the rest of the walk to the castle. As they passed the library with its two statues in black marble, Andy wondered if the others had made it through. He thought of trying to mind-speak, to see if he could reach them, but Loki had warned him Devon was sometimes able to pick thoughts out of the air.

It was getting close to noon. Soon Bowen would begin his distraction. He prayed that everyone was in position.

*   *   *

Earlier that morning, Donella and the others had been in the Kensington cemetery, staring at the tomb of Redlin. The front entrance, which butted up against the hillside, was made entirely of white marble. The lintel was borne up by two iconic columns, and the door was made of a dark black wood. An inscription was chiseled into the marble above the door: *Think not of our brother as dead, but rather as journeyed to the next world.*

"That inscription is probably very close to the truth," Loki commented.

"Did you have this tomb put here?" Paolo asked.

"No, it was the people of Kensington," Loki replied. "The library curator at the time picked out this spot himself, which stands to reason why there is a tunnel here."

"The people of this city must have loved him, to erect such a tribute," Cleo said, marveling at how pristine the tomb was. It seemed like time had not touched it; she assumed some enchantment must have been laid upon it.

"Redlin was an intellectual," Loki said. "He spent a lot of his time here, but that is not to say he ignored the other races of Vasara." He pondered for a moment before continuing. "People always think of me as cranky and cantankerous, always chasing after causes. Devon was thought to be too aloof. But Redlin, he was a people person. He would immerse himself in the daily lives of those with whom he came in contact. You are right, Cleo. He was greatly loved."

"Any ideas as to how we get in?" Dain asked, eyeing the lock on the door.

"Not a problem," Loki said with ease. He pointed his finger at the keyhole, and a small burst of energy shot from his fingertip and penetrated the lock, causing it to burst apart and fall to the ground.

"I've said it before," Bart chimed in, smiling. "You and Andros are handy people to have around."

Donella opened the door, and everyone stepped inside. She closed it behind them just in case someone wandered by and noticed the open door. She took the comb out of her hair and transformed it. Then, using her staff, she caused the sphere to glow with a subdued light that made everyone look pale and ghostly.

The tomb was actually quite spacious. An effigy on the floor depicted a man on his back carved out of stone. The hair was short and wavy in appearance, and he seemed to be wearing a robe with a wide belt chiseled around his midsection. His eyes were closed, his hands folded across his chest. His visage was carved in a peaceful expression, in harmony with the way he had lived his life.

"Is that what he looked like?" Dain asked, adjusting his sword to keep it from digging into his side.

"More or less," Loki said, shrugging his shoulders.

"So, where is the tunnel?" Leah asked.

"My guess is under the effigy," Loki responded. "The only problem now is finding the mechanism that opens it."

"Couldn't you use your magic?" Paolo prompted.

"I probably could, but now that we are starting to get close to Devon, I should use my magic as little as possible. I would be willing to bet he has wards set up to tell him when anyone is channeling the source."

Donella looked down at the effigy. The face was kind and fatherly. "Do you think Devon would know if I used Braylynn's power?"

Loki pondered that as he looked over at the green-eyed Summoner. "You know, I believe he might not. In any case, I think it is worth the risk."

Donella lowered her staff so the sphere was touching the effigy. As she opened herself up to Braylynn's power, the stone began to move. As it slid across the floor and the air below escaped, little eddies of dust swirled around the opening. Once it was wide enough, Donella raised her staff and peered down at the now-revealed stairs.

"After you, my dear," Loki said, smiling. "You have the light."

They descended the stairs; Leah and Dain brought up the rear. The tunnel ran straight as an arrow. After twenty minutes of walking, they came to the end.

"What if someone is in the library?" Bart asked, holding his bow with a godstone arrow nocked on the string.

"The library doesn't open its doors until noon. The only one in there should be the curator," Loki replied. "Go ahead, Donella. Open it."

Donella slowly pushed on the bookshelf and stepped into a room with several long tables and high-backed chairs. The room featured twenty-foot ceilings with bookcases covering every bit of wall space. A rail ran along the top with a ladder attached for reaching all the books up high. Once everyone was in the room, she closed the bookshelf with a wave of her hand.

"We need to find the curator quickly," Loki said hurriedly. "Even though the library doesn't open until noon, the staff will be arriving shortly."

"Leave it to me," Leah said, leaping into the air and flying down the hall. A few minutes later, she was flying back with a most reluctant curator kicking his legs in midair. He had dark hair and a bushy brown beard. His scholarly robes were getting wrinkled from flailing about as Leah dropped him unceremoniously at Loki's feet.

"What is the meaning of this?" the curator sputtered. "How did you get in here?"

Loki grabbed him by his shirt collar, jerking him to his feet, and gave him his most menacing look. "We will ask the questions here, and your survival might depend on your ability to answer. What is your name?"

"Yellen," he replied indignantly.

"Very good. See how easy that was? Now, where do you stand in regards to Devon?"

"I've no love for him, but I obey the laws," Yellen responded.

"I'll buy that. Final question. Where is the tunnel that leads from the library to the castle?"

"What are you talking about?" Yellen cried.

"Wrong answer," Loki said, emotionless. "Dain, run him through."

"*Are you crazy?*" Yellen screamed. Dain had pulled his sword from its scabbard and started to approach Yellen. "I'm telling you, there is no tunnel to the castle."

"Are there any tunnels from the library?" Loki asked, looking at him sharply.

"No!"

"Wrong answer. Finish it, Dain."

"Wait a minute," Leah said, putting a restraining hand on Dain's shoulder. She looked over at Donella. "You have the ability to read people. Does he speak true?"

"He does," Donella replied.

"How can that be?" Bart said. "He said there are no tunnels from the library, and we know that is a lie."

"Bart, we know he is oath-bound not to reveal the tunnels of the curators to anyone but another curator," Donella explained. "But a tunnel to the castle he knows nothing about."

Yellen looked at Donella aghast. "Who told you of the tunnels of Redlin?" he whispered, as if some great trust had been betrayed.

Donella saw where his thoughts were going, and her green eyes burned fiercely into his as she replied sternly, "A curator who put her life at risk to rescue the first dragon in Vasara in more than fifteen hundred years. Were it not for her sacrifice, Devon might have conquered another world already, while solidifying his control in this one. It is her whom we are trying to save."

Yellen blinked twice. "Forgive me. All this has been most unsettling. Redlin gave the curators those tunnels as a means of protection. To hear that you know of them took me by surprise." He paused a moment as he looked around at all assembled there. "I can see that something out of the ordinary is happening, and if it will help you in your struggle against Devon, I will give what aid I can. I am no hero, unlike the curator you are trying to save, but neither am I a coward."

"Well spoken, sir!" Loki said, slapping him on the back and knocking him forward several paces. "You have earned a reprieve from Dain's splitting you up the middle."

"I'm glad to hear that," Yellen said, rubbing his shoulder. "But I was not lying when I said I know of no tunnel going between the library and the castle."

"Then I guess that means we have to find another way in," Paolo said, frustrated.

"I don't think so," Loki said with assurance.

"What do you mean?" Bart said. "You heard Yellen say there was no tunnel."

"What he said was that he didn't know of any," Loki corrected. "Now that I know of these tunnels, there are certain people Redlin would want to help, such as the curators and the king and queen. My brother took great care in making sure the royal line would continue. I have to believe he would have made an escape route out of the castle. And it only makes sense that it would lead here."

"So how do we find it?" Donella asked.

"Ah, that is a good question. Let's go to the rotunda where there is more light, and I can think."

They made their way to the central part of the library. A huge, round desk sat in the middle. Several ledgers lay on the desk to record books checked out. Loki slowly paced around the desk, deep in thought.

"Any idea how long he's going to be?" Leah whispered to Donella. "People are going to start arriving soon."

"Not a clue," she whispered back.

"Loki, we don't have all day for this," Bart said impatiently.

"*Shhh!*" Loki responded. "I need to think of how Redlin might have acted. If all the entrances are operated by the same type of mechanism, then there is a book somewhere in this library that is the key."

"But there are thousands of books here," Cleo put in. "How will you know which one?"

"If I am given a moment to think, I believe I can narrow it down based on what I know of Redlin." Everyone remained quiet as he continued pacing around the desk. About the third time around, he stopped suddenly and looked up at Yellen.

"Yellen, in what section would we find the books on faeries?" Loki asked.

"Follow me. I will show you." Yellen led them down a hall marked *Magical Beings*. After they passed four rooms, they came to a door painted forest green. The plaque on the top was marked simply *Faeries*. Yellen unlocked the door and led them inside. Like every other room in the library, the walls were covered from floor to ceiling with books.

"Now what?" Leah said in dismay. "We don't have time to pull on every single book in here."

"We are not going to," Loki explained, smiling mischievously.

"All right, old man," Bart said, catching the look in Loki's eyes. "What craftiness are you going to dazzle us with this time?"

"I asked Yellen to bring us here because there is one other race that is dear to Redlin. The faeries. Or at least one faerie."

"What do you mean?" Donella asked, puzzled.

"There was a faerie whom Redlin loved, a princess. Her name was Luel. She disappeared around the same time that he did. For all I know, they could be together. In any case, I am guessing that a tunnel of this importance would be controlled by a book about something just as important to his heart. Thin, I know," he said, shrugging. "But it is all I can think of that gives us the best chance."

"So how are you going to pick the right one?" Dain asked skeptically.

"Why, with magic, of course," Loki said, smiling.

"But I thought you said Devon might be able to sense you," Leah said.

Loki smiled triumphantly. "This is the part where he dazzles us with his brilliance," Bart said, rolling his eyes.

"Quite right, Bart. Quite right," Loki exclaimed. He turned toward Donella. "I am going to need your help with this, dear," he said in a fatherly voice.

"Of course," she responded. "What do you need me to do?"

"I want you to create a shield of Braylynn's power around this room. That should mask the small amount of power I will draw from the Five."

"Got it," she said. Donella wove an invisible barrier in the shape of a square and pushed it out to encompass the entire room. "Ready," she said.

Loki folded his arms across his chest and, with eyes closed, slowly started spinning. His feet came off the floor, and his rotations became faster and faster. He was almost a blur. Eventually, he came within inches of the ceiling when his turning slowed. He dropped down one shelf from the bookcase he was facing and floated over to pull out a book. As he pulled on it, there was an audible click, and a section of books on the far side of the room opened to reveal a darkened passageway beyond. Loki settled back down to the floor with a satisfied expression on his face.

"How did you know?" Paolo asked, clearly amazed.

"I used the magic to scan quickly every title in this room. Then, taking what I know of Redlin, I picked the most logical choice, *Understanding the Heart of a Faerie*."

"And why is that the logical choice?" Bart asked.

"Because Redlin is a hopeless romantic," Loki responded, walking over to the nearest shelf, pulling a red leather book, and tossing it to Bart. "See for yourself."

Bart read the title aloud, *"Faerie Sonnets* by Redlin."

"That is some of the sappiest stuff you'll ever read," Loki explained.

"I think it's time we got going," Cleo said, adjusting her swords on her back.

"Quite right," Loki said. "Donella, where is Andros now?"

Donella turned her sight inward as the dragon eye started to glow. "He is by some trees. He can see the bridge from where he is standing."

"He will be starting across soon. Come, we must be in place before he reaches Devon."

One by one, they filed into the passage that led to the castle. Yellen stayed behind to close the entrance, since his absence from the library would raise suspicions. After twenty minutes of walking, they came to a wooden door.

"All right, Cleo, I think it is time to use that talisman Andros gave you," Loki said.

She took out the small disk her brother had given Andros. As she focused her thoughts on the disk, an image was revealed of the room they were about to enter. It was a bedroom, richly furnished; it must have been the king and queen's. Outside the door that led to the hallway, two guards were posted. "The room is empty," she reported. "Two soldiers guard the door outside."

"Where is Andros now?" Loki asked, directing his question to Donella.

"He has started across the bridge, accompanied by a Raptor," she replied.

"We need to get in position. Dain, can you and Paolo render those guards unconscious without making any noise?"

"No problem," Dain said with confidence. "What say you, sire? Care for a little action?"

"Lead on, General. I'm ready," Paolo replied.

Cautiously, they opened the door and tiptoed in. Hugging the wall, they came adjacent to the outer door. Dain looked at Paolo and held up three fingers. Paolo nodded his head in the affirmative that they would go on three. Peering carefully through the door, Dain could see both men staring straight ahead. He looked at Paolo and started the countdown. On three, they both jumped out without a sound and hit each guard on the head with the hilt of their swords, knocking them out cold. Grabbing them under their arms, they dragged them back into the room. Loki and the others, seeing everything was all right, came in and congratulated the two men on a job well done.

"You two get into their uniforms while the rest of us look for something to tie them up with," Loki said. After the guards were gagged and bound, Loki turned toward Donella. "We will stay here. The treasure room is right next door, in the tower. Once Bowen starts his attack, we will break in and neutralize any guards inside. You and Dain must leave now, so you are in position to do whatever it is you and Andros have planned."

"How do I get to the tower?" Donella asked.

"The tower is in the westernmost part of the castle. Follow this wall and take any stairs going up. You might have to look out a window now and then, to get your bearings."

Now came the most dangerous part of their mission. Donella wondered if they would all make it through this alive. Braylynn had told Andros they had the power to free Abby but not what it might cost. She decided not to think about that. "Are you ready, Dain?" she asked.

"Ready," he replied.

Leah walked over and gave her a hug. "Be safe, sister. I don't want to lose you."

"You stay safe, as well, Leah, and if you see Zana, don't go after her without me," she said, her green eyes afire with vengeance.

"I promise we will go after her together." Leah turned to Dain. "I shall be extremely put out with you, sir, if anything should happen to my sister," she said with one eyebrow raised.

Dain pushed her blonde hair behind her pointed ears and lost himself for a moment in her eyes. "I do not plan on either one of us dying today, even if a host of demons stands in our way. Take care, love. I will come find you in the woods across the bridge when this is done." He kissed her lips and made ready to depart.

"Are you sure that is where Andros said to meet?" Bart asked. "Devon is going to be hot on our heels."

"We need to plan our next steps quickly," Paolo explained. "And we can't do that if we have to waste time searching for one another. Diminitus, Ala, and Acacia should have enough horses ready for us when we come out so we can get away as quickly as possible."

"I feel like this whole enterprise is riding on a knife's edge," Cleo said.

"It is," Loki said. "You two be careful," he said to Donella and Dain. "The gods be with you."

"And the goddess," Leah added.

Donella and Dain quietly slipped out the door and down the hall, while the others waited for the sound of cannon shot to strike the ocean side of the castle wall.

CHAPTER 19

ANDY FOLLOWED Lieutenant Nyle through the myriad halls in the White Castle to the upper tower, where Devon waited. Earlier, as they had walked through the town, Andy had looked toward the open market. With his dragon sight, he'd seen Diminitus busily working on a broken wagon wheel. Ala and Acacia were a few stalls down, selling herbs. *At least they are in place*, he'd thought. Now he needed a way to be able to locate Donella.

After climbing several flights of stairs, they came to a long hallway with several rooms and darkened alcoves splitting off it. At the end was an oaken door. Andy remembered the other side of that door from his arrival in Vasara.

As he walked past one of the alcoves, something warm struck his cheek. Andy smiled to himself. Using magic, Donella had just blown him a faerie kiss, and when it hit his face, images of Laurel Hollow flooded his brain. This was her way of telling him she was in place and ready.

Nyle knocked on the door. That hollow-sounding voice Andy had heard when the raven brand first touched his skin told him to enter. He didn't know what to expect or how he should feel upon first seeing Devon. All thought of that went out the window when he saw Abby lying on the floor with blood pooled around her head.

"She is alive," Devon said, his golden eyes never leaving Andy.

"What did you do to her?" Andy demanded through gritted teeth. Devon turned his head to the side, showing Andy three angry red welts along his cheek.

"She was trying to get me to kill her so you wouldn't have to choose. She almost succeeded."

Andy couldn't help feeling this was entirely his fault. To see her like this was almost more than his heart could stand. Suddenly, he found he had the desire to kill Devon. He brought his eyes level with Devon's. The resolve and steel in Andy's spirit were more than enough to overcome the wizard's hypnotic stare.

"So, what do you want exactly?" Andy asked.

"Very simply, for you to walk through the door opposite the one you came in and go home."

Andy could feel the raw power in the room. Devon seemed calm and poised, but Andy knew he was a coiled spring, waiting to unleash the power of demons on him, if necessary. He would have to be careful that he didn't trip that spring too soon.

"And if I walk through that door, you'll just let Abby go?"

"Yes."

"What if I refuse?" Andy asked, stalling for time.

"Then you both will die."

Andy was silent for a few moments, pretending to weigh his options.

Devon spoke again. "I will even free your brothers, if that will help you to decide."

Andy's eyes narrowed. "What do you know of the other dragons?"

"I sent them to where they are now," he said matter-of-factly. "And there they will remain until I set them free. It is not a pleasant place, I assure you."

Andy felt a tugging on his mind not unlike the feeling he'd had when he stood before the arch that had brought him to Vasara. It was a strong desire to go home. To forsake these people and return to his mother and father; to walk along the banks of the Hudson River once more in peace and contentment. But his eyes were open now, and his mind was awake to his dragon nature. Devon's magic fell flat. He must have realized it was not working, because the attack stopped. Devon tried reasoning with Andy.

"Listen, boy, you don't belong here. This is not your fight. Why should you make all the sacrifices?" Like honey being drizzled slowly onto the tip of the tongue, Devon was trying to make his words as pleasing as possible. But Andy was having none of it. Any convincing Devon had hoped to achieve was lost the moment he caused pain to Abby.

"You might as well save your breath. If I am being asked to make any sacrifices, it is because of you." Andy threw down the gauntlet. "You have taken a throne that is not yours and murdered its king and queen. The gods only know how many more you have murdered in your quest for power." He decided to let him have it between the eyes. "You also don't need to pretend to care for my welfare and desire for home. Loki has told me what your brand means and what power it gives you, should I go back to my world. I have already made up my mind. No matter what happens, I will not give you a toehold there."

Devon's face went red with rage, especially with the mention of his meddling brother's name. Then he seemed to get control of himself and chuckled softly. Andy became wary.

"You foolish boy," Devon said with a smirk. "You actually had a chance of surviving all of this, had you just gone back. But you made a mistake, coming this close to me. It doesn't matter what condition you are in when you go across. I can throw you through the door myself. As long as there is just one heartbeat on the other side, then I have won."

Andy knew the time for discussion was over and decided to land the first blow. Fire shot out of his upraised hands and streaked toward Devon. The flames, however, hit an invisible barrier in front of the wizard, leaving him unscathed. He laughed as the flames were deflected straight up into the ceiling.

"Did you not think I would be prepared?" Devon said mockingly. "I know the dragon's power, and if I were just an ordinary wizard like Loki, you might have had a chance of defeating me. Did Loki tell you that another reason the Five created dragons was to keep the wizards from abusing their power? But I assure you, I am no longer an ordinary wizard." His eyes started to glow even more brightly, and Andy knew he was gathering his strength to strike.

Donella, I need you now! The oaken door burst asunder as the Dragon Summoner stepped through. The silver in her jet-black hair gave off such luminescence that the light in the room was twice as bright as before. Her green eyes were hard and focused. In her hand, lightning danced as she gathered it like a ball and flung it at Devon's shield.

Devon was knocked back a few steps by this unexpected visitor but did not lose control. "Very clever," he said. "I don't know how you got in undetected, but it matters little. I had a feeling you might show up, ever since Zana came running back here with her tail between her legs."

Donella, ignoring his words, leveled her staff and shot bursts of energy at Devon as she ran to get behind him.

Who's watching the door? Andy was worried someone might sneak up behind them.

Dain, Donella replied between shots. Andy felt much better, knowing that the Border Lands general was guarding their back. His musings, however, took his focus off Devon for an instant, and Andy took a blow to the chest. Again, as with Braylynn, he was propelled up and back until he slammed into the wall. He thought Braylynn had hit him hard, but with Devon, it was like he was a piece of iron in a smithy, with the wizard being the hammer and the wall the anvil. No wonder Braylynn had tested them as she had.

All of a sudden, the sound of cannon fire was heard in the distance, followed by explosions against the outer castle wall. They were coming fast and fierce. Andy started to worry Bowen might try to level the castle. When he had caught up with Bowen and explained his plan and the fact that Abby was a prisoner, every sailor to a man had wanted to lay waste to the castle because of Devon's outrageous behavior. To them, Abby was a seaman's sister, and they would not let this assault go unpunished.

Devon paused and shielded himself once more as he listened to the cannons. Then a slow smile crept upon his face.

"So, you thought to distract me. Have me drop my guard or run to the battlements, I suppose," he said with disdain. "My army is more than a match against any invasion you can dream up. They don't even need me to lead them. Now, how about we finish what we started here."

Devon was right: it was a distraction. But the wizard didn't yet realize the distraction was for Cleo's benefit. Hopefully, most of the guards would empty out of the castle, giving the others freedom of movement to find the stone.

Andy reached for his non-dragon weapon of choice and brought into being his fire whip. He cracked it several times over Devon's head, trying to shake him. He looked over at Abby, who was thankfully still unconscious. Some of the fire from his whip had dripped extremely close to her.

Donella, can you shield Abby? I'm worried that she might get hit.

She didn't answer or hesitate as she took her talon spear out of the strap on her arm. After extending it, she threw it over to where Abby lay, and it came to rest along her side. Putting a hand to her necklace, the green stones started to glow as she drew on the elements of Earth and nature. She pointed her staff at the spear and directed the flow of power, causing shoots to appear all along its length. They were growing rapidly and intertwining, making an enclosure between the floor and wall, encasing Abby.

That is the best I can do, she said, fending off more of Devon's lightning strikes.

Devon started pouring on the attacks, lashing out simultaneously at Andy and Donella. Andy took a hot, searing blow across his forearm that would leave him with a scar for the rest of his days.

I think we need to do it now, Andy said. He'd had an idea that he thought had a pretty good chance of success. He had worked out the logistics with Donella in the glade, practicing against the lizard creatures.

We need some kind of distraction, Donella replied.

I don't know if we can make that happen, Andy said. *Devon is on his guard, now that Bowen has begun his assault. Does Dain know the plan?*

Yes, he's prepared.

Andy had been giving his idea a lot of thought. It had been Devon's golden eyes that inspired him, but he needed to time this right. If Devon managed to shield himself, their element of surprise would be gone.

Andy and Donella started moving closer together so Devon would be looking in one direction only. The wizard was throwing energy blasts at an alarming rate. It took them every bit of concentration to protect themselves.

We are just going to have to do it and hope for the best, Andy said.

Just then, they heard the cry of a raven right outside the door. It was piercing, as if someone were holding its leg while it flapped like mad, trying to escape.

"What the...?" Devon heard the cry and glanced toward the door, thinking one of his ravens was in mortal danger.

"Now!" Donella said

Andy turned body and spirit inward. He ran the forest path and plunged himself into the source. He knew he was extremely vulnerable right now, but this was the only place that would protect his dragon eyes. Donella was also looking through his eyes to protect her own eyesight. When Andy had all the power he could contain, he channeled it back to Donella. He was banking that Devon's golden eyes were very sensitive to bright light.

Donella's power flooded her being and joined with Braylynn's power through the sphere. The sphere illuminated with the brightness of three suns. Devon tried to shield his eyes, but it was too late. The shriek of pain coming from the wizard was unlike anything Andy had ever heard.

He felt Donella cut off the power to the source and assumed it was all right to come back. When he looked at Devon, he gave a shuddering wince and let out a curse. Blood was streaming from Devon's blackened eye sockets, and his breath was coming in raking gasps. He looked around sightlessly.

"You will die, boy!" he hissed, blood mixing with spittle as he spat out his words. "The only care I have now is your destruction and that of everyone you love. I'll pull someone else from your world, but your time here is over." He raised his hand to strike when suddenly he paused and tilted his head as if listening. "*No!*" he screamed, and in a flash of fire and smoke, he vanished.

"Where did he go?" Donella asked, astounded he would leave.

"My guess is he is headed to where the others are. He must have sensed that they have the stone."

"Is yellow eyes gone yet?" said a familiar voice from the doorway. Andy and Donella looked over to see Tera sitting on the back of Pan. The silver-haired faerie slid off the faun's back and ran to embrace Donella.

"Tera! However did you get here so fast?" Donella asked, giving her a big faerie hug.

"Pan brought me," she said, smiling, "along with a hundred other fauns who are creating havoc all throughout Kensington."

"That was you making those raven sounds?" Donella asked.

"Yep," Tera said, clearly proud of herself.

"Tera, thank you for your help," Andy said. "Your distraction turned the tide for us."

"No problem," she replied.

Pan's hooves made an audible clicking sound against the stone floor as he walked over to where the others were standing. Dain was right behind him, sword drawn and walking backwards to make sure nobody surprised them from behind.

"I know there are a lot of questions here," Pan said in his deep booming voice, "but we need to move fast."

"Yes," Andy agreed. "We need to get Abby and leave. Donella, if you would, please."

Donella walked over to the enclosure she had made around Abby. Touching her necklace again, she caused the talon wood to decay and fall apart. Brushing the debris away, she put a hand on Abby's forehead and poured the goddess's healing power into her.

Andy knelt down and picked her up in his arms as she began to stir. She looked into his eyes as her own began to well up with tears. She reached up, put her arms around his neck, and buried her face in his chest as the sobs came. After a few minutes, Abby composed herself.

"I thought I would never see you again," she said in a tired voice.

"I'm sorry," Andy said, the pain and guilt evident on his face from the suffering he felt he'd caused.

Abby managed a weak smile and touched a hand to his cheek. "It is not your fault. I know you wouldn't have left me unless it was beyond your power to stay."

"Can you walk?" Andy asked.

"I don't think I can. I feel extremely weak."

"Give her to me, Andros," Pan said, holding out his arms. "I can carry her as if she weighed no more than a leaf." Andy handed her to the king of the fauns.

"You have a lot of friends who I have never met, Andros," Abby said, looking at the others. Andy made introductions as much as time would allow. They exited the room. In the hall were two guards, slain by Dain's sword. Andy didn't give them a second look but proceeded down the hallway. As they passed the last alcove, there came a shout to halt from behind. Andy looked back and saw Tolbert emerge from a side hallway with three guards.

"Stay where you are!" Tolbert commanded.

Andy had had enough of this idiot. He started to walk back when Dain restrained him.

"We need to get out before Devon comes back," he said urgently.

Andy let out a curse. "You're right, General. Let's go." He made to leave when he checked his stride. What caused him to pause was the sight of Lieutenant Nyle walking toward them with his sword drawn.

"Nyle! Don't let them escape," Tolbert shouted.

Andy noticed that Nyle's eyes were fixed on Tolbert and not on himself. Nyle stopped in front of Andy. "You may leave, Lord Dragon. I will take care of this."

There was nothing Andy could think to say. He and the others sped past Nyle and down the stairs.

"You *traitor!*" Tolbert screamed. "You let them go!"

Nyle gave Tolbert his Raptor's smile. "Let us finish our duel, Tolbert. Your friends may join in if they wish," he said, giving his sword a flourish.

*   *   *

As soon as Bowen started firing, Loki and the others ran to the treasure room door. "Quickly, Cleo," Loki said hurriedly. "How many?"

Cleo concentrated on the disk. "There are five. Two on either side of the door against this wall, two on the far wall, and one is pacing," she replied.

"Bart, can you hit the one who is moving?" Loki asked.

"Sure, not a problem," he replied with confidence.

"Leah, you can get to the far ones the quickest."

"I'll take care of them," she replied with a grim expression.

"And Cleo and Paolo will take the other two," Loki finished. "I'll blast the door. Get ready."

Leah moved into position, ready to be the first in and then fly over to the guards by the far wall. Bart had knocked an arrow and set himself to follow her. Loki lifted his hand and made a pushing motion, causing the door to fall in; the guards were momentarily stunned into disbelief. Quick as a cat, Leah flew in and, using her spear, rendered them unconscious in seconds. Bart shot his man on the run, burying an arrow in his chest. Paolo and Cleo made short work of the guards who remained. Loki surveyed the scene and, after the two unconscious guards were securely bound, began the search for the stone.

The treasure room was inaptly named. It was more a room of historical artifacts than of money or jewels, although there were plenty of those, as well. Many paintings of various styles adorned the walls. Statues large and small representing all the races of Vasara were scattered throughout the room. There were several long wooden tables with crowns, necklaces, rings and other jewelry upon them. Many artifacts of wood, stone, and steel made their way through history to come to rest in this room.

A flash of red caught Cleo's eye. On a wooden pedestal in the far corner of the room, the stone of the Pillar of Fallon twinkled in its diamond case.

"There it is!" she said, pointing excitedly. The red stone was shaped like a crystal ball, and its size was such that it would rest comfortably in the palms of both hands. Flames danced just under the outer surface, as if it were alive and breathing. Cleo was awestruck at seeing something that none of her race had set eyes upon in fifteen hundred years.

"How do we get it out of there?" Paolo asked Loki.

"I can open the case," Loki said, eyeing the stone intently. "The question is how much time we will have before Devon comes after us. I can feel the magical wards that surround it, so he will most certainly know when we have taken it."

"Why don't we just take it, pedestal and all?" Bart suggested while cleaning off his arrow.

"The pedestal is held down by magic, and, short of destroying it, I doubt we could budge it." Loki thought for a moment, scratching his chin. "I was afraid it might come down to this, but I can see no other way."

"What do you mean?" Cleo asked, suddenly wary of the tone in his voice.

"I mean I am going to buy you time to escape by engaging Devon here," Loki said solemnly.

"No, Loki!" Paolo said earnestly. "We can find another way."

"We don't have time," he stated simply.

"Can you beat him?" Bart asked.

"With that demon inside him, no," Loki replied.

"So you will throw your life away," Leah said pointedly.

"This is bigger than me, Leah, or you, for that matter. We do what we must. Bart, I need to tell you something." They walked a little bit away from the others where he spoke softly. "I want you to give Andros a message for me."

"Certainly," Bart replied. "Whatever you want me to do."

"Tell him not to lose heart and that I love him like a son. Also tell him to remember what I said in the woods outside Fenner. 'Just because a man looks harmless, doesn't mean he is'."

"I will tell him," Bart assured him. He clasped Loki's hand in farewell. "Good luck, old friend."

"Thanks. Come, let's get this over with." They walked back to the stone. "The only one who needs to be here when I do this is Cleo. The rest of you should wait by the door and be ready to flee." They all bid him farewell and did as he asked. "Are you ready?" he asked Cleo.

"Yes," she replied, taking the pouch off her belt that would hold the stone.

Loki closed his eyes as he put both hands on either side of the case. The case started to take on an orange glow, as if it were being heated. A slight ringing sound filled the air like a finger being rubbed around the rim of a crystal glass. All of a sudden, there was a loud crack like a whip, and the case was no more.

"Take the stone, Cleo," Loki said hurriedly.

Cleo put the stone in the pouch and bolted for the door to where the others waited. She glanced back and saw Loki move into the middle of the room to await his confrontation with Devon. The last image she saw of him was with his head down, as if in prayer. Once she was through the door, they all dashed down the hall and headed for the castle gate, avoiding the tunnel through which they had entered lest they be trapped.

*　*　*

As soon as Cleo joined them, Leah told the others to make their way to the outside.

"Aren't you coming?" Bart asked.

"No, I am going back to see if I can help Loki," she replied.

Leah flew back to the treasure room while the others made their way outside. As she neared the door, she could hear two voices talking, one of which she knew was Loki's. She cautiously peered around the door and looked in. Devon had his back to her while Loki faced the open door. He must have seen her, because he gave a very slight shake of his head. Leah tried to sneak in behind Devon when, to her astonishment, she found she could not move. She looked back at Loki, who gave her a barely discernable side to side motion of his head, warning her to do nothing.

"You should have stayed out of this, Loki," Devon said.

"You made that impossible, brother," Loki returned. "You betrayed our masters and aligned with the enemy. It is my duty and obligation to stop you."

"I'm going to kill you," Devon stated. "You know that."

"Aren't you taking a risk?" Loki asked. "You don't know who the gods will choose to replace me."

"It doesn't matter anymore. Any wizard they choose will not be a match for me. I'm going to kill your pet dragon, as well. Farewell, Loki." Devon let loose a burst of fire that enveloped Loki. Leah could no longer see him, only a column of flame. As the flame died down and disappeared, the only thing left on the floor was a pile of ash.

Leah stared in horror. Free to move and speak once more, she let out a curse. Devon heard her and whipped his head around. Leah jumped and flew down the hall just moments before two lightning strikes came streaking out of the treasure room and hit the wall where she had just been standing.

* * *

Diminitus was having a hard time keeping the horses from bolting. The market square was absolute pandemonium. Once the cannons had started firing, people began running for cover. When the fauns arrived, everyone started running for their lives. They would have been safer staying where they were, since the fauns were only engaging the soldiers. Ala and Acacia were having just as much trouble keeping their own horses under control. Every now and then, Acacia would hand off her horses to Ala while she dealt with a robber or looter. Two men already lay dead at her feet, having mistakenly thought the women were easy targets.

"Here they come!" Diminitus said, catching sight of Paolo and the others emerging from the castle gate. Bart was bringing up the rear, his bow singing as he shot arrow after arrow at the pursuing soldiers. Diminitus did not see Andros and Donella with them nor Pan and Tera, whom he saw go in when the fauns arrived.

"Where are the others?" Diminitus asked Paolo when they reached him.

"I don't know," he said breathlessly. "As soon as we got the stone, Loki made us leave."

"Where is Loki?" Acacia asked, coming over to stand next to her husband.

"He stayed to fight Devon so we could escape," Cleo added. "Leah went back to try to help him."

Fauns were everywhere. A group of them had gone over to fight the soldiers who had been chasing Paolo and the others.

"You should leave now," Diminitus said. "I'll stay and wait for the others. Acacia, you and Ala go with them. I can handle the remaining horses."

"Right. We'll meet you in the woods just beyond the bridge," Acacia replied.

They mounted up and raced for the city gates. Luckily, the archers were on the battlements shooting at the ships, so the way across the bridge was clear. After Diminitus saw them make good their escape, he turned his attention back to the castle gates. "Where are they?" he wondered aloud. No sooner were the words out of his mouth than he saw Pan's huge form emerge, carrying a young woman.

"Over here!" Diminitus shouted. They altered their path and met up with him.

"Did the others get out?" Andy asked worriedly.

"Yes," he replied. "The only ones left are Leah and Loki."

"Where are they?" Donella asked.

"From what I understand, they were fighting Devon."

"My god!" Andy exclaimed. "They'll be butchered. I have to go back."

"I'm coming with you," Dain said.

Just then, they saw Leah flying out of the castle as if the hounds of hell were after her.

"Quickly, we need to get out of here. There are Raptors behind me," she said hurriedly.

"Where is Loki?" Andy asked.

"He's dead," she replied sadly. "I'm sorry. I will tell you every-thing, but we must leave now. Devon will be coming."

Andy stared woodenly back toward the castle. He couldn't believe Loki was dead. "That can't be true," he said. "Loki can't die. I need him. Surely the prophecy wouldn't let him die." He started walking back toward the castle when he felt a hand on his shoulder.

"There is nothing we can do, Andros," Donella was saying to him. "He gave his life so we might escape and end this once and for all. Do not let his death be in vain."

Andy just stared at her as if her words didn't register.

"Andros." It was Abby talking now. He looked over at the girl he loved in the arms of the big faun, and rational thought started to come back to him. "Donella is right," she said urgently. "We must leave."

"There they are!" Several Raptors came rushing out of the castle. They never knew what hit them. Andy, taking out his vengeance on them, thrust both hands forward as fire shot out and consumed them.

"By the Five!" Diminitus exclaimed.

"Go," Andy said with dead eyes. "I have to signal Bowen. Pan, recall your fauns."

Pan held Abby in one arm as he took a horn hanging from a belt on his waist and gave a mighty blow. The sound echoed off the buildings, making fauns stream from every direction and trot across the bridge.

Dain and Diminitus mounted and rode toward the woods with the faeries and Pan following. Andy changed, causing everyone around him to run in terror at the sight of the black dragon. He still couldn't believe Loki was gone. He leaped into the air and started flying straight up, giving out a roar for the loss that he felt. When he was high enough, he started his descent, belching fire before head-ing east.

The ships, seeing the signal, broke off their attack, and set sail for the Mistral Islands to await the final battle.

CHAPTER 20

WHEN ANDY JOINED the others in the woods, they made a quick camp to discuss the events that led up to today. The fauns set up around the perimeter to watch for enemies. He forced himself to put aside his grief for the moment to concentrate on the revelations being shared.

Pan told of how he had left Parma to cause as much havoc to Devon and his soldiers as he could. Just across his border, he'd found Valencia and Tera waiting for him as they journeyed north. Valencia had explained to Pan that Tera was fit and able to travel as long as she didn't fly for long periods. Pan at first objected to this, but Valencia had told him Braylynn had foreseen that Tera would be needed at the castle.

"She was right about that," Donella commented.

Next, Leah told of what she saw of the encounter between Devon and Loki.

"He didn't fight back at all?" Andy asked, puzzled.

"Not that I saw," she responded. "I think his main aim was to delay Devon while we escaped."

Bart then told Andy of the message Loki had given him, which puzzled him even more. His heartfelt sentiments lifted his spirits, but his message of "just because a man looks harmless, doesn't mean he is" baffled him.

Time was moving on, and Andy knew they had to leave, but he needed a moment to himself first. He asked Abby to come a little ways deeper into the woods with him. They found a small stream and sat on the grass near its banks where the water burbled soothingly.

"Andros, I'm sorry," Abby said as he pulled her close to him. "I know what Loki meant to you."

"Thanks, Abby. And I'm sorry for what you were put through because of me."

She looked into his hazel eyes. "The only one who deserves blame in all of this is Devon." Reaching her hand behind his head, she brought his lips to hers and kissed him passionately. Eventually she pulled back, leaving Andy breathless. Her smile held a little mirth as Andy tried to regain his composure.

"Wow," he exclaimed. "Kiss me like that again, and I might forget what it is we are supposed to be doing."

"Well, you'll not get another one until Devon is defeated," Abby told him pointedly. "It will give you incentive to finish this. Now, why are we here? Not that I'm complaining."

"I want to walk the forest path to the source, and I want you to watch over me while I do."

"Of course. Lay your head in my lap." Andy did this. It was peaceful and relaxing as he closed his eyes while Abby ran her fingers through his sandy brown hair.

* * *

Andy walked the path slowly, letting the healing balm of this otherworldly forest wash over his soul in an effort to assuage his grief. He didn't hurry, because time was different here than in the waking world. It seemed that he could spend an hour here sometimes, but only a few minutes would have passed in the normal world. He believed that the time spent here was determined by need. The more time that was required, it seemed, the more was given, without affecting real time.

As he started getting closer to the source, he saw a figure. For a moment, hope flared in his being, but it was quickly extinguished when he saw it was Braylynn. His features went from hope to despair when he saw her. When he reached her, she gave him a comforting embrace.

"I'm sorry I'm not Loki," she said, letting him go.

"No, it's all right," he responded. "I just thought maybe his spirit would come here."

"Don't lose heart, Andros," the goddess told him.

"That's what Loki said, but I feel alone and afraid without him." Tears stood in his eyes as he looked at the goddess.

"Perhaps I can help with that." With a kindly smile, she looked back down the path, and Andy followed her gaze. It was Donella walking toward them. Andy was stunned.

"How is it possible that she is here?" he asked her.

"She is able to come at my invitation."

"Braylynn asked me to come," Donella said when she reached them. "I hope it's all right I'm here."

"Of course. It seems fitting that you should be able to come here, since you are linked to dragons." Andy was glad Donella was here. It comforted him to know they shared in his grief.

He watched as Donella gazed at the source, hypnotized by its constant movement. He could tell that she longed to touch it, but it was not for her. He wondered if she could, since he had channeled some of that power into her.

"I have asked Donella here for a reason," Braylynn said. "It is time for her to have her memories back."

"That's great!" Andy said. "But why here?"

"Because you are a part of this," the goddess replied.

"What does that...?" Andy started, but he never finished. Braylynn put a hand on their foreheads.

"Donella, it is time for you to remember, and Andros, it is time for you to see."

A red nimbus surrounded the three of them. For Donella, it was like a dam had been raised and her memories, like water, came rushing back in. With Andy, it was like filmy gauze had been ripped in two, allowing him to see clearly who was on the other side.

"Em?" Andy blinked several times. "Em, it is you," he said, catching her up in a rough embrace and spinning her around. "I can't believe I didn't notice. Actually, probably the fact that you are a faerie threw me off a bit." He smiled, his eyes filling with tears and brimming over with joy that he was with his sister.

Emilia was silent for a moment, and her expression wide-eyed.

"What's the matter, Em? Don't you remember?" Andy asked, concerned.

"Yes, I do," she said slowly. "I remember… everything." Her eyes met Braylynn's knowing look. Andy saw something pass between them in that glance.

"What is it?" he asked.

"It is nothing," Braylynn said. "Time will reveal all, but not now."

"So are you Donella now?" Andy asked with a smirk.

"Now, you listen here, brother mine. Dragon or not, I'm still your older sister, and I'll have none of your sass." She smacked him on the shoulder and then smiled as she hugged him to her.

How he had missed his sister, he thought.

"Her name has always been Donella," Braylynn said. "I wrote it in the stars long before she was born."

Andy started to ponder something. "Did you cause Emilia to lose her memory?"

"I did," she replied. "I also clouded your mind so it wouldn't register that Donella was your sister."

"Why?" Emilia asked.

"With your brother, Devon believed he had only one route to your world," Braylynn explained. "He did not know you had come with Andros. You are my creation, so I was able to hide you as you came through."

"But why make her forget who she was?" Andy asked.

"Because her conscious mind would have given her away," she said. "Devon is sometimes able to sift through thoughts, and he would have seen where she was from. It would have given him a second option when he thought he had only one."

"That makes sense, I suppose," Andy said, scratching his head.

"There was another reason," Braylynn said, looking into Emilia's green eyes. "Had you come here with all your memories intact, you would not have accepted your faerie nature or your sisters'. You would have considered yourself an outsider. With the Dragon Summoner, it is all about connections. And the connection to your faerie sisters is just as important as your connection to the Summoner's clothes and talismans."

"Yes, I can see that," Emilia said.

"You two must go back now. Devon will be amassing his armies to destroy you. He is wounded deeply, and his obsession for power and dominance has slipped into madness."

"Will we win?" Andy asked.

"I cannot see that. But you have the power. Remember, you are the first Dragon Summoner and dragon that can join their powers."

"I remember," Emilia said.

"It is because you share the same blood that this is possible," Braylynn explained.

"That brings up a point," Andy said. "How is it that we are brother and sister, and yet I am a dragon and Emilia is a faerie?"

"As I said, all will become clear in time, but not now." She put a hand on each of their shoulders. "Take care of each other, and be safe." She turned and walked back down the forest path. A mist enveloped her until all they could see were her blue wings and then even those faded into the white fog.

"She is amazing," Andy said wistfully. He turned back toward his sister. "It's weird, we have been together all this time, but I feel like this is the first time I have seen you."

"I know what you mean," Emilia responded. "I've really missed you, Andy, although, because of my memory loss, I didn't know how much until this moment."

"I'm sorry I got you into this."

"You didn't get me into this," she said. "We were brought here to this place and time in order to make the difference in the freedom of Vasara. Braylynn was right. If events hadn't happened as they did, I don't believe I would have come to look at these faeries as my own family."

"Come on, Em. Let's finish this and go home," Andy said.

"I'm not exactly sure I know where that is anymore," she said, looking at the raw energy of the source.

"Come on, we'll figure it out." Turning, they walked back the way they had come.

* * *

Andy opened his eyes and found Abby still stroking his hair and looking down at him. She smiled, and it was like the sun just cresting the horizon at sunrise. He sat up and took her hand.

"Abby, there is someone I want you to meet." They got up and raced back to where the others waited.

Everyone was astounded when Andy informed them that Donella was his sister. There were congratulations all around plus some confusion about calling her Emilia or Donella. Emilia told them that, as the Dragon Summoner, Braylynn had given her the name Donella, and that is what she would go by.

Emilia gave a private apology to Abby for summoning Andy when she did. Abby told her she understood. Emilia hugged her and told her how glad she was that Abby gave her brother such happiness.

Bart brought everybody's attention back to the business at hand. "Well, lad, where do we go from here?"

"First and foremost, I have to get Cleo to the Border Lands so she can return the stone and free up the Border Lands warriors," Andy responded. "Bart, I need you to go to Fenner and tell Maccus to get his riders to Albion."

"Albion?" Diminitus said incredulously. "Why in the name of the gods would we want to go there? They are nothing but farmers and sheepherders."

"I will let Abby tell you. It was her idea, after all," he said, smiling. They all looked expectantly toward Abby.

"Albion is a sham," Abby explained.

"I don't follow," Diminitus said.

"The people of Albion have no real protection, so they went to the other extreme."

"Meaning what?" Diminitus interrupted.

"Dim, just let her finish," Dain said, getting frustrated. Diminitus scowled but remained silent.

"They sing praises to Devon day and night in a shrine they built," Abby continued. "They swear undying loyalty to him, but it is all a lie. The Barons of Albion have always portrayed themselves to Devon as ruthless tyrants of the common folk, even sending reports of beheadings of traitors. But not a single person has ever been executed there. They do this so Devon will leave them alone and they can live as they wish, and for fifteen hundred years, this has worked. There is only a token garrison there."

"But would they welcome us and the troubles we bring?" Paolo wondered.

"They have been waiting for the day when they no longer need to pretend," Abby explained. "There are underground caves and tunnels where they have been storing weapons since Devon came to power. They have just been waiting for everyone to unite. And someone to lead them," she said, looking at Andy.

"How do you know all this, Abby?" Bart asked.

Her face took on a sad aspect. "My father told me shortly before he was killed. I don't know how he knew, but he would not have told me if he didn't know it for a fact. He also told me, if I ever needed protection, I would find asylum there."

Just then Dain raised up his hand, commanding everyone to silence. He cocked his head to the side, listening.

"What is it?" Leah said, whispering.

"A rider approaches," he replied. Soon everyone else heard the hoof beats, as well.

"Bart, get an arrow ready," Dain said urgently. Bart took out one of the godstone-tipped arrows, set it on the string, and aimed it down the trail. Dain and Leah went on opposite sides to cut off any retreat. There were noises of twigs breaking and leaves crunching as the rider bounded into view. At the sight of everyone, the rider reined in his horse. The raven symbol, visible on his shield as the horse swung around, let everyone know what he was.

"Don't move, Raptor," Bart said, his voice like ice. "Twitch even a muscle and your heart is mine."

With Dain holding his sword drawn and Leah keeping her spear at the ready, they came out of concealment and blocked the trail to the rear. Andy stepped forward and placed himself between Bart and the horse.

"Lower your bow, Bart," Andy said calmly. "I know this man."

"He is the one who allowed us to escape," Dain said.

"Lieutenant Nyle. I see you came out on top in your fight with Tolbert," Andy said.

"Tolbert has joined his ancestors," Nyle replied. "I came to warn you. Devon is mobilizing his armies. You had better leave while you can."

"That was our intention," Andy said, watching the Raptor closely for signs of a decision for or against them. "And what is your intention, Lieutenant?"

"I have been a soldier all my life," Nyle began. "I have never questioned my superiors or Devon. But lately, I have been seeing signs of decay and rot in the ruling order of Vasara. When men like Tolbert are the type of man preferred to become a baron, then something is seriously wrong." He met Andy's eyes. "I am not going to lie to you. I have killed men without mercy in what I believed to be the line of duty. Now I am starting to question that duty. You told me I deserve a better master. Very well, Lord Dragon. I choose you."

"Now hold on," Andy said quickly. "That is not what I meant."

"Whether you meant it or not is irrelevant," Nyle said. "For good or ill, I have made my choice. Whether you accept me or not is up to you."

This was a hard decision for Andy to make. Should he let this Raptor join them and possibly turn on them at a crucial moment? He would be putting everyone's life at risk, if he were wrong. He wished Loki were here.

What do I do, Em? he asked his sister, mind to mind. *Should I trust him? I do not detect any deceit in his words.*

Andy thought for a moment. As a Raptor, he probably knew this land really well. He made up his mind. "I will trust you, Lieutenant. Do you know a quick way to Albion?"

"There are some secret paths the Raptors use that I can lead you through."

"Excellent. Okay, this is what we will do. Bart, you go to Fenner and get the riders. Leah, bring the faeries to Albion as quickly as you can."

"I will talk with Valencia," Leah said. "She will know how best to proceed."

"I am going to go back to Black River, Andros," Ala said. "If there is a battle coming, we will need the healers."

"Acacia and I will come with you, Ala," Paolo said. "We need to inform the villagers and also see if Brayton has returned."

"I will send some of the fauns with you, for protection," Pan offered.

"That sounds like a good idea," Andy agreed. "All right, Cleo and Emilia will come with me, and the rest will follow Nyle to Albion."

Andy took Abby aside. "I hate to leave you again."

"Don't worry," she said, putting on a brave face. "I will be fine. Besides, I think I am going to be needed in Albion, if the people there are to believe us. I have a feeling my father's name will help convince them that we will not betray their secret."

He kissed her and hugged her tight before letting her go. Andy watched them all go their separate ways in order to set in motion the events that would, hopefully, lead to the end of Devon's reign. He turned back toward his sister and Cleo.

"Are you ready?" he asked them.

"I am ready, Andros," Cleo said, "although a little apprehensive about flying."

"Don't worry," Emilia told her. "He is very good at keeping riders on his back."

Andy gave himself some room as he made his change. The black dragon lowered his long neck as Emilia flew Cleo into position on his back. When both were settled, Andy leaped into the air, powerfully thrusting his wings as he gained altitude. He circled once and steered a course across Lake Pleasant. Hopefully, they could accomplish everything in time. Andy had a feeling that Devon was going to strike hard and fast in the hope that one blow would settle it all.

CHAPTER 21

IT TOOK A DAY for Andy to traverse the distance across Lake Pleasant. He arrived in Bolivar just after sunrise. The back of Lyson's house had an enormous walled-in courtyard that Andy felt he could land in quite comfortably. He circled once before touching down, much to the astonishment of the staff who supported the place and who had obviously never seen a dragon. He waited until Cleo and Emilia were off his back before changing back to his human shape. Lyson was standing in the doorway when they set down and rushed out to meet them. He was not wearing his traditional military garb. Instead, he was dressed in a simple yet elegant black silk robe with a white shirt underneath. He also had a belt of gold disks encircling his waist. Hanging from this was his serpent-hilt sword. Cleo reached him first and gave her brother a fierce hug. She then reached into her bag and brought out the stone.

"By the gods," Lyson exclaimed. "I never thought this would happen in my time. Well done, sister."

"Thank you, Lyson," Cleo replied, "though it would not have been possible without the help of Andros and his sister, Donella, who also happens to be the Dragon Summoner."

"Welcome, Donella," Lyson greeted. "It is a pleasure and honor to meet Braylynn's Dragon Summoner." He took her hand and kissed it, and when Lyson lifted his head, Andy saw Lyson go wide eyed as he gazed upon Emilia.

"It is a pleasure to meet you, General," Emilia replied, smiling politely.

Andy secretly smiled to himself. Lyson seemed to be smitten with his sister, but Emilia, with all her powers of insight, didn't appear to notice. He didn't know if Lyson fully realized it, either. Andy had a suspicion of some goddess intervention; he imagined Braylynn liked to meddle when it came to affairs of the heart.

"Well, Andros, it appears you were successful all around," Lyson said as congratulations.

"Not without its cost, General," Andy replied sadly. "Loki didn't make it." The pain was still raw, and it hurt him to tell of it.

"I am sorry, Andros. I will miss that old wizard. Come inside. You can tell me all, and then we can discuss the next steps."

They went into the library where Andy had first met Cleo. Lyson poured wine for everyone and sat down. Andy told his tale from when they first left the Border Lands until the recovery of the stone of the Pillar of Fallon. Emilia told of her part, as well, up to the point when she'd summoned Andy.

"Where is Tori?" Cleo asked her brother.

"She is at the training yards, with your Vipers."

"Who is Tori? And what are Vipers?" Andy asked.

"Tori is my right arm," Cleo explained with pride and affection. "She is also my best friend and second-in-command. The Vipers are an elite fighting force, made up of the best warriors from each regiment in the Border Lands army. There are thirty of us. We take on the riskier missions." She downed her wine and stood up. "Come with me. I will introduce you."

Lyson had horses waiting, and they mounted up and rode to the outskirts of Bolivar, to the training yards. Emilia declined her horse and said she preferred to fly. The yards were quite extensive and represented every form of terrain the warriors might be required to fight upon.

At the bottom of the hill, in one ring about the size of a football field, were seven riders. Scattered throughout the field were wooden dummies, resembling what Andy assumed were demons. The warriors were in an inverted-V formation, meaning the riders on the outermost legs of the V were in the lead positions. At the point of the V was a female rider with no helmet on, her hair blowing free in the wind. She rode a white palfrey and kept her position in the center at the extreme rear.

"What are they doing?" Andy asked Cleo.

"They are doing what we call a 'Flying V,'" Cleo explained. "It is a deception maneuver. Tori, in the center, will pick out the demon she deems to be the biggest threat. They start out in a V to spread the demons into a line. When the riders on the wings reach the demons on both ends of that line, they peel off and circle back to the center, behind Tori. Each subsequent rider will do the same, so by the time Tori reaches what we call the boss demon, the V will have become a spear that will overwhelm it. Once they have ridden him down, Tori falls back, and the V reforms around her while she looks for the next target."

Andy watched as the maneuver unfolded. They had such precision and grace, it was like watching a piece of art in motion. The wingmen detached from the V with such incredible speed and agility that he was amazed the horses didn't simply roll over from the angle they were forced to make. As Cleo said, the last rider fell in behind Tori just before she reached the target. She had a godstone-tipped spear that exploded the wooden demon upon impact. The rest of the riders followed in her wake so that nothing remained but a few splinters of wood.

"That was the most amazing thing I ever saw," Andy said in awe. Cleo just looked at him and smiled with pride. She then gave two quick whistles, and the riders, without missing a beat, turned and galloped up to where Andy and the others watched. It was clear who the leader was. The riders formed two columns of three, with the woman on the white palfrey leading the way.

With his dragon sight, Andy was able to watch them the whole way up as if they stood right next to him. He could see that Tori was a beautiful woman. Unlike Cleo, who wore her hair braided, Tori's dark hair hung free with waves in it like the ocean during a tempest, its length falling just below her heart. Her dark brown eyes drank in and delighted in the life around her but also lent her face a mischievous air. Her light olive skin was smooth and flawless.

Tori's face was flush from the tactics they had just performed. The sweat on her brow and her winsome smile gave her face such a glow of excitement and adventure that Andy thought this was someone who just enjoyed being alive and was in harmony with every living thing around her. He was friends with her before she even spoke a word.

"Welcome back, boss," Tori said in a lighthearted manner, as if Cleo had not been out risking life and limb against what was probably the most powerful being in Vasara. "I take it you were successful, being that you are here."

"Was there ever any doubt?" Cleo responded, smiling.

"Not in my mind there wasn't." She jumped down and embraced her friend and commander.

"I wish you had been able to come with me, Tori," Cleo told her as they separated. "What the...?" Just then, Cleo started shaking and wiggling, patting and searching her leather armor. She reached under her shirt and pulled out a small white snake with a red stripe down its back. "Tori!" she shouted indignantly.

Tori was on the ground, roaring with laughter. The other riders were trying hard to suppress their smiles. "That's for not bringing me along," Tori said, trying to regain control.

"Does she do this often?" Andy whispered to Lyson.

"Oh yes," he replied. "Tori is quite the practical joker."

"Are you all right, Percy?" Cleo addressed the snake. The snake's tongue darted in and out, touching Cleo's nose.

"You're on a first-name basis?" Emilia asked, taking a step back. She was not a big fan of snakes.

"Percy is kind of like our mascot and good luck charm," Cleo explained. "Someone always carries him into battle when we ride."

"It's good to have you back, boss," Tori said, wiping her eyes.

"Yes, well, if you have gotten hold of yourself, we have some introductions to make," Cleo said, letting Percy curl around her arm. "This is Donella, Braylynn's Dragon Summoner."

"We are honored, Summoner," Tori said, inclining her head in a very formal manner. "The bond between warriors and faeries is long, and no one now alive has ever met someone of your abilities since the last Dragon Summoner perished fifteen hundred years ago. I hope that I may one day be able to fight by your side."

"It is a pleasure to meet you, Tori," Emilia said, warming up to this free spirit. "And I have a feeling we shall be fighting together a lot sooner than either one of us would wish."

"You may have noticed a black dragon earlier," Cleo continued, adding to her introductions. "This is Andros. He is that dragon.

"Andros the Black," Tori said, giving a deep bow. "A great honor it is to meet you."

"Why do you call me that?" Andy asked.

"Because it is who you are," Tori replied simply with an impish smile.

"Tori likes to give names and titles to people as the mood takes her," Cleo explained. "I imagine the name is supposed to inspire fear in a person's enemies. She calls me the Red Harpy," Cleo said, rolling her eyes.

"Scoff if you like, Cleo," Tori said, pushing her hair back behind her neck and then crossing her arms. "But no matter what other titles he has, it is Andros the Black that everyone is going to remember."

"We can debate that another day," Lyson said, interrupting. "Right now, we have plans to make. Let's go to the tavern. It's close."

"Sounds good to me," Tori said cheerily. She turned toward the other Vipers. "Herne, you and the others head back. We will be along shortly."

"You got it," he said, saluting smartly before he and the other riders wheeled their horses around and headed back to the training camps.

The tavern was a one-room structure with a high ceiling and wide beams. The bar ran the length of one wall, and a fireplace adorned the center of the opposite wall. Tables and chairs were scattered throughout. The clientele seemed to be mostly warriors along with a few of the regular folk of Bolivar. There was a thin, smoky haze in the air from some of the old-timers' pipes.

Tori bought everyone ale, and then they sat at the nearest table. She took a long draw from her tankard before setting it down on the table with a thunk, and then she leaned in close and spoke quietly.

"Lyson told me what you went after," she began, "but we didn't want to tell the others until we were sure of your success. I assume that the object of your quest is in that pouch at your side."

"It is," Cleo responded.

"We need to get it to the pillar as soon as possible," Andy added. "The Border Lands warriors need to set out quickly before Devon overwhelms us."

"There is something you need to know," Tori said soberly, putting all mirth and mischievousness aside. "I believe the demons know you have it."

"How would they know?" Emilia said. She had her wings tucked in and was wearing one of Cleo's cloaks so as not to draw too much attention.

"I don't know, but there is a score of them hovering around the pillar, and we can't move them off. I also think one or two may be demon lords. They have concentrated a lot of power there."

"Tori and I have been discussing tactics," Lyson said. He gave a sidelong glance to Tori.

"What is it?" Cleo said apprehensively, noticing the look.

After a moment's pause, Tori answered. "All the Vipers are going to attack at once, and when the demons are all engaged, you put the stone back."

"No!" Cleo shouted, drawing the attention of everyone in the room. "That is suicide," she whispered fiercely, "and I will not allow it! We will find another way."

"We looked at every other way, boss," Tori said. "This is the only one I can see that gives us the best chance at success."

Cleo's blue eyes flashed green, which tended to happen when great emotion was conflicting within her. She seemed about ready to accept the fact that there might be no other way when Andy spoke up.

"Did you consider my sister and me in your planning?" Andy asked Tori.

"No, we didn't," Tori answered. "Does that mean you are going to join this fight?"

"I don't see why not," Emilia said. "Braylynn told us the whole reason for the Summoner-dragon link is battle advantage, and it looks like that is what we need right now."

"Yes!" Tori said, pounding her fist on the table, jostling everyone's drink and startling the tavern patrons once more.

Just then, there was some movement by the front door and some busy whispering. Andy looked up to see a faerie with red wings had just entered. Emilia followed his gaze, and an expression of joy came over her face.

"Brie!" Emilia exclaimed as she jumped up and hugged her faerie sister.

"Hello, Donella," Brie said smiling. "I hope we haven't come too late."

"Whatever are you doing here?" Emilia asked in wonderment. She noticed Brie was dressed for battle.

"Valencia sent us," Brie replied. "She thought you might need some help."

"Us?"

"There are thirty faeries that came up with me. They are on the outskirts of Bolivar at Faerie Hall."

"I am so glad to see you," Emilia said, taking her by the hand. "Come over and meet the others."

Introductions were made, and Brie went on to tell everyone why she was there. She told them Valencia had received instructions from Braylynn that their help would be needed here and so they had set out from Laurel Hollow four days ago. Tori found it interesting that there were just as many faeries as there were Vipers.

They discussed several battle plans for the next couple of hours, eventually deciding on a plan of action, then Lyson, being the general he was, leapt onto the nearest empty table to address those in the tavern.

"Warriors!" he shouted. All talking ceased and every eye turned to him. "For fifteen hundred years, we have waged constant battle against the demons, ever since Devon stole one of the stones from the

Pillars of Fallon." He paused, building up the moment. "Today, my sister Cleo has returned from a quest to return to us that very stone."

Cleo, sensing the timing was right, stood up and unveiled the stone for all to see. A deafening cheer went up from every throat in the tavern, and instead of dying down, it became a chant that drifted outside. Those nearest the door left to spread the word, and the sound of celebration seemed to come from every corner of Bolivar.

Lyson held up his hands for over five minutes before the crowd started to quiet down once more.

"Today we fight a battle unlike any we have fought before. The demons know we have the stone, and they will sacrifice any of their number to insure it never reaches the pillar, thereby limiting their numbers passing through the corridor. But it will avail them little, for joining our ranks will be thirty of Braylynn's faeries." Another cheer went up at that news, and Brie smiled to hear it.

"Also fighting with us," Lyson said, once order had been restored, "are two beings the likes of which have not been seen in Vasara since Devon stole the crown." Once again, he paused for dramatic effect. "I give you Andros the Black, Dragon of the Five."

"I told you," Tori whispered to Cleo.

"*Shh!*" Cleo said.

"And also Donella, Dragon Summoner of Braylynn," Lyson continued. "They have agreed to join in our struggle. With their help, we cannot fail!"

The crowd erupted once more. Many gathered around Andy and Emilia, pumping their hands and slapping their backs in gratitude. Afterwards, Lyson told all officers in the room to gather at his home for further instructions. He then sent messengers to all off-duty officers to make their units ready. No one was sitting this fight out.

"Get the Vipers ready," Cleo told Tori. "I will meet you at the Corridor."

"You got it, boss," she said as she stood, downed the last of her ale, and headed for the door.

Brie turned toward Emilia. "I am going to go with Lyson, so we can coordinate the attack with the faeries. Be careful out there. I've sent some crows out to scout around, and they tell me the number of demons is vast."

"I will be careful, dear Brie," Emilia said, giving her a parting hug as if it might be their last. Andy gave his sister a nod as she brought her green eyes up to meet his, letting her know he wondered the same: how many friends were going to die today?

*   *   *

Emilia sat on the grass beneath a tall evergreen tree. Her eyes were open, but it was not the scene in front of her face that she was seeing. The dragon eye was glowing brightly as she saw the battlefield through Andy's eyes. They had decided to see how things lay before the actual operation started.

The Corridor was a flat expanse with small shrubs and sparse knife-edge grass. The image before her eyes, though, was like a picture from hell. Demons of every size and description dotted the plain like ants. Some walked, some flew, and others slithered, using their hands, claws, and teeth as often as their clubs and spears.

Warriors, men and women, engaged the demons from every position. It was more of a melee than any kind of coordinated attack. The demons, like the lizard creatures in the glade, disappeared into a vaporous cloud when fatally struck.

What do you think? Emilia asked her brother.

This won't be easy, he replied with apprehension. *I am going to fly close to the pillar.*

She watched as he flew to the southeast corner of the Corridor. Emilia could see the pillar standing tall, the bright sunlight reflecting off its white surface. Surrounding it were many demons. Standing right next to it were four cloaked beings, which Emilia assumed must be demons, as well.

Andy was circling high and heading back when shots of fire hit him in the head. He roared in pain as he started spinning out of control. Emilia, seeing and feeling what had happened through the link, sprang from her sitting position and started to streak across the

Corridor. Pulling the comb out of her hair, she brought Braylynn's staff to bear on any demon that got in her way. She could see her brother still spiraling as he drew closer and closer to the earth. She started flying up toward him.

Andy, you need to change! she screamed in his mind. *I can catch you, but not if you're a dragon.*

Emilia's words penetrated as she saw Andy change back into his human self. With his arms and legs spread out, his descent seemed to slow as his sister flew up from underneath and grabbed him under the arms.

The dragon mark on her leg became incandescent as it glowed with power. Emilia reached inside herself and sought out the power of the red dragon that was a part of her. She had it. She wrapped her legs around Andy's while she held his chest and flew like a comet crossing the heavens. Several of the flying demons got in her path only to dissolve into vapor.

Emilia was searching the ground for a place to land when she saw Cleo's Vipers assembling beneath a grove of trees, so she altered her course to land by them. When she touched down, Cleo and Tori rushed over.

"What happened?" Tori exclaimed, having drawn both her swords in the event that demons were in pursuit. "Are you hurt?"

"I'm all right," Andy said, waving everybody off. "I injured my pride more than anything else. Although it would have been a lot worse if my sister hadn't saved my butt. Thanks, Em," he said, giving his sister a gratified smile.

"What hit you?" Cleo asked with her swords drawn, as well.

"Demons with magic surround the pillar," Emilia told them.

"It is as I said," Tori remarked, sheathing her swords. "There are demon lords on the field of battle. We will need to rethink our strategy, boss."

Andy rubbed his head. It still throbbed from the blow. "No, my sister and I need to rethink our strategy. You should proceed as planned. The demon lords will be our responsibility."

*   *   *

The horses stomped their hooves with impatience. Those warriors not already engaged with the enemy waited at the jump-off point at the beginning of the Corridor. Lyson looked up and down the line. He had never seen armor and shield shine so brightly. Everyone knew the importance of this fight, and every face bore the grim determination of the knowledge that they might be trading their lives for its success. The warriors had formed a square around Cleo and her Vipers; the plan was to get them, unmolested, to the pillar. Brie and her faeries were in the extreme rear. When the march began, they would provide aerial cover.

Cleo and Tori were in the middle of a circle of Vipers. Should Cleo fall, Tori would pick up the burden of getting the stone back on the Pillar of Fallon.

Lyson looked up, scanning the sky for the black dragon with the Dragon Summoner astride him. This was to be the signal to move. Andy had told him to ride once he saw the dragon fire and heard the dragon's roar. Lyson, however, looked not so much for the signal as he did for the green-eyed faerie whose face he could not seem to get out of his head. He turned toward his sister and, catching her eye through the ranks of warriors, lifted his sword to his face in silent salute. Cleo saw and returned it. Tori looked dead ahead, the wind blowing her hair, while the rest of her seemed carved from stone, so still in her determination. Lyson was glancing back at Cleo when he saw something white flash around her throat. He smiled as he realized Percy was going to have a front-row seat in the battle. *May he bring us all luck*, he thought.

Lyson heard the roar before he saw him, and, as the sunlight gleamed off his golden talons, Andy sent a jet of flame skyward. Lyson raised his sword. All his commanders followed suit. Hands grasped their reins tight. The chomp of bits and heavy breathing through the nostrils gave testament to the readiness of horses and warriors.

The swords dropped, and, as one, the warriors sprang forward into the Corridor. The air was stale and smelled of sulfur. The number of demons for the first couple of miles was light, and Andy blazed back and forth with his fire, getting them out of the warriors' path. But then, the attacks became more frenzied. Demons en masse attacked the columns from all sides. Those warriors on the outer fringe had to separate in order to fend off the monsters. The first demons they encountered were as tall as the average man but covered with scaly skin and had claws on their hands and feet. Most were on the ground, but those that flew and tried to penetrate the inner ring were quickly dispatched by the faeries.

Lyson tried hard to steer them toward the pillar. He looked up and saw Andy and Emilia fighting many demons at once. These demons had no magic, so their only asset was to attack in large numbers. Lyson's heart nearly stopped when he saw a score of flying demons knock Emilia off Andy's back and swarm on top of her.

"Donella!" he yelled as he wheeled his mount over to where she was trapped. As he got close to the mound of demons on the ground, climbing on top of one another like ants scurrying into their anthill, he could see an orange glow blossoming in the center of the pile. Suddenly, an ear-splitting crack and the smell of burnt flesh filled the air, as the demons were blasted upward and turned into black vapor. Emilia got to her feet and brushing herself off when Lyson dismounted.

"Are you all right?" he asked with concern.

"Yes," she said, smoothing out her dress and wiping a hand across her brow. "I was careless and tried to take on too many at once. A mistake I will not make again."

Andy circled to where they were. *You're not hurt, are you?* he asked worriedly. *Lyson, can you help her back?*

I'm fine, Emilia said. *Nobody needs to help me back. I'll be right there.*

"Donella, are you sure?"

"Yes, General, I am fine!" She immediately regretted her words. "I'm sorry, Lyson. I'm mad at myself more than anything else. Forgive me."

"I understand," he said, smiling. "There are many times in battle when I have felt the same way." He put an affectionate hand on her shoulder and looked deep into her green eyes. Emilia broke eye contact first.

"There is no time for this, General. Everything hangs in the balance right now."

"You are right, of course," he said, stepping back. He quickly mounted as the demons, overcoming their confusion, started moving toward them. He looked at her one last time. "I will see you at the pillar." And, digging his heels into his horse's flanks, he galloped away.

*   *   *

Emilia watched as Lyson rode to rejoin the column. She was a little shaken by the way he had looked at her. There was little time to dwell on it, though, as more demons came rushing in. She took to flight and started blasting the demons below her.

What happened down there? Andy asked his sister when she caught up with him.

I don't want to talk about it, she responded crisply. Andy let it go and started talking about the plan at hand.

We need to get rid of some if not all of the demon lords before Cleo and Tori get there. Any ideas?

"I don't believe we can take them all at once. I think we will have to lure them away one at a time. I have a strong feeling they can fly, so, if we can get them to chase us, we should be able to take them out."

Let's just hope we can get enough of them in time, Andy said.

"If we can remain the main threat to them, it should give Cleo the opening she needs."

A lot of people are going to die, aren't they?

Emilia didn't answer. What could she say? She settled back down on his back, and they winged their way toward the demon lords. They needed to end this quickly.

*   *   *

Cleo kept looking toward the sky for more attacks. They had been harassed several times by flying demons since starting, but the Vipers had been able to fight them off. Tori had a gash on her forearm from a demon raking a claw across it before losing its head to her swords. The outer riders kept peeling off as they were engaged, leaving a ring two columns deep with half the distance to the pillar left to go. Pretty soon, it would be the Vipers alone. Lyson had been able to stick with them so far.

"Can you see Andros?" Cleo yelled to Tori.

"He was heading east with a demon lord on his tail," she yelled back. The pounding of the horses' hooves against the hard-packed dirt made a thunderous noise as they galloped on.

The warriors of the Border Lands were second only to the riders of Fenner when it came to horsemanship. The warriors also had special talents granted to them by the gods. When fighting on horseback, they were able to lay the reins of their horses on the saddlebow, leaving both hands free to wield weapons as they guided their horses with just a gentle nudge of the knees.

The Vipers had special saddles with saddlebows that could release another set of stirrups on the same level as the top of the saddle. This allowed them to fight from a standing position on the back of the horse. The Vipers were the only warriors in Vasara who'd trained long enough to truly master this form of riding, and Cleo and Tori were the best.

Cleo could see the pillar now. As she thought, the Vipers were pretty much alone, except for five or six warriors and her brother Lyson. She looked up to see Andy and Emilia battling two demon lords at once. She watched as they separated, causing the demons to split up, as well. Blasts of fire and lightning lit up the sky. She figured there was probably only one demon lord left at the pillar. Soon she and Tori would put their plan into action. They were the only ones who knew what would happen. It was necessary because believability was key in this situation.

The last of the demons surrounding the pillar started to surge forward to meet the Vipers' threat. The demon lord faced Cleo, his face cloaked in shadow and his hands clasped together in front of him. Cleo tapped her temple twice, letting Tori know she was ready. Tori gave a silent nod. She looked as if she wanted to convey more, but instead set her face in a grim expression for the task that could wind up killing them all.

The Vipers were a tightly trained unit, so, when Cleo gave a command, no one took time to question it, which could have proved disastrous in battle. She gave one now.

"Vipers, left!" she ordered.

On the next hoof beat, all horses made a shallow, arcing, ninety-degree turn. All except one. Tori turned right and headed out of the circle. Before she reached the edge, Cleo smashed a hand down on her saddlebow, extending her stirrups. The stirrups were designed to lock her feet into place, preventing her from sliding out. Each rider knew a special twisting motion that would free her feet in a hurry, if need demanded it. Cleo grabbed the front of her saddle to lift her legs up and slide into the stirrups. She then stood up in full view for all to see.

"Cleo, are you mad?" Lyson screamed. "You are going to get yourself killed!" He wheeled his horse hard left to follow.

Cleo untied the strings and opened the pouch at her side to take out the stone. Once she had the stone in her hands, she held it above her head. The demons screamed wildly when they saw it and made a mad rush for it. The Viper circle finally broke, as each warrior was engaged by several demons. Above the din and roar came an inhuman scream, high and piercing above all the rest. The demon lord by the pillar started to fly toward Cleo. The demons could come close to the Pillars, but, because they were made by the god Fallon, they could only get within five feet of it, so any stone on a pillar could not be removed by a demon. A stone off a pillar was a different matter, and the demon lord saw the chance to bend the power of the stone to his will.

Cleo gave a glance back and smiled. The bait had been taken. The demon lord, sensing something wrong, slowed his advance. All of a sudden, he felt a power emanating behind him. He looked back at Tori, who stood up in her stirrups, about to place the stone on the pillar.

"Tell me how this feels, you spawn!" Tori yelled as she placed the stone back where it belonged.

The demon shrieked in anger, but his cry was suddenly cut off as a golden talon emerged from his chest. The demon looked down dumbly at the protrusion before his essence was blown away on the wind and Andy climbed higher.

As soon as Tori placed the stone on the pillar, a ray of red light shot out from it to connect with the western stone. That stone illuminated to connect with the stone in the north and so on, until all the stones were connected once again. When it was complete, a great cry came out of the throat of every demon in the Corridor, and then, suddenly, they disappeared. The abrupt silence was deafening. All the warriors looked at one another in amazement.

* * *

It was a solemn group who gathered at the pillar. It seemed no one had escaped without a wound of some kind. Emilia was helping out where she could, using the goddess's healing power for those who were not beyond help. Brie and some of the other faeries were helping her locate the more seriously wounded.

"It was a high price, Cleo," Tori said, looking somberly at the carnage around her. After all the counting was done, more than five hundred warriors lay dead. Ten faeries also lay among the fallen.

"How many Vipers?" Cleo asked.

"Ten wounded and three dead."

"Cleo," Emilia called. "One of your Vipers is asking for you."

Cleo and Tori walked over to where Emilia stood over a fallen warrior. His armor was rent in many places, and blood was pooling beneath him.

"Herne!" Tori cried, rushing over to kneel beside him. "You hang in there. Everything is going to be all right." Cleo looked with sad eyes at Emilia, who shook her head in the negative.

"No, dear Tori," Herne replied weakly. "I go to Fallon's paradise now, where I will be waiting for you so that we may ride again side-by-side." He turned his eyes toward Cleo. "I hope I have served you well, boss."

"You were one of the best, Herne. We will never forget you."

"Thank you for that, and farewell." He closed his eyes as his breathing became more labored. He gave one last shuddering breath and died.

"The cost was indeed high, sister," Lyson said quietly, placing a hand sympathetically on her shoulder.

Just then, a captain of Lyson's command rode up.

"General, do you wish us to bury the dead?"

"No, Captain, there are far too many. Let a funeral pyre be built instead in the center of the Corridor."

"It would take weeks to get enough wood into the Corridor to achieve that," Tori remarked.

"If you can get them all into the center, I can take care of the rest," Andy told them.

"Yes," Lyson said. "It is fitting that a dragon, a creature of all five gods, sends them home. Thank you, Andros."

It was sundown by the time all of the fallen had been brought into the center of the Corridor. Still no demons had ventured in from the Plains. The word had gone out, and everyone within a half-day's travel came to pay their respects to the warriors who'd given their lives at what would come to be known as the Battle of the Stone. Afterwards, masons would erect a replica of the pillar and stone as a memorial to the dead.

A huge circle had formed around the fallen, although they were far enough away so as not to be burnt. They heard the dragon's lamenting cry come from the east, where the pillar whose stone had been bought and returned with the highest price of all.

Andy circled several times and then came to hover over the dead. He let loose with his dragon fire, which was ten times hotter than any wood fire. He sprayed them for several minutes. When his flame was out, he gave a thrust of his powerful wings and wheeled off to the west.

Emilia then stepped forward and closed her eyes as her green necklace started to glow. She made small swirling motions with her hands, causing the sand around the ashes to funnel up and form a pyramid, and, when the shape was perfect, a white-hot beam shot from her palm and turned the sand to crystal. As she let it go, the moonlight reflected off the sides of the pyramid, giving it an otherworldly glow. There was no crying. No mournful songs or chants, just a profound quiet for the voices that had been silenced.

* * *

Andy and Emilia were sitting outside in Lyson's courtyard, watching the sun come up. They rose early and took their coffee outside. Brie stopped by and told them the faeries were leaving immediately and would see them in Albion. Lyson had joined them shortly after Brie left.

"We will need to leave soon," Andy said. "When can your people be ready to move?"

"We are always in a state of readiness," Lyson explained. "The first regiments will move out tonight. Some will go south and meet up with you in Albion. Others will go north and come down from Dragonsgate. We will take out every garrison we can on the way."

"Remember, give them a chance to surrender first," Emilia said.

"You have a kinder heart than I do, Donella," Lyson said. "I prefer not to leave enemies behind me."

"I know, General, and it is sound military thinking. But everyone should have a chance at a choice of living in a Vasara without Devon's rule," she explained.

"I understand." He looked at her as if he were trying to etch her face and features into his memory. "You said in the Corridor this was not the time. Is now the time?"

Emilia could see something close to pain on his face, but his military exterior would not let it through. She seemed to be growing fond of this Border Lands general, and she didn't exactly know why that should be. She gave him what hope she could.

"I promise we will speak when all has been settled."

He seemed to accept that. "'Til then," he said as he kissed her hand. He reached out to shake Andy's hand. "I will see you at

Albion." And with that, he turned and walked back inside. Not long after, Cleo and Tori came out to see them off.

"Well, Andros the Black, it looks as if we will have the chance to fight side-by-side one more time," Tori said with a little too much enthusiasm, Andy thought. Going up against Devon again did not thrill him at all.

"Tori and I will be on the boats," Cleo said, "so we shouldn't be too long behind you."

"I will send Bart to meet you in Black River," Andy said.

"I'll tell you, Andros, I miss that crazy archer," Cleo said, smiling. "He was a great traveling companion, and he could always make me laugh."

"Yeah, we certainly could've used his bow here."

"We should make ready to go," Emilia said.

"Farewell, Summoner," Tori said, giving her a hug. "I look forward to fighting with you again, as well."

"Goodbye, Tori. I... What...?" Emilia started shaking her clothes wildly, trying to get out whatever was in there. Eventually, Percy fell to the ground as Tori held her sides, laughing. Cleo and Andy were laughing, as well. "Tori, you do that again, and I will turn you into a toad and have Percy eat you!"

"Can she do that?" Tori asked Andy, wide-eyed.

"I have no idea, but I wouldn't test her on it." Andy could tell Emilia wasn't mad at Tori. She just didn't like snakes all that much.

"Don't be too mad, Donella," Tori said good-naturedly.

"Oh, I'm not mad, Tori. Just know, I owe you one," she said, narrowing her eyes.

Andy moved into the middle of the courtyard and made his change. Emilia flew over and landed on his back, taking her position at the base of his neck as Andy lifted off and flew toward Albion.

CHAPTER 22

ABBY WAS WALKING down the main road through Albion when a dark shadow passed overhead. Looking up, her heart surged in her breast as a black dragon flew to the outskirts of the town. She ran to her horse, which was tethered just up the street by the town's stables. Once in the saddle, she galloped out of town in the direction she'd seen the dragon fly.

If anyone had told her that, one day, she would fall in love with a dragon, she would have told them they were out of their mind. When she came to the edge of the wood to a clearing, she could see two figures walking toward her. One paused a moment upon seeing her and then started to run. Abby galloped to where they were and, when she reached them, flung herself from her horse and into Andy's arms. Andy held her tight, stroking her hair. They didn't say a word to each other. Abby pulled her head back to better look into his hazel eyes. Then, putting her hands on the side of his head, she pulled him in to give him a kiss he wouldn't soon forget. Emilia coughed lightly from behind, and Abby pulled away.

"Oh, I'm sorry, Donella," Abby said, her cheeks slightly flushed.

"That's all right, Abby," Emilia replied, smiling and giving her a hug. "I can understand your distraction."

"Yes, *umm*... How are things coming along here, Abby?" Andy asked, somewhat flustered.

Emilia laughed loudly. "Andy, sometimes you can be such a goofball. I'll wait for you two up ahead."

"I'm sure I don't know what you mean by that!" he shouted after her. "Are you all right? All injuries healed?" he asked, scrutinizing her closely.

"Oh, yes. Ala arrived day before yesterday and started ladling some foul concoction down my throat, so it was either get better or endure that stuff for several more days," she said, wrinkling her nose at the thought of it. She hooked her arm into his as he grabbed the reins of her horse, and they walked back to town. She filled him in on who was there and where they were meeting on a daily basis to discuss the strategies of the day. Devon had wasted no time in unleashing his forces upon them. Nyle had led them at a furious pace in order to reach the Tear River and across the Wizard's Bridge.

"What is the Wizard's Bridge?" he asked her when Emilia rejoined them.

"I read about it many years ago. It was made by the three wizards. By joining their powers, they made a bridge of magic that was to benefit all of Vasara. It disappears to allow ships to pass through, as well as provide a commerce route between the northern and southern halves of Vasara. One thing no one realized, though, is that, it seems when Vasara is under attack, it will not allow an enemy to cross."

"Why is that?" Emilia asked.

"No one knows. This is the first time it has ever happened. Whenever Devon's troops step onto the bridge, it vanishes, and they fall into the river. So now, they stay on one side, and we are confined to the other. There are archers along the banks, so even the faeries will not attempt to cross over."

"Is Valencia here then?" Emilia asked.

"Yes. We will see everyone at Baron Weylin's manor."

* * *

They walked into the north end of the town of Albion, to an inn. The name on the sign out front read *Bella's*. Music and raucous laughter drifted out onto the street. The building was two stories, the top floor dedicated to rooms for rent. Attached to the back was a kitchen with a smoke stack coming off the roof that filled the air with the pleasant aroma of cooking vegetables and meats. Andy suddenly realized how hungry he was. He would need to find dinner soon or else go out and hunt. Andy also caught a whiff of roasting coffee beans and smiled. He remembered Loki telling him there were coffee bean growers in Albion, the best in the land.

There were several wool and clothing shops, since sheep were the main commodity here. The streets were awash with every race in Vasara, most citizens gathered there for the coming confrontation.

When he and the girls reached the center of town, Andy noticed the remains of a fallen statue on the ground.

"What happened here?" he asked, picking up some of the fragments.

"The people of Albion couldn't wait to throw off their cloak of deception when we told them all that had transpired at the White Castle," Abby explained. "The few garrison soldiers who were here were rounded up and imprisoned. The local population took great delight in smashing this statue of Devon to pieces. They used to gather around it and sing praises to it. Now, they sing some rather crude, off-color songs," she said, smirking.

They came to the baron's manor, which actually was more like a public hall than a personal residence. Abby explained that the barons of Albion felt they should not live in splendor from the exploits of the local population. Therefore, they had designed the manor with the idea that it belonged to the people. A modest residence for the baron and his family was in the rear, a fact never made known to outsiders, however.

The trio climbed the steps to the main doors. As Abby opened the doors and they all stepped inside, every head in the room turned to see who had entered.

"Donella!" a female voice from the left cried out. Emilia looked and caught a flash of autumn-colored wings moving through the crowd as the queen of the faeries made her way toward them. Emilia ran to meet her halfway and embraced her.

"You do not know how happy it makes me to see you here, my queen," she said, her eyes glistening.

"Well, I'm not about to let my subjects face a danger that their queen would not," Valencia said, smiling. "It is good to see you, Andros," she said, hugging him as well. "I take it you were successful in the Border Lands."

"Yes, we were," he replied. "Let's go to where the others are, and I will fill you all in. Then you can tell us how things stand here."

The main hall into which they walked had mostly staff and messengers milling in it. In a large room off to the side, they found Dain, Leah, Paolo and a short, balding man with merry eyes and a long pointed white beard who Andy assumed must be Baron Weylin. Hugs and greetings were exchanged all around, as well as introductions.

"It is a pleasure to meet you, Lord Dragon," Weylin boomed cheerily. He had a deep, clear, and resounding voice. Andy had no doubt he could be heard from far away. He gave a slight wince at the title the baron used.

"Please, Baron, just Andros is fine. If anyone is deserving of a title, it is Paolo here," Andy said, nodding in Paolo's direction.

"All in the gods' good time," Paolo interjected, smiling. "For now, you are the leader of this avalanche of freedom you've started."

Andy, feeling exhausted, plopped down into a deep-cushioned chair near the hearth, where a fire merrily burned. One person who was noticeably missing was Bart. Andy asked Dain about that.

"He's down at Bella's with Diminitus, drinking and dicing," Dain said, running his fingers through his hair. "He was the last one across the Wizard's Bridge. The Raptors were hot on his tail when he came out of Fenner. They almost caught him at the bridge, but it started disappearing right behind him as he rode across."

"This bridge is the strangest thing I ever heard of," Andy commented. "I wish Loki were here to tell us about it." He paused for a moment as he gazed into the fire and thought of his friend. "Where does everything stand right now?"

"Paolo, can you bring the map over?" Dain said.

The future king of Vasara, if everything went as planned, spread the map out on the low table by the fire while everyone leaned over it.

"This is where the bridge is," Dain began, pointing to a spot just below the mouth of where Lake Pleasant emptied into the Tear River. "Devon's archers occupy the northern bank, to make sure nothing flies over. There are also small detachments spread out every five miles or so down the length of the Tear. Raptors are out there, as well, but they are hard to spot."

"How do you know this, if you are trapped here?" Emilia asked.

"We have our scouts," Dain said, winking.

"Scout, you mean," Leah said, crossing her arms. Emilia burst out laughing. "What?" Leah asked, puzzled as she raised an eyebrow.

"It's nothing," Emilia said, smiling, "You just reminded me of someone."

"Who?"

"Oh, you'll meet her soon enough. I think you'll find you have a lot in common."

"We could cross the bridge if we wanted to," Dain continued, "but then we would be picked off piecemeal. Leah flying by herself can find holes in their lines."

"Did the Fenner riders make it across?" Andy asked.

"No. Bart was a day or so ahead of them, after he delivered his message."

"I found Maccus," Leah added. "He wanted me to thank you for waiting and to let you know Lily had twins."

Andy looked down and smiled to himself. He was glad he didn't have to tear Maccus away from his family before his children were born. It may have seemed small in the scheme of things, but to Andy, it was a steady, burning ember in the heart of his soul that warmed his spirit, knowing that, in spite of everything, life kept happening as it always did, even though the mighty would rise up to shake the very foundations of the earth.

"They make small raids into any encampments they find," Leah continued. "It's harassment, mainly."

Andy thought that should help somewhat. At the very least, it would keep Devon's troops from being well rested, if they were constantly on alert. He started feeling restless all of a sudden, as if time had become his enemy.

"What are your thoughts, Andros?" Valencia asked, sensing his mood. She happened to be standing next to a window that the setting sun was pouring through, and it made her red hair look like it was on fire.

"I am feeling like we need to strike soon," he replied.

"I have to agree with you," Dain confirmed. "Devon's army is seasoned and organized. They can last a long time. We on the other hand have no supply trains to feed and equip us for any sustained period." He looked at Andy soberly. "We probably only have the ability to hit Devon once."

"I agree," Paolo interjected. "The blow we strike must be the one that ends it."

"What does that mean exactly?" Emilia asked.

"It means when we leave here, we go straight for the White Castle and cut off the head of the snake," Dain answered, adjusting the sword on his hip. "The common soldier has no love for Devon, so it is hoped they will desert. The rest we will have to fight until they surrender or die."

"There is something else you should know, Andros," Paolo said.

"What?" Andy said, not liking the sound of what might come next.

"Valencia, could you bring the arrow over?"

The faerie queen walked over to a small bookcase that had an arrow resting on top of it and brought it over to Andy. He took it in his hands and immediately felt how heavy the thing was.

"My god!" he exclaimed. "How is it possible this thing can fly?"

"There is some magic involved in it, that's for sure," Dain said. "It is fired with an overly large crossbow. We only saw one archer using it, a giant of a man with huge arms. But look at the arrowhead."

The head of the arrow was cone-shaped, but instead of being smooth, there were razor-sharp fins etched into its surface. It would spin like a drill. It was a cruel-looking device.

"One of the fauns was hit with this," Paolo said with a look of disgust, remembering the sight. "It blew a hole in his chest two-hands wide."

"It is our belief," Valencia said, "that this is meant as a warning for you."

"I don't understand."

"What she means, my friend," Paolo said, "is that we think this arrow will pierce the armored skin of a dragon."

Up until now, Andy had thought he was pretty much immune to the attacks of the common soldier. It was a sobering thought to realize he could be shot out of the sky like that.

"Well, we're just going to have to make adjustments for this in our planning. We will spend the next few days going over it," Andy said, standing up. "Cleo and her team should be here by then. Lyson's warriors coming from the south around Lake Pleasant will probably come in by week's end." Thinking of Cleo made Andy realize something about the ships.

"With Devon's army amassed on the other side of the river, they won't be able to dock in Black River."

"I know what you're thinking," Dain said, "but don't worry. Bowen was able to sneak a couple of ships into the lake, and they will inform the other captains to land at the docks not far from here."

"Excellent," Andy said. "Now I need to eat something before I pass out."

"Let's go to Bella's," Abby said. "The food is excellent and there are rooms for you and your sister."

* * *

The inside of Bella's was dimly lit but extremely clean. This was due to the fact that the owner, for whom the tavern was named, was a stickler for cleanliness. Bella ran a tight inn, and anyone who even smelled like they hadn't bathed in a week was denied entrance. She was a short, matronly woman with brown hair always done up in a bun. She'd never married. The inn was her husband, she would say, and more demanding than any man. She had three serving maids in her employ plus one huge, hulking brute named Sloane.

Sloane was a one-man security force. Standing at almost seven feet tall with muscles bulging from his large frame, he towered over the largest of patrons. His head was completely bald, and he wore a gold earring in his right ear. Sloane also had a wicked-looking scar going down the side of his neck that lent a fearsome aspect to his already intimidating looks.

Andy struck up a friendship with Sloane almost immediately. To kind and respectful people, Sloane was a gentle person. Only when someone chose to offend Bella or her inn did his other nature come out, and those people tended to find themselves on their backsides in the middle of the street.

Andy also found out that Sloane had a weakness for the female voice raised in song, and Abby was able to bring the man to tears. Sloane told him that Abby sang at the inn every night, and the place was always packed. Abby was a treasure, he told Andy, and he would be extremely angry with anyone who allowed harm to come to her. He gave Andy a hard look.

"Don't worry, Sloane," Andy said, raising his hands. "I want to keep her out of danger just as much as you. But she does have her own mind about such things."

"That's true," he responded.

Andy was amazed at how everyone wanted to be Abby's protector. They all loved her in their own way. Actually, he wasn't really amazed when he thought about his own affection for her.

Shortly after arriving at the inn, Andy found Bart and Diminitus, just as Dain had said, drinking and shooting dice, with Diminitus's voice going up an octave after each throw as he accused Bart of cheating.

After their game, Bart filled him in on his meeting with Maccus.

"I'm a little worried about them being out there all alone," he said, "especially with the Raptors roaming around unchecked."

"I know," Andy said. "And there is no telling when the Border Lands warriors will be coming down from the north. I do have an idea to get them some help, though," and he outlined his plan for Bart. He then told Bart to check the docks periodically over the next couple of days for Cleo's arrival. Bart assured him he would.

* * *

On the morning of the second day, Andy found himself in the middle of Lake Pleasant, swimming with the tagen, when, all of a sudden, the tail of one wrapped itself around his leg and started to pull him to the bottom. He struggled frantically but couldn't free himself. In his panic, he opened his mouth to scream only to have water come rushing in.

I can't breathe! I'm going to drown, he thought. Then the oddest thing happened. Someone was calling his name, and he caught a faint smell of rotten eggs. He woke up in the inn as a cloaked figure stood over his bed, his hands squeezing Andy's throat to cut off his air. Andy tried kicking and hitting to no avail. It did not even occur to him to reach for the source.

Running feet sounded on the stairs and then down the hall. The door was kicked in, causing one of the hinges to splinter off the frame. Tori was there with both swords out and her eyes drawn down in a feral look.

"*Ahh!*" she yelled as the twin blades sliced through the cloaked stranger's head and stomach. The hands let go, and the figure dissolved into black smoke that let out a careening wail as it floated through the beams of the ceiling.

Andy sat up, gasping for breath. The room was suddenly crowded now as everyone rushed to see if he was all right. Ala sat beside him and looked intently into his eyes.

"Andros, are you all right?" Abby said with a fearful look.

Andy, nodding his head and taking big gulping breaths, tried to signal he was all right and to give him a minute.

"I'm okay," he managed to say in a raspy voice. Just then, a gale-force wind blew in the shutters of the window. "That would be my sister," he mumbled, smiling weakly.

Sure enough, Emilia flew into the room, her staff blazing white. Leah was close behind her.

"Andy, I felt it through the link. Are you all right?"

"I'm fine, Em. I just need to catch my breath. Tori saved my life," he said, looking at her with gratitude. She just smiled and winked at him as she sheathed her swords.

"You've got the gods' own luck, lad," Bart said. "If Tori and Cleo hadn't arrived today and been downstairs, we never would have known that thing was here."

"How did you know?" Andy asked her, his breathing much easier.

"I could smell the sulfur. It was very faint, but I knew it had to be demon-related."

"Tori has the sharpest senses out of all of us," Cleo added.

"You mean you didn't smell it?" Ala asked.

"None of us did," Bart said. "That is why we were all surprised when Tori took off running up here."

"Tori," Cleo said, tilting her head toward the door and exiting.

"Are you sure you're okay?" Emilia asked again.

"I'm a little shaken, but I'll be all right."

"I want to go talk to Cleo about what that thing was," Leah said, heading for the door.

"I'll come with you," Bart said.

"If you're all right, I'm going to go down as well," his sister added. She transformed her staff and placed the pearl comb in her hair.

"Sure, I'll be down once I get myself together."

Ala kept checking him over. She pronounced him fit and told him it was okay to get dressed.

"You have some angry welts where he grasped your neck," she said. "I have a paste we can put on it that will help."

"Thank you, Ala."

"No need for thanks, Andros. It is what I do, after all," she said, smiling, as she got up to fetch the medicine.

Andy came downstairs about ten minutes later with Abby, wearing a scarf around his neck to keep dirt out of the paste Ala had applied.

"I can fix that, if you want," Emilia told her brother.

"I know," he said. "I just feel that, for minor stuff, I like to let my body heal itself." Emilia smiled at him. "Did you introduce Tori to everyone?"

"Just Leah," Bart said. "Everyone else was here when we came in."

They all sat down at one of the long tables in the common room.

"So what was that, Cleo?" Andy asked. "Was it a demon?"

"That is what Tori and I have been discussing. I think you should prepare for the worst, Andros."

"What do you mean?"

"It was a demon and not a demon," Tori added.

"Tori, you're not making sense," Bart said.

"Watch your tone, archer," Tori said dangerously. "Unless you would care to have your hand on the floor and never be able to draw a bow again."

"What is it with you warriors and cutting off hands?" Bart said indignantly.

Cleo burst out laughing. "He means no offense, Tori."

Her face softened. "I'm sorry, Bart. Sometimes I just snap."

"What do you mean exactly, Tori?" Emilia asked.

"What I mean, Summoner, is that thing we encountered is related to demons in some way, but it is not like any demon we fight in the Border Lands. If it were, even someone with a cold should have smelled him. His scent was masked. I just barely caught it. Also, there should have been a trail of bodies from the Plains to this inn, because a demon's only goal is to cause death and destruction."

"This one," Cleo said, "sought out Andros specifically."

"Devon, you think?" Abby asked.

"My gut tells me no," Tori said. "This is new to us, and I don't believe Devon knows anything about them."

"Them? You think there is more than one?" Leah asked.

"I do."

"Well, I haven't got time to worry about it," Andy said, rubbing the back of his neck and scratching at the scarf. "If it is not related to Devon, then it is not our focus."

"Whatever you say, Lord Black," Tori said, smirking.

"Will you stop that?" Andy said. "Now, the first order of business is to get the Vipers across the Tear."

"Why is that?" Leah asked.

"The riders of Fenner need help. How would you like to go up against the Raptors?" Andy asked Tori.

"The viper and the raptor are natural enemies." Tori smiled mischievously. "That should be fun."

This time, Leah had to laugh. "I like this girl!"

"I thought you might," Emilia said, smiling.

Bart looked over at Andy with some skepticism. "How do you plan to get them across?"

"With an illusion," Andy replied.

"Would you care to explain that?"

"Better yet, I will show you." He looked toward the inn's kitchen door and concentrated. "Abby, walk through the kitchen door please."

Andy had been practicing with Abby, so she knew what to expect. She walked up to the swinging oak door but, instead of pushing it, walked right through it and disappeared.

"Well, I'll be!" Bart exclaimed. "Where did she go?" Andy let go of the illusion, and Abby appeared standing in front of the real kitchen door.

"That is an amazing thing, Andros," Cleo said, "but how will this help us?"

"My sister and I will work together to create an image exactly like our side of the bridge—trees, grass, sky, and so on. We will push it forward as you ride behind it. We cannot mask the sound of your horses' hooves, but I am hoping they will be too perplexed to act."

"Also, we will have a few other distractions as you ride across," Emilia said.

"What exactly would that be?" Tori asked.

"Pan and his fauns will be firing arrows into their ranks as you ride."

"Sounds like you have it all worked out," Cleo said. "When do we do this?"

"At dusk, when the light will not be so good for them," Andy responded.

* * *

Andy saw Pan as he trotted down the path to the edge of the wood where they waited with the Vipers. Looking between the trees, they had an excellent view of the Wizard's Bridge. It was made out of gray stone and ran level from one shore to the other. Looking up and down the river, he could see the archers that lined the banks. This was not going to be easy. Not only did they have to duplicate the scenery that was directly in front, but also that on the sides, as well, to prevent those a little farther down the river from seeing them from a side angle.

The sun had just set, and it would soon be time to start. The bridge was wide enough to hold seven riders abreast. The Vipers would assemble into four ranks, with Cleo and Tori alone in front. There would be one more to join them. Nyle would go as well. Cleo was apprehensive at first, but Andy vouched for his trustworthiness, telling her his knowledge of the Raptors would be invaluable.

"Andros!" Pan boomed. "We are ready and just await your signal."

"Okay, Pan," Andy said. "We'll be ready soon ourselves." As Pan left, Andy called for Tera. She was to be the signal. Once everything was ready, she would play a special note that only Pan could hear. When the arrows started flying, the Vipers would begin their run.

"Andy!" Tera squealed. "Shall I blow it now?"

Andy couldn't help smiling. Out of all the inhabitants of Vasara, Tera was the only one who called him by his nickname. She said, since Donella was his sister and she was Donella's sister, then he was her brother, as well. He tried to tell her it was probably more complicated than that, but she would hear none of it.

"Not yet, Tera. Soon," he said. "I just want you close by, so I won't have to come find you."

Andy started to look around at everything Devon's archers would see from their side of the river, fixing in his mind's eye every leaf and blade of grass. He also looked closely at the air around him. This bit of knowledge he'd learned from his study of the Hudson River School artists back home. They painted landscapes in exacting detail, especially atmospheric conditions. For this illusion to work, he needed to duplicate any little haze, fog, dew, or mist. It wouldn't do to have a picture that didn't mimic the conditions around it. He felt he had it. Just then, Emilia came flying in.

"Are you ready?" she asked when she landed.

"Yes. I'm just going to have a word with Cleo."

Cleo was doing one last check of her horse's hooves and saddle cinch when Andy walked up.

"We're all set," Andy said, looking at the assembled Vipers. It was inspiring to see the ordered ranks of riders, every eye set and looking straight ahead. These were professional soldiers who knew their task and would not shrink from it. One thing he noticed that was different about them was that they were all wearing studded wristbands with extremely sharp points. He asked Cleo about this.

"We normally don't wear them," she said, "because they are of little use against demons. Men are a different matter."

Andy shuddered to imagine what it might feel like to be hit by that.

"Once your brother gets here, the rest of us will set out for the White Castle. I'll get word to you somehow, and then meet us there with the Fenner riders."

"We will try to have the Raptors neutralized by then," Cleo said.

"Good luck to all of you," Andy said soberly.

"Don't look so glum, Master Dragon," Tori said cheerily. "We'll see you at the castle to crown a new king."

"I hope so." He turned toward Nyle. The Raptor did not look happy with what he was about to do. "Are you all right, Lieutenant?"

"Do not worry about my loyalties, Lord Dragon. But know I take no pleasure in hunting down men I once called brothers."

"I understand," Andy said. "Hopefully they will surrender or at least be taken prisoner." Nyle looked at him as if that were unlikely. Andy walked back to where his sister waited.

"I'm ready whenever you are," Emilia said confidently.

"Okay, let's do this. Now, Tera," Andy said. Tera flew up to a high limb and blew on her pipes. No sound could be heard, but Pan obviously got the signal because his fauns burst out of the woods and started shooting arrows into the ranks of Devon's archers.

Pan and his fauns had been harassing the enemy since arriving in Albion, so it was no surprise to the archers on the other side. Andy hoped the routine would lead them to believe nothing was amiss or out of the ordinary. They started returning fire when the fauns came in range.

The fauns had a slight advantage, because they could fire on the run, giving the enemy nothing but moving targets. It was like watching a dance as they weaved in and out, firing past one another with such precision that no faun ever fell from a friendly arrow.

Andy started to create his illusion. Unlike the illusion at the inn, this one would have to change slightly as it moved forward. He closed his eyes as he used the source to paint the image he had in his mind. He could feel Emilia doing the same with Braylynn's power. Beads of sweat started to break out on his forehead. This was taking a lot of concentration to hold together. Emilia looked at him and gave a slight nod of her head.

Cleo, you can move in, Andy mind spoke.

As quietly as possible, the Vipers moved out from the cover of the trees and into the space surrounded by Andy's illusion. There was no outcry from the other side, so Andy assumed it was safe to proceed.

Slowly at first, the riders moved forward at a measured pace to keep from bursting through the illusion. Fauns were fighting on either side of the bridge, and they could see the Vipers had begun. Pan moved out into the battle. He gave a long hard blow on his horn, the sound echoing off the nearby hills. The archers didn't know what to make of this call and looked behind them anxiously for any attack from the rear. The fauns raised their fighting level to cause as much distraction and noise as possible. Before the echoes died down, Pan blew again in hopes of masking the sound of hoof beats on the bridge.

Cleo and Tori had just reached the halfway point. She lifted a hand, and, as one, the Vipers dropped their reins and drew their swords.

Andy saw the move and knew that soon they would break through the illusion and make a dash across. *Twenty more yards.* He needed to hold it together a little longer, but he was losing it. He could see some of the archers looking across the bridge in puzzle-ment. *Ten more yards.* Andy's head felt like it was going to explode. Cleo had started to gallop. A cry from the enemy rang out as the Vipers suddenly appeared on the bridge and made contact with the first rank of soldiers. Swords flashed left and right, and bodies were trampled as they rode past.

The archers fighting the fauns could not disengage, lest they be slain themselves. The center contingent of soldiers who manned the bridge didn't stand a chance. These were warriors used to fighting demons, and they cut the men down like a harvester cutting wheat. Andy watched as they rode into the hills. It was a bloody carnage right down the center of enemy lines. In the fifteen hundred years Devon had been in power, his army had never faced such a foe. Andy smiled as he fell to his knees in exhaustion.

"Are you all right?" Emilia asked, breathing heavily herself.

"Yes. Help me up. Tera! Sound the all clear."

"You got it, Andy," Tera said, and this time the notes she played could be heard. It had a very uplifting, victorious sound to it.

"Now what?" Emilia asked.

"Now we go talk to Dain on how to proceed from here, because, to tell you the truth, I haven't a clue." Holding onto his sister, he turned back toward Albion to go find the ex-general of the Border Lands warriors.

CHAPTER 23

EMILIA AND ANDY had reached the center of town when they noticed Valencia walking toward them. Her eyes were looking at the ground, as if she were deep in thought.

"Are you all right, Valencia?" Emilia asked when they reached her.

"Oh, Donella, Andros. I'm sorry, I didn't see you. Everything went as planned?"

"Yes, it did," Andy replied. "We were just on our way to Baron Weylin's to talk to Dain."

"I will be there shortly myself," Valencia said. "Donella, may I speak to you for a minute?"

"Of course, my queen," Emilia said with compassion, sensing Valencia was struggling with some inner question.

"I'll meet you both at the manor," he said as he walked away.

"What is it, Valencia?"

She started walking again, and Emilia followed. Their steps brought them to a small park area. The grass was neatly trimmed and flowers lined the paths that meandered throughout. There was an old stump, left from a tree that had been struck by lightning years ago. Valencia sat on this while Emilia sat cross-legged on the ground, her green wings catching the gentle breeze.

"What is your plan when this is all done, sister?" the queen asked.

Emilia was taken aback for a moment by the question, not because it had been asked, but because she never really considered it. She just assumed she would go home. However, now that the issue had been voiced, she found herself pausing to think about it.

"I have to go back," she answered finally. "There are some questions back home that I need answers to."

"I thought that might be your decision."

"Why are you asking, Valencia?"

Now it was the queen's turn to pause before answering.

"I'm not sure how much you know of the lineage of the royal houses of faeries, and there is really not enough time to explain it adequately, but I am the last of my house."

"I still don't see…"

"Should I not return from this battle, it is my duty as queen to have a successor chosen. I had thought to ask you, should I fall."

Emilia's green eyes went wide. She was dumbfounded that the queen actually thought her capable to rule. "I have no idea of how to be a queen."

"Not yet, but all the qualities needed to rule I can see in you." She looked up at some birds singing in a nearby tree. "There is a certain stamp in the character of the royal houses. It doesn't make us better than anyone else. it's just what Braylynn put in us to rule effectively. I cannot say for sure, but you seem to have that stamp."

Certain things suddenly started to make sense to Emilia.

"I do not believe anything will happen to you, Valencia, but I think that, should the need arise, a successor will be revealed."

"How do you know this?" Valencia asked, looking at her intently.

"I am prevented from saying, but rest assured, everything has been taken into account."

Valencia visibly relaxed. "I believe what you say, Donella, and now I can enter this fight with an unburdened heart." She stood up. "Come, sister. Let's go make sure your brother hasn't committed us to some impossible task." Emilia smiled at the thought.

* * *

Andy was standing on the balcony of the second floor in Weylin's house in the back of the manor, looking west. It had been four days since Cleo and the Vipers had left. Leah would fly out from time to time to learn what she could, but all she heard were rumors of their passing. The Vipers were definitely on the offensive, taking the fight to the Raptors whenever they could. From what she had gathered, two Raptor units had been entirely wiped out.

Gray clouds covered the sky that morning, giving the day a dreary, depressing look. Andy heard the sound of sandals on stone behind him and turned to see Weylin.

"Good morning, lad," Weylin said, putting a firm hand on his shoulder and smiling. "Not thinking negative thoughts, are you?"

"No, not really," he said. "It's just sometimes the enormity of all this tends to overwhelm me." He looked the jolly baron in the eye. "I'm sorry we got you and your people messed up in this."

"*Ha!* Son, we have been waiting to get messed up in this for fifteen hundred years." He put his hands on the balcony rail and scanned the horizon. "People have always assumed we were cowards, Devon's lapdogs, and we fostered that belief for our own survival. There is not a person here who hasn't longed for this day, to be able to rid ourselves of that characterization."

"I guess it hasn't always been easy, having everyone think you're cowards."

"Let me tell you a story, Andros," he began. "The baron at the time of the king's overthrow was named Orin. He loved his king and queen. When they were boys, King Baldric and Orin went through arms training together. They were like brothers. I don't believe Devon knew this, or I'm sure he would have killed Orin. When Devon summoned all the barons and Orin saw which way all the others were leaning, he knew he had to hide his feelings or he and his people would perish."

Andy continued to look west as Weylin spun his tale about how Orin went back to his people and convinced them to feign allegiance to Devon.

"Orin was a broken man after that day," Weylin said. "He felt he'd betrayed his friend and king. So you can see why we are so elated. Even though Orin did what he felt was necessary, we have never gotten the stench of that betrayal out of our nostrils until this moment."

Andy looked at Weylin. Tears stood in his eyes, and his jaw was firmly set. The man had transformed from his usual kindhearted self into a serious, committed avenger. Andy could tell, when it came time to march, Albion would lead the way.

"Come inside, Andros. It is time we settled this matter. I bring you word that our scouts from the south have returned. Your Border Lands warriors are only a half day's march from here."

Andy followed Weylin into the house, where they waited for Lyson and the news he would bring.

*   *   *

Andy, Leah, and Dain were looking over a map when Lyson walked into Weylin's library.

"Dain!" Lyson exclaimed when he entered.

Dain looked up upon hearing his name and a smile crept across his face as he bounded over to Lyson and clasped his hand, giving him a firm pounding on the back.

"Lyson, you old war dog," Dain said in greeting. "I heard you had been made supreme commander, and it shows." He laughed.

"It's good to see you, too, General," Lyson said good-naturedly. "I hope we didn't miss anything?"

"Nope, not a thing," Andy said, smiling. He felt so much better having another tactical mind there.

"You're right on time, as usual," Dain said. "Come on over and meet Leah."

"Ah yes, I have heard much from Donella about you," Lyson told her, "although your reputation as a skilled fighter is known throughout the Border Lands."

"Thank you, General," Leah replied. "And I, of course, have heard of your battle prowess, as well."

"Is Donella here?" Lyson asked Andy.

"She's with the queen," Andy said. "They should be here soon."

"Lyson, sit down and have a drink," Dain said, wrinkling his nose. "And, maybe later, a bath. You smell like you've been in the saddle for a month."

"Always a true friend, Dain," Lyson said, raising an eyebrow. "You would smell the same, if you'd been on a forced march for five days, fighting skirmishes all along the way."

"Were there a lot of encounters?" Andy asked.

"A lot, yes," he said, pouring a glass of wine and then sitting down, "but nothing in great numbers. Hit and run tactics, mostly."

Lyson continued to explain all that happened from the time they'd left the Border Lands until they'd arrived in Albion. He told Andy that there were only small villages along the southern part of the lake and few garrisons, but Devon still maintained roving patrols, and it was these that Lyson would encounter. He also told them that Dain's cousin Jana was leading the warriors around the north end of the lake.

"When did you promote her to general?" Dain asked.

"Shortly after you disappeared. She seemed the logical choice, since she was your second-in-command." He smiled at Dain mischievously. "She might have some choice words for you, since you didn't even bother to write her."

"Lyson, you know how I am with writing."

"Oh yes, my friend. As I recall, I always had to fill out your reports." Leah laughed at that.

"It's as I told you, love. I'm a fighter not a poet."

"What has been happening here?" Lyson asked.

Dain filled him in on Cleo's arrival and the departure of the Vipers. Andy also told him of the demon-like creature that had tried to kill him. He asked Lyson if he had ever heard of such a thing.

"No, I haven't. But I would go with Tori's assessment. If she doesn't think it is from the Border Lands, then I believe her."

"Abby is in the library here in Albion, seeing if she can find anything," Leah added, moving her wings back and forth slightly to stretch the muscles in her back.

Just then, the door opened, and the queen and Emilia entered followed by Acacia and Paolo. Andy saw his sister's eyes meet

Lyson's and could tell there was definitely a connection between them. Whether they would do anything about it remained to be seen. The greetings were cordial but somewhat formal, Andy thought. He wondered if, like Dain, Lyson had already, in his heart, sworn allegiance to the future monarchy of Vasara.

The door opened again, and Abby came walking in with her head down, looking at a battered, leather-bound book.

"Andros, I think I may have found something. I…" She looked up and saw who was in the room.

"Lyson!" she said, running over to him. He stood up and gave her a crushing embrace.

"It is good to see you, Abby," he said with a genuine smile. "I heard you have been through quite the trials after you left our lands."

"Oh, nothing worth mentioning," she said offhandedly. Lyson had to laugh at that.

"What have you found, Abby?" Andy sked his sweetheart, who had a stray lock of brown hair that kept falling into her eyes. Her forehead and cheeks were smudged, as if she had been climbing up a chimney.

"Oh, yes, well, while I was searching through the books in the library, I happened upon this one quite by accident. I'd gone to throw a log on the fire when the tile I was standing on next to the hearth broke at the corner. It was loose, and I could feel air coming up, so I knew the space below must be hollow. I pried the tile up, and this book was lying in a carved-out niche underneath. It was wrapped in oil cloth and inside a stone box."

They all gathered around to look at the flowing red script on the cover. The title read, *The Betrayal of Parma as Chronicled by Lorcan of the Alfar*."

"Alfar!" Leah exclaimed. "I didn't even know they knew how to write."

"More importantly, why would this book be in Albion?" Lyson pondered.

"When Parma had a functioning government, there was a trade route between Albion and the Wilds," Valencia said.

"I've heard the name, but what exactly are Alfar?" Acacia asked.

"They are very fierce and wild wood elves," Dain explained. "Small, about a child's height, but very nimble and extremely fast. They have the ability to hide in such ways as to seem almost invisible."

"What do they have to do with this creature that attacked Andros?" Valencia asked Abby.

"Well, according to this," Abby explained, "and, mind you, it was very difficult to read because time has eroded a lot of the words, this Lorcan witnessed the overthrow of the Parma government and the destruction of its main capital. The part that pertains is here." She began to read aloud.

"'As I saw the last wall of the house of the Ministers of Justice collapse, a great hole opened. Dust and ash came billowing out. I was standing on a hill a short distance from the destruction when I saw them. In a column of twos, ten hooded and robed figures emerged from the hole. I could not tell what they were, but they walked upright like a man. No other characteristics did I notice except one. As they came forth and passed below my place of concealment, I caught a slight odor of sulfur.'"

Abby stopped reading and looked at the faces around her.

"Do you think it could be the same thing?" Donella asked of no one in particular.

"The fact that this Lorcan recorded a sulfur smell makes me tend to believe yes," Lyson answered. "They are not ordinary demons, otherwise they would not have behaved in such an orderly fashion."

"That would mean these things have been around for a long time," Paolo said.

"But why has word of them not surfaced before now?" Andy wondered.

Emilia's face paled slightly, and Lyson noticed it.

"What's wrong, Donella?" Lyson asked.

"I know where they came out," she said. "Do you remember the ruins we camped at in Parma?" she asked Dain.

"Of course. And I remember saying nothing living would enter there."

"Exactly. These demon-like creatures, or whatever they are, emerged from that spot. I remember when we walked through it, Parma felt like an open wound that was still bleeding. These creatures have some connection to the betrayal."

"But why attack Andros?" Leah asked.

"That I don't know. Maybe they sense him as a threat yet to come. Anything is possible."

"Well, it doesn't matter," Andy said pushing, his hair back out of his eyes. "If they have been around since Parma fell, then they were here long before Devon committed his murder and probably have nothing to do with him. In any case, I can't worry about it now."

Just then, hoof beats clattered outside, one of Pan's fauns who had asked to see Andy.

"My Lord Dragon," the faun said, "my master begs me to tell you he had to leave for Parma and that we would come under your leadership."

"What?" Andy said, not believing it. "Why?"

"He did not say, only to give you that message."

"It might have to do with those demon things," Abby said. "I ran into Pan on my way over here and told him what I had found. He did seem troubled by it."

"Great, what else can happen today?" Andy did not like having to go to battle without the king of the fauns.

"General! General!" a voice shouted from the hall. An Albion soldier, who not long ago had been a farmer, came running into the room. "General, Devon's archers and soldiers have left."

"What do you mean they left?" Dain looked at him sharply.

"It has been very quiet across the river all morning," the soldier began. "We thought they had just pulled back beneath the cover of the trees. But as the noon hour came and went without any sign, we rode across the bridge to check. We found fire rings with ashes showing they'd left shortly after dark yesterday."

"What? How can that be?"

"Leah!" Andy said running out the door. Leah was already in flight and out the open window.

"Where are they going?" Lyson asked.

"Leah is going to fly low and check the forest for signs," Emilia replied, "while my brother searches from a higher altitude." Her eyes took on a distant look as the eye on her crown started to glow. "There are no signs of them yet. I can see Leah as she flies through the large gaps in the trees." Emilia pushed her dark hair behind her pointed ears and cocked her head sideways, as if straining to hear something. "They are coming back," she announced after a few minutes.

"Did they see any sign of them?" Paolo asked.

"No."

There was a commotion out in the yard as Andy came in to land. Leah flew through the window as Andy walked back inside.

"You saw?" he asked his sister. She nodded her head in the affirmative. "I think the soldier was right. They probably left right after sunset."

"But why would they leave?" Acacia asked, tugging at her long braid.

"I have a theory," Lyson said, "if you'll permit me."

"Please," Andy said.

Lyson started pacing as he organized his thoughts. "When Cleo took the stone back from Devon, I believe it was his intention to stomp you out quickly, before you could organize any resistance, and also before Cleo got to us with the stone." He stopped pacing and looked at Andy. "He had to know that, if we were successful in getting the stone back on the pillar, then the warriors would be freed up to come after him. But Devon's soldiers hadn't counted on the Wizard's Bridge confounding them."

"And now he has warriors converging from the north and the south," Dain added, as though seeing where Lyson's thoughts were going.

"Exactly. So now he has pulled all his troops back to Kensington, which he hopes will have the effect of neutralizing our numbers and strength."

"I don't understand," Emilia said.

"The Palatine Bridge is the only way across the chasm to the White Castle," Lyson said. "It is easily defended. Which means the initial assault will come from the flying races of Vasara."

"Dragons and faeries," Emilia said.

"I'm afraid so."

Valencia looked hard at Andy. "Well, Andros, I said before, any attack involving faeries would need to include a way to neutralize the archers. Any ideas?"

Andy swallowed hard. He didn't have a single one.

CHAPTER 24

THE AIR WAS HOT and sticky as Andy looked out from the edge of the forest toward the open plain that ran to the chasm and the Palatine Bridge. Granite walls ran along either side of the bridge, and on them, the archers were clearly visible.

It took a week from when Lyson arrived in Albion to reach this spot. The next day, Cleo and the Vipers appeared, along with the riders of Fenner. They had erected a command tent in a clearing not far from where Andy now stood.

Maccus had told Andy how he and his riders had engaged the enemy daily, whittling away their numbers. Things appeared to be going well until they got to Dragonsgate. Devon had split his forces. Half went toward Albion, while the other half went to Dragonsgate. There was already a heavily fortified garrison, and when Maccus got there, they were outnumbered four to one. They'd been encircled and almost met with disaster. Fortunately, the Vipers had arrived and were able to provide an escape. It was not without cost. Maccus lost a third of his riders, including his good friend Red. Dain's cousin Jana was now charged with liberating Dragonsgate.

Andy had sent a third of the faeries with Bowen. Bowen had come to him with a great idea. If they could keep the archers busy at the front gate, he would bring a force of faeries around the back by sea and take them by surprise. If his calculations were correct, Bowen should be in the sea and close to position. Once they saw Andy flying, they would launch their attack as soon as the opportunity presented itself.

Ravens circled out on the plain. Bart was fifty yards down from him, shooting arrows at them. He had said he probably wouldn't be able to hit any, but at least he would annoy the hell out of them. Cleo had laughed at that and decided to join him.

Andy could see the high tower of the White Castle and knew Devon was there, looking at him. A chill crept up his spine. He pulled up the sleeve of his dragon shirt and saw goose bumps on his arm. Fear made his knees shake. He didn't know if he could do this. He started breathing fast and shallow. Suddenly, he felt a hand on his shoulder and gave a sharp intake of breath. He turned quickly and then sighed with relief.

"What is the matter?" Abby asked, concerned. "You didn't even hear me come up."

"Oh, Abby," he said, holding her close, "I'm starting to lose my nerve. He has so much power. I don't know if I can beat him."

Abby pulled her head back so she could look into his hazel eyes. Placing both hands on the side of his face, she told him, "Yes, he has power, but he is alone. Your friends are here to help you bear this burden. The prophecy has brought everything together to help you win."

Andy visibly relaxed. He pulled her shirt down slightly off her shoulder to see the black dragon mark. He traced its outline, knowing they were linked in a way he didn't fully understand. "We can win, yes. But will I live? I so much want to live, Abby."

She looked at him with compassion. He could tell such thoughts had occurred to her as well. "We'll just have to leave that in the hands of the gods," she said quietly, as she rested her head on his chest.

Andy looked down to where Cleo and Bart were shooting and saw Tori ride out from the woods. She stopped and spoke briefly to them before wheeling her horse around to ride up to where he stood, her dark hair streaming in the wind.

"Andros, I bring word from Dain," she said. "They want you to come back to the tent to go over the plan one more time."

"I'll be right there."

Tori started to ride away but then stopped and turned back toward them. "Something just occurred to me. If you two lovebirds get married someday, will your kids be dragon babies?"

"Tori!" Abby said, shocked. They could hear Tori's laughter drift back to them as she continued on.

"She loves to do that," Andy said, smiling. He took one last look at the castle. "Abby, I think my biggest fear is that Loki is not here to help me. I always assumed that, at this point, we would be together. I miss him a lot. Almost as much as I miss my own mother and father. I've been suppressing these feelings so I can still function, but I feel like I might be losing my grip."

"Don't hold your feelings in, Andros," Abby told him. "True healing cannot begin until it comes out. Go to that special place of yours. Maybe that will help. I'll watch over you while you are there."

"That's a good idea, Abby. I don't know why that thought hadn't occurred to me."

"Just stick with me, Edward. I'll steer you straight," she said winking.

He laughed. She liked to tease him sometimes by using the name he had given her when they first met.

Together they walked back to the command tent, Andy feeling much lighter in spirit than when he had walked outside.

*   *   *

The tent was crowded. Everyone stared down at a map of Kensington on the table. It seemed to Andy every race and province was represented. Abby was right: all his friends were there to help him through the fight that was coming.

Ala spoke about where the healers would be set up to care for the wounded. Andy had never seen the healer clothed in what he assumed was military garb. It looked like someone had taken a healer's robe and cut it into two pieces to form a shirt and pants. She also wore a dark red leather breastplate embossed with a white dove with outstretched wings. Ala had told him this designated them as noncombatants when they ventured onto the field of battle to tend to the wounded and dying.

"When do you think we should start the battle?" Andy asked Dain.

"Dawn. Just as the sun comes up and is shining right in their eyes. This will give the faeries the best chance of success."

The plan was that a contingent of faeries would fly as high as they could on this side of the chasm. The intent was to have the archers looking up then have Andy create an illusion at ground level to allow a force of faeries to slip into the chasm. Then the illusion would shift to cover them and prevent the archers from seeing what waited below. When the time was right, the faeries in the chasm would fly straight up, hugging the rock face. It was hoped the archers would not see them until the faeries were staring them right in the eyes on the wall.

Once the archers near the bridge were taken out, the warriors would cross, followed by Pan's fauns. Maccus and his riders would remain on this side of the chasm, to help cover and give warning from any possible attack from the rear. Many patrols were still roaming about out there. After everyone was inside, there was no further plan, except to neutralize as many of the enemy as possible. The only objective was the overthrow of Devon, which was Andy and Emilia's task.

There was a stirring at the front of the tent. Andy looked back to see that Acacia had entered. She was clad all in white, from her tunic to her trousers, which flared out by the ankle of her soft leather boots. Upon her head, she wore a pearl band that came to a point in the center with a red jewel affixed to it. Her long hair was braided as usual, with black ribbon tied every six inches. On her hip, her rapier gleamed brightly. Her face glowed with pride and joy as she stepped to the side and allowed Paolo to enter.

Andy stood in awe of how regal he looked. He was encased in armor from head to foot, but instead of the gleaming silver steel associated with most armor, Paolo's was black. The gauntlets and foot covers were gold in color, as was the intricate scrollwork around the breastplate. In the center of the breastplate was the emblem of his house, a rearing white unicorn with yellow fire coming out of its mouth. The image was striking, as was the man who bore these adornments.

He wore no visor or helm, but a circlet crown of obsidian black rested on his head. And on his hip was a sword, its scabbard colored in gold, as well. Every warrior in the tent took a knee at once, followed by everyone else.

"Rise, friends," Paolo said. "Today I assume my birthright. Descended from Taiyo, I claim the throne of Vasara." The crowd stood up and cheered as one. He raised his hands, bringing silence to the tent. "Tomorrow I will lead the vanguard across the Palatine Bridge and take back what the usurper stole fifteen hundred years ago." Paolo stopped speaking as the crowd in front of him started to part and a lone man walked up. It was Lieutenant Nyle, his face resolute and his eyes focused on the man before him. He pulled his sword from its sheath, and there were a few muttered gasps from the crowd. Paolo, however, did not flinch or show any outward sign of worry. Nyle turned the point of his sword and touched it to his chest, the hilt coming to rest in Paolo's outstretched hand. Nyle's eyes held Paolo's.

"Sire, I have worked and fought hard in the labors of your enemy," he said in a calm and unwavering voice. "If any man here has a claim to my life, it is you. You may kill me, if that is your desire, but if it is not, allow me to ride at your side at the head of your army, for I would share the danger with my lord and king."

Paolo then showed his worthiness. "Take a knee, Lieutenant." He took Nyle's sword and rapped him smartly on the shoulder. "Rise, General Nyle, and take your place by my side. Today, you become the King's Royal Protector from this day on. It shall be the role of you and all your heirs after you. Rise, General, and take thy place." Nyle stood and took back the sword Paolo offered.

"He was destined to be king," Emilia whispered to her brother.

"Yes," Andy replied. "He has the love and loyalty of everyone here."

"In the battle coming," Paolo began speaking again, "you are to kill as few as possible. I know this is hard to do, but the men on those

walls are only doing what they think is their duty. They are not traitors. The barons, who my scouts tell me are holed up with Devon,
are another matter. They will face punishment for the crimes they
have perpetrated against the people under their charge." Another
cheer went up at this pronouncement. "Go now," he said after it
had quieted down again, "and prepare for the dawn. Tomorrow, for
good or ill, all will be decided."

He pulled out his sword, and, to the astonishment of many, its
godstone blade shone with a brilliant radiance as a sunbeam peeked
through a hole in the tent, illuminating its surface. The crowd
erupted in jubilation again.

"By the gods!" Lyson exclaimed.

"What is it?" Andy asked.

"It is King Baldric's sword. It was thought to have been lost or
stolen after his death. Taiyo must have gotten hold of it and made
sure it was passed down to his descendants."

It was some time before things settled down in the camp. But
then, that feeling of a calm before the storm pervaded the place, and
they waited for the dawn.

*   *   *

The day of the battle was a perfect day in terms of the weather. The
sun would soon crest the hills, and there was not a cloud in the sky.
The heat and stickiness of the previous day was gone. It was as if
the gods wanted everything to be perfect. Andy thought it would be
like most battles he had read about or seen in the movies: gray and
disgusting, matching the moods of the soldiers. But the promise of
the new day instead filled everyone with hope. Andy wondered if
this was how the prophecy would set the conditions, to give the best
possible chance of success.

Paolo, Lyson, Dain, and Abby stood by his side at the edge of the
woods, where he had been standing the day before. Abby would
help Ala, so she had on one of the breastplates the healers wore. She
also had strapped to her hip the rapier Lyson had given her. Her

brown hair was tied up in a ponytail to keep the errant breeze from blowing it in her face.

"Where is Donella?" Lyson asked, staring at the wall of archers.

"She is with Valencia and the faeries who will be providing the initial distraction. Once I change, she will join me as we go after Devon." Andy felt totally unprepared for this.

"The sun is up, Andros," Paolo said, looking at him solemnly.

Andy felt a momentary panic. Once he gave the signal to start, they would not stop until it had been decided. He summoned up his courage and looked behind him. Tera waited, biting her lip. Andy gave her a silent nod. She nodded back and, instead of any flippancy or foolish laughter, blew him a faerie kiss then pulled her fist over her heart in salute. She then lifted off the ground, blowing her pipes and creating the natural sounds of the forest.

* * *

Valencia heard the sounds of Tera's pipes.

"Ready yourselves, sisters," she said.

The faeries were dressed in their battle gear, consisting mainly of soft leather shorts and half-chest leather breastplates. On their feet, they wore soft leather shoes with straps crisscrossed up their calf muscle and tied off below the knee. No other protection did they have, except for spears and knives. Faeries relied heavily on their ability to maneuver quickly in dangerous situations.

Valencia gave a nod to Emilia, who pointed her staff up and just over the heads of the archers. As she focused, a green burst of energy shot forth to explode over the heads of the men on the walls. Then the sound of a hundred wings beat the air, as the faeries burst into the open and started to climb. They zigzagged as much as possible to prove a difficult target.

The archers, after feeling there were no more energy bursts coming at them, started shooting. There was only a single row of archers on the wall, so there was not a constant volley of arrows, but there were still plenty of them flying through the air.

Valencia, when she was not busy batting away arrows with her spear, kept a close eye on her faeries. Most were doing fine, although several had fallen to shots in the leg and chest. She could only pray they would be all right.

Every archer she could see seemed to be engaging the faeries in the air. She caught movement below her. Leah, leading a contingent of faeries, was running for the chasm. *Andros and Donella must have started their illusion*, she thought.

In groups of ten, they plunged into the chasm as Valencia's contingent kept the archers occupied. When the last one was in, Valencia saw the retreat signal from Emilia explode over the head of the archers again. The faeries in unison turned and flew back to the safety of the trees. Valencia altered her flight to bring herself down next to Andy.

* * *

"How was it out there?" Andy asked her.

"The fighting was hot, but I see the objective has been met."

"Yes, and we haven't a lot of time before they figure out what that diversion was for," Dain added.

"I am surprised they haven't used any cannon," Lyson said.

"Bowen was telling me that they moved them to the far wall behind the castle when the ships attacked, during the retaking of the stone," Andy told him.

"I believe it is up to you now, Andros," Paolo said, putting a hand on his shoulder.

Andy could see the confidence and trust this man placed in him, and he took courage from it. "Right. I will blast the gates, and that will be Leah's signal to begin her attack."

"My faeries and I will join you to bring their bows skyward once again," Valencia added.

"Are you ready, Em?" he asked his sister.

"I'm ready," she replied, her green eyes blazing, and the silver in her hair shining bright like the sun.

"I'll meet you at the castle." Andy turned back toward Paolo. "Don't wait too long, sire."

"Do not worry, Andros the Black. We will cross quickly," he said, smiling.

Tori strikes again, Andy thought to himself. There was no point delaying any longer. He ran into the open field. The archers saw him and started to fire. Andy thrust his palms forward, and balls of fire shot out to hit the walls as he ran. Then, in what seemed to take only a second, a black dragon with gold talons stood where the young man had been. A mighty roar came from his throat as his powerful wings lifted him off the ground and away.

As soon as he changed, the faeries took to the air again. The arrows came in earnest once more. Andy circled the field and sent a blast of fire at the gates, which exploded on impact, sending metal and granite hurtling through the air, some striking the archers and soldiers nearby.

Shortly after the gates exploded, it looked as if paint were streaking up the walls of Kensington. In actuality, it was Leah and the many-colored wings of the faeries that followed her out of the chasm. The archers were taken totally by surprise, as they each suddenly found themselves staring a vengeful faerie in the face. They were either knocked unconscious or impaled on the talon spears.

Valencia began to lead her faeries across the chasm. Cannon fire could be heard from the far side of Kensington, but they were not aimed toward them. Andy saw Paolo and the warriors begin their charge across the bridge.

He had just flown over the wall when he realized their one mistake. Hiding in ambush in the streets, alleys, and building tops were the remaining archers.

Valencia watch... Ahh! Just then, Andy felt a searing pain. He looked and saw that an arrow had pierced his wing. It had to be one of those special arrows. He scanned the ground quickly, and then he found the source. A huge, hulking soldier with a crossbow was taking dead aim at his chest. He had to veer away. Hopefully, Valencia would see the archers in time.

* * *

The sea was a tempest as cannonballs, shot from the battlements, landed in the water next to the Grey Morning. Bowen was shouting orders to the crew to bring her about and give the soldiers manning the walls a broadside. The air was hot and smelled of gunpowder. Four other ships were in the battle with Grey Morning, pounding the cannon positions. There was a fifth ship, but a lucky shot had taken out her mizzenmast and forced her to leave the engagement.

"Brie!" Bowen yelled as he frantically turned the ship's wheel.

Brie was in the bow, conversing with some seagulls. Upon hearing Bowen's voice, the red-winged faerie flew back to the stern. "What is it, Captain?" she asked when she touched down next to him.

"You should probably have your faeries get ready," he said, straining against the wheel.

Brie gave a couple of quick whistle,s and all the faeries assembled on the port side. The plan was to have all available ships shoot a broadside at the same time and the faeries would follow the cannon shot in. It was hoped the soldiers manning the cannons on the walls would be too busy ducking to have a chance to fire back as they passed over.

"Can you fly faster than a cannonball, Brie?" Bowen asked her, smiling and looking more like a roughish pirate than a man of commerce.

"It will be a close race, Captain," she said, giving him a wink.

"Kellen!" Bowen yelled to his boson.

"Aye, sir!" Kellen yelled from the bow.

"Get ready to signal the other ships to fire at my command!"

"Aye, sir!"

"Good luck, Brie," Bowen said with a gentleness that surprised her.

"Thank you, Captain. I'll see you on the other side." He gave her a nod.

"Cannons ready!" Bowen shouted. Kellen held a green flag and started to wave it slowly.

"Aim!" The faeries flexed their legs as if they were about to sprint.

"Fire!" Kellen's flag came down, and four ships let loose with a broadside. As soon as the cannons roared, the faeries flew through the plumes of white smoke at a speed that astounded the sailors. The cannonballs hit their mark just before the faeries sailed over the wall and into Kensington.

The sight that met Brie's eyes was one of utter chaos. She could see warriors, faeries, fauns, and Devon's soldiers all in one big melee. Citizens of Kensington were running everywhere to try to avoid the fighting. She also spotted archers hiding behind buildings, shooting faeries out of the air. A great rage came over her. She reached down and pulled out her spear and extended it. The rest did the same, as Brie pointed out their targets. They altered their trajectory and came in behind the archers, who never saw their adversaries as they were impaled on the talon spears.

*　*　*

Andy settled back down on the other side of the chasm after being struck. *Em, I need you!* he called out. His sister was the only one who could hear him from any kind of distance.

I'm coming! she replied.

Watch out. One of those dragon archers is over there.

I see him. I'll take care of it.

He saw his sister hover and aim her staff down. A bright, white beam of energy shot out and exploded on the other side of the wall where Andy could not see. Emilia then flew over to where he had landed.

"I got him," she said aloud when she stood next to him. "Are you hurt?"

He put a hole in my wing. Can you patch it up?

"No problem." She touched her staff to his injury, and the hole in his leathery wing closed. He let out a loud roar of pain.

Damn! That burns!

"Oh, don't be such a baby." He gave a low, sulky growl at that. "We can't help on the battlefield anymore. If there is to be an end, we need to go after Devon now."

You're right. Hop on.

Andy leaped into the air and circled around the forest to gain speed before taking aim on the tower where he knew Devon would be. He barely registered the battle raging below as he came closer to the castle.

Standing on a balcony on the upper tower was Devon, dressed in red with a white cloth across his ruined eyes. The only thing those golden eyes would ever see again was a white light. But Devon didn't need his eyes to see. He had his magic for that and the aid of his demon.

Andy sent a jet of flame at him only to test what he figured to be true: Devon was shielding. He laughed as their attack proved fruitless.

Any ideas? he asked as they veered away.

"Actually, yes. We'll blow out the balcony he is on."

Great idea. No wonder you're the oldest.

Emilia turned on Andy's back and aimed her staff back toward the castle. She released her energy, and the balcony exploded in a shower of dust and stone. Devon had seen what was coming and managed to jump back inside before the balcony collapsed. Just then, several fireballs came flying out of the castle.

"You better climb!" Emilia said.

Andy started climbing into a loop as the fireballs narrowly missed and exploded into the forest beyond, setting the trees ablaze.

Hold on!

At the top of his loop, Andy rotated so he was right side up and headed back towards the castle. As he raced past the tower, he whipped his tail and smashed the roof off. Devon, seeing he was vulnerable in this position, destroyed the walls of the tower so he would have an open shot. It looked as though he stood upon a pedestal. Andy opened his mind to him.

Surrender now, Andy said. *There will be only one outcome, if you keep this up.*

I don't think so, he spat. *There is only one thing that will bring me joy now, and that is the death of you two. Can you hear me, Summoner?*

I hear you, Emilia replied.

I will give you a gift before you die. Devon looked down toward his feet and seemed to be speaking. Suddenly, a door in the floor opened, and a bedraggled looking Zana stepped out. The black-winged faerie looked like she had been the object of some fierce punishment. Devon was pointing at them, and Zana suddenly stood more erect. She removed the small stick strapped to her arm and extended her talon spear. Waving it in a challenge, she flew a short distance away from the castle.

Emilia transformed her staff back into the pearl comb and put it in her hair. Extending her own spear, she jumped off Andy's back.

What are you doing? Andy said. *It's a trap. Get back here.*

Stay out of this.

Oh gods! Andy thought, as he flew away from Devon's sudden onslaught.

*   *   *

Emilia knew she was not thinking rationally. But when she saw Zana, the mark on her leg started to burn. The red dragon within her had awakened. This was her enemy. She had killed Layla, the Dragon Summoner before her, and almost killed Tera. It was time for vengeance.

Zana started to fly toward her. Emilia closed the distance quickly, and, with an ear-splitting crack, the two spears connected. The fairies' eyes locked as they separated. They seemed to hang in a frozen moment. Zana suddenly let out a wild scream as she spun her spear over her head. Then, flying toward Emilia, she brought it down to smash her skull.

Emilia got her spear up in time to block it. Zana had a wild, haunted look in her eyes as she beat her spear again and again against Emilia's. Out of the corner of her eye, Emilia saw that familiar flash of yellow and lavender. Leah was flying up to help her. Unfortunately, Zana saw her eye movement and knew what it meant but did not break off the attack. She waited, and when she felt Leah almost on top of her, she turned her spear on Leah.

"*Leah!*" Emilia yelled, hoping to stop her from being impaled. But Leah was no novice to combat flying. Suddenly, she just was not there. What actually happened was Leah dropped low and gashed Zana's leg as she flew by. Cursing, Zana sought her wound while Emilia, sensing an opening, brought her spear to bear on Zana's unprotected back.

But Zana was no novice, either. She had more than two thousand years of fighting experience that she honed daily. She knew what Emilia's move would be, and, without turning around, she swung her spear behind her back and blocked the blow. Emilia was about to follow it up when a buzzing went past her ear. Several more followed, and she looked down to see a handful of archers who had taken aim on all three faeries. Zana let out a cry as one of the arrows pierced her arm.

"You bastard!" Zana yelled, looking over at Devon. Emilia could see Devon' wicked smile on his face. He meant to kill them all.

Zana raised an open hand toward Devon, and a feeble black beam shot out. It lacked strength and intensity and died as it reached its target. Devon laughed. He must have used some magic, because now his voice was clearly audible.

"I see you have been spying on me, Zana," Devon said casually. "But you have not perfected it. And the demon you must have conned into entering your body is not very strong, probably just an imp. Let me show you how it is done." He started to laugh insanely, and some of his soldiers looked up at the unsettling sound.

He thrust out both hands, and two black streams went racing toward Zana. She hovered, with eyes wide open, as her death streaked toward her. But then, the beams impacted with a bright luminescent shield. Zana looked over at Emilia in surprise. Her pearl staff was out, blocking Devon's assault.

"What are you doing?" Leah screamed from behind her. Emilia looked at Leah with chagrin. Turning back toward Zana, she spoke only a single word.

"Go." The voice was hers, but it seemed to be overlaid by another.

Zana only took a moment before her survival instincts kicked in, and then she turned and fled to the south.

"Why did you do that?" Leah asked, totally perplexed. "She was as good as dead!"

"I don't have time to explain. I need to go help my brother." And with that, she flew back to Andy to finish this once and for all.

* * *

Andy had several scorch marks along his scaly hide from some of Devon's direct hits. The wizard had managed to effectively repel all of his assaults. After he broke off for the last time, he watched Devon's exchange with the faeries. Like Leah, he was baffled by his sister's sudden intervention to save Zana's life. Now she was heading back this way.

What happened? he asked her.

We'll talk about it later, she said crisply.

Well, I'm not having any luck here.

Let's hit him from both sides at once.

Okay. I'll come from the right.

Emilia nodded as she flew off to attack from the left. Andy circled back across the chasm to give himself some speed as he closed in. He looked down at the utter chaos below. People were running everywhere. He saw one old man dart in and out of the battlements, looking for cover. How he came to be there, Andy did not know, but he prayed he would be all right.

He made his turn and started heading back toward the castle. His sister had lightning dancing in her hand. She shaped it like balls which she threw at Devon. They expanded as they got closer, encircling Devon and releasing their energy. Andy brought fire into the mix. Devon was straining, but he managed to protect himself. They kept it up for a while but made no headway. Then, from the battlements, an energy blast came hurtling in, and, with the combined effect of all three attacks, Devon sank to one knee, finding it difficult to attack and block three strikes at once.

"What the...?" Devon exclaimed. Then Andy heard a voice he hadn't dared hope to hear again.

"You look like you're having a little difficulty, brother," Loki exclaimed.

Loki! This was the old man he had seen running along the battlements. That was why Loki had given Bart that message about the harmless-looking man: to let Andy know he was still alive.

"No need to yell, lad. It's good to see you, too."

"That's impossible!" Devon shrieked.

"Oh, my dear brother," Loki said, shaking his head. "You never learned that sometimes the simplest tricks are the best. The only thing you succeeded in killing was an illusion." Loki wasted no more time talking, as he rejoined Andy and Emilia in their attacks on the evil wizard.

Suddenly, Devon started muttering to himself.

What is he up to now? Andy said. He still couldn't believe Loki was there.

I don't know, lad, but whatever it is cannot be good.

Devon finished his muttering and drove his fist into the stone at his feet. Black rock shot up and closed him up like an egg. The trio could not penetrate it, no matter what they tried. They broke off their attack and regrouped. Emilia landed on the battlements next to Loki while Andy circled overhead. She ran over and hugged the old man.

Any suggestions? Andy asked.

I think all we can do is wait to see what he does next, Loki replied.

It wasn't long before, all of a sudden, an explosion of the rock shell enclosed Devon. Debris went flying everywhere, striking people and fighters below. Some of it struck and bounced off Andy's back.

As the dust started to settle, a figure began to stand erect. He was more than seven feet tall. The facial features were Devon's, but the body had changed. His torso was bare and, muscles rippled on his chest and arms. His beard was gone, and his once-black hair was now as yellow as the summer sunshine and came down to his shoulders. The white band around his eyes was gone, and two black orbs stared out of the sockets. His fist clenched a staff of iron with a blue crystal affixed to the top. He pointed it to where Loki and Emilia stood and let loose a blast of blue energy.

Emilia jumped just in time, but Devon's strike hit the stone at Loki's feet, sending him hurtling through the air and slamming him into the castle wall, where he fell unconscious. Emilia quickly flew onto Andy's back.

What is that? he asked.

"I'm not sure, but I think he is starting to let the demon have more control. Fly out a ways. I have an idea."

I don't like the sound of that.

He flew back over the chasm one more time. As he did, he looked back and saw Devon shooting at the people below him. Friend or foe, it didn't matter. He was set on destroying them all.

"This is far enough," Emilia said, jumping up and running to the middle of his back where his wings joined his body. "Start turning." She took out her talon dagger and sliced both of her palms. The blood ran freely and fell onto Andy's back. He could feel it trickling between his scales.

What are you doing?

"It is all about connections!" she shouted. And with that, she lay down on his back, and with each blood-soaked hand stretched out toward a wing, she slapped them down on his dragon scales, using magic to hold herself in place.

Andy was suddenly aware of a foreign presence in his mind. His body started to buck and lurch, as if he were trying to dislodge an unwanted rider.

Em, what's going on?

"Don't fight it!"

In his mind's eye, he saw it: a red dragon keeping pace with him, flying as he flew and turning as he turned. It was as if they were joined together. It turned its head, and the malevolence in its eyes could be felt throughout his entire being. Andy also felt the strength of the red dragon added to his own.

Draw as much energy as the two of you can hold! his sister's thought came to him.

Now he understood. He pushed himself into the source while maintaining his link to the red dragon. Suddenly, he found he could keep drawing way beyond what he usually drew before feeling like he would split at the seams. He circled higher and higher as he drew more and more. Feeling he could hold no more, Andy went into a steep dive and started to angle towards Devon. The wizard gave a guttural roar as he saw Andy descend and, leveling his staff, shot an intensely powerful blue beam directly at Andy's head.

Andy opened his mouth and let loose all of that stored energy in one shot. What came out of his mouth was a beam of black and red, twisting together as it met the blue beam. There was no pushing back and forth of energies. Andy's beam obliterated Devon's and then went on to blow a hole in Devon's midsection. He stared down dumbly, not exactly sure what had happened. As Andy flew past him, he whipped his tail and cut the evil wizard in two.

He felt a tremendous release of strength. He could barely hold his wings outstretched, let alone move them to fly up. With what little stamina remained, he glided back across to crash land in the clearing from where the battle started. His sister fell off his back and rolled several yards. He lifted his head and saw Abby and Ala running toward him. Tera and Diminitus were close behind.

"Are you all right?" Abby asked, frightened.

No, he said to her weakly. *I don't even have the strength to change. How is Emilia?*

"Ala is checking on her," she said, stroking his dragon head.

Just then, Andy heard a terrible sound. A scream he had heard from hundreds of demons in the Corridor of the Border Lands. He lifted his head higher and swiveled his long neck to look back at the battlements where Devon had been standing. With his dragon eyes, he could see the demon that Devon had enslaved was free. And this wasn't just any demon. According to what Loki had told him, this was a Demon High Lord. Vast magic was his to draw on, and he was in his true form within the borders of Vasara.

They were lost. Andy couldn't even fly, let alone grasp the source. Despair filled him as the demon started throwing fireballs from has talon claws at the people gathered below, while that hideous cry bellowed from his mouth of double-row razor teeth.

* * *

Valencia stood on the library steps and watched Andy cut Devon in two. She gave a sigh of relief as the body fell back and moved no more. A great cheer went up from all the people who witnessed it. She could scarce believe that they had won. The cost, however, was extremely high on both sides.

The archers, for some strange reason, would not surrender. The queen wondered if Devon might have used magic on them, because the faeries had been forced to kill every last one of them. Her spear was bloodied on both ends. That thought alone weighed heavy on her soul. The regular soldiers gave up when they saw all was lost, once Paolo and Dain along with Lyson and the warriors had routed them. The majority of the officers were being held within the library itself.

Leah flew in and landed next to the queen.

"He's done it, Valencia!" Leah said, her face smudged and her legs bearing cuts from the recent engagements with the enemy. "Andros has slain Devon. And it appears they were just in time, because they crashed over on the other side of the chasm."

"Yes, I saw," she responded, running a hand through her auburn hair. "But my heart is still unsettled." Just then, she heard the shriek of the demon and understood why.

"By the goddess," Leah exclaimed, looking up at the monstrosity. The cheers in the street soon turned to screams of horror as fireballs rained down on the city. The citizens of Kensington ran in every direction, seeking cover.

Then Valencia stared in wonderment as the scene before her suddenly froze. Leah herself had her hand raised in mid-gesture and stood like a statue. She watched as the goddess of the faeries came walking up the library steps, her deep blue wings standing out in stark contrast to the white marble everywhere. Tears were in her eyes as she stood beside Valencia. Valencia, too, had tears coming down her cheeks.

"Must it be so, Mother?" she asked, lowering her head, her faerie wings folding in.

Braylynn gently lifted her chin to look into her hazel eyes. "I'm afraid so, my daughter," she replied with compassion.

"This is the longest incarnation I have been in," Valencia said, her voice thick with emotion, "and I have loved these more than any others." She looked over at Leah and put a caressing hand on her cheek. "Will this be the last time?" she asked, tears streaming down her face now.

"My heart breaks every time, as well, dearest. As for the end, I do not know. As long as the prophecy exists, you will."

Valencia took her spear and laid it at Leah's feet. She then kissed Leah's cheek. "Remember me," she whispered into Leah's pointed ear. She then turned and hugged her goddess. Letting go of the embrace, she started to walk down the steps. Valencia turned to look back, but she already knew Braylynn was gone. The frozen moment ended, and everything resumed its normal pace.

"Valencia?" Leah said, concern written all over her face. Valencia couldn't answer. Instead, she flew off toward the forest. "*Valencia!*" Leah screamed. She tried to fly after her but found her legs would not move. She started to shriek and yell.

"Leah, what's wrong?" Tori said as she rode by, blood splattered all over her armor from her hand-to-hand combat.

"I'm getting sick and tired of being tied down with magic!" she cursed at the sky.

*   *   *

Diminitus held Emilia's head while he lifted a cup of water to her lips. She seemed to be coming out of it. Abby and Ala looked at her closely.

"Donella, are you all right?" Diminitus asked.

"Yes, just very weak," she said, rubbing her hand across her forehead. Then she heard a terrible shriek. "What was that?"

"The demon that possessed Devon, it's free now."

"We need to do something!" She started to rise.

"Just you sit down, missy! There's nothing you can do in your current condition."

"Donella, look!" Tera had flown over and was pointing toward the sky just overhead.

"It looks like Valencia," Emilia said.

It is Valencia, Andy confirmed.

Emilia's dragon eye started to glow. She was looking at Valencia through Andy's eyes.

"Something is not right."

"Why do you say that?" Ala asked.

"She has a resigned look on her face, as one who is about to meet their fate."

Valencia was directly overhead as she started her turn back towards the castle.

"Something is happening. She's changing."

They could all see her now, as her flame-colored wings started to grow beyond the lengths of her arms. Her wings now resembled those of a bird instead of a faerie. The edges fluttered like dancing flames. Her red and gold hair started to grow down her back and along the entire length of her body. Valencia's face transformed, as well, and became that of a bird. They all stood with open mouths as her whole being burst into flames.

"My god!" Diminitus exclaimed. "I can't believe it!"

"What?" Emilia asked.

"Valencia is the phoenix, the first of all creatures born at Vasara's creation, and there can only be one reason she is in flames."

"What reason is that?"

Diminitus looked at her sympathetically. "She is going to sacrifice herself to destroy the demon."

"No!" Tera yelled and started to fly after Valencia.

Emilia pulled out her comb and transformed it into her staff. With what little energy she had, she created a shield around Tera to hold her in place as if she were in a bubble.

"Let me out! Let me out!" she said, beating against the shield. Her cries became pitiful sobs as Emilia brought Tera over to where she was sitting. When the bubble was on the ground, Emilia released her and held her while she wept.

Emilia looked through Andy's eyes again, as Valencia burned brighter and brighter. The demon saw her and started to throw fireballs. Valencia just absorbed the balls into her own flames. The demon howled in rage, and its body started to grow. Then, quick as oil sliding down a pipe, Valencia plunged into its gaping maw, causing the beast to explode, bits of charred flesh flying everywhere. There was no sign of Valencia.

For several heartbeats, it seemed as if the world held its breath, not believing a great evil had departed. Then, as realization set in, a great cheer went up from everyone in Kensington.

On the other side of the chasm, the tone was more somber, as the small band of friends wept for the faerie queen. Emilia looked up as she heard the mournful cry of ravens. Devon's birds were heading south, following the path Zana had taken. Emilia put her head on top of Tera's and held her close, and then she let grief take her.

Chapter 25

ANDY WAS STANDING on the portico just off the main hall that looked out onto the courtyard gardens. It had been two months since Devon's defeat, and most of the battle scars inflicted on the city of Kensington had been cleaned away.

Paolo had fought a bloody battle right here in these very gardens against General Kyle, leader of the Raptors. The general had been killed by Nyle, himself. Dain and Lyson were with him, as well, and together they defeated the entire castle guard.

Tori, with great delight, had told Andy how the Vipers, along with the fauns and Weylin's people, had helped the faeries destroy the archers. From what she said, they would not surrender, and when their arrows were spent, they turned to their swords and fought on to the death.

Andy saw a couple of figures walking on the stone path in a far corner of the garden. With his dragon sight, he could see the green wings of his sister, with Lyson walking beside her. They seemed to be having this continual talk ever since Paolo's coronation two weeks after the battle. After he took the White Throne, there was a week devoted to mourning the dead.

Whenever Andy thought of that, he thought of Valencia. He was very saddened by her death, but it could not match the grief of the faeries, his sister included. Tera had played what she called a faerie death song on her pipes the entire week. It was both mournful and beautiful. Emilia had not said a word to him during this time. As a point of fact, he'd hardly seen her at all. He figured she must have wanted to be alone.

Lad, are you in here? Loki's voice came into his head.

I'm outside by the gardens.

"Ah, I see you," he said aloud from inside the hall. "Doing some quiet contemplation, I see."

"Yes," he replied. He looked over at his friend and mentor. His black hair seemed to have some new gray streaks. Loki was holding a tankard of ale and puffing on a long-stemmed brown pipe. Andy smiled at this man who was like a father to him. It had nearly ripped his heart out when he had believed him to be dead. The thought brought his own father to his mind. He felt the need to go home. It would be time to leave soon.

"You are thinking of home."

"I am. I think my time here is almost done.

"Actually, I was thinking the same thing. That is what I have come to talk to you about."

Just then, the gate set inside the ivy-covered east wall opened, and Leah and Dain stepped in to walk the garden paths.

"I take it your sister and Leah are friends again?" Loki said, pointing with his pipe.

"Yes, after the mourning period was over. She was able to make Leah understand that the choice to destroy Zana was taken away from her. She believes the prophecy caused it to happen."

"Your sister has incredible insight. I for one believe her. It could very well be that Zana has some part to play in a future event."

"Which means more trouble."

"That could be a long time away, my boy," Loki said, putting a hand warmly on his shoulder.

Leah and Dain caught up with Emilia and Lyson, and they walked together. Andy felt a pang of loneliness for Abby. She was tied up in the hospital with Ala and her healers, caring for the last of the wounded who remained there. She said she would come later, while the sun was still out.

"I've been wondering something," Andy said.

"What's that, lad?"

"Is Valencia truly dead?"

Loki thought for a moment before answering. "That is a complicated question. Valencia, the queen of the faeries, is dead. But all that she was will be reborn from her ashes. She will never be Valencia again, but all that is Valencia will live on in a new form."

"What form is that?"

"No one knows, except maybe Braylynn. The phoenix was created by her and her brother, Cael. They made her as a kind of ace in the hole, so to speak. The final trump card, after every other card has been played. The last resort, if you will."

"I actually think I understood that." Andy smiled.

"Brilliant, lad! You see, stick with me, and wisdom is bound to rub off," he said with a laugh.

"Where are the ashes now?"

"I'm sure the wind has carried them off to whatever place fate has decided they will go."

"You said you wanted to talk to me about my leaving."

"Yes. I have noticed you become restless the past few weeks, and I surmised you would be going soon. Before you leave, I would ask a favor."

"I will do anything you ask me, Loki."

"Thank you, lad," he said with a fatherly smile. "Later this evening, I want you to meet me in the woods at the source."

"Sure. Any special reason?"

"A new wizard is to be chosen. And as the only dragon in Vasara, you should be there."

"Any idea who that is?"

"Not a clue."

"I will come," Andy said.

It was just after sunset when Abby and Andy walked back to his room. They sat on the floor by the fire and stared at the flames. Andy had his head in Abby's lap while she ran her fingers through his hair. He loved to enter that other place like this, so relaxed and content.

As he entered the woods, he could see Loki not far down the path.

"Let's go stand by the source before the others get here," Loki said when he reached him.

"Others?"

"Yes, there will be other witnesses who will be allowed to come here. Don't ask me who they are, because I don't know. The power of the gods selects them."

They stood before the source, its five rays rotating like a ship's wheel.

"I always feel a great loneliness for my brothers when I come here," said a voice out of nowhere. Andy was so startled, he jumped on the other side of Loki. Then Braylynn was suddenly there.

"My god, Braylynn, you scared the hell out of me!"

"I'm so sorry, my young dragon," she said affectionately.

"Don't you believe her, lad. She loves to show off." Braylynn laughed at that.

"Do you know who else is coming?" Andy asked her.

"I don't want to spoil it," she replied. "I will tell you this. One of those attending will be the next wizard to replace Devon."

"What if that person doesn't want to be a wizard?"

"Whether the person knows it or not, they have already accepted the position in their heart. My brothers' power would not bother, otherwise."

The first person to arrive was Abby. Andy was so stunned to see her there that he ran down the trail to meet her. He hugged her to him and asked how she was able to get there.

"Last thing I remember was staring down at your face in my lap when a great heaviness came over my eyes. I think I must have fallen asleep, and then I was here. Is this where you go?" she asked, looking around wide-eyed as he took her hand to walk back to Loki and Braylynn.

"Yes, this place is the power source for dragons and wizards. The next wizard is about to be chosen. I guess you are one of the invited guests."

Abby had never met Braylynn, and she seemed a little shy at first in front of the goddess. That soon disappeared as Braylynn enfolded Abby in her arms and wings with her goddess embrace.

The next to arrive were Emilia, Leah, and Tera. Tera had not seen Braylynn since Valencia's death and she flew straight to her arms and started to cry anew.

"I miss her too, Tera," Braylynn said soothingly, stroking her silver hair. After her crying subsided, Tera looked into her blue eyes and saw tears standing there and knew she shared her grief.

"I'm sorry, Braylynn. I will be brave," she said, smiling.

"There is no need to apologize, Tera," Braylynn said, putting her down gently.

"This is very strange, Braylynn," Leah said, looking at the source nervously as if it would lash out at her for daring to come. "Why are we here?"

"I will explain when the rest arrive."

Paolo, Acacia, and Dain were followed shortly by Bart, Cleo, and Maccus. And last came Lyson, Ala, Tori, and Diminitus.

"Any idea why I'm here?" Maccus whispered to Andy.

"Braylynn will explain," he whispered back to the Fenner chief.

"This better be good, Braylynn. You're interrupting a very peaceful sleep, which I don't get too often," Diminitus complained crankily. Braylynn just smiled at him.

"To start off with," Braylynn began, "you have all been brought here because of your struggle and sacrifice in defeating Devon, and you have merited this high honor to witness the appointment of the next wizard. Others also serve the dual purpose of representing one of the gods. There is at least one son or daughter of the Five among you."

"That explains it," Maccus said, satisfied.

"Wait a minute, Braylynn," Diminitus interrupted. "No one here represents Cael."

"You are wrong, Diminitus. Though you have never known it, and you never bothered to ask as far as I can tell," she said, raising an eyebrow, "you are a son of Cael." She paused to allow that to sink in. "Have you never thought why it is that you have been able to live in Parma for so long unmolested?"

"Why, that...," he sputtered, about to launch into a criticism of the Vasara deity.

"Moving along," Braylynn continued before he could get going, "the five representatives must stand in a semicircle in front of the source."

"I was afraid she was going to say something like that," Maccus said to Bart.

"Courage, Maccus. I'll be right behind you to back you up," Bart said, slapping him on the shoulder.

"Somehow that doesn't make me feel better, old friend."

"I will call out your names and you will stand by the marks on the ground. For Aditya, Maccus of Fenner. For Fallon, Cleo of Bolivar. For Rafael, Ala of Black River. For Cael, Diminitus of Parma." Diminitus was still muttering under his breath as he walked forward. "For Trystan, Paolo of Kensington."

Those named took their places in front of the source.

"The rest of you, form a loose semicircle behind them. The power will flow through the five representatives and enter into the chosen one."

"Does the wizard have to be a man?" Tori asked Loki.

"Nope, a woman works just as well," Loki answered.

"You don't mind if I stand a little closer to you? There is little chance of you being chosen twice, and I would much rather wield a sword than magic."

"I have a feeling, my dear, that, if you're the one to be chosen, where you stand will make no difference," Loki said, smiling.

"It has begun," Braylynn stated.

Everyone looked at the source. The five beams radiating out of the center started to turn back and forth, as if searching. The colors seemed to alternate between black and silvery white. After several minutes, the source just stopped, like it was frozen. Everyone's hair started to move as if pushed by a gentle breeze, except there was no wind. It was the raw living energy of the source reaching out.

Those in front stared wide-eyed as the beams shot out and into their bodies. Then, as one, they turned around and raised a hand straight at Dain. The energy from those upraised palms did not shoot out like a killing blast. Instead, they seemed to almost float, as they wound their way like a corkscrew and encircled Dain's body.

Dain held his arms out and seemed to slightly come off the ground, like he was being held up. His face transformed. Years fell away, and years were added, giving him that stamp of indeterminate age that all wizards bear. The colors then dimmed as they melted into his being. Dain had an expression of awe and wonderment. Loki was the first one to bring him back to those around him.

"Welcome, brother," Loki said. "The choice is well made."

"I… I don't know what to say," Dain said.

"It will be awhile before it all makes sense to you. Don't try to take it all in at once."

Everyone was then offering their congratulations to Dain. There was a lot of pounding on the back and hugs before all was said and done. Tera had absolutely showered him with kisses. Dain then walked over to Leah and took both of her hands.

"Well, love, I guess we don't have to worry about me dying before you do."

She had forgotten about that, and when the realization dawned, her eyes went wide.

"Oh, Dain!" she said, wrapping her arms around his neck and hugging him fiercely.

"That is just so beautiful," Acacia said to Ala, dabbing at her eyes.

"Oh brother," Diminitus said, rolling his eyes.

"Dim, I am going to make a wish in this place where all the power of the gods and goddess have currently come together, and maybe it will come true," Ala said mischievously. "I wish for you to meet a woman who you are so smitten by that you will not be able to think of anything else for the rest of your long, long life."

Diminitus was horrified. "Braylynn, make her take that back!"

"I'm sorry, did someone say something?" Braylynn said, feigning ignorance.

"Ha-ha!" Tori laughed. "Good one, Ala."

Several of the others were smirking as well.

"I guess I will have to tell your cousin you will never be coming back to command," Lyson said to Dain. "Just make sure you write this time."

"It is time for most of you to go back," Braylynn said. Then she held the gaze of each person in turn. A soft blue-green glow seemed to emanate from her body. "Please know this, I and my brothers are eternally grateful and proud of the sacrifices you have made in our service. You did it all out of love, and you are the perfect stewards for this world we created. Go with our blessings." Every person there felt his or her heart and mind caressed by the touch of the goddess. After she said this, everyone disappeared, with the exception of Andy, Dain, Loki, and Emilia.

"How do you feel?" Andy asked Dain.

"I feel like my old self and yet wholly different at the same time. It is very confusing."

"That old man over there can help you with that," Andy said knowingly, pointing a finger and smiling at Loki.

"So what will you do now?" Emilia asked Dain.

"I don't know," he said, looking up at the source and thinking. "I imagine I will go with Loki for a little while, until I come into my powers." He paused as he looked back at them. "When I entered Valencia's service, I never felt totally whole. I knew I would never be a Border Lands general again, but I never expected to feel like a soldier without a country. This, though, feels right. So, whatever I do, I know I am where I was meant to be."

"And it is because of that that you were able to accept this responsibility suddenly thrust upon you," Braylynn said, kissing his forehead. "Be well, Wizard Dain. You have a long road ahead of you." And with that, she faded away, leaving the four alone.

"Andros, why don't you and Donella head back? Dain and I will stay awhile, so he can get acquainted with the power of the Five."

"Sure thing. We'll see you back at the castle."

Andy and Emilia walked back down the forest path, leaving the two new brothers to get to know one another. Andy felt sure that some kind of wizard bond had formed between the two, and though they knew each other, in a way this was the first time they had ever met. Andy smiled to himself, because Loki was not alone anymore.

* * *

The summons came two days after Dain's anointing. Andy and Emilia were to present themselves to Paolo at the noon hour. A lot of emotions were going through Andy. He was going home today. He wondered what he would find when he went back. Would things be as he'd left them? Not that it really mattered, because he was no longer the same.

He felt apprehensive about going back. He was as much a part of this world as the other. Braylynn had come to see him and Emilia last night to tell them of some hard truths, the worst of which was he could not transform into a dragon at his home in New York.

"An altogether different god rules that world," she had said, "and we don't trespass uninvited in another god's domain."

The thought made him cringe inside. Loki was right: he was a dragon that could turn into a human, and he wondered if he would not go mad if he could not touch his dragon self. Braylynn had assured him he would not.

Emilia had asked her if some other faerie was to be the Dragon Summoner. Braylynn told her no, that she would remain the Summoner for a long time to come. They then exchanged one of those knowing looks that Andy knew meant they were keeping some things to themselves, and dragons weren't privy to them.

He had just put his dragon pants on when the door to his room opened, and Abby stepped inside.

"Well, aren't you just the handsomest thing," she said with a smile and a raised eyebrow as she looked him up and down.

"Good thing you didn't come in any sooner, or I'd been standing in my underwear," he said, laughing.

"That might be interesting." She walked over to him and pulled his head down to give him a kiss. She stepped behind him so she could trace his raven brand with her finger. Little electric shocks seemed to travel throughout his body whenever she did that.

"You look beautiful," he said, his mouth suddenly dry. Abby had come in wearing a dark blue dress that was made from a very thin fabric. It seemed almost like silk and was bare at the shoulders. It came down just below her knees and hugged her body. The dark blue brought out the whiteness of the pearl necklace she was wearing. On her wrists were gold armbands with hoop earrings to match.

"Do you like it?" she said, modeling it for him. "Acacia picked it out for me."

"It suits you perfectly."

Abby sensed something in his voice that wasn't quite right.

"What's the matter, Andros?"

"It's just strange to me. When I first got here, I was confused and scared, and now that I'm leaving, I am confused and scared."

"Braylynn said everything would become clear once you were back, and then your confusion will end."

He looked into her brown eyes. "You haven't changed your mind about coming with me?"

When Andy had felt it was time to go home, he had talked long with Abby about what they should do in relation to each other. For Abby, there was no question; she was going with him if that were possible. She had no real family to speak of in Vasara. The goddess had assured them it was possible. Andy had almost fainted with relief when he'd realized he didn't have to choose.

"No. I think I made my mind up that day in the tunnel of the library at Dragonsgate. I was leaving behind all I knew because of you, and I have never regretted it."

"Together then." He smiled that she hadn't had second thoughts.

Just then, there was a knock at the door. Andy quickly pulled on his shirt lest some other female see him half-naked.

"Come in."

A female it was, but only his sister, who had seen Andy in every form of undress since he was a small boy. But he was older now and had some sense of modesty.

"I hope I'm not interrupting," Emilia said, entering. She was wearing her Dragon Summoner clothes, and her staff was out.

"Abby and I were just talking about going home."

"I, for one, am glad you're coming, Abby. Hopefully you will be able to keep this young adventurer from his wanderlust."

"Don't count on it, Donella. The months I've spent on the road with your brother have been the most exciting of my life, after years at the library. It might just be him who has to hold me back," she said with a smile.

"Oh great," she said, rolling her eyes.

"What about you and Lyson?" Andy asked her.

Emilia's eyes took on a hurt look. She pushed her dark locks behind her pointed ears before answering.

"It's complicated," she said. "We both have feelings for each other, but we also have things to attend to in different worlds. He could not leave as Abby can, and I must go back." She paused a moment as if thinking of something else. "I did promise him that, if I ever did make it back to Vasara, we would see how things stood between us. Enough of that, though. Are you almost ready?"

"Yep, I'm ready now."

"You're going dressed like that?" Abby asked. "This is to honor you both. Don't you think you should dress more formally?"

"Loki told us we had to wear these," he said. "Something about badges of honor."

And, as if mentioning his name summoned him, Loki was at the door, knocking then entering without waiting for an answer.

"Aren't you ready yet?" he asked.

"It's getting like Grand Central Station in here."

"Whatever that means," Loki responded. "Come, everybody is waiting. Abby, you walk with me. Wait at the doors of the hall until you're announced, and then come in. Abby?" Loki held his arm out to escort her.

"I will see you inside," she said, kissing his lips and then departing with Loki.

Emilia was smirking at him.

"What?"

"Nothing, dear brother." She chuckled to herself.

Andy looked at his sister and thought how different she was from the person who stepped through the arch at Bannerman's Castle. In fact, he couldn't believe how different he was.

"We will never be the same again, Em. Will we?"

"No, we won't. But if it helps any, I think we have become what we were supposed to be all along. There are some questions that I need confirmation about, and back home is where I will get that. And I don't know if it will be possible, but I mean to come back here."

"Well, one thing I know, when we go back, Mom and Dad are going to freak out!"

"Ha-ha!" Emilia burst out laughing.

"Sure, laugh. You're old enough that they won't ground you."

"Andy, you are a treasure. You killed a demon-possessed wizard, and you're worried about being grounded. I think you will find them very understanding."

"I hope you're right."

"Come on, let's go see our friends," she said, holding her hand out. Andy took it, and together they walked to the Great Hall.

* * *

The huge oaken doors were open wide. Loki and Abby were announced and proceeded down the aisle, with onlookers on either side. A herald stood at the door to announce those going through.

The herald, dressed in the livery of the castle guard, stepped forward into the hall and rapped his staff loudly on the floor three times.

"Donella, the Dragon Summoner!"

As if on cue, twenty faeries took flight and aligned themselves into two ranks of ten by the door. They all extended their spears in unison and touched them tip-to-tip, forming a tunnel of talon spears. Leah and Brie were at the head of the ranks as Emilia stepped inside the hall.

Tera flew in from the side and placed herself in front of Emilia and, as she walked forward, threw petals from a basket to the floor at her feet. Andy learned later that the petals were from the fire rose, Valencia's favorite flower.

As Emilia passed beneath them, the faeries flew down to walk behind her as soldiers following the leader they loved. She reached the front of the dais, where Paolo and Acacia stood next to the White Throne. Off to the side were their children. The eldest, Brayton, a younger version of Paolo in looks, stood one step higher than the rest on the dais, as the heir to the throne.

The herald once again rapped his staff on the floor.

"Andros the Black," he called out.

"Tori strikes again," Andy muttered to himself as he rolled his eyes.

Andy heard the rasp of steel sliding from sheaths, and, as Emilia had had a tunnel of spears, he had a tunnel of swords. The Vipers provided the honor guard for Andy's entrance with Cleo and Tori at the head.

Tori winked at him as he walked by and gave a knowing look, as if to say, "I told you so." Percy was in attendance, as well. Andy could see him wrapped around Tori's wrist.

There was great cheering during the whole time the heroes made their way to the dais. Andy looked up to see Paolo smiling at him. Acacia was positively beaming. Paolo raised his hands to silence the crowd.

"Today we gather to honor and bid farewell to Andros and Donella," he began. "They have delivered this world from more than fifteen hundred years of oppression." He looked down and addressed them directly. "There is nothing we have that would be payment enough for what you have done for us, but we promise that your deeds will never be forgotten. Bards already are putting your exploits to song. And as long as there is a tavern, inn, or hall, these songs will never die."

He turned and nodded to his wife, who was wearing a wine-colored dress with a gold belt and a crown made out of a single diamond. Acacia turned toward her son, Brayton who was carrying an ornate wooden box to her. Taking it from her son, she turned and held it open for her husband.

Paolo lifted out of the box two medallions on chains of godstone. On the one he put around Andy's neck was the image of a black pyramid with gold lightning bolts emanating from it. On Emilia's was the image of a white swan in flight.

"Are those what I think they are?" Loki whispered under his breath to Paolo.

Paolo nodded but gave Loki a look that said they would discuss it later.

"Wear these in remembrance of Vasara and all the friends who love you." He turned them both around to the adoration of a thankful people. Paolo then announced they would have one last feast before the saviors departed.

There were a lot of tearful farewells with those who would not be accompanying Andy and Emilia to the room with the door that opened into that other world.

Maccus made his way to Andy.

"Well, Andros, I guess this is goodbye and maybe forever for us."

Andy had a huge lump in his throat. "Yes, but I want you to know I will never forget you, ever. I don't know the lifespan of dragons, but however long it is, I will make sure the name of Maccus of Fenner is always remembered."

Maccus grasped Andy's forearm. "And every heir to my house will know the story of Andros the Black and how it was because of him they can live as their ancestors did, free." He hugged Andy to his breast and, with tears standing in his eyes, turned and left the hall to ride for home. It was to be the last time Andy would ever see the Fenner chief. Andy looked over and saw Bart walking toward him.

"There goes one of the best of men," Bart remarked to Andy.

Andy could only nod; he didn't trust his voice just now.

"I see your sister is over making her goodbyes."

He looked to see Emilia hugging Brie and several other faeries he did not know.

"Ho, Andros!"

Andy turned around and smiled as the familiar form of Captain Bowen came striding over.

"Thank you for everything, Captain," Andy said, shaking his hand. "You were always there when we needed you most."

"No problem, lad. No problem. Listen, I know you will be shoving off soon, but the boys and I were wondering if Abby might not mind giving us a song of farewell, before you take the most beautiful voice in Vasara out of this world."

"Are you sure you are in the mood for crying, Captain?"

"Lad, 'tis tears of joy and well worth it to hear that voice in song."

"I'm sure she would be delighted. I will go and ask her."

Abby was more than delighted. On the far side of the hall opposite the dais was a huge hearth that could easily fit four grown men standing up. A small fire was lit that gave the darkened corner an otherworldly light. Tera stood with her to accompany on her pipes, as did a Kensington bard strumming his harp.

Abby sang about two lovers separated by a war. The last sight the woman has of her beloved is of him waving from the stern of his ship as he sails into the morning mist. News reaches the woman that he has gone missing, so she sets sail herself to find him, going from port to port for many years. When there is no word of him, stricken by grief, she sails alone to the end of the world, where the great waterfalls are, and plunges over. The man eventually returns and, when he learns of his love's death, follows her path to join her, so that they will live together through eternity.

When Abby's song was finished, there were a few moments of silence, for no one wanted to disturb the enchantment that had settled over them. There were very few dry eyes. Paolo, being moved in his spirit by Abby's song, rose from his chair and walked over to her. He took the necklace that bore the mark of his house, a prancing unicorn, from around his neck and placed it around Abby's neck. He kissed Abby on both cheeks then turned to face the crowd.

"Today, with all of you as my witnesses, I make Abby of Dragonsgate one of my daughters and a princess to the realm."

There was a gasp from the crowd, which then erupted into cheers, for everyone had been just as moved as Paolo. Acacia came over and hugged and kissed her. Abby, for her own part, had tears coming down her face, for a mother and father had claimed her to stand in place of the ones that were taken from her.

Andy was overjoyed at the happiness and good fortune of his beloved. Bowen's crew then hoisted Abby onto their shoulders and paraded her around the hall.

As things settled down, everyone made their final farewells, then those chosen to see Andy, Abby, and Emilia off went to the room where it all began.

Braylynn was waiting for them when the door opened and they stepped inside. Emilia ran over and embraced the goddess. Braylynn returned her hug, but then her eyes went wide as she sensed something. She held Emilia out at arm's length.

"What is around your neck?" she said sternly. "Take it out now!"

Emilia, taken aback by this sudden display, nervously lifted the swan medallion for the goddess to see. Braylynn's eyes narrowed.

"Paolo! What is the meaning of this?"

"I was about to ask him the same thing once we got up here," Loki echoed.

"What is it? What's going on?" Andy asked, totally perplexed.

"Did he tell you what these are?" Braylynn said.

"No," Andy answered.

"I was waiting until we were up here," Paolo said. "These are not just ordinary adornments," he said to Emilia and Andy. "The power of two ancient gods from some other world resides in them."

"How is that possible?" Cleo asked.

"Let me tell it from the beginning," Braylynn stated, casting dagger eyes at Paolo. "It will save time and questions. Just after my brothers and I created Vasara, two rocks, one black and one white, came shooting down from the sky to land in the ground upon which this very castle now stands. Trystan found them and, upon touching them, realized the energy force of two gods, actually one god and one goddess, resided in the stones. He realized that, if these forces were released, it could rip the fabric of our world and who knows how many others. To keep them from getting in the wrong hands, he melted the stones very carefully, so as not to release their power.

This process took several hundred years in a forge that he made and hid. Once melted, he crafted them into their present form. He did this so it would be almost impossible to release them."

"Almost?" Tori said.

"Nothing is truly impossible," the goddess told her. "Before this castle was built, a crypt was erected with a special door that would only open for Trystan or the king and his heir. In there, he placed these two medallions. So now the question is why has the king removed them?" She looked hard at Paolo.

"One thing they should also know," Paolo said, "is that to open the door, the king or his eldest child, who is the presumed heir, must place his hand on the clear orb embedded into the lintel of the door to prove their blood is of the same line as the first king of Vasara. The magic also knows who the eldest child is. A second or third child cannot open it."

"You keep saying eldest," Diminitus said, "instead of just the heir. Why?"

"Because something has happened that there can only be one explanation for."

"What has happened?" Andy asked.

"The orb that allows you to open the door also shows you images of every other person who has tried and the order in which they tried. There were several images of Devon trying and failing. The last one who tried was a tall, hooded figure. He did not fail. I saw the door open, but to keep it open, your hand has to maintain contact until it rises to the very top, otherwise it will close again. He was stopped. Devon must have discovered him, because I saw the hooded man blown asunder."

"I still don't see what this has to do with the eldest child," Diminitus said.

"I think I see where you're going with this," Loki said.

"Prepare to be amazed, lad," Bart said mockingly. Loki pretended not to hear him.

"Taiyo's bloodline currently ends with you and your son Brayton. And if the two of you can open the door, there shouldn't be any others who can, unless there is another eldest child."

"Loki, that makes no sense!" Diminitus said. "How in the world can there be two eldest children?"

"Think, Dim. The answer is staring you in the face."

"Twins," Ala said.

"Yes," Loki said.

"But even with twins, one is always born first," Bart chimed in. "Unless... My god, no," he said as realization dawned.

"Yes," Paolo said soberly. "Somewhere in history, a queen of Vasara was carrying twins, and she was killed so both babies could be brought out through her abdomen at the same time."

"You mean it was planned," Leah said in revulsion.

"That has to be it. And as far as the magic is concerned, there will always be two heirs, unless that other branch is destroyed," Loki said. "Magic can sometimes take things quite literally. Since both children were the eldest, the conditions would be met for the line of either child."

"Which brings us back to why I gave the medallions to Andros and Donella," Paolo said to Braylynn. "The crypt is no longer safe, and aside from yourself, who would not take them, these two are the most powerful beings in Vasara. Also, they will take this power to a place where the members of that other bloodline cannot get it." Paolo paused as he watched Braylynn mull that over. "It is my responsibility as king and my right to do this, goddess."

She looked sidelong at him. "You are correct, of course. It is your right, and there is a certain logic to it, until some better plan can be thought of. But I do not like that you involved my Summoner without consulting me first."

"Will you ever forgive me, Braylynn?" Paolo said with a smile.

"I'll think about it," she said primly. "Now, I think we have delayed our good friends long enough."

Andy took that as the cue that it was time to go. He looked around at the people he had come to love and respect. His eyes welled up at the thought that he might never see them again.

Courage, lad, Loki spoke to his mind. *I have a strong feeling you will be back.*

Andy looked over at him and smiled. He walked over and embraced him. When they separated, Andy noticed where he was. It was the exact spot where Devon had branded him and where Loki had pulled him to freedom. He thought it fitting somehow.

Leah and Dain walked over to Andy.

"Be sure to watch out for our sister, Andros. I should hate to have to kill you, should something happen to her." Andy knew she was only kidding, because she was smiling as she said this.

Dain hugged him to his chest. "If you can come to the place of the source from your world, call for me and I will meet you there."

"I will. I promise."

"I guess this is the end of the road for us, lad," Bart said from behind him.

Andy gave him a hug and pounded his best friend on the back several times.

"I'm not sure if I ever said it, but thanks for saving my life. I'm not sure how many times it was."

"Five or six at least."

Emilia was off to one side, talking to Lyson. He spied Ala and Acacia talking to Abby and went to say goodbye.

"I never thanked you for saving my sister's life," Andy said to Ala.

"It was my honor, Andros. I'm glad I was able to do it."

"Yeah, but she made us frantic until you did," Diminitus added.

"Dim, you're such a wet blanket," Acacia said.

"A wet...," he started to sputter.

"I am going to miss you very much," Emilia said. She had glided up silently to land right next to Diminitus and plant a kiss on his cheek.

"Well, I'm going to miss you too, lass," he said with surprising tenderness.

The goodbyes took longer than expected. Everyone had something special they wanted to convey, just in case this was the last time they saw one another. Tera didn't want to say much; she just wanted lots of hugs and kisses.

Cleo and Tori had given them gifts from the Vipers. Tori wanted to give Abby her twin swords, since she didn't have any magic to protect herself. Emilia convinced her that they would not have magical powers, either, and swords would not look right where they were going.

"It is time," Braylynn announced. She walked over to the far door and opened it. A gray mist filled the doorway, making it impossible to see what lay beyond.

Braylynn gave her blessing to each in turn and spoke private words to their minds. Aloud she told them not to be afraid, that the crossing over would not be like when Devon had pulled them in.

"One last word of caution," Braylynn said. "Never let those medallions out of your sight. It would be best to wear them always."

"We will," Andy promised. "Thank you, Braylynn."

"No, my young dragon, thank you," she said, the warmth of her eyes boring into his very soul. "Don't forget what I said. Though you are the youngest among your brothers, you will be chief among them. Now you must go. Farewell."

Andy, Emilia, and Abby each held hands and slowly started walking toward the door. Just then, Andy heard a commotion behind him. He looked back and saw Tori patting her hair.

"Tori, what are you doing?" Lyson said.

"Something is in my hair," she replied frantically. Then she started screaming as ladybugs by the score went running out of her hair and down her neck and dissolved into the floor.

"I think we better pick up the pace," Emilia said, suppressing her mirth.

"Summoner! I owe you one!" Tori yelled. "I hate bugs!" The rest of the room erupted in laughter, and it was the last thing Andy heard as they stepped into the mist.

Braylynn had been right. They felt as if they were walking on a concrete road with no sound but their own breathing. As they continued walking, Andy could see it was starting to get lighter up ahead, and then, as if they had just blinked their eyes, the scene in front of them was clear. They were back on the island at around the same time of day as when they left.

"Is this it?" Abby said in wonder. "Is this where you live?"

"Well, not exactly," he replied. "Our house is on that side of the river, up on that hill," he said, pointing.

All of a sudden, there was a loud noise, and Abby jumped and clung to Andy.

"What the hell was that!" she exclaimed.

"That's just the horn from that oil tanker over there."

Abby looked toward the opposite shore and saw an enormous metal ship gliding down the river. "I see there is a lot I will need to get used to."

"You'll do fine. You'll see," Andy assured her.

"Andy!" a voice called out. "Emilia!"

"That sounded like Dad!" Andy said. "Dad?" he shouted.

"Andy!"

He looked up toward the house ruins, where he saw a figure emerge onto the path. From the size and shape, he knew it was his father. Andy took off running as his father did the same.

He met him halfway and locked him into a fierce embrace.

"Dad, I'm so sorry. You and Mom must have been worried sick."

Andy's dad looked at his son as if seeing him for the first time. He could tell something had changed in him.

"I'm sorry we were gone so long, but I can explain everything."

"Calm down. It was only a couple of hours, and I knew you were hiking by the river, but when you weren't home in time for dinner, your mother insisted I come looking for you. I saw your tracks going down to the water, and I feared the worst. But something told me to check the island, so I got a boat and rowed over. I had just started looking up here when you appeared."

"That doesn't make sense, Dad. We've been gone for months."

His father seemed to hesitate, and then understanding lit up in his eyes. "I think I know what happened."

"How?"

"Well..."

"Dad!" Emilia yelled as she jumped into her father's arms.

Abby was running with Emilia, but as they got closer, she started to hang back a bit, as if she didn't believe what she was seeing. Andy saw her and went to grab her hand.

"Abby, you have to come meet my dad." He felt her reluctance, as he almost had to drag her closer. He looked at her and saw her eyes go wide. "Abby, what's wrong?"

Andy's father was looking at Abby now. "You are from Vasara, aren't you?" he said.

"Dad, how did you know that?" Andy said, whipping his head around.

"Because he is the Wizard Redlin," Abby said with an awestruck voice.

"What are you talking about?" Andy said, starting to shake. "That's not possible!"

"Every curator knows the image of Redlin, Andros. It is him."

Andy didn't believe it. He wouldn't believe it.

"Dad?" Andy said in a small voice. His father looked painfully at him.

"He is Redlin," Emilia said.

Andy's knees hit the ground as he buried his face into his hands, and his world turned upside down one more time.

THE END

Here ends Part I of the Vasara Chronicles

Acknowledgments

I want to thank my team at Booktrope: April Gerard, Ellen Margulies, Kathryn Galán, and Greg Simanson. Your dedication and expertise in your field have given my book a fresh, new start, taking it to bolder and higher heights. You never shied away from the challenge and, in the process, opened my mind to the many moving parts of getting a book published. I used to think the author had the hardest job, but you have shown me otherwise, and I have grown and matured because of that, as well as developed a deeper sense of all you do.

I want to give thanks to my family, without whom this book would not even exist.

I would also like to acknowledge the many authors and artists who have followed me along on this journey, giving ideas and critiques when I needed them most. It is a wonderful community of human beings and an honor to be considered a member.

I need to acknowledge my niece Becca, who helped to name my world. We were sitting in my living room, throwing names around, when she said the word that clicked in my mind: *Vasara*. When I heard it, it was as if I knew that that had always been its name.

I used to think writing was a solo effort. But I think, for most authors, this cannot be true. Many family and friends have knowingly and unknowingly provided me with material help to make my story a living, breathing tale. There are too many to individually name, but I will be forever grateful to each and every one.

About the Author

Roland Capalbo calls New York home. He lives in the picturesque Hudson Valley, an area so rich in beauty, history, and folklore, an author has an abundance of inspiration to draw from. Roland is married with two kids who constantly provide inspiration for the creation of story lines.

He draws his ideas from the people in his life and from the nature that surrounds him. Always a big reader of the fantasy genre, he has sometimes come across a book whose plot he just didn't like and, in his head, proceeded to rewrite the scene. This is where his desire to create his own worlds began.

Roland's first book was a bedtime story he had written for his five-year-old nephew, called *The Magic of the Pony Man*. It was in this book that the idea for his first full-length novel, *The Dragon and the Faerie*, was born. He is currently writing the sequel, titled, *The Dragon's Redress*.

Roland's favorite quote:

I like nonsense. It wakes up the brain cells. Fantasy is a necessary ingredient in living, it's a way of looking at life through the wrong end of a telescope. Which is what I do, and that enables you to laugh at life's realities.

—Theodore Geisel